DEFY
THE
NIGHT

DEFY THE NIGHT

BRIGID KEMMERER

BLOOMSBURY

NEW YORK LONDON OXFORD NEW DELHI SYDNEY

BLOOMSBURY YA
Bloomsbury Publishing Inc., part of Bloomsbury Publishing Plc
1385 Broadway, New York, NY 10018

BLOOMSBURY and the Diana logo are trademarks of Bloomsbury Publishing Plc

First published in the United States of America in September 2021
by Bloomsbury YA

Bloomsbury books may be purchased for business or promotional use. For information
on bulk purchases please contact Macmillan Corporate and Premium Sales Department at
specialmarkets@macmillan.com

Library of Congress Cataloging-in-Publication Data
Names: Kemmerer, Brigid, author.
Title: Defy the night / by Brigid Kemmerer.
Description: New York : Bloomsbury Children's Books, 2021.
Summary: The kingdom of Kandala is recovering from a devastating plague
but the cure is rare and expensive, so a girl hatches a plan to infiltrate
the castle and bring the corrupt system crashing down
Identifiers: LCCN 2021017795 (print) | LCCN 2021017796 (e-book)
ISBN 978-1-5476-0466-1 (hardcover) • ISBN 978-1-5476-0467-8 (e-pub)
Subjects: CYAC: Fantasy. | Courts and courtiers—Fiction. | Magic—Fiction.
Classification: LCC PZ7.K3052 De 2021 (print) | LCC PZ7.K3052 (e-book) |
DDC [Fic]—dc23
LC record available at https://lccn.loc.gov/2021017795
LC e-book record available at https://lccn.loc.gov/2021017796

ISBN 978-1-5476-0984-0 (exclusive edition A) • ISBN 978-1-5476-1036-5 (exclusive edition B)
ISBN 978-1-5476-1045-7 (exclusive edition C) • ISBN 978-1-5476-1-0464 (exclusive edition D)

Book design by Yelena Safronova
Typeset by Westchester Publishing Services
Printed and bound in Great Britain by the CPI Group (UK) Ltd, Croydon CR0 4YY
2 4 6 8 10 9 7 5 3 1

To find out more about our authors and books visit www.bloomsbury.com
and sign up for our newsletters.

For Mrs. Pat Bettridge
and
Mrs. Nancy Vaughan.

Two amazing teachers
who showed me
just how powerful
the written word can be.

THE KINGDOM

The Kingdom of Ostriary

TRADER'S LANDING

SUNKEEP

STEEL CITY

THE POLITICAL LEADERS OF KANDALA

NAME	ROLE	SECTOR
King Harristan	King	Royal
Prince Corrick	King's Justice	Royal
Barnard Montague (deceased)	Consul	Trader's Landing*
Allisander Sallister	Consul	Moonlight Plains
Leander Craft	Consul	Steel City
Jonas Beeching	Consul	Artis
Lissa Marpetta	Consul	Emberridge
Roydan Pelham	Consul	The Sorrowlands
Arella Cherry	Consul	Sunkeep
Jasper Gold	Consul	Mosswell

*Sometimes called "Traitor's Landing" after the former king and queen were assassinated by Consul Montague, leaving Harristan and his younger brother, Corrick, in power.

THE OUTLAWS

NAME	ROLE
Tessa Cade	Apothecary
Weston Lark	Steelworker
Lochlan	Rebel
The Benefactors	Unknown

THE CURE

The only known cure for the fever is an elixir created from dried Moonflower petals, a plant native only to two sectors: Moonlight Plains and Emberridge. Moonflower petals are strictly rationed among sectors, and quantities are limited.

Those with means can purchase their own supply.

Those without, cannot.

DEFY THE NIGHT

CHAPTER ONE

Tessa

The hardest part of this job isn't the stealing. It's the escaping. At best, it takes me two minutes to scale the wall out of the Royal Sector, but the night is cold, and my fingers are starting to go numb. Dawn is only an hour off, and sentry spotlights slide along the high stone walls at irregular intervals. I clutch my father's old apothecary pack tight under my arm, clinging to the darkness, waiting for an opportunity.

Several of the sectors have electricity in the wealthy areas, or so I've heard, but the spotlights here are brighter than any candle has ever been—even brighter than the bonfires the towns light to burn their dead. The first time I saw them, I stared like a fool until I realized those lights meant danger. I spent days trying to figure out some kind of pattern to the surveillance, until I admitted that to Weston. He snorted and said there was no pattern, just bored men spinning a light around a pole.

They've been spinning this light pretty steadily for the last hour.

I flex my fingers and mentally adjust my estimate to three minutes—then bite my lip and think. The light has been returning to this section of wall at least every two.

Wes is probably at the workshop already, waiting. He can scale the stone wall in half a minute. Thanks to his height, he can leap, catch the high spires with his treble hook, then brace against the wall to bounce to the top like a cat. I'd be jealous, but it's kind of entrancing to watch.

Not that I'd ever tell him. I'd never hear the end of it.

Entrancing, Tessa? It's just a wall. Nothing like this. And then he'd climb a tree or do a cartwheel off the workshop roof or walk on his hands.

And then I'd have to punch him, because that would be better than him seeing the blush creeping out from under my mask, because *yes*, all of that is equally entrancing.

I need to stop thinking about Wes. This sentry light needs to stop spinning. I need to make my rounds, or we'll lose days of healing. Some people don't have days. A few might not even have hours.

I have to get out of here first. If I'm caught with a pack full of Moonflower petals, King Harristan and his brother, Prince Corrick, will tie me down in the palace gardens and let the birds peck out my organs.

Suddenly, the light stops, way down near the corner where the wall dips into shadow because of a slope. It's where the amateurs always try to make their escape.

I'm not going to waste an opportunity. I tear out of my hiding place like a rabbit scared from a glen, my own treble hook already swinging. I can't fling it all the way to the spires like Wes can, but I can reach the brackets that sit midway. The hook whistles up at the wall ahead of me, and I leap before it pulls taut. My boots scrape against the stone as I climb, slipping a little on the granite. I reach the bracket, the tiniest little ledge, but it's enough to brace against while I pull the treble hook free and swing for the top. It clangs onto the spires, and up I go.

The light begins to move.

I suck in a breath and urge my feet to push me faster, higher. The pack bounces against my ribs as my feet slip and shift against the wall. My hands are burning where the rope slides. The light sweeps close, and it's suddenly blinding.

Then I'm over the wall, half rappelling, half dropping to the forest ground like a sack of oats. I give the rope a jerk and the hook falls beside me, a little jingle in the gravel at the base of the wall. Dirt and debris cling to the homespun wool of my skirts, but I don't dare move to brush it away. I can almost taste my heartbeat as I hold my breath and wait for the sentries to ring the alarm.

But no. Brightness glides along the edge as the light continues on its path.

I swallow my heart and wind up my hook. A crescent moon hangs high in the sky, but the barest hint of purple gleams at the horizon, a reminder that I hesitated too long, and time grows short. I slip through the forest with practiced ease, my feet silent on the fallen pine needles. I usually smell fire from the woodstove by now, because Wes always beats me back. We have a system: he starts the kettle and grinds the petals so we can make the elixir, while I weigh and divide the powder into the appropriate dosage.

Then he bottles the liquid as it's ready, I wrap it into our packs, and together we make our rounds.

But today, there's no smell of wood smoke.

I get to the workshop, and there's no Weston.

I think of that light stopping on the wall. My heart is in my throat again.

Wes isn't stupid. He wouldn't try the corner. I didn't hear an alarm anyway.

But he's still not here, and I'm already late.

I light the fire and try not to worry. I can hear his voice telling me to keep calm. *Mind your mettle, Tessa.* They're the first words he said to me on the night he saved my life, and he's said them a dozen times since.

He's fine. He has to be fine. Sometimes we can't meet at all, and one of us waits at the workshop for fifteen minutes before running solo. Mistress Solomon occasionally keeps me late, brewing and measuring and weighing the herbal remedies that she promises her customers will work—but they rarely do. Sometimes Weston's master needs him at the forge early, because some spoiled sports-man needs a new sword or a horse has thrown a shoe. It's happened before.

But Wes was here earlier. And he's always back first.

The workshop is tiny and warms quickly from the fire. There's no electricity out here, so the workshop is dim, but I don't need much light for this. I busy my hands to keep from worry, grinding each petal into dust, careful to scrape every speck onto the tray of my scale. Even dry, they're fragrant. The elites pay dearly for every fraction of an ounce, then waste it by drinking the elixir three times a day, even those who show no signs of disease. *Preventive measures*, the king calls it. Once a day is usually plenty, and I have my notes to prove it. Even Wes was distributing too much in the beginning, until I showed him that we could help far more people with less. My father would have called it a waste. A waste of good treatment when those who can't afford it are dying.

Then again, my father was executed for treason and smuggling, so I don't call it anything at all. I just do what I can.

I glance out the window. The purple horizon has taken on the faintest hint of pink.

I glance at the door, as if that will make Wes appear.

It doesn't. The kettle whistles. I divide the water into tiny measured cups and add half an ounce of ground petals to each, along with two drops of roseseed oil for the cough, which I measure out almost as carefully as the Moonflower petals themselves. I try not to steal what I can come by honestly, but roseseed nearly costs me a week's wages, so I don't even let Wes measure it.

Once the petals and roseseed have dissolved, I weigh in a bit of turmeric, which can bring down a fever enough to let the medicine work better, but I have to add a sprig of mint and a pinch of sugar, too. Adults don't usually need much convincing to swallow the tincture, but we can't risk wasting it on children who might spit it out.

From the Royal Sector, horns blast and shouts cry out, and I jump so hard that I overturn a cup. They've caught someone.

Wes.

I should run and see. No, I should run and hide.

My muscles refuse to do either.

Mind your mettle, Tessa.

I need to move. I need to finish. When the Moonflower is

combined with the other ingredients, the elixir works better—but then they're only good for a few hours after brewing. I need to finish our rounds, even if I have to do it alone.

The horns continue to blow. Shouting echoes in the distance. They're going to wake half the sector. My breath has become a low keening from my throat. I imagine Prince Corrick being called down to deal with the traitor. The sentries aren't gentle. Weston's easy smile will be a grimace of pain. I'll hear his screams from here. They'll tear him apart with the tiniest knives imaginable. They'll stuff his mouth with burning coals. They'll feed him alive to the royal lions. They'll burn each limb, one by one, until he loses consciousness from the—

"Lord, Tessa, you hardly need me anymore."

I shriek and overturn another cup. There he is, in the doorway, his blue eyes bright behind the mask, his smile easy.

Weston sees the mess I've made and rolls his eyes. "Or maybe you do." He moves forward and sets the cup upright. "Did you already put the powder in that one?"

I don't know if I want to hug him or hit him. Maybe both. "You're late. I heard the horns. I thought—I thought they caught you."

"Not today." He pulls the sleeves of petals from his pack, then follows them with three apples, along with a twist of sugared dough that's still warm from an oven. "Here. The baker was out back scolding his daughter, so I swiped you some food."

He was late because he brought me *breakfast*. Not just any breakfast either. Food from the Royal Sector will be the finest imaginable. The apples will be injected with honey, the twists of dough made with real butter and laced with cream and sugar.

My mouth opens. Closes. I frown and turn away. My throat is tight for an entirely new reason. "That's very kind of you, Weston."

" 'That's very kind of you'?" he scoffs. "My, aren't we feeling proper this morning."

"I need to finish the elixirs."

"I'll finish. You eat."

"I'll eat in a minute." The horns continue on the other side of the wall, but now I can ignore them. Probably another smuggler. We'll likely see his skin suspended beside the gates tomorrow, after the king and his brother are done with the body.

"Fine." Weston takes an apple, kicks back in the only chair, and props his booted feet up on the worktable. He wears a wide-brimmed black hat above the mask that stretches over his eyes, but he tips the hat back now that we're in the workshop. I only ever see him by firelight, so I can't tell exactly what color his hair is, but he usually needs a shave by now, and the faint beard growth always seems reddish brown when he sits near a candle, matching the dusting of freckles near the edge of his mask. The skin around his eyes is smudged with kohl or soot, making the blue brighter than any eyes I've ever seen. My own eyes are hazel green, my brown hair in a tight braid under my cap. Wes always says I look like a cat in my mask and my black jacket. Once, when I was feeling brave and cocky, I told him he should see me without the disguise so he knows what a proper young woman looks like, but his face went grave.

"Never," he said. "It's too dangerous. If we know what the other looks like, the information can be gained under torture. I won't do that to you." He paused. "And I sure don't want you to do it to me."

That was the first time I realized that Weston Lark probably isn't his real name. He likely assumes Tessa Cade is fake, too, but it's not. When we met two years ago, my parents had just been killed in front of me, and I was too racked with grief to come up with another name.

"You're quiet," says Wes. He loudly crunches the apple, and I want to smack it out of his hand. "What's wrong?"

"Nothing." I bottle the elixir I've already made—usually his job—and pour new cups of water to begin the process again.

Behind me, I hear him shift out of the chair and stand. He comes close enough for me to catch his scent, like the woods and the cinnamon from the bakery—but also something heavier underneath, something unmistakably Wes. "Tessa."

I jab an elbow into his midsection, and I have the satisfaction of hearing him grunt.

"What was that for?" he demands.

"You made me worry."

"But I brought you breakfast." His voice is rich and deep behind me.

I ignore him.

He leans in until his breath brushes against the sliver of skin between my hair and the high neck of my jacket. The other apple appears in front of me, wrapped up in his long fingers. "It's a really *good* breakfast," he taunts.

I take the apple. Sugar dusts the skin. It's warm to the touch, and I wonder if the honey inside is warm, too.

Despite myself, I take a bite. The honey is warm. "I hate you," I say with my mouth full.

"That'll probably work out for the best." He flicks my hat up a few inches and grins. "Now eat quick," he says. "We have rounds to make."

CHAPTER TWO

Corrick

I've been listening to my brother's breathing for hours. There's a new sound each time he inhales, a faint stuttering in his lungs. In the Wilds, they call it the death rattle, because it means the end is near.

Here in his chambers, I'm unwilling to use the word *death* at all. I'm unwilling to even think it.

He doesn't have a fever. There's no cause to worry.

I can't even convince myself.

Sunlight blazes through the open window, and birds trill in the trees. Harristan shouldn't be sleeping this late, but I hate to wake him. To everyone outside the doors to his rooms, we've been deliberating over paperwork all morning. I've called for food twice, enough to feed a dozen people, but most of it sits untouched. Flies have begun gathering on the sliced fruit, and a bee drones over the pastries.

Harristan coughs faintly, and his breathing eases. Maybe

that's all it was, a tickle in his throat. A tightness in my own chest loosens, and I run a hand across the back of my neck, finding it damp.

A faint breeze nudges at my papers with enough insistence that I tuck most of them under the weight of the lamp before they can scatter across the desk. One of us has to work. I've been making notes along the margins of a funding request from one of the eastern cities, looking for omissions and inaccuracies in their statement demonstrating the need for a new bridge. I expected to get through only a few pages before Harristan would wake up, but now I've gone through the entire report and it must be nearly midday.

I tug my pocket watch free and glance at the glittering diamonds embedded in its face. It *is* midday. If he doesn't appear at the meeting of the sector consuls, there will be talk. I can only silence so much.

As if my thoughts wake him, my brother stirs, blinking in the sunlight. He frowns at me and sits up, shirtless, then runs a hand down his face. "It's late. Why didn't you wake me?"

I listen to his voice carefully, but there's no roughness to his tone, no sign of any difficulty breathing. Maybe I imagined it. "I was just about to." I move to the sideboard and lift the kettle. "The tea has gone cold." I pour a cup anyway and carry it to him, along with a thin corked tube of Moonflower elixir that's darker than usual. The palace apothecary doubled his dosage last week when the coughing started again, so maybe the medicine is beginning to work.

Harristan uncorks the tube, drinks it, and makes a face.

"There, there," I say without a lick of sympathy.

He grins. That's something he only does when we're alone. Neither of us smiles outside these rooms very often. "What have you been doing all morning?"

"I went through the request from Artis. I've drafted a refusal for you to sign."

His expression turns serious. "A refusal?"

"They're asking for twice what a new bridge would cost. They hid it well, but someone got greedy."

"You hardly need me anymore."

The words are said lightly, but they hit me like an arrow. Kandala needs its king. I need my brother.

I lock away my worries and fold my arms. "You need to dress—and shave. I'll call for Geoffrey. I've said we were too busy for you to bother earlier. Quint has requested an audience with you twice, but he will need to wait until after the evening meal, unless—"

"Cory." His voice is soft, and I go still. He only ever calls me Cory when we're alone, one of the few reminders of childhood we have left. A nickname from when I was small and eager and trailing after him everywhere he went. A name that was once spoken in gentle fondness by our mother or encouraging praise by our father, back when we believed our family was beloved by all. Back before anyone knew about the fever, or the Moonflower, or the way our country would change in ways no one expected.

Back when everyone expected Harristan to have decades before he'd take the throne, that he'd rule with firm kindness and thoughtful care for his people, just as our parents did.

But four years ago, they were assassinated right in front of us. Shot through the throat in the throne room. The arrows pinned them upright, their heads hanging cockeyed, their eyes wide and glassy as they choked on their own blood. The image still haunts my dreams sometimes.

Harristan was nineteen. I was fifteen. He took an arrow in the shoulder when he dove to cover me.

It should have been the other way around.

I stare back into his blue eyes and look for any sign of sickness. There is none. "What?"

"The medicine is working again." His voice is quiet. "You don't need to play nursemaid."

My smile feels a little wicked. "Cruel Cory playing nursemaid? Never."

He rolls his eyes. "No one calls you Cruel Cory."

"Not to my face." No, to my face, I'm Your Highness, or Prince Corrick, or sometimes, when they're being especially formal, the King's Justice.

Behind my back, I'm called worse. Much worse. So is Harristan.

We don't mind. Our parents were loved—and they were loving in return. It led to betrayal and death.

Fear works better.

I move to the closet and pull out a laced shirt to toss at my brother. "You don't want a nursemaid? Then stop lazing around. There's a country to run."

—◆—

The midday meal is already arranged on the sideboard when we enter. Roasted pheasant drips with honey and berries, nestled among a dense bed of greens and root vegetables. A few feathers have been artfully placed along the gilded edge of each platter, held in place by a glistening drop of crystalized honey. Though the stewards stand in silence along the wall, waiting to serve, the eight other Royal Consuls are engaged in lively conversation by the window. I'm the ninth, but I have no interest in lively conversation.

There used to be ten, but Consul Barnard led the plot to have my parents killed. He would have killed us, too. After Harristan saved my life, I saw Barnard coming after him with a dagger.

My brother was on top of me, his breath panicked and full of pain in my ear. I pulled that arrow out of Harristan's shoulder and stabbed it right into Barnard's neck.

I blink the memory away. The consuls fall silent when we enter the room, each offering a short bow to my brother before moving to their chairs, though no one will sit until Harristan does, and no one will eat until we both have taken a bite.

The table is shaped like a rectangle at one end, narrowing to a point at the other, like the head of an arrow. Harristan eases into his chair at the head of the table, and I ease into mine, directly to his right. The eight consuls ease into theirs, leaving one seat empty. It's the one directly beside me, where Consul Barnard used to sit. The Trader's Landing sector has no new consul, and Harristan is in no rush to appoint one. In whispers, the people often call it Traitor's Landing, after what Barnard did, but no one says it in front of us. No one wants to remind the king or his brother of what happened.

They respect my brother—as they should.

They fear me.

I don't mind. It spares me some tedious conversations.

We've known everyone in this room for our entire lives, but we've long since doused any comfort born of familiarity. We saw what complacence and trust did to our parents, and we know what it could do to us. When Harristan was nineteen, blood still seeping through a bandage on his shoulder, he ran his first meeting in this room. We were both numb with grief and shock, but I followed him to take a place standing by his shoulder. I remember thinking the consuls would be sympathetic and compassionate following the deaths of our parents. I remember thinking we would all grieve together.

But we were barely in the room for a full minute before Consul Theadosia snidely commented that a child had no place attending a meeting of the King's Council. She was talking about me—but her tone implied she was talking about Harristan, too.

"This child," said Harristan, "is my brother, your prince." His voice was like thunder. I'd never heard my brother's voice like that. It gave me the strength to stand when I so badly wanted to hide under my bed and pretend my world hadn't been turned upside down.

"Corrick saved my life," said Harristan. "The life of your new king. He risked himself when none of you were willing to do the same, including you, Theadosia. I have named him King's Justice, and he will attend any meeting he so pleases."

I went very still at those words. The King's Justice was the highest-ranking adviser to the king. The highest position beside Harristan himself. Our father once said that he was allowed to stay in the people's good graces because the King's Justice handled anything . . . unsavory.

Another consul at the time, a man named Talec, coughed to cover a laugh and said, "Corrick will be the King's Justice? At fifteen?"

"Was I unclear?" said Harristan.

"Exactly what justice will he mete out? No dinner? No playtime for Kandala's criminals?"

"We must be strong," said Theadosia, her voice full of scorn. "You dishonor your parents. This is no time for Kandala's rulers to be a source of mockery."

You dishonor your parents. The words turned my insides to ice. Our parents were killed because the council failed to uncover a traitor.

"He looks like he's ready to *cry*," said Talec, "and you expect to hold your throne with him at your side?"

I *was* ready to cry. But after their statements, I was terrified to show one single flicker of weakness. My parents were killed by someone they trusted, and we couldn't allow the same to happen to us.

"No dinner and no playtime," I said, and because Harristan sounded so unyielding, I forced my voice to be the same. I felt like I was playing a role for which I'd had no time to rehearse. "You will spend thirty days in the harvest fields. You are to fast from midday until the next morning."

There was absolute silence for a moment, and then Theadosia and Talec exploded out of their seats. "This is preposterous!" they cried. "You can't assign us to work in the fields with the laborers."

"You asked for a demonstration of my justice," I said. "Be sure to work quickly. I have heard the foremen carry whips."

Talec's eyes were like fire. "You're both children. You'll never hold this throne."

"Guards," I said flatly.

I remember worrying that the guards would not obey, that the council would overthrow us both. That we *would* dishonor our parents. After what Barnard had done, every face seemed to hide a secret motive that would lead to our deaths.

But then the guards stepped forward and took hold of Talec and Theadosia. The doors swung closed behind them, leaving the room in absolute silence. Every pair of eyes around the table sat wide and staring at my brother.

Harristan gestured at the seat to his right—the seat just vacated by Talec. "Prince Corrick. Take a seat."

I did. No one else dared to say a word.

Harristan has held on to his throne for four years.

We're later than usual today, and the food is likely going cool, but he's in no rush to eat. When my father ran meetings, there was a sense of jovial ease around this table, but that's always been lacking during Harristan's reign.

He glances at me. "You have the response for Artis?"

I place a leather folio on the table before him, along with a fountain pen. He makes a show of reviewing the document, though he'd probably sign a letter authorizing his own execution if I placed it in front of him. Harristan has little patience for lengthy legal documents. He's all about grand plans and the broad view. I'm the one who dwells in details.

He signs with a little flourish, lays the pen to the side, and shoves the folio down the table to Jonas Beeching, an older man with a girth as round as he is tall. I guarantee he's dying to eat, but he eagerly flips open the cover. He's expecting a positive response, I can tell. He's practically salivating at the idea of bringing chests full of gold back to Artis this afternoon.

His face falls when he reads the refusal I drafted. "Your

Majesty," he says carefully to Harristan. "This bridge would reduce the travel time from Artis to the Royal Sector by three days."

"It should also cost half as much," I say.

"But—but my engineers have spent months on this proposal." He glances around the table, then back at us. "Surely you could not make a determination in less than a day—"

"Your engineers are wrong," I say.

"Perhaps we can come to some sort of compromise. There— there must be an error in calculation—"

"Do you seek a compromise, or do you suspect an error?" says Harristan.

"I—" Jonas's mouth hangs open. He hesitates, and his voice turns rough. "Both, Your Majesty." He pauses. "Artis has lost many lives to the fever."

At the mention of the fever, I want to look at Harristan. I want to reassure myself that he's fine. That the rattle in his breathing this morning was all in my imagination.

I steel my will and keep my eyes on Jonas. "Artis receives a ration of Moonflower petals, just like the other sectors. If your people need more, they will need to buy it just like anyone else."

"I know. I know." Jonas clears his throat. "It seems the warm weather is causing the fever to spread more quickly among the dockworkers. We are having difficulty keeping ships loaded and staffed. This bridge would reduce our reliance on the waterways and allow us to rebuild some of the trade that has been lost."

"Then you should have asked for an appropriate amount of gold," I say.

"Artis can't build a bridge without healthy workers," says Arella Cherry, who sits at the opposite end of the table. She took over for her father when he retired last year. She's from Sunkeep, a sector far in the south that's bordered by the Flaming River on the west and the ocean to the south and east. Her people fare the best from the fevers, and it's thought that Sunkeep's high heat and humidity make them less susceptible—but the heat is so oppressive that their population is by far the smallest of any of Kandala's sectors. She's soft-spoken, with rich russet-brown skin and waist-length black hair that she keeps twisted into a looping knot at the back of her head. "Medicine should factor into their proposal."

"Every city needs healthy workers for all projects," says Harristan. "Which is why each city receives a ration of medicine for their people. Including yours, Arella."

"Yes, Your Majesty," she says. "And my people fare well because of it." She pauses. "But my people are not attempting to construct a bridge across the Queen's River in the dead heat of summer."

Her voice is quiet and deferential, but there's a core of steel beneath her gentle voice and soft hands. If she had her way, Harristan would seize Allisander's lands along with everyone else's, and he'd distribute Moonflower petals with abandon. We'd also be thrust into a full-on civil war when the other consuls refused to yield their territories, but she's never keen to acknowledge that side of things. That said, she's one of the few people at this table I enjoy a bit of conversation with.

Unfortunately, the last woman who weaseled her way into my thoughts also tried to poison me and Harristan at dinner. It wasn't the *first* assassination attempt, but it was definitely the closest anyone has gotten since our parents were killed.

So romance is off the table for me.

Allisander Sallister clears his throat. He sits almost directly opposite me, and his face is pale, with pink spots over his cheeks that look painted on. His hair and brows are both thick and brown, and he wears a goatee that he's clearly enamored of, but I think looks ridiculous. He's only a year younger than Harristan, and they were friends when they were boys. My brother had few companions when we were children, but Allisander was one of the few who had the patience to sit in the library and move chess pieces around a board or listen to tutors read from books of poetry.

But then, when they were teens, Allisander's father, Nathaniel Sallister, requested additional lands from a neighboring sector, claiming his farmlands yielded better crops—and would therefore yield better profits, and greater taxes for the Crown. Our father, the king, refused. Allisander then made a plea to Harristan, leaning on their friendship, asking him to intercede on the Sallisters' behalf—and still, our father, a fair and just man, refused.

"We cannot force one sector to yield lands to another," he said to us over dinner. "Our lands were divided by law, and we will not unjustly take from one to give to another."

He made Harristan reject Allisander's request personally. Publicly. At a dinner with all the consuls present.

In retrospect, I think Father meant to send a message, that it was unfair to seek favoritism through his children, and he wouldn't play those kinds of games.

But Allisander took it personally. We didn't see him in the palace much after that.

Not until last year, when his silver-hoarding father stepped down. Harristan had hoped Allisander would be a new voice for his sector, the key to distributing more of the Moonflower petals among the population.

Instead, he's worse than his father was. Under Nathaniel Sallister, Moonflower prices were expensive, but stable. Allisander never misses a chance to negotiate for more. Harristan doesn't like to think that their controversy as teenagers would have anything to do with the way Allisander barters now, but I have no doubt.

I spend a lot of time at these meetings imagining ways to irritate him.

"A new bridge along with extra medicinal rations would give Artis an unfair advantage at trade," Allisander says.

"An unfair advantage!" Jonas sputters. "You and Lissa control the Moonflower, and you want to accuse me of seeking an unfair advantage?"

Allisander steeples his fingers and says nothing.

Jonas isn't wrong. Allisander Sallister represents the Moonlight Plains, and Lissa Marpetta represents Emberridge—the two sectors where the Moonflower, the only known treatment for the fevers that plague Kandala, grows.

Therefore the richest sectors. The most powerful.

Also, the reason all my imagined irritants for Allisander stay in my head. I can hate him and need him as an ally at the same time. "Regardless of advantage," I say, "your motives in your proposal were deceitful, Jonas."

Allisander glances across the table at me and gives a small nod of appreciation.

I nod in return. I want to throw the fountain pen at him.

Roydan Pelham clears his throat from the other end of the table. He's pushing eighty, with weathered skin that can't seem to decide if it's more beige or more sallow. He's served on this council since my grandfather was king. Most of the others seem to grudgingly tolerate him, but I rather like the old man. He's set in his ways, but he's also the only consul who seemed genuinely concerned for us after our parents were killed. No one dotes on Harristan—or me, for that matter—but if anyone could be considered doting, it would be Roydan.

"My people suffer as greatly as Artis's," he says quietly. "If you grant this petition, I will seek the same."

"You have no river to cross!" says Jonas.

"Indeed," says Roydan. "But my people are just as sick."

My brain wants to drift. This is a common argument. If the proposal from Artis hadn't started it, something else would have. The fever has no cure. Our people are suffering. Allisander and Lissa won't yield the power and control granted to them by their lands and holdings—and as much as Harristan would love to be able to seize their properties, the other consuls would never stand for it.

Harristan lets them argue for a few minutes. He's more patient than I am. Or maybe he's just better rested. I did let him sleep till noon, when I've been up longer than the sun.

Eventually, my brother shifts his weight and inhales, and that's all it takes for them to shut up.

"Your petition was rejected," Harristan says to Jonas. "You are free to file another before we convene next month."

The man sucks in a breath like he wants to argue, but his eyes flick to me, and his mouth claps shut. My brother's temper has a limit, and no one here wants to find it.

"When your people are suffering," Arella says fearlessly, "it would not be inappropriate for the Crown to help make them well."

Harristan looks down the table at her. "At what cost? All of

Kandala is suffering. The supply of Moonflower petals is not endless. How would you choose, Arella? Would you sacrifice your doses? Your family's?"

She swallows. She wouldn't. None of them would.

I think of Harristan's cough this morning, of his fever last month, and I can't even blame them.

I wouldn't either.

"We will dine now," says Harristan, and the silent attendants shift away from the wall to begin serving the food. For a short while, the only sound in the room is the clatter of silver against china. But under it all, I catch the low hiss of Jonas's voice, spoken under his breath to Jasper Gold, the consul from Mosswell.

"They're heartless," he says.

I freeze. From the corner of my eye, I see Harristan's fork go still as well. It might be a coincidence. I wait to see if he'll acknowledge the words.

He doesn't.

And because I'm *not* heartless, I don't either.

CHAPTER THREE

Tessa

On a good day, Weston and I can make over a hundred deliveries of the elixir. I once thought we'd be better off making our rounds separately, because we could hit twice as many families, but Wes insists that one of us should always stand as lookout—and honestly, the stoppered vials get so heavy that I doubt I could carry enough for one hundred homes by myself.

Some days it feels impossible. Thousands are suffering. Possibly tens of thousands. We hardly make a dent—and sometimes we're too late, or we can't steal enough, or someone falls ill so quickly that the medicine refuses to work.

Those are the worst, when someone goes from mild body aches to dead between one visit and the next.

Today, we're able to get started on our rounds quickly, because we built up a good stash of crushed petals yesterday, so we don't need to waste time thieving. I won't admit this to Wes, but I'm still a little shaky over the few moments he was late. He'd never let me hear the end of it. As it is, we're walking through the woods while he whistles under his breath. He probably thinks I don't know the melody, a bawdy tavern song about a sailor wooing a maiden, but my father used to sing them all the time when he was busy crushing roots and measuring medicines, just because they would make my mother blush and giggle.

Thoughts of my parents still have the power to make my throat tight, so I shove them away and kick at pebbles in the path.

"You shouldn't whistle that song," I say. "It's vulgar."

He glances over and knocks the brim of my hat down a few inches. "Love is never vulgar, Tessa."

"Oh, you think it's a song about love, do you?"

"Well, I'm certain the maiden feels *something* for the sailor. Why else would she be removing her underthings?"

Now my cheeks are heated, and I'm glad for the darkness and the mask. I don't want to give him the satisfaction of hearing me giggle. "You're incorrigible."

"On the contrary. I am *highly* corrigible." He fishes an apple from his pack and offers it to me. "Breakfast?"

I blink at him. We didn't have time to go into the Royal Sector this morning. I don't like the thought of Wes going without my knowledge. Some days I wonder what I would do if he simply . . . vanished.

I shouldn't be so attached. I know I shouldn't. But since my parents were executed, the only constant in my life has been Wes. The thought of fate yanking him away, too . . . I almost can't bear it.

He must be able to read my expression in the forest shadows, because he says, "I saved one from yesterday."

"Oh." I hesitate. My stomach is still empty, but men who work in the forges don't get a lot of opportunities to eat, and I'm sure Wes is no different. "No—you have it."

He doesn't argue, and he bites into it, his crunching loud in the early morning air. "You sure?" he says, holding it out. "The honey's gone cold, but it's still sweet."

When I hesitate again, he picks up my hand and presses the fruit into it. "Lord, Tessa. Just share the apple."

His fingers are warm against mine, and I try not to think about the fact that his lips were just against this piece of fruit. I twist it to bite at a different spot.

He starts whistling that stupid drinking song again. I roll my eyes and take a second bite.

Many of the sectors in Kandala have open borders, with the exception of three: the Royal Sector, where the king and his brother and all of the elites live, plus Moonlight Plains and Emberridge, where the Moonflower grows. Those sectors are heavily guarded and walled off, and also boast the healthiest—and wealthiest— populations. The Royal Sector sits in the center of Kandala, though, bordered by five others. Mosswell sits to the north, which is mostly livestock and produce. Artis is east, known for its massive lumber trade because of the proximity to the Queen's River. The Sorrow-lands is a vast sector to the west, composed mostly of desert.

South of the Royal Sector are Steel City, home to metalworkers and machinists thanks to its proximity to the iron mines, and Trader's Landing, which has a bustling market that runs parallel to the Flaming River for miles. It's sometimes called Traitor's Land-ing, ever since their chief consul killed the king and queen.

The lands immediately surrounding the Royal Sector are heavily wooded and difficult to travel, dense with underbrush and brambles and thorns—the best place for our workshop, especially since it's far from the main gates, and our little wood fire never makes much smoke.

Beyond the woods are the lands where most of the sectors come together to surround the Royal Sector like spokes on a wheel. The area is densely populated because of the closeness to the Royal Sector—and it's also dense with poverty, illness, and armed guards watching for smugglers and troublemakers. My father used to say that the royal elites would sneer and call these lands the Wilds, a slur against the people forced to live and work there. But the people claimed the name for their own, and now living in the Wilds is almost seen as a point of pride, where sector borders are blurred and the people all feel united by desperation.

We always start in the Steel City part of the Wilds, because it's closest to our workshop, and I think Wes is less worried about getting caught by anyone he might know. We trade lookout at each house, because we can't just leave the vials and vanish into the night. We wake each person, make sure they drink every drop, then take our vials and leave. Leave no evidence, Wes always says. No proof.

The streets are empty and quiet in the early morning darkness, but Wes isn't whistling now. We slip from house to house in the shadows.

At the fifth house, I step up onto the porch just as a low moan sounds from inside. I hesitate with my hand an inch from the wood.

Weston is instantly at my side, appearing out of the darkness. "Tessa. What's wrong?"

The moan sounds again, and he freezes.

Mistress Kendall lives here with her son, Gillis. Kendall's husband died two years ago, but she and Gillis haven't shown any sign of the fever since, and they were two people I've felt we were helping. Gillis is thirteen, and he works as a runner for the forge closest to here. He's a hard worker, and he often whispers that he wants to join me and Wes once he's old enough. We haven't seen him in a week because his mother said he's been making early morning runs for supplies—but it means he's been missing the doses we bring.

Wes taps at the door lightly, and for a moment, we hear only silence. Then a fractured sob from inside.

Wes's eyes meet mine. I swallow.

He closes his fingers around the latch and eases the door open. Kendall is kneeling on the floor in the dark, a body wrapped up in blankets by her knees. She snaps her head up with a gasp.

Gillis. I suck in a breath, too. Wes puts a finger to his lips and shakes his head, and I'm not sure if it's at me or her. Probably both.

"Tessa," Mistress Kendall cries out anyway, half yelp, half sob. "Wes. He's dying."

Dying.

Not dead. Yet.

I stride forward and drop to a knee beside her. Gillis's eyes are closed, and his dark hair is matted with sweat. That's usually a good sign, meaning the fever has broken, but I think it has more to do with the blankets she's got wrapped around him. I'm surprised we didn't hear his breathing from the door. The death rattle in his chest is clear.

My own chest tightens. "Can you sit him up?" I whisper. "We brought medicine."

But we'll be too late. I can see we'll be too late. He's not even conscious. There's no way he can drink a dose—and little chance it'll do any good at this point.

Kendall nods hurriedly, and Wes meets my eyes. His expression is resigned, but he gets an arm under the boy's shoulders to help. Gillis's small body flops lifelessly, his head lolling against Wes's shoulder. I fish one of the vials out of my pack and pull the cork free. My fingers are trembling.

"Gillis," says Wes, and his voice is very low, very soft. "Gillis, open your eyes."

We all hold our breath. Hoping. Praying. Waiting.

In the beginning, when the fever began to steal lives, many people believed that it spread through close contact, especially since it seemed to affect those in the Wilds before striking the elites in the Royal Sector. The gates to the Royal Sector were kept locked for weeks. But my father kept records of those who grew ill, and as cases began to appear at random, even among those who closed themselves away, it quickly became apparent that the fevers had nothing to do with close contact. I've kept up my father's books, and there's no pattern to it. The illness might take one life—or a dozen.

It might leave an entire family unscathed—or it might leave a half-dozen bodies waiting for the next funeral pyre.

A sob breaks free from Mistress Kendall's chest again. Just when I've begun to give up hope, Gillis coughs hard, then blinks. "Ma?" he croaks.

Kendall gasps. "Gillis! Oh, Gillis!" She presses her hands to his cheeks. He blinks again slowly.

"Shh," says Wes. "The night patrol will hear. Tessa?"

I take a deep breath for the first time since we came through the doorway. "Here." I hold out the vial. "Gillis, you have to drink."

He coughs wetly. "Yes, Miss Tessa."

While Wes helps him drink, I dig through my pack hurriedly, pushing the vials of elixir aside, looking for my bottle of morningwood oil. A few drops will help rouse a drunk or someone with a head injury, but I've learned that it will also help the Moonflower elixir work more quickly.

Mistress Kendall is kissing his forehead, his cheek, her breath shaking, her hands fluttering. "Oh, Gillis," she whispers against his temple.

His hand lifts weakly to touch her cheek, but I pull the dropper of morningwood free. "This too," I whisper.

His dry lips part, and I tap three droplets into his mouth. His throat works as he swallows.

"There," says Wes. He finds Gillis's hand and gives it a squeeze. "You'll be slipping through the shadows with us in no time."

Gillis blinks, but then a slow smile finds his mouth. "Promise."

"I promise."

Mistress Kendall presses a kiss to his cheek again, murmuring nonsense, but the love in her tone is pure and clear. I put a hand on her shoulder. She looks at me, tears gathering in her eyes.

Gillis coughs, hard, then tries to inhale, but the muscles of his neck stand out as he fights for air. His fingers dig into Wes's arm.

"Slow," Wes says, but I can hear the concern underlying his tone. "Slow, Gillis. Breathe."

The boy's jaw clenches tight, and his back arches, his fingers grasping at nothing.

Then he flops back against Wes's shoulder, his entire body limp.

Kendall is frozen. I'm frozen.

Wes is the one who moves, laying the boy flat, pulling the blankets free. He presses two fingers to Gillis's throat, then drops to put an ear against his chest.

Gillis doesn't move.

Wes looks up. His eyes are blue pools of sadness.

"No!" Kendall's voice is a sudden shriek, full of rage and pain and fear that echoes in my own chest. "No!"

Somewhere in the distance a dog starts barking.

She keeps screaming. "This is their fault! That horrible king or his horrible brother or any of those other horrible people who live on the other side of that wall. I hate them! I hate them! I hate—"

Weston grabs her arm and slaps a hand over her mouth. His voice is a low rush of words. "Kendall. Get a hold of yourself."

"Wes," I whisper.

"It's treason," he snaps at me. "If the night patrol hears, they'll kill her, too."

"I don't care," she moans. She's sagging against him. "Let them kill me. Let them see what they've done to my boy."

I take a long, shuddering breath. "Kendall—I'm so sorry."

"He was just a boy." She inhales, then seems to steel herself, and she runs a hand against her son's face. "It's their fault, you know." Rage fills her voice again. "They sit in there healthy, and they leave the rest of us to live or die."

We've heard this a hundred times. We'll hear it a hundred more.

It's why we do this. Because she's right.

Wes pulls a vial from his bag and holds it out. "You need to take yours, Kendall."

She takes the vial in her shaking hand, and I think she's going to pull the stopper and drink it, but instead she moves to hurl it into the darkness. I gasp.

Always quick, Wes snatches it out of the air before it goes far. "Don't let your grief make you stupid."

His voice isn't unkind, but she flinches and all but crumples onto her son's body. "Give it to someone who wants to live. I don't."

I hesitate, then put a hand over hers. "Kendall," I whisper. "Kendall, I'm so sorry."

She turns her hand to clasp mine within hers. "You know what it's like," she says. "You lost someone, too."

"Yes," I say. My father. My mother. I'll never be able to erase the moment of their death from my memory. Unbidden, tears form in my own eyes.

"Someone needs to stop them," says Kendall, her breath shaking. "Someone needs to stop them, Tessa."

"I know," I say. "For now, we do what we can."

She nods, then lifts my hand and kisses my knuckles.

"You should drink your medicine," Wes says gently. "Gillis would want you to."

"Gillis can't care anymore." She draws a shuddering breath. "Go. Both of you. Don't waste your potions on me."

I inhale to refuse, and her face contorts with fury. "Go!" she shouts. "Go! You remind me of him. *Go!*"

I jerk back.

"Tessa," says Wes. He catches my elbow.

I don't want to leave. We shouldn't leave her like this, a broken husk of a woman sobbing over the body of her son.

But Wes is right.

"We'll tell Jared Sexton," I say to her quietly, referring to a woodworker a few houses away. He's big and burly—and usually the one who drags bodies to the pyre for burning. "I'll check on you tomorrow."

She doesn't answer. She's sobbing into her hands now.

We slip away into the shadows, our feet practiced at making no sound on the pathways. Weston must see or hear something, though, because he quickly jerks me into the pit of darkness by the corner of the next house. My back is against the building, and he's all but pressed against me, his head ducked, partially blocking mine.

"What—" I begin, but his eyes jerk to mine, and his head shakes almost invisibly.

I peer past him. There's little light, but now I can hear the booted footsteps of the night patrol. Wes was right—they likely heard Kendall's screams, and now they're here to check it out. It's too dark for me to see her. Maybe they won't see anything, and they'll pass by.

But no. Kendall comes flying through her door. "You killed him!" she screams. She has a rock in each hand. One flies, and a man cries out. "You tell that pig of a king and his evil brother that they'll burn for their—"

A crossbow fires. The arrow hits with a sickening sound. Her voice goes silent, and her body drops.

I whimper. Against me, Wes goes rigid.

One of the patrolmen kicks her body.

"Leave it," says one of the others. "They'll find her."

Another one spits at the ground. Maybe at her. "They'll never learn."

"Tessa." Weston's voice is a bare hiss in my ear. "Mind your mettle, girl. They'll kill you, too."

His weight is against me, pressing me into the wall, his hand over my mouth. I don't realize I'm struggling against him until I stop. My eyes meet his, and when I blink, he goes blurry.

"I know," he whispers.

My breathing shudders. I clench my eyes closed. His hand comes off my mouth.

I press my face into his shoulder, shaking with tears like a child.

After a moment, his hand presses to my cheek below the mask, his thumb brushing away the tears that slip down my face. "I know," he says again. "I know."

At some point, my tears slow, and I realize that Wes is nearly holding me, and I want to stand right here in this circle of his comfort, because the idea of anything else is too terrible. The thought feels immeasurably selfish in the face of what happened to Kendall and Gillis, but I can't help it. Wes is warmth and safety and . . . friendship.

He draws back at exactly that moment, his hand falling to his side. He's looking into the distance, his eyes searching for trouble. "We should head west now. The night patrol is already keyed up. I don't want to take a chance. If we have time, we can double back and do the rest."

I swallow and try to force my thoughts into some kind of coherent pattern. "Yes. Sure." I sniff back the last of my tears and swipe at my face. I'm full of sorrow now, but I know from experience that later it's going to rearrange itself into rage. "Should we—should we do something about her body?"

"No," he says. He reaches out to straighten my hat. "They're right. Someone will find the body."

"Weston!"

"Shh." He puts a finger to his mouth, and he shakes his head. "I'm not being callous. We can't help her anymore, Tessa." He adjusts his pack, the vials clinking. "We do have rounds."

"Right." I swallow. "Rounds."

We head into the darkness again, shifting silently through the night. Weston's usual lighthearted banter is gone. His whistling is silent. The air is heavy, as if we carry the weight of what happened along with us.

"I hate the king," I whisper. "I hate the prince. I hate what they've done. I hate what Kandala has become."

My voice is so soft that I wonder if he can even hear me, but after a moment, Wes reaches out to take my hand. He gives it a squeeze, for just a second longer than necessary—the only sign that this affected him as profoundly as it did me.

"Me too," he says.

Then he lets go and nods at the horizon, any hint of vulnerability gone. "Morning is coming. We'll have to step quick."

CHAPTER FOUR

Corrick

When Harristan was very young, he was weak and sickly. He fell ill often. This was before the fevers had begun to terrorize our people—before I was even born. I've heard rumors that my mother and father were relieved when she became pregnant with me, because there was a time when they worried Harristan wouldn't survive, that they'd be left without an heir. Our parents spent so many years coddling him that they never seemed to stop, even once he grew out of his childhood illnesses. Weeklong hunting trip? Harristan remained behind in the palace, while I was free to gallop off with Father and the nobles. Journey to distant sectors? Harristan would ride in the carriage, protected from the sunlight and the cool air, while I would ride with the guards and advisers, feeling far older than I was when they included me in their banter.

You'd think this would breed resentment between the two of

us: Harristan's born of envy for my freedom, and mine born of envy for all the attention he received. But it didn't. No, resentment never bred because Harristan was good at *sneaking*. Sneaking out of the palace, sneaking away from watchful eyes, sneaking out of his gilded prison, as he used to call it.

Resentment never bred because he always took me with him.

We'd wait until the moon hung high overhead, then dress in the plainest clothes we owned, stuff our pockets with copper coins, and sneak out of the Royal Sector. He taught me how to watch the patterns of the guards, how to sprint through the gates in the shadows, how to tell which smiles were genuine and which smirks meant someone was going to try to trick you.

Some of the elites will sneer about the dangers of the Wilds, but when we were younger, the Wilds were full of magic and adventure. Music would play until late in the night, dancers spinning by firelight. We'd pick at roasted meat with our fingers and drink home-brewed ale that was so much better than the dull wine served in the palace. We'd climb trees and shoot arrows and dodge the patrolmen. And the people! So many people. Fortune-tellers and jugglers and metalworkers and dancers and farmers and artists. We'd listen to stories and sing bawdy drinking songs, and even though no one knew who we were—because who would expect the heir and his brother to be laughing around a bonfire in the middle of the night?—we were always welcome, because no one was a stranger in the Wilds.

Sometimes now, as King's Justice, I'll see a face and wonder if it was someone I knew as a child. I'll wonder if the thieving woman I'm sentencing to a month of hard labor in the limestone mines is someone who once poured me an extra cup of ale. Or if the

Moonflower smuggler I'm condemning to die by fire is the man who once read the lines in my hand and told me I'd live a long and happy life, winking as he promised I'd have a big-breasted woman at my side.

I don't like dwelling on thoughts of the past.

Honestly, I don't like dwelling on thoughts of the present either.

They're heartless.

Jonas's words from yesterday's council meeting are haunting me. I keep wondering if Harristan heard him. I don't want to ask. For as close as we are, some of his thoughts are better left a secret, just like my own.

It's late, and my windows are dark. My brother likely retired long ago, but despite how early I wake every morning, I always have a hard time finding sleep. I have another request to read, another plea for money, this time from Arella. She turned it in after Jonas's proposal was rejected, and it's brief and rather hastily written, so there's a part of me that wonders if it's being done in retaliation somehow. Or maybe she senses that silver sits ready to be spent, so she should grab it before Jonas can reorganize.

I sigh and rub at my eyes.

When a knock sounds at my door, I look up in surprise. "Enter."

A guard pushes the door open. "Your Highness. Consul Sallister requests a word."

I pull my pocket watch free and glance at the face. I want to ask if Allisander is aware that it's nearly midnight, but he likely knows and doesn't care. He's one of the few people who could demand an audience at this time of night and have it granted.

I sigh, then shuffle the papers together and lay them facedown on my desk. "Send him in."

Despite the late hour, Allisander is still buttoned up in all his finery from the day. I've long since abandoned my jacket, and my sleeves are rolled back. He takes in my dishabille and says, "Forgive me. I did not realize you had already retired."

"I haven't."

He waits for me to indicate that he may sit, but I don't.

"The smugglers have grown more bold," he says. "I am receiving word of interrupted deliveries, of thievery on the road, of supply loads being raided. And that is outside the Royal Sector. You know it has long been a problem within your own walls."

I take a sip from my cup of tea. "When smugglers are caught," I say, "they are punished severely."

"The rains have been heavy this year. Our crops are not as plentiful as they were last year. Combined with raids on our deliveries, we may have a supply issue."

"Does that mean you *do* have an issue, or you *might*?"

"The promise of a problem is nearly as bad as the problem itself, Corrick."

His father used to be a pain in the ass, but there's something worse about hearing these words from someone not much older than I am. His tone is patronizing. His use of my given name is patronizing. His stupid goatee is patronizing. I have no idea how my brother was ever friends with this man.

I set down my cup. "I can offer armed guards for your supply runs into the Royal Sector."

"I will gladly accept them. We will also be increasing our prices by twenty percent."

"Twenty percent!" The absolute gall. He heard me refuse funding to Artis because they already suffer for lack of medicine, and now he's raising his prices. I don't know if this is simple greed or if it's rooted in humiliation, as if he takes any opportunity to retaliate against Harristan.

Either way, I want to throw my tea at him. I settle for raising an eyebrow and tracing my finger around the rim of my cup. "You believe your crops have suffered that much?"

He shares what he must think is a conspiratorial smile. "We must protect our supply." He hesitates. "If you feel that our pricing is too extreme, I can speak with Lissa. We can try to work within our current constraints."

His voice is pleasant, unchanged, but I hear the veiled threat. Kandala needs their Moonflower crops. All of us do.

I think of Harristan's coughing in his sleep yesterday morning, then quickly shove the thought out of my head before any shred of worry can manifest in my eyes. "No need," I say. "Your position is understandable." I pause. "I imagine Consul Marpetta will be raising her prices as well?"

Lissa Marpetta rarely says much in our council meetings, but it's always assumed that she will act in accord with Allisander. Her sector, Emberridge, provides half as much of the Moonflower petals as his—but it's enough for her to carry a great deal of influence.

"I believe so," he says. "Of course we will happily pay taxes on our revenue, as always. If our supply runs remain safe, this could be quite a benefit to the Royal Sector—and therefore to all of Kandala."

He thinks he's doing us a favor. As if the bulk of these taxes won't come straight from our own coffers when we buy our own supply.

Sometimes I wish I knew how my father would have handled this kind of conversation. Or rather, how Micah Clarke, the previous King's Justice, would have handled it. Father was a well-loved and temperate man, known for kindness and fair ruling. But maybe that was a luxury afforded to him by allowing someone else to handle the more challenging political intrigues.

Either way, I have no idea. Micah was killed when our parents were. And our people weren't suffering like this when Father and Mother were in power. The fevers had only just begun to spread. People weren't making choices between whether to feed their families or buy medicine.

Another rap sounds at my door, and I sigh. Does no one sleep? "Enter," I call.

The guard swings the door wide. "Your Highness. Master Quint would like a—"

"Yes, yes, yes," says Quint, shoving past the guards with no regard for whether I'll even see him. "I don't need to be announced." His red hair is a bit of an unruly mess, as usual, and I doubt his jacket was fully buttoned at any point today. He takes note that we're not alone and all but skids to a stop. He gives a brief nod to me, and then to Allisander. "Your Highness. Consul."

Aside from my brother, Quint might be my favorite person in the palace. He's young for his role as Palace Master, but he was apprenticed to the last one, and when the man wanted to retire, I told Harristan to give Quint a chance. He's honest as the day is long, and he keeps secrets better than a dead man. He's also got enough energy for half a dozen people, talks twice as much as necessary, and has little patience for pomposity and presumption. He annoys Harristan to no end. He annoys pretty much everyone to no end.

I rather love him.

Allisander's mouth forms a line. "Master Quint. We are in the middle of a *private* conversation."

Quint blinks like that's quite obvious. "I see that." He makes no move to leave.

Allisander inhales with clear intent to speak words that will chase Quint out of here.

I pick up my cup of tea. "We're nearly done, though, are we not, Consul?"

His mouth snaps shut. He doesn't scowl at me, but almost.

I offer him an indulgent smile. "I believe we've come to an understanding."

It's the best sentence in my arsenal of courtly lines, because it means absolutely nothing, yet somehow always makes people believe I've acknowledged their point.

It does the trick now, too, because Allisander's expression smooths over. "I'm glad to hear it."

"I'll draw up an order for guards for your supply runs in the morning."

"Early, Corrick," he says pointedly. "We'd like to return to the Plains before midday."

I go still. He can raise his prices and make pains about his supply runs being in danger, but just like my brother, I have a limit. Allisander Sallister may have money and power, but he does not rule Kandala—or me.

He must read the change in my expression, because he says, "At your convenience, of course. With my thanks." He pauses, then adds, "Your Highness."

I set down my cup. "You'll have it in the morning."

Once the door swings closed behind him, Quint drops into the opposite chair. "Does he want to be fed to the royal lions?"

"Don't tempt me." Though really, it's not tempting. I ordered it as a sentence once, for a man who'd killed an entire family in order to hoard their supply of Moonflower petals. Watching the lions tear him apart while he screamed for mercy was the most horrific thing I've ever seen. Even Harristan, always stoic since we watched our parents murdered, had later said to me, "Don't do that one again."

"Sallister wants more guards?" says Quint.

"Among other things." I take in his tousled appearance and try to determine whether he looks more harried than usual. It's possible Quint doesn't even know it's so late. "Have you eaten? I can call for a meal."

"Ah—no. I dined with Consul Marpetta at . . ." He pulls out his pocket watch and frowns at the face. "That can't be right."

I smile. "You sleep less than I do."

"No one sleeps less than you do."

True enough. "I'll send for food. Wine too?" I stand and move toward the door. "Or should you be sober for whatever you came crashing in here about?"

"A runner just arrived at the palace. The night patrol in Steel City unearthed a group of smugglers. Two were killed in the fray. The other eight have been taken to the Hold."

I stop and look at him. "That's a large pack."

"They had quite the operation, from what I understand."

Quite the operation. It's rare to have outlaws and smugglers working in larger groups. Ten is unheard of. The risk of discovery is simply too great. The punishments too severe.

Maybe Allisander wasn't exaggerating about the threat to his supply runs. I was going to make him wait, but now I'll be sure to draw up an order before I go to sleep.

"Does Harristan know?" I say.

"No."

My brother will want to issue a statement early. He'll expect me to make an example of them all.

At least one of us is sleeping.

"I'll call for food," I say. "Send a message to the Hold. I want to speak to the patrolmen who captured them. Tell them I'll want to question the prisoners after sunrise. Separate them if they haven't already done so. I don't want them conniving a story."

Quint has taken a piece of paper from the desk, and he's been writing since the moment I began speaking. He's good at his job. "Shall we make a public announcement?"

"Not yet." My thoughts are reeling. Eight all at once. We'll be lucky if we don't start a riot. "Tomorrow. Midday."

He glances up. "Should I wake the king?"

I think of Harristan's cough. The fever. He needs to sleep. I blink the thoughts away. "No."

Quint nods and rises, taking his paper with him. "I'll see to it."

I follow him to the door. He pauses with his hand against the handle and turns to look at me. "You asked about wine . . ."

"I'll order plenty."

CHAPTER FIVE

Tessa

I shouldn't be daydreaming about Weston. It's the least productive way to spend my time. I should be focusing on measuring thimbleweed for Mistress Solomon's ointments, or thinking about how many houses we missed this morning since Wes said it wasn't safe to sneak into the Royal Sector. I should be thinking about how many coins I have in my purse, and whether it would be too indulgent to buy some sweets from the baker.

I should be mourning Mistress Kendall and Gillis. But thoughts of their deaths fill me with more rage than sorrow, and my hands begin to shake, until it's all I can do to avoid flinging rocks at the patrolmen myself.

Thoughts of Wes are safe, and nearly as indulgent as the sweets would be. He was pressed so tightly against me yesterday morning, his palm against my cheek, his voice so soft in my ear.

When we were in danger, my brain whispers at me. It was not a romantic moment.

I don't care.

Karri, the other assistant, is grinning at me over her own scale. We're the same age, but instead of the freckled tan skin and brown hair that I have, Karri's skin is a rich, deep brown, with shiny black hair she wears twisted in a rope that reaches her waist. "What are you blushing about?" she says.

I bite the inside of my lip. "Nothing."

She leans in against the table and drops her voice, because Mistress Solomon doesn't like it when we gossip. "Tessa. Do you have a sweetheart?"

I try not to blush. Instead, my traitorous cheeks burn hotter. "Of course not."

I would never hear the end of it if Weston knew I was blushing over the idea of him being my sweetheart. Never.

"What's his name?" she says.

I blink at her innocently. "Whose name?"

"Tessa!"

I add some thimbleweed to my bowl and begin to smash it with the pestle, grinding it against the stone. "It's nothing. There's nothing."

She pouts, but her brown eyes are twinkling. "Tell me about his hands."

Unbidden, my thoughts summon the image of the apple held between his fingers.

I sigh. I can't help it.

She bursts out laughing. "You have a sweetheart."

I glance at the front of the shop. "Shh."

"If you won't tell me his name, will you tell me what he looks like?"

Words come to mind so quickly that it's a miracle they don't fall out of my mouth. *He looks like revolution. He looks like compassion. Blue eyes and gentle hands and quick feet and a core of strength and steel.*

I grind hard with my pestle, and Karri laughs again. I wonder how dark my cheeks have gotten.

"I can't wait to meet him," she says.

That will never happen. I sigh for an entirely different reason now.

"Is he from Artis?" she asks.

I have to give her something, or she'll never stop rooting for information. "Steel City," I say.

"Steel City! A metalworker, then."

"Hmm." I add more thistleroot to my bowl.

"Steel City?" says Mistress Solomon. She's caught wind of our conversation, and she leaves the front of the shop to come peer at what we're doing. "Are you talking about the smugglers?"

"What smugglers?" says Karri.

"There was an announcement from the Royal Sector at midday. They caught a pack of smugglers from Steel City. Ten of them, all from the same forge."

My blood goes cold.

Mistress Solomon tsks under her breath. "We're lucky the night patrol looks out for the people, you know. Those criminals deserve everything they get. We all get our allotment of medicine. No one needs to be greedy."

I bite my tongue. Not everyone gets an allotment of the Moonflower petals, and she well knows it. Only those who can pay for it. That's how she makes such a market from her ointments and potions—it's cheaper to buy from her. It's cheaper because it doesn't really work, but I can't say that if I want to keep my job. Back when the healing effects of the Moonflower was first discovered, there were hundreds of charlatans who tried to pass off other leaves and petals as the Moonflower—but when the king put as strict a penalty on fraud as he did on smuggling, the fake petals quickly went away. It's easier to just steal it than to grow and nurture something that simply looks the same.

There are plenty of shop owners like Mistress Solomon, though. People who can't cure the fevers, but who claim to "help" with symptoms. I wouldn't work for a true swindler, but Mistress Solomon seems to mean well. Most of the potions we create are for frivolous things like clear skin or shiny hair or trouble with sleep. Sometimes her mixtures won't work, but I know what will, and I adjust my measurements accordingly.

I keep notes in my father's notebooks of what cures the fevers—the Moonflower—and what doesn't: everything else.

My ears are still ringing with what Mistress Solomon said: ten smugglers were captured. All from the same forge.

Weston. He doesn't work with anyone else. I know he doesn't.

But Weston isn't even his real name. And if that's not real . . . maybe I don't really know anything for sure. Maybe the ten of them are people like Wes, who pretend to be working solo with friends in other sectors who don't know the truth.

I have no way to find him. No way to ask.

I swallow. "Did they read off names?"

"No. Six men, four women. Two of the men died in the capture."

I feel dizzy. "When—" I have to clear my throat. "When were they captured?"

"They didn't say. Yesterday, today, does it matter?" She sniffs haughtily. "You're overgrinding that thistleroot, Tessa."

"Oh. I'm sorry." She's wrong, but she won't like me saying so. She doesn't like the idea of an impertinent young woman telling her how to run her business—which is how the last girl was let go. I need this job. No one thinks an eighteen-year-old girl from the Wilds could be a real apothecary. My father would have found these tinctures and remedies ridiculous, and he would have told Mistress Solomon to her face—but my father isn't here to pay my rent, so I obediently drop the pestle on the worktable and scrape out the powder.

When she moves away, Karri is eyeing me. Her voice drops very low. "Is your sweetheart a smuggler?"

"What? No!" I'm sure my face is redder than fire now.

She goes back to her herbs, tossing a small handful into her bowl. "Mother says a lot of them are just trying to feed their own families. She's heard stories of men who promise the moon, getting women to help them, and really it's all for a half-dozen mouths to feed at home."

I scowl into my bowl. My stomach is churning, tying itself into knots. I don't know what's worse: Wes dead at the hand of the King's Justice, or Wes having a family at home.

What a thought. Dead is worse. Of course.

I always thought he was close to my age, but maybe he's older. I only ever see him in the dark, with kohl-smudged eyes hidden behind a mask. He could easily be twice my age, I suppose.

"Be careful, Tessa," says Karri.

I glance up. "I'm always careful," I say. And then I perfectly measure my medicines to prove it.

———◆———

Once the dinner bells begin ringing through the streets, Karri and I are free to go. She lives at home with her family, while I've lived alone in a rented room in a boarding house since my parents died. She watched me all afternoon and invited me to dinner, probably thinking my "sweetheart" must have been one of the captured men. I can't take her pitying glances for one more moment, so I turn her down and head home.

I stop in at the confectioner's anyway, deciding it isn't too much of an indulgence if I can hear any more gossip. As I hand my coins across, I say, "Can you believe they caught so many smugglers?"

The clerk nods sadly and says, "They'll all be put to death tomorrow, I reason."

That icy grip on my spine refuses to loosen, especially when she adds, "I understand they'll be doing it at the gates. You know that will draw a crowd."

I wish I had a way to find out if Wes is part of it. He can't be.

But . . . Steel City. A forge. That's too close.

I try to bide the time in my room, but the air is too stifling and my nerves are too jangled. I'll never sleep. I head for our workshop hours before we're supposed to be there and light the fire. I thought this would be better, to sit somewhere and wait, but it's worse. Every inch of this space is wrapped up in two years' worth of memories of Wes. *That's where he sits while I measure. That's the spot where he burned his finger on the woodstove. That's the window that broke during the winter storms, the one Wes boarded over while the snow swirled in.*

I fall asleep in the chair, sitting up, tears on my face. When I sleep, I dream. I dream of my parents, the night they were caught by the night patrol. I remember how I was ready to burst from my hiding place, ready to tackle the patrolmen myself. Wes caught me and kept me out of sight that night—but in my dream, he's caught, too, his body jerking as arrows pierce his flesh. I dream of Wes's body hung from the gates or his head on a stake. I see him broken and burning in a pile of bodies, while onlookers yell, though some cheer. I dream of him screaming for me, shouting warnings while they beat him with clubs, smashing his bones.

"Tessa. *Tessa*."

I open my eyes and there he is. For a moment, I think this is a new dream, that I've been so worried that my imagination has conjured him into this space, and I'll wake up for real and the workshop will still be empty.

But he's not. He's real and solid and his blue eyes are bright as ever behind the mask. My eyes well with relief, and I don't even bother to stop the tears from running over.

"You're crying?" he says, and he sounds so startled about the fact that I'm *crying* over him that I want to punch him right in the face.

Instead I lurch forward and throw my arms around his neck.

"Tessa," he says. "This is so sudden."

"Shut up, Wes. I hate you."

"Ah yes. Quite obviously."

I giggle through my tears against his shoulder. I should let him go.

I don't.

He doesn't either.

I want to ask if he knows about the people who were arrested, but instead, all that comes out of my mouth is, "Do you have a wife and a house full of children to feed?"

"No. Do you?"

I sniff and draw back to stare at him. For all his teasing, his eyes are serious, searching mine.

"You were right," he says.

"About the children?"

He grins. "No. No children." He shakes his head at me like I'm addled. "No, you were right that I should see you without your mask."

I gasp and slap my hands to my bare cheeks.

Weston's grin turns wolfish. "I regret not taking you up on the offer earlier."

I sink back into the chair and press my hands over my eyes, but of course it's too late now—and truly, he was the one who never wanted to see me. "I was . . . upset. I wasn't thinking. I was so worried." My voice breaks on the last word.

He drops into the opposite chair. "Tell me all your fears."

"I thought you were one of the smugglers who got captured."

His face goes still, and his eyes seem to shutter. "I'm not a smuggler, Tessa."

"I know. I know you're not. *We're* not." I have to swipe at my eyes. "I just—they were from Steel City, so I thought maybe—"

"You see every single petal I take from the Royal Sector." His eyes have gone cold. "I've never sold anything that we've taken. What we do—"

"Wes! I know."

"*What we do*," he repeats, his tone as sharp as I've ever heard it, "is not the same as what the smugglers do. I'm not in this to line my pockets."

"I know," I cry. "Wes, I know." I sniff. "Me too. But it's all the same to the king and his brother."

He draws a long breath, then runs a hand down his face. When he looks back at me, his eyes are no longer so hard. "You're right. Forgive me."

I press my fingers into my eyes. "And I know you always tell me not to grow attached, but you're the only true friend I have, especially since—since—" My voice breaks again. "Since my parents—"

Wes takes hold of my wrists, so gently. "Tessa."

When he pulls me against him, I don't resist, and he holds me for the longest time. We hold each other. This is so different from the other day, when we were pressed into the shadows beside a house, hiding from the night patrol. Now it's just me and Wes, in the warmth of the workshop, our workshop, holding on as if we can keep out all the evils of the world.

"They'll be executed." His voice is so quiet. "At midday."

I nod against him. "I heard." I draw back and look up. "Do you think they deserve it?"

He hesitates, and his eyes are shuttered again. This isn't something we ever talk about. Our conversations revolve around how to avoid detection. How effective the medicines are, and whether a little browning on the petals makes a difference. How frivolous and wasteful the elites are. We discuss the people we lose to the fever, and the people who live.

We don't discuss what could happen, because I'm right. The king wouldn't care that we're stealing to help people. If we're caught, we'll be executed right next to the smugglers.

"I think . . . ," he begins, and then he shakes his head. "I think we're wasting time. Do you have your mask? The patrols have doubled because of—"

"Wes." I swallow and catch his arm. His voice was so harsh when he said, *I'm not a smuggler, Tessa.* "Do you think they deserve it?"

"I think that very few people truly deserve what they get, Tessa." He pauses, and for the briefest moment, sadness flickers through his eyes. "For good or for bad."

I think of my parents, executed in the street for doing the very thing Wes and I do. I think of Gillis, dying for lack of medicine, and Kendall, killed to leave an example. I think of the executions to come, and what that will mean for the people left behind.

I think of Weston risking his life to save mine, once upon a time, stopping me from falling to the same fate as my parents. I think of how he risks his life every night to bring medicine to people who need it.

"You only deserve good things," I whisper.

He gives a small laugh without any humor to it and looks away. "Do you think so?"

I catch his face in my palm and turn his gaze back to mine. As usual, his jaw is a little rough and a little warm, the fabric of the mask soft under my fingertips.

"I do," I say.

I wait for him to pull away, but he doesn't. Maybe we're both shaken. Maybe what happened to Kendall and Gillis has left us both reeling. The air between us seems to shift, and his eyes flick to my mouth. He inhales, his lips parting slightly. "Lord, Tessa . . ."

My thumb slips under the edge of his mask, shifting it higher.

Weston hisses a breath, and his hand shoots out to capture my wrist. I give a small yip of surprise at the suddenness of it.

His eyes clench closed. He lets me go. Takes a step back.

"I'm sorry," I whisper. I'm such a fool. He's always been so clear about where we stand. About where *he* stands.

"Put your mask on," he says roughly. "We'll lose the darkness."

I swallow and turn away, digging between the books in my apothecary pack until I find it. I tie it into place over my hair with shaking fingers. When I reach for my hat where it hangs on a hook by the window, Wes catches my arm and turns me around.

I suck in a breath, but he puts his hands on my cheeks to lean in close, and I all but melt into a puddle on the floor. My back hits the wall of the workshop, and my head spins.

Then Wes's mouth hovers above mine, and I lose all rational thought. His thumb traces my lower lip.

"Not never, Tessa," he says, and his voice is so rich and deep that he could be speaking straight to my heart. "But not like this."

I stare into his eyes, wide and guileless and pleading.

And ever the fool, I nod.

He pulls me forward and kisses me on the forehead.

I sigh. "I really do hate you."

"Always for the best." He takes a step back, puts my hat on my head firmly, then flicks the brim of his own up an inch. "Eight people will die at midday. Let's see if we can get enough medicine to spare twice as many this morning."

CHAPTER SIX

Corrick

Harristan never visits the Hold. If he wants to see a prisoner, they're dragged into the palace in chains and deposited on the floor at his feet. To my knowledge, he's never set foot inside the prison since the day our parents died. Possibly not even before.

I, however, am well acquainted. I know every guard, every cell, every lock, every brick. When I was fifteen, already drowning in grief so thick I could barely breathe past it, I quickly learned how to block emotion once I stepped past the heavy oak doors. We couldn't afford one single moment of weakness, and I would not be the one to cause my brother's downfall. I have heard every manner of scream without flinching. I have listened to promises and threats and curses and lies—and occasionally, the truth.

I have never hesitated in doing what needs to be done.

Today, Allisander has accompanied me to the Hold. After learning of the smuggling operation, he delayed his return home.

Both he and Lissa have stated that they will remain in the palace until they can be certain there is no danger to their supply runs.

I've often imagined Allisander walking through these halls, but in my imagination, he's usually in chains, a guard prodding him with a blade, instead of how he looks right now: exasperated and huffy, with a handkerchief pressed over his nose and mouth.

"Is there nothing you can do for the *smell*?" he says.

"It's a prison," I say to him. "The residents aren't motivated to make it pleasant."

He sighs, then winces, as if it required more inhaling than he was ready for. "You could have brought them to the palace."

"The last thing I need is eight martyrs being marched through the Royal Sector." I glance over. "I told you they're a sympathetic lot."

He glances back and seems to be taking shallow breaths through his mouth. I have to force my eyes not to roll.

"Did they reveal the names of any other smugglers?" he says.

"No." We reach the end of the hallway, which leads to a descending staircase. The guards here snap to attention and salute me. The smell is only going to get worse, but I don't warn Allisander.

"Nothing?" he demands. "And you questioned them thoroughly? You were convincing?"

"Are you asking if I tortured them?"

He hesitates. Most of the consuls—hell, most of the elites, if not most of Kandala—don't like what I do, but they say nothing because they believe it keeps them safe. They don't mind it as long as they don't have to talk about it. They'll wrap it up in pretty language and dance around terms like torture and execution by asking if I'm *encouraging forthright answers* or *terminating a risk to the populace.*

Allisander is bolder than most, though, and his hesitation only lasts a second. "Yes. That's precisely what I'm asking."

"No."

"Why not?"

Because despite all outward appearances, I'm not cruel. I don't delight in pain. I don't delight in any of this.

And they're all sentenced to die. The penalties for theft and smuggling are well known, and each prisoner knew it before they stole the first petals. Half of them are terrified. I only had to question one to discover that they were working together in the loosest sense of the word. One outright fainted when the guards let me into her cell.

Cutting off their fingers or whatever Allisander is imagining feels like overkill.

"In my experience," I say, "those who are facing execution are not eager to share information that will help their captors."

He's frowning behind his handkerchief. "But there could be more. Our supply runs could be at greater risk than we expected."

"They're roughshod laborers, Consul, not military strategists. From what I can tell, they're not very organized." It's likely the reason they were all captured so quickly.

We reach the bottom of the staircase. While the palace and many of the homes in the Royal Sector have been wired for electricity, the lowest level of the Hold has not. Outside, it's morning, but down here, it's dim and cold, lit by oil lamps hung at odd intervals, with gray walls and black bars. There are twenty cells, but they're never occupied for long.

"Go ahead," I say. "Question whoever you'd like."

He looks at me like he was expecting . . . more. As if I were going to walk down the line of cells and personally introduce him to each captive.

I lean against the opposite wall, fold my arms, and raise my eyebrows. "You can't very well do it after they're dead."

Allisander starts to sigh, thinks better of it, and turns for the first cell.

This one holds a man named Lochlan. He's not more than twenty-five, with coal-black hair, pale, heavily freckled skin, and arms bearing a lifetime of burn scars from a forge. When I questioned him, he stared back at me fearlessly and refused to say a word. This is the kind of man Allisander would torture, but I know it wouldn't make any difference. I've seen Lochlan's type before, men who think they can survive an execution through sheer force of will.

They can't.

He's sitting in the back of his cell, glaring darkly at both of us, but when the consul approaches the bars, Lochlan rises to his feet and comes forward. His expression is similar to one I'd wear if I were free to make my feelings for Consul Sallister known.

Allisander clears his throat as if he's addressing a dinner party. "I would like to know the names of any associates you—"

Lochlan spits right in his face. Some hits the handkerchief, but most hits Allisander right between the eyes.

He sputters and swipes at his face, then takes a step forward, rage transforming his features. "You will pay for that, you stupid—"

"Consul!" I start forward, but I'm too far. Lochlan has already reached through the bars to grab the front of Allisander's jacket. He jerks him face-first into the steel. Blood blossoms on the consul's face.

"I know who you are," Lochlan is snarling. Down the hallway, the other prisoners have been drawn to their own bars by the sound of the commotion, and those who can see begin yelling.

"Kill him!" they scream. "Kill him!"

Lochlan jerks Allisander against the bars again, and it's clear he needs no encouragement. "You're the killer. I know what you're doing to your people."

The guards are nearly upon us, but Lochlan rallies to jerk Allisander against the bars again. This time might really be a killing blow. I draw back a fist and throw a punch right into Lochlan's wrist where it extends through the bars. The bones give with a sickening crack. He lets go and drops back, screaming, clutching his arm to his chest.

Allisander falls to his knees in the hallway, choking on blood and mucus and arrogance. Rust-colored dirt from the floor is in streaks on his pristine clothing. His breathing is broken and hitching, marked by a thin whimper every few breaths. I stare down at him for a second longer than necessary.

Perhaps I delight in *some* pain.

I drop to a crouch in front of him. "Look at me," I say. "Is your nose broken?"

"I want him dead." His voice is thick and nasally, but he doesn't glance up.

"He will be," I say. "But I can't kill him twice. Now look at me."

He spits blood at the ground, then draws a ragged breath and looks up. A lump is already forming above his left eyebrow. He'll have two black eyes, and his lip is split, but his nose looks straight as ever. Pity.

The guards have filled the hallway now, chasing the other

prisoners back from their bars. Lochlan is curled on the floor of his cell, dry-heaving over his broken arm. One of the guards has a hand on the cell door, but he looks to me, waiting for an order on whether he should take action.

I shake my head, and the guard gives a brief nod before stepping away. I draw my own handkerchief from a pocket and hold it out to Allisander. "Here."

He takes it, somewhat sheepishly, and presses it to his mouth. I rather doubt he needs me to tell him he shouldn't have stepped right up to the bars like that, so I don't.

I straighten. "So," I say brightly, and he blinks wearily up at me. "Who would you like to question next?"

———

Harristan is fit to be tied.

"Why would you bring him there?" he demands. "What were you thinking?"

"I was thinking that our richest consul made a request, and I sought to honor it."

"Well, now he's requesting a spectacle." My brother is pacing the floor along the windowed wall of his chambers. The weather has turned overcast, promising rain and lending enough shadows to match his mood. "He's requesting that we send a clear message to anyone else who might be considering a similar plot."

For all my brother's anxious movement, I'm motionless in a chair. "We're executing eight prisoners, Harristan. It'll be a spectacle."

He stops and looks at me. Some unspoken emotion passes between us, a mixture of regret and loss and fury, but he blinks and it's gone. His voice goes quiet. "How are you going to do it?"

In moments like this, I sometimes wonder if Harristan regrets that moment with Allisander from so long ago, as if our father yielding to Nathaniel Sallister then would have somehow staved off Allisander's manipulations now.

I doubt it. I think he'd be worse.

I think we'd be forced to *do* worse.

I inhale to answer, but a sharp rap sounds at the door. Harristan doesn't look away. "Enter," he calls.

The door swings wide, and a guard says, "Your Majesty, Master Quint would like—"

"No," says Harristan. His eyes still haven't left mine.

"Oh, let him in," I say.

My brother sighs and glances at the doorway. "You have ten minutes, Quint."

Quint was bouncing outside the door like an eager puppy, documents and folios clutched to his chest, but now he comes bustling through. His jacket is unbuttoned, his hair unruly. He never bothered with a shave this morning, so his pale jaw is dusted with red. "I only need nine."

"I'm counting."

Quint sets down his materials and launches into a litany of issues in the palace, from a shortage of straw bedding for the royal cattle requiring a decision on whether to substitute wood shavings, to a disagreement among the kitchen staff about whether Harristan prefers ivory tablecloths trimmed in green or burgundy tablecloths trimmed in gray. My brother casts me a withering glance when Quint shifts into a request from the Royal Sector to ring the dawn bells at two hours *past* dawn so people aren't woken so early.

"Could they really be called *dawn* bells, then?" I say.

Harristan sighs. "I feel rather certain we've passed nine minutes."

"It's hardly been eight and a half," I say. I really have no idea.

Quint makes a note on his papers. "I do still need to address the matter of pardon requests we've received this morning."

Harristan waves a hand. "You're done, Quint. Draft the usual response."

"But—"

"Out."

"I'll just leave them with you, then." Quint shoves most of the paperwork he was carrying toward the center of the table, then turns for the door.

"Wait!" says Harristan. "Leave what with me?"

I lean forward and take the top piece of paper from the pile. It's scribbled and unsigned, but requests can be made at the palace gates by any citizen.

We're all dying. You're just killing them quicker.
Show mercy.

I skip to the next one.

Free the rebels from Steel City.

I flip through a few more. Some are hastily written, some are more eloquent, but they all beg for the same thing.

"Pardon requests," I say hollowly. We always get a few—but never to this extent.

"How many are there?" says Harristan.

Quint hovers by the doorway. "One hundred eighty-seven."

I set down the letters and look at my brother. "As I said. A spectacle."

"One is from Consul Cherry," says Quint.

That gets Harristan's attention. "Arella?" he says. "I thought the smugglers were captured in Steel City." That's firmly Leander Craft's territory, while Arella speaks for Sunkeep, far in the south.

"They were." I push aside the thinner parchments and scribbled pleas until I get to the folios at the bottom. Arella's is black leather, the cover stamped with Sunkeep's sigil in gold: half a sun descending into a rolling sea.

To His Royal Majesty, the Esteemed King Harristan,

I write to you in regard to the men and women imprisoned on charges of smuggling and illegal trade. While I recognize that true crime deserves punishment, these men and women are not criminals. They are acting out of desperation to help their families during a time of need. I humbly request that you might find it in your heart to pardon them.

We of Sunkeep are willing to welcome them into our territory if you will grant clemency.

Yours in service,
Consul Arella Cherry

I read it out loud, and Harristan looks at Quint. "You dragged me through twenty minutes of nonsense when this was sitting on the table?"

My brother's voice could cut steel, but Quint doesn't flinch. If anything, he looks somewhat incredulous. "I brought a day's worth of issues to you and attempted to fit them into nine minutes. As per your request."

Harristan swipes the leather folio out of my hands, but he's still glaring at Quint. "I gave you *ten*."

Quint opens his mouth to argue, but I have no desire to see him as the ninth victim today, so I say, "Did Leander issue a request?"

"No," says Quint.

Harristan scans the letter I just read, then snaps it shut and looks back at the Palace Master. "Anyone else of importance? Or were you going to tell me tomorrow?"

"The usual elites from the Royal Sector," Quint says. There are a few families who request a pardon for every captive. They're always denied, but they always ask.

Quint glances at the pile. "A few others are from influential families. Many requests came from the Wilds. No other consuls."

I look at the folio in Harristan's hands. I'm surprised Arella submitted her request this way, instead of coming to speak with me directly. "Is Arella still here?" I say.

"She left at dawn," says Quint. He pauses. "She and Roydan shared a carriage."

Harristan goes still at this news. After a moment, he says, "That's enough, Quint." He sets the folio on the table.

"Your Majesty." Quint offers a quick bow, then escapes the tension of the room.

We sit in the silence for a long moment, until Harristan eventually eases into the chair across from me. He picks up one of the pardon requests, reads it, gently sets it aside. Then another. Then another.

I wait.

He reads them all.

He's been the fierce king for so long now that I sometimes forget how he was when he was the beloved crown prince, the boy who was sheltered and coddled and doted upon. I remember he once told me he was glad that Father took me along for hunting trips, because he'd go pale at the sight of blood, and he hated the idea of putting an arrowhead into a living creature.

When he finally looks up, I see a glimpse of that boy in his eyes.

I lean in against the table. "Allisander was already going to raise his prices before this happened. You have nearly two hundred pardon requests sitting here, but I imagine you'd have three times as many decrying their crimes."

He holds my gaze. "Arella requested a pardon for smugglers on the same day Allisander claimed his supply chain is being attacked. He won't be happy. It pits her against him."

I snort. "Who's not against Allisander?"

"You," he says.

I lose any shred of humor. "Only in public." I frown. "And you well know that."

"In *public* is all that matters." He pauses. "It likely pits her against Lissa Marpetta, too. I find it interesting that she shared a carriage with Roydan."

Roydan Pelham. Some at court might think the old man was after Arella because she's young, cultured, and beautiful, but I've known Roydan my entire life, and no one is more devoted to his wife than he is. He's also played court politics for so long that he wouldn't be seen climbing into a carriage with Arella unless it meant something. "Their sectors border one another."

"Exactly." He pauses. "It's a risk to stand against Allisander. Especially now."

"Arella's people have always fared the best against the fevers," I say. "Maybe she feels like she has less to lose."

Harristan runs a hand across his face. He wants to pardon the prisoners. I can see it in the set of his jaw. I don't know what about them has drawn his sympathy, whether it's the number of captives, or the quantity of requests we received, or if it's simply that he's as tired of violence and treachery as I am, and he longs to be kind to someone. Anyone.

Kindness killed our parents.

Harristan coughs behind his hand, and my attention sharpens. I go stock-still.

His breathing sounds fine. His color is good. He's fine.

I think it again, more emphatically, as if I can will it to be true. *He's fine.*

"If they go free," I say slowly, "Allisander will see it as the Crown taking a stand against him, too." *Again*, I think. "We aren't just talking about affecting the supply to the palace, Harristan."

"I know."

"We're talking about the entire Royal Sector. We're talking about all of Kandala."

"I *know.*"

"We can't side with criminals," I say. "This is the first time we've seen a larger group attempt to organize. If we're lenient, it will lead to more raids, to more thefts, to more—"

"Cory." His voice is quiet. "I know."

I say nothing. We're in agreement, then.

We've come to an *understanding*.

I sigh. So does he.

My brother pulls his pocket watch free. "We're two hours from midday. You never did tell me how you're going to do it."

My thoughts turn dark, a black cloak already dropping across my mind to stave off any emotion. I do what needs to be done.

"Wait and see."

CHAPTER SEVEN

Tessa

I have no desire to see eight people hung or garroted or chopped into bits or whatever other horrible fate the king and his brother will come up with, but Mistress Solomon wants to see the executions, and she expects Karri and I to join her.

"It's right to see people punished for their crimes," she says to us. "We could all use a reminder that there are punishments for those who take what they haven't earned. We have a duty to be grateful for all our rulers do to provide for us."

I remember my parents, killed for trying to bring more medicine to the people. I consider Mistress Kendall, executed in the street for crying out in her grief, or poor Gillis, who definitely didn't deserve to die because his mother was too poor to buy medicine for them both.

I'm not sure what I feel, really, but it definitely isn't gratitude.

There are wagons full of people heading for the gates to the

Royal Sector, so Karri and I hitch up our homespun skirts and climb onto the first one with space available while Mistress Solomon pays an extra coin to sit up front near the driver. We're pressed together at the back, sharing a bale of hay to sit on, but I don't mind. The day is overcast and cool, with a hint of mist in the air.

Karri leans close. "Have you seen your sweetheart?" she murmurs. "He's not one of them, is he?"

I meet her gaze. "No. He's not." I remember Wes's eyes, almost hurt when I said I thought he was caught up with the others from Steel City. "He's not a smuggler."

"He's well, then?"

I think of Weston in the firelight, his thumb tracing over my lip like it was something precious, and I press my fingertips to my mouth. I could almost taste his breath as he said, *Not never, Tessa. But not right now.*

Karri grins and bumps me with her shoulder. "He's well."

I wonder if he'll be somewhere in the crowd today. He said a lot of the forge workers would likely be in attendance, but whether he meant it in solidarity or in judgment, I couldn't tell.

Probably just like everyone else flocking to the gates: partly horrified, partly curious.

Partly relieved, because someone else's downfall generally means your own isn't imminent.

I don't grin back at Karri, because it feels odd to smile while we're being carted along to watch someone else die. Wes wasn't among them, but I wonder if he knows them, or if he knows someone close to them. No one in Kandala is a stranger to what happens to smugglers, but always before it's been one or two, like Wes and me. Never a group.

When the fevers first began taking lives, it wasn't long after King Harristan had come to power, naming his brother, Prince Corrick, as King's Justice. Father was a true apothecary then, providing real medicines and elixirs, not like the potions and herbs that Mistress Solomon dispenses. He knew how to ease an ache or salve a burn or calm a colicky infant. Mother and Father weren't anxious about a new king, at least not at first. King Harristan and his brother were young, but the royal family was loved. We were all shocked by the assassination—and all of Kandala mourned along with the brothers.

That is . . . we all mourned until people began to fall sick and die. Father tried tinctures and poultices and every combination of herbs he could think of, but nothing worked—until a healer in Emberridge discovered that the petals of the Moonflower could reduce the fever and allow the body to heal itself. Within a fortnight, word had spread to all the sectors. Fights broke out over supply of the Moonflower. Raids and thievery became common. Deals were worked in back alleys and shadowed sitting rooms, where gold or weapons or anything of value would be traded for a few days' doses. Emberridge and Moonlight Plains, the only sectors where the plant grew, quickly hired enforcers to guard their borders, and later they built a wall.

At first, King Harristan tried to maintain order, but desperate people take desperate actions, and there was never enough medicine to go around. We had people knocking on our door at all hours of the night, begging for whatever Father could do for them, and I'd mix elixirs and potions and teas in the hope that anything else would work.

Nothing ever did.

Out of desperation, Father found a smuggler who was willing to cut our family in on whatever he stole, provided we gave him half our proceeds from selling the medicines to Father's patients.

Father would charge half and gave all the money to the thief. He always said it was more important to save everyone we could. That a few extra coins in his pocket wasn't worth the cost of a few more bodies on the funeral pyre. It was then that he discovered that spreading the medicine among more people would still save lives. He tried to share his records with the king, but there were too many apothecaries, too many theories, too much fear and death and pain. Everyone was afraid to take less.

Then King Harristan struck a deal with the Emberridge and Moonlight Plains sectors, using royal funds to provide doses for the people of Kandala, allocated by sector. It wasn't enough—there was never enough—but it was something.

King Harristan also promised a death sentence for thievery, smuggling, and illegal trade.

His brother, Prince Corrick, the King's Justice, made good on that promise.

Brutally. Publicly. Horribly.

But it was effective. Within a month, order had been restored. Many people had access to medicine.

Many, but not all.

Father tried to continue helping, Mother at his side.

And then they were caught. Sometimes I wonder if I was lucky that they fought back, that they were executed in the early dawn hours by the night patrol. That they didn't have to stay in the Hold, waiting to die, knowing their daughter would have to watch.

Lucky.

Karri squeezes my hand. Her gaze has turned pitying. "I find it upsetting, too," she whispers.

Not like I do. Her parents never do anything wrong. They're almost afraid to take the medicine allotted to them, as if they're being greedy. But she means well, so I squeeze back.

The gates to the Royal Sector are closed, but a massive wooden stage has been dragged into place before it. I'm too far away to see much detail, but the stage is high enough for everyone to get a good view. Eight armored guards stand in a line, crossbows in hand. At their feet kneel the eight prisoners. They're all in muslin tunics, with burlap sacks tied over their heads, so I can't tell who's a man and who's a woman. They must be bound in place somehow, because two seem slumped, their heads hanging at an odd angle.

I wonder if those two are already dead. One has a stain at the front of the burlap, something soaking into the material. Blood, maybe, or vomit.

I have to look away. My throat is tight.

The road is mobbed with people, and I've already lost sight of Mistress Solomon. People mill and churn, and gossip runs high. The emotion of the crowd is overwhelming, pressing against me like something alive.

"Look," says a man nearby. "That one's pissed himself."

I don't want to look, but my eyes are traitors and they shift to the stage anyway before quickly flicking away. The man is right. I wonder how much terror you need to feel before that would happen.

It's not a hot day, but I feel sweaty and sick.

The burlap is awful. The guards are awful.

The king is awful. The prince is awful.

I want to rush the stage. I want to grab a crossbow. I want to lie in wait and fire a bolt right into them both.

It's a ridiculous thought. I'd be dead before I got anywhere close. I swallow hard, and rage pushes away some of the emotion churning in my gut, replacing it with white-hot fury. It allows me to look up, to lock my gaze on those prisoners.

If they have to die, I can watch it happen. I can remember them. My soul burns with a promise that things will get better. That they have to get better.

I wish Weston were here. I'm better with the medicines, with the dosages and the treatments and our patients, but he's better in the face of violence and danger. He's cool and reserved when I'm hot and rattled.

I look around the crowd, at the hundreds of people who've gathered, and I think he must be here somewhere. It gives me some comfort. I search the faces around me, looking for the ice blue of his eyes, for the faint freckles I know dust his cheeks below where the mask sits.

Men are everywhere. Blue eyes are common. So are freckles.

I close my eyes and whisper a prayer. *Oh, Wes. I need you.*

He doesn't appear. But horns blare, and conversation quiets almost immediately. Figures ascend what must be a set of steps on the opposite side of the stage: more guards, these with armor trimmed in purple and blue, signifying them as members of the palace guard. One carries a staff; the other carries the flag of Kandala, a panel of blue and purple split diagonally, with a lion encircled in white sitting directly in the center. They're followed by two more guards who are heavily armed.

Then King Harristan appears, though as usual, he's too far for me to see much more than dark hair, booted feet, and a long black jacket that nearly reaches his knees. A silver crown sits on his head, glinting in the sunlight.

A herald calls out, "His Majesty, the highly esteemed King Harristan."

For a moment, I can see more clearly, because people are dropping to a knee, and Karri is pulling at my hand.

I don't want to kneel to him. I want to spit at him.

I imagine what Wes would say. *Mind your mettle, Tessa.* My knee hits the cobblestone of the roadway. Karri squeezes my hand again.

"Rise," says King Harristan, and his voice is loud and clear. It's all he says, before stepping back to stand between his guards. He's probably bored. Irritated that this bothersome little execution is taking him away from a game of chess or a luxurious bath or whatever ridiculous diversions he enjoys while the rest of us are out here in the sectors, trying to survive.

We rise. I can taste bile in my throat. I focus on not breaking Karri's fingers with my right hand. The fingernails of my left hand are cutting into my palm.

Another man arrives on the stage. His hair is lighter than his brother's, more red than brown, but from here, his eyes are shadowed and dark, unreadable. He also wears boots and a long jacket, but no crown sits on his head. He doesn't need one. He wears his role like a mantle, some kind of invisible weight that clings to his frame, echoed in every step. This is Prince Corrick, the King's Justice. He's not usually the one to swing the blade or light the fire or draw the arrow, but he's the one to give the order to kill. The executioner.

"They're very handsome, don't you think?" whispers Karri.

NO, I DO NOT THINK.

"They're horrible," I whisper.

Her head whips around, and I watch as her eyes flick from face to face to see if anyone heard. "*Tessa.*"

I swallow and refuse to take it back.

After the herald announces him, Prince Corrick moves to stand parallel to the prisoners. His voice is cold and carries an edge. "You have been charged with smuggling and—"

"Don't let them do this!" one of the prisoners yells. It's a man's voice, but it takes me a moment to figure out which one has cried out. "There are hundreds of you! Thousands! The Benefactors will get you medicine! Don't let them do this!"

Beside me, Karri goes rigid. The guard behind the shouting prisoner cracks him on the back of the head, and the prisoner sprawls face-first onto the stage, his hands bound behind his back. He doesn't stop yelling. "Rise up!" he shouts. "Rebel! Don't you see what they're doing? Don't you—"

The guard fires his crossbow. I'm too far to hear the impact, but the body jerks and goes still. The crowd sucks in a gasp.

Another prisoner takes up the shouting. This time it's a woman's voice. "You can stop this! Listen to the Benefactors! You can stop this! You can—"

The guard hits her next, and she goes skidding forward onto the wood of the stage. The other prisoners have started shouting, too, cries for rebellion, for defiance.

No one cries for mercy.

A man shouts from somewhere in the crowd. "They're just trying to survive!" A woman yells, "We need their medicine!" More shouts join theirs until the crowd begins to shift, and it's impossible to know where all the cries come from. Karri and I are shoved apart as people begin to surge forward.

"Fight them!" rages the woman on the stage. "Fight back!"

Another guard fires his crossbow. Her body jerks like the man's did, but it must not have been a killing blow because she begins using her legs to shove her body forward. The other prisoners must sense an opening, because the others are fighting their bonds, struggling forward on the stage—at the same time as citizens are storming forward. The sound has surged into a roar of angry shouts and panicked cries as people are jostled and shoved. An elbow catches me in the temple, and then a shoulder drives into my rib cage. I've completely lost sight of Karri. Guards have taken the stage now, blocking the king and his brother from view—if they're still there at all. Crossbows fire wildly, but the prisoners were right: there are maybe two dozen guards on the stage, and there are hundreds of citizens.

A man barrels through the crowd, and I'm knocked aside. I feel myself falling, and I try to find purchase, but there's nothing. A booted foot catches my jaw, and I taste blood. Another steps on my leg.

Then a hand has a hold of mine, surprising strength in its grip.

Wes, I think.

But no, it's Karri. She pulls me to my feet, then pulls me back, away from the stage. Her lip is bleeding. Tears glisten in her eyes. "We have to get out of here."

She doesn't need to tell me twice.

Chapter Eight

Corrick

Six months before our parents were killed, there was an assassination attempt. The fevers had only just begun, but I was hardly aware of a problem. Then, my parents were still well loved, and I'd just begun to attend their meetings with the consuls. My brother had been attending for years, and I'd heard stories about them all. Allisander's father, Nathaniel Sallister, was full of bluff and bluster, and he challenged my father on every issue.

I remember being presented with my own folio, my own fountain pen. At my side, Harristan was doodling horses and dogs in the margins of his own folio—but I could tell he was listening to everything said. I read every word twice, hoping to have an opportunity to share my "worldly" insights on something. Anything.

By the time the meeting pushed past two hours, however, I was bored and looking for any excuse to leave. I'd begun sketching caricatures of the consuls in the margins of my folio, complete with Nathaniel urinating on a pile of papers. Harristan glanced over, choked on a laugh, and drowned the sound in a sip of water.

Stop it, he mouthed at me, and I grinned.

Across the table, my mother gave us both a look, but her eyes were twinkling.

Then a crash and a shout echoed from the hallway, and the twinkle disappeared from her eye. Everyone at the table went silent. Another shout, followed by many more. My father was blocking my mother against the wall. Harristan grabbed my arm and shoved me behind him, but I wrestled to get in front of him.

"You're the heir," I hissed, like he needed a reminder.

Something hit the door with a loud *thunk*, and it didn't matter which of us was in front, because my father gave an order, and two guards blocked us from view. My heart was in my throat—but what's worse is that I remember being more worried that Consul Sallister would see my drawing than of anything happening.

Wood cracked and split, and men poured into the room. Crossbows fired almost instantly. The men fell—all except one.

Micah Clarke, the King's Justice before me, caught one by the arm. He twisted it up behind the man, then slammed him facedown on the table, right where I'd been sitting. My eyes were wide, and I could hear Harristan breathing.

My mother peeked out from around my father. "Why?" she whispered. "Why are they here?"

Micah looked at my father. I don't know if he was waiting for permission, or an order, or something else entirely.

But my father looked away.

The man wrenched his face up from the folio and inhaled. Later, Micah would say he was going to spit at my parents, but to me, it looked like he was going to speak.

He didn't get the chance to do either. Micah drew a blade and cut his throat. Blood poured all over my drawings.

We never found out who sent them. It's long been rumored that they were the first attack sent from Trader's Landing, but we've never been able to prove it.

I think about that day sometimes. The way my mother seemed confused. The way my father looked away. The way my brother kept trying to drag me behind him.

The way everyone was afraid, except the King's Justice, who was forced to act.

Today, I expect Harristan to be furious after the riot outside the gates, but he's not.

I am.

Listen to the Benefactors.

I don't know what that means, but I've been turning it over in my head since the guards dragged us off the stage.

The consuls requested a meeting the very instant we returned to the palace, but my brother has been making them wait. He's been quiet for hours. Thoughtful. Contemplative.

The longer he sits quietly and thinks, the more agitated I become, until I'm the one pacing his chambers.

Three of the prisoners escaped during the melee. Five were killed, but three slipped into the crowd when citizens began swarming the stage and the guards moved to protect Harristan and me. One of them was Lochlan, the man who smashed Allisander's face against the bars.

The consul is probably boiling with rage. I'm surprised steam isn't pouring from the other side of the door.

As if on cue, someone raps at the door. "Enter," calls Harristan.

One of the guards swings the door wide. "Your Majesty, Master Quint would like to remind you that the consuls are gathered—"

"They can wait," says Harristan.

The guard nods. The door swings closed.

"You can't hide in here all day," I say to him. "We need to address this."

"I'm not hiding." Harristan doesn't move. "Do you think it was planned?"

"Which part?"

He looks at me. "All of it." He pauses. "There were cries for revolution in the crowd, Cory."

You can stop this!

Fight them! Fight back!

I run a hand across the back of my neck and sigh. "I heard them."

"Everyone heard them." He hesitates as if he has more to say, but he falls silent. He's so quiet that I can hear the clock ticking on his desk. After a moment, he coughs, and my head snaps around.

That makes him glare. "Stop that. I don't need a nursemaid."

I study him, looking for telltale signs of the fever. His cheeks aren't flushed, and his eyes are clear. I listen to his breathing anyway.

His eyes narrow. "If you want to worry about something, worry about what we're going to tell the consuls."

"I thought that's what *you* were spending all this time thinking about."

"Allisander will be furious."

"Undoubtedly."

"Lissa will be as well."

"I've already offered guards for their supply runs."

"They're going to want more. More assurance. More promises. More . . . *more.*"

Then I realize what he's been waiting for. What he's not saying. He asked for a spectacle this morning—and he got one. Not the one he wanted, surely, but it was a spectacle all the same. Now he wants another one. Something that will appease the consuls and stop the populace from thinking revolution is an easy path.

He's been waiting on me.

I finally stop pacing and look at him. "Then let's give them more."

─ ◈ ─

Allisander only has one black eye, but the bruising across his jaw and forehead seem to make up for it. It must have been too painful to shave around that perfect goatee, because it looks like he started before giving it up. Poor baby.

The pain doesn't stop him from railing at me during the consul meeting. "They were all to be taken care of," he snaps. "Now you've let three get away."

"I didn't let anyone get away," I say evenly. "They're not the first to escape, and they surely won't be the last."

"They can reorganize," he says. "They'll be after our supply runs. You'll see." He slams a fist down on the table. "You promised me, Corrick."

"I've offered additional guards." I glance across the table at

Lissa Marpetta, who's been sitting in silence while Allisander has a tantrum. "For your supply runs as well."

"Who are these Benefactors?" she says, looking down her nose at me coolly.

"I have no idea."

"*No idea,*" thunders Allisander. "No idea, yet you felt no need to torture them during questioning—"

"It's concerning," Lissa says quietly, her voice at complete odds with Allisander's, "that your guards were unable to complete their duties in time."

"Those guards should be tried for treason," Allisander snaps.

"Those guards kept your king alive," says Harristan, and there's enough of a chill in his voice to remind them who's in charge here. It draws some of the tension out of the room, though displeasure still hums in the air around us.

At the end of the table, Roydan clears his throat. "Consul Sallister. You wish to punish a dozen guards for failing to stop a thousand people from rushing the stage?"

Arella Cherry adds, "Should we assume you punish your own guards when your supply runs are attacked?"

Allisander turns his glare on her. "My sector is no business of yours." He pauses for a rage-filled breath. "I understand that you asked for these smugglers to be *pardoned.*"

She doesn't flinch, and her eyes are ice-cold as she regards him. "People in these sectors are dying, Consul Sallister. They're not criminals. They're desperate."

"We can't keep them alive if outlaws keep raiding our supplies," says Jasper Gold, Consul of Mosswell. "I've heard reports of missing dosages from within the Royal Sector. Escaped prisoners always embolden others. Especially if they're being funded by someone with means."

His words drop like a rock. Most of the people with means in Kandala are sitting at this table—or they're close to someone who is.

"Are you implying someone here knows about these raids?" says Roydan. He sounds truly concerned, as if insurrection from within our own circle only just occurred to him.

Arella makes an exasperated noise. "You think these rebels are well funded? They were barely more than children!"

Jonas Beeching clears his throat. "Those *children* were old enough to commit a crime." He glances at Allisander. Jonas is still smarting from his bridge proposal being rejected, and he very obviously wants to keep friends at this table. "They should be stopped at all costs."

Allisander turns a glare his way. "You were just seeking twice as much silver as you needed, were you not? Perhaps we should investigate *your* finances, Consul."

I want to roll my eyes.

"Enough," says Harristan. "We've doubled the number of patrols in the Wilds. We've mandated searches of the forges in Steel City, and we've offered a significant reward to anyone who can provide the identity of the three smugglers—or anyone else involved in the trade of stealing Moonflower petals."

Quint's eyes almost bugged out of his head when he took down the orders. It's a reward large enough to provide medicine for a family for an entire year.

"Are you still offering them refuge in Sunkeep?" Allisander snaps at Arella. "Maybe we should start there."

"Go ahead," she says evenly. "I am not harboring criminals."

"We need swift action," says Lissa. "Do you not agree, Your Majesty?"

"I agree," says Harristan. His gaze shifts to me.

My thoughts have been spinning with shock and anger since the moment we lost control of the crowd, but now that I realize what is expected of me, a cool certainty takes over my thoughts. "Swift action?" I say. "Or swift justice?"

Allisander looks across the table at me, and I can tell he's remembering the moment in the Hold, when Lochlan jerked his face into the bars and I broke the man's wrist with my bare hands.

I wonder how much of Allisander's fury is rooted in the fact that Lochlan is one of the prisoners who escaped.

"Both," he says, and his tone is vicious.

I've never backed away from brutality, and I don't now. I hold Allisander's eyes and nod. "Consider it done."

Chapter Nine

Tessa

This time when I head for the workshop, I'm wide awake, my mask tied firmly in place, kohl darkly smudged around my eyes. My jaw aches, but I ignore it. My chest burns with anger and rage at the king, the prince, the horrible way we're all treated for doing what we have to do to survive.

My mind burns with the need for action.

The night patrol has been doubled, and even though I carry nothing more than my apothecary books, I slip through the woods with extra care. I won't bother to light the fire while I wait for Wes, because I don't want to take any chances. My heart has been tripping along in my chest all night.

When I get to the workshop, however, I don't need to wait. Wes is there already, leaning against the doorway, barely more than a shadow.

I stop short in surprise, but he straightens, then lets out a breath. "Tessa."

All the horror I've felt all day seems to evaporate when I see that he's still safe.

"Did you see?" I say softly. "Were you there?"

He doesn't need me to be specific. He nods, and his voice is grave. "I saw." He pauses, then glances out at the early morning darkness. "The patrol is everywhere. They're searching the forges."

It's unusual for Wes to sound unsettled, and that makes *me* unsettled. I swallow. "I heard."

His eyes return to meet mine. "It's a risky night for thieving and delivering."

"It's always risky," I whisper.

"I heard that three got away. There's quite a reward for their capture." He pauses. "For the capture of any outlaw."

"I heard that, too." Everyone who came into the shop this afternoon was talking about it.

Wes says nothing; he just looks at me.

It takes me a moment for realization to smack me across the face, and I draw back. "You think someone might turn us in."

He snorts, then runs his hands over his jaw. "It's a lot of money, Tessa." A hint of his familiar grin skips across his face. "I'm surprised you're not waiting here to turn me in."

"How do you know I'm not?" I tease, though everything is so serious that the words fall a bit flat.

Any hint of a smile vanishes, but there's a gentle warmth in Wes's voice when he says, "Because you wouldn't."

I blush, and I'm glad for the mask and the darkness. He's not wrong. I tug my treble hook from my pack and spin it in the night air. "We're losing the darkness."

He catches the hook with his nimble fingers, forcing it still. We stand there in absolute silence for the longest time, connected by the narrow length of rope. His eyes are heavy and dark and intent, and I wish I could read his thoughts. I'm glad he can't read mine.

I swallow and try to keep my mind on business. "Who are the Benefactors? Do you know?"

"No." He pauses. "I thought you might."

I shake my head. "We can ask when we make our rounds."

Wes says nothing for a moment, and when he speaks, his voice is very low. "There are calls for revolution. The king won't allow it to stand. They'll make an example of anyone they catch."

"They always do."

He snorts. "I don't think we've seen the worst they can do."

"You're afraid." I breathe.

His eyes skip away, and his jaw tightens. "I'm not afraid for me."

For me? Or for others in the forges? I'm scared to ask. "Wes."

"I've seen the atrocities they commit, Tessa. I've heard the stories." His eyes meet mine again, but now they've shuttered and gone dark. "I saw what happened by the gates. That's mild compared to what they'll do next."

I've seen the same atrocities. Heard the same stories. My heart flutters in my chest. I think of Mistress Kendall and all she lost. I think of the dozens of other families we bring medicine to, of all the people who will die without the medicine we bring. "We can't stop, Wes. People . . . people count on us."

His eyes close. "I'm not talking about forever. But perhaps—"

"No!"

"Tessa—"

"We can't!" I say fiercely. "We'd be sentencing them to death ourselves! We—"

He uses the treble hook to jerk me forward, and his hand slaps over my mouth. "You are aware they've *doubled* the night patrol, yes?"

I nod at him, wide-eyed. He lowers his hand.

"We can't stop," I whisper, though my voice is no less adamant. "We can't."

"We can." His eyes blaze into mine. "We can't help anyone if we're dead. Rebellion won't stop the fevers."

I swallow and think of my parents. My father did everything he could to make sure everyone had access to medicine. It led to their deaths, so maybe that should be a warning to me.

It's not. It's a legacy. "If you don't want to go, then stay here." I jerk my treble hook out of his hand. "I have people to help."

"Tessa!" he hisses behind me, but I don't stop.

My throat is tight with so much emotion. Anger. Fear. Worry. Disappointment.

I hear nothing, but he suddenly appears at my side, as quick and agile as a cat. "You're going to get us both killed," he says under his breath.

"If you're so scared, go home."

"I am not scared." He catches my arm and hauls me to a stop.

I look up into his eyes, flecked with sparks from the starlight. "When there are calls for revolution," I say to him, "we should be riding at the front, not hiding in the shadows."

His voice is so rough. "All we do is hide, Tessa."

"Maybe it's time we stopped. We don't know who these Benefactors are . . . but maybe they're onto something good. Something right."

He's so silent, so still, his eyes intent on mine.

"Maybe it's time to make a difference another way," I whisper, because everything feels so dangerous to say aloud.

When he says nothing, I lift a hand to touch the edge of his mask. He's so still, especially when the tip of my finger slides under the edge.

Just when I think he's going to let me tug it free, his eyes flick open and he ducks his face away. His voice is low and rough when he says, "Go back to the workshop. Heat the water. I'll make the run."

"Wes—"

"I'm faster. Don't look at me like that. You know I am." He pulls a small pack from his bag and presses it into my hand. "Here. There's a bit left from yesterday. I found some extra roseseed oil, too. Start the water and measure what you can. If we're quick, we can bottle the elixirs and make our rounds before daybreak."

His eyes are boring into mine, so I nod quickly.

I close my fingers around the pack and take a step back. I can't tell if he's angry or determined or we're both just fooling ourselves into thinking we can make a difference.

"Go, then," I say, and my voice almost breaks.

Something in his eyes fractures. "Lord, Tessa. Don't you understand? I'm not afraid for me. I'm afraid for you."

My heart is pounding so hard I have to press a hand to my chest.

Without warning, he strides forward, catches my waist in both hands, then presses his mouth to mine.

For a moment I'm breathless and startled, but my body quickly catches up. I yield to his touch, softening in the circle of his arms. A fire lights in my belly, racing through my veins until I'm warm all over. He's solid and he's strong and he's Wes, and I've imagined this moment so many times, but my imagination never did it justice.

Minutes—hours—days before I'm ready, he pulls away, his eyes full of stars again. He taps me on the nose. "Mind your mettle and keep your head down. I'll be back in an hour."

I'm pressing a hand to my mouth, my thoughts spinning. For all my talk of riding at the front of the revolution, I want to call him right back to find some decent shadows for the foreseeable future.

But his treble hook is already spinning free of his hand, whistling through the air to catch the edge of the wall. Without a backward glance, Wes is over the top, and I'm on my own.

—◆—

I light the fire and balance my scales, but my thoughts are still in the woods, remembering the feel of his lips against mine over and over again, the sound of his voice as he said, *Lord, Tessa*, before stepping forward to pull me against him. Or the way he said, *I'm not afraid for me*, while holding my gaze so steadily.

He still ducked away when I went to move his mask—but he kissed me. I've been tangled up with fury and regret and fear since the riots outside the gates to the Royal Sector, and maybe I still should be, but . . . Wes. Oh, Wes. His hands were so warm and his voice was so lovely and deep and his mouth was just . . . I sigh. All my talk of revolution and riding at the front, and now I just want to spin in circles while I mix my medicines.

But we're still taking action. We're not backing down from that horrible king and his awful, cruel brother. We're saving the people who need saving.

Fight back, one of the prisoners said.

We are. I'm not strong enough to rush a stage or attack the king or take down a patrolman in the woods, but I know how to save lives. Wes said that all we do is hide, and he's right, but what we do while we're hiding is what matters. What we do together is what matters.

Together. I press a hand to my chest to keep my heart from fluttering.

The kettle begins to whistle, and I take it off the fire just in time, pouring it carefully into the vials I've lined up.

In the distance, the alarm rings out in the Royal Sector, and I freeze in place. I set the kettle down and move to the window of our workshop. I can see the lights from here when they burst over the edge of the wall.

It's fine. He's fine. He really is faster than I am, no matter how much I don't want to admit it. They're looking for smugglers everywhere, so anyone could have tripped the alarm. He was fine the other day, so he's surely fine tonight.

I swipe suddenly damp hands against my homespun skirts and go back to the table. When I pick up the kettle, the lid rattles, and I realize I'm shaking.

I take a long breath and steady myself. He'll be back any minute, his usual cocky grin on his face. He'll poke me in the side and roll his eyes and tell me to hurry so we can grind more powder from the petals he's stolen. We'll spare a moment to think of whatever poor soul was caught, and we'll thank our lucky stars that we have another night together, helping people.

Together. My heart flutters again. This time, however, dread crowds its way into my chest. How long has it been? An hour? Or not quite? The alarms continue to blare in the Royal Sector, the lights spinning as they seek their prey.

Wes. Oh, Wes.

The elixirs have blended. I carefully pour the liquid into the vials and stopper them closed. The alarms fall silent.

I can hear my heart racing. I move to the door, my ears straining against the cool, early morning silence. Wes never makes a sound, so I expect him to jump out from behind a tree, or leap off the roof, or something equally foolish that will make me startle and then laugh and then punch him in the gut.

He doesn't.

My stomach is a pit of fear now. I can't draw a deep breath. I grip tightly to the doorframe until my fingers hurt.

Between the trees, the first hint of sunlight breaks the horizon. My throat closes up. I can't breathe at all.

It's been more than an hour. A lot more.

My fingers feel numb, and I can't tell if it's from the doorframe or the gasping breaths that are fighting their way into my lungs. I dive back into the workshop. I need to go after him. I need to find him. They take them to the prison first. To the Hold. I can get him out. I can—I need—I want—I need—

Light catches my eyes through the window, and a cry breaks free of my chest. Sunrise is happening, a new day beginning, heedless of my panic. My hand is already wrapped up in the rope of my treble hook, my pack falling over my shoulder.

Mind your mettle, Tessa.

A tear squeezes free of my eye, catching in the mask. I freeze in the doorway. I can't go out like this. Not in the sunlight.

I can't go after him.

I drop in the doorway of the workshop. Something in my chest gives way, and suddenly I'm crying into my skirts, shuddering against the doorway.

He's going to find me like this, and I'll never hear the end of it.

I'll take his teasing, and gladly, if he could just appear.

Please, Wes. I don't realize I've whispered the words until I hear my shaking voice. *Please, Wes.*

He doesn't appear. Sunlight streaks through the woods.

I can't keep sitting here in the doorway. We're in a remote part of the forest, but hunters and trappers aren't completely foreign in this area.

I jerk the hat off and tuck it down in my bag. I use the mask and some of the boiled water to scrub the kohl off my cheeks and eyes. I rebraid my hair and straighten my skirts, then tuck away the medicine, the bowls, and the kettle under the floorboards.

Please, Wes.

I hesitate in the doorway.

Nothing.

Maybe he had to run back to his forge. Maybe he couldn't risk coming this way. Tomorrow morning he'll be waiting with a good story for me.

"What was that?" he'll say, teasing. "I was right? We should have waited a few days?"

My throat refuses to loosen. My chest is caught in a vise grip.

I can't stay here. Mistress Solomon will be waiting for me. Karri will know something is wrong. My eyes feel raw.

I walk, forcing my pace to remain sedate. Just a girl out for a walk in the Wilds, heading to work early. No one of importance. I keep my ears open for the night patrol, but the city is beginning to come to life around me as I near more populated areas, and suddenly, I'm not at risk.

A woman and her daughter are hanging laundry between two trees, and I catch a few of their words as I pass. The girl shakes out a pair of trousers and hands them up to her mother. "Da said the prince is going to leave the body hanging there until he catches them all."

"He can hang up all he likes," says the woman. "You keep your eyes on your tasks. Those outlaws have nothing to do with us."

"Yes, Ma."

The prince is going to leave the body hanging there.

"You lost, girl?"

I jerk my head up. I've stopped, my hand braced against a tree. The woman is peering at me. I need to keep walking. I need to get out of here.

"The prince caught an outlaw?" I say, and my voice breaks.

"It's none of our business," she says curtly, but her daughter steps forward and says, "Yes! My da said they hung him from the gates, but he wouldn't let me see—"

I run. My feet dig into the path as I sprint for the gates to the Royal Sector, skidding around trees. I can't breathe. I can't stop. People are staring, looking up in surprise as I tear through the Wilds. Someone is going to grab me, to stop me, to announce that I'm not where I'm supposed to be.

No one does. And suddenly, I'm there, at the gates.

The girl was right. There's a body, hanging by its neck, the head hanging crooked. The face is bloated and purple, the clothing dark.

There's a mask across his face. A hat I know so well. A pack I've seen a hundred times strapped across his chest.

A treble hook hangs from the rope knotted around his hand, swinging gently in the breeze.

A dagger hilt sticks out from each eye socket. Blood has soaked into the mask, which means they did it while he was alive.

Trapped between the hilts is a blooming Moonflower.

This can't be real. This can't be real.

I don't want to keep staring, but I can't stop.

I'm not breathing. I can't breathe. My heart needs to stop beating. I need to stop feeling.

He didn't want to go. He was right. It was too risky.

He went for me.

The gate guards have taken notice of me, and one of them calls, "Guess he won't be making it home for supper, will he, girl?"

They all laugh.

My fingers curl into fists. I want to hit the guards with every ounce of my strength and fury. I want to light them on fire. I want to burn the palace to the ground. I want to steal every petal of every Moonflower in Kandala and watch the elites wither and die from the fevers.

I want to put daggers in the eyes of the king and his brother.

Mind your mettle, Tessa.

It's like his voice is in my head, and I choke on a sob. One of the guards must hear, because he peels away from the gate.

I need to run. Wes would want me to run.

That thought spurs me into action. I dig my feet into the trail again and run as fast and as far as I can, leaving a path of tears behind me.

CHAPTER TEN

Corrick

For as harried as he always seems, Quint is rather good at chess. It seems like the kind of game that would frustrate him, as so much time is spent sitting quietly and waiting on an opponent, but maybe it gives him an excuse to be still. Tonight, I'm the one who needs something to force me into stillness. I'm restless and antsy and troubled.

My windows are dark, and the fire burns low beside us, meaning I should probably be sleeping. So should Quint. My brother went to bed hours ago.

I rarely resent Harristan, but every now and again I wish he could bear the weight of this role, that he could be the one to look every prisoner in the eye as they take their last breath or say their last words or beg for everything I can never give them.

I shift my rook forward and wait, watching as Quint surveys the board.

He'll win. He usually does, but tonight I'm distracted and unsettled, so Quint has an advantage. Allisander and Lissa left after dinner, which should be a relief. With evidence of smugglers running loose and whispers of revolution in the street, it's not. I can't remember a time when the Royal Sector felt as if it held its breath like this, waiting, but the anxiety has bled into the palace, sharpening tempers to a razor's edge.

A knock sounds at my door, and I pull my pocket watch free. It's an hour till midnight.

"Enter," I call.

The guard swings the door wide. "Your Highness. Consul Cherry requests an audience."

Quint looks up from the board. "Should I send her away?"

It's tempting, but Arella has never come to my chambers, and I'm curious. "No." I run a hand across my jaw and sigh. "Send her in," I tell my guard.

Allisander always blows into my room like a thunderstorm wrapped up in silken finery, bringing demands disguised as requests, so I'm surprised when Arella eases in like a breeze, stepping quietly, her dark hair unbound, her body encased in a simple velvet gown that reveals every curve yet leaves plenty to the imagination. She curtsies to me, her fingers gracefully lifting the heavy velvet of her skirt. "Your Highness."

I don't move. "Arella."

Quint stands and offers her a nod. "Consul Cherry."

Allisander would ignore him, but Arella nods back. "Master Quint." Her eyes fall on the chessboard. "Do forgive me for interrupting your game."

I trace a finger over the top of my wineglass. "We'll see."

Quint is waiting to see if I'm going to send him out. He knows everything that goes on in the palace, and there are no secrets between him and me, but many of the consuls act like he's a nuisance and ask for privacy.

Arella doesn't. "I've seen the display you left at the gate."

"I'm hoping everyone has seen it. That's why I left it there." I glance at Quint. "It's still your move."

He eases back into his chair. He glances at me and then back at the board.

He might be the only one in the palace who knows how very much I hate this. All of this.

Arella isn't easily distracted—or put off. "Someone will climb up there and steal the flower."

"Good. Then we'll have a second body. My brother is disappointed we don't have three strung up there already."

In all honesty, I actually think Harristan was disappointed we caught one so very quickly. As much as he wants to appease his consuls and offer a show of strength, he doesn't like the thought of rebellion. When the smugglers were hiding in the darkness, it was easy to see them as criminals, as individuals clearly doing wrong.

It's hard to bring down the sword of justice on a thousand citizens who scream for rebellion and mercy in the bright light of day.

Arella appears to be choosing her words carefully, so I speak into the silence to say, "You've been spending a great deal of time with Consul Pelham."

I watch her for a reaction, but she offers none. One perfectly manicured eyebrow lifts. "Jealous, Corrick?"

"Of an eighty-year-old man?" I smile. "Maybe."

She doesn't smile back. "I find we have similar goals."

"You and Roydan? Tell me more."

"No."

"Check," says Quint.

I glance at the board. He's moved his knight into position to capture my king, but that's easily solved. I move one space to the right and look back at Arella. "Allisander and Lissa believe you are making a statement in opposition to them."

"How lucky for me that I don't pander to Consul Sallister and Consul Marpetta, then."

That statement is a little too barbed, and I lose the smile. "Why are you here, Arella?"

"Your people are suffering," she says. "These whispers of rebellion are not an attack on you and your brother."

"They're not whispers," I say.

"People are desperate. They're dying."

"Check," says Quint.

I sigh and move my king again. "I know people are dying."

"Your brother may wear the crown, but everyone knows two consuls rule Kandala."

My voice gains an edge. "You should watch your words."

"Or what? You'll throw me into the Hold?"

I inhale a breath of fury, but Quint says, "Check."

"Damn it, Quint!" I shove my king one more space to the left, then stand to face Arella. "I know our people are dying. So does Harristan. I am doing my best to keep them alive."

"Hmm. Would the man hanging from the gates agree?"

Her confidence would be impressive if it weren't all being used to stand against me. "You requested a pardon for the eight smugglers who were imprisoned."

"Yes. I did." Her eyes don't flinch away from mine. "Do you think your presentation before the sector gates would have ended in cries for revolution if your brother had granted it?"

I go still.

Outside my window, lights flash, and the faint sound of the alarms carries over the quiet of the night sky.

"Another prisoner," says Arella. She all but spits the word at me. "Another body for your wall."

"Another warning to other smugglers," I snap. "A promise to the people that their medicine supply will be kept safe."

"The medicine only a privileged few receive?"

My voice is tight. "We grant as much of the supply as we can, and you well know it."

"True strength is not determined by how brutal you can be," she says, and her tone is still quiet, but full of steel. "True leadership is not determined by killing those who oppose you."

"True leadership is not determined by slipping into the prince's chambers in the dead of night either," I say. "You could have gone to Harristan at any time, Arella. I notice you waited until the others were gone, and you bring your pleas to me instead of my brother."

To my surprise, she laughs. "I told you, I care nothing for Lissa and Allisander." She pauses, and her voice drops again. "I care for my people. I care for your people." Another pause, and she takes a step closer. "You are the King's Justice, not his executioner. I thought someone should remind you."

My jaw is tight, and everything I want to say would be a betrayal to someone who matters.

So I say nothing.

Arella frowns, then offers a curtsy. "Thank you for granting me an audience, Prince Corrick."

Once she's through the door, I take a long breath and run my hands back through my hair. I look at Quint, who's sitting impassively beside the chessboard.

"What?" I say.

He inhales as if to answer, then shakes his head. He reaches out and knocks over my king. "Checkmate."

CHAPTER ELEVEN

Tessa

I lose track of how many days pass. Maybe four, maybe five, maybe an entire month. I go to work, I mix the potions for Mistress Solomon, and then I walk woodenly back to my rented room where I fall into bed. The vials and scales and bottles for real remedies sit untouched on my side table. Herbs and leaves and petals dry up and crumble on their own, worthless.

I haven't returned to the workshop. Every time I try, my breathing goes short and my legs refuse to work. Too much . . . Wes.

I haven't listened to the names of those lost to the fever, read at the end of each week. There are many, though. Without Weston and me delivering a daily dose, the number of people dying has surely risen.

The guilt is almost as bad as the loss. I've hardly eaten. I've hardly slept.

When I do, I dream of Wes, of the warmth in his hands or the light in his eyes or the promise in his words. And then the dreams shift into nightmares, where a man in black drives daggers into Wes's eyes while he lies there screaming for mercy.

I hope he didn't beg. I hope he didn't give that evil prince the satisfaction.

This is the only thought that chases away some of my sorrow, letting rage pour in to fill the gap.

Weston's death is different from my parents.

Weston's death is different from them all.

I wish I'd listened. I wish we'd stayed in the workshop.

I want to wish he hadn't kissed me, but I can't. Every now and again, I touch my fingertips to my lips, as if the feel of him still lingers there. My throat always closes up and I choke on my tears, but I can't move my fingers, as if this tiny memory will soon be gone, too.

"Tessa. *Tessa.*" Karri's whisper takes a moment to break through my thoughts.

I clear my throat. "Sorry."

She studies me with clear concern. She's asked me a dozen times what happened, but I've already risked so much. I can't tell her anything. The night patrol is still doubled. I've heard rumors of other bodies stretched along the gate, but I have zero desire to discover what Wes's remains have been reduced to, so I haven't gone to see.

She knows something happened, though.

Her eyes flick down to the thimbleweed roots I'm grinding together. It's supposed to be a tincture to help someone with their complexion. As if someone's skin matters while people are dying.

"That's too much," says Karri, her voice a hushed whisper. "You'll end up killing someone."

Good. Maybe I'll spare them from the fever. Or the king.

It's a dangerous thought, and one I've had too often lately. I dump out my bowl to start over.

"Tessa!" cries Mistress Solomon from across the room. "That's my best thimbleweed!"

I can't make myself care. Wes is dead. My parents are dead. The world is gray and empty and cold. I cut a new stretch of root.

She hurries across the shop to stand over me. "Honestly, girl, your brain is gone lately. You're not with child, are you?"

I nearly burst into tears and choke on them to stop any from falling. With child. As if. *As if.* Without warning, I snort with laughter, and a tear snakes down my cheek.

She's staring at me, mouth partially agape. So is Karri.

I swipe at my face haphazardly. "Sorry. No. What?"

"That order is for the Royal Sector!" she says. "You'd best pay attention!"

Knowing it's for someone in the Royal Sector makes me want to light it all on fire. I grind at it half-heartedly.

But then my brain seizes on what Karri just said. *You'll end up killing someone.* I glance down at the pile of discarded grindings. She's right. The wrong combination can turn a tincture to a poison without much effort. There's a reason I insisted on measuring and weighing the elixirs Wes and I used to distribute.

I'm not entirely sure what I'll do with the discards, but I sweep the grindings into a length of muslin and wrap it up to tuck it into my pack.

I don't have a plan. I don't even have an idea, really. I just have rage and sorrow burning up my insides.

"Well, that's useless," Mistress Solomon says. "The rest of the month, I'll be collecting your wages."

My head snaps up. I may be wrapped up in sorrow, but I do know that I can't afford to lose more than half a month's income. "Let me make the delivery," I say to her. "Please don't take the thimbleweed from my pay."

"Don't be ridiculous, Tessa." She's already moving away.

"Please?" I say. "Surely a courier to the Royal Sector would cost more."

She glances back at me. She'll do anything to avoid paying for something.

I rest a hand over my stomach for half a second, until her eyes follow the motion, and then I jerk it away and clear my throat.

"Oh, Tessa," breathes Karri. "I wish you'd told me."

I swallow. I didn't consider that I'd be lying to Karri. She's so good and kind and warm that it feels like a crime.

"He abandoned you, didn't he?" she says knowingly, and I realize she's remembering our talk of how so many of the smugglers are just stringing stupid girls along.

Abandoned me. No. Wes didn't abandon me. If anything, I abandoned him. My throat closes up again.

Karri reaches out and gives my hand a squeeze. "You come round to the house tomorrow, and Mother will brew you some of her tea for the early sickness. She swears it helps."

Maybe it's safer if this is what she believes—that I'm just a silly girl who made a silly mistake, but now it's all over. I have to sniff back waiting tears. "That's very . . . very nice. Thank you."

Mistress Solomon draws herself up. She likely has a few thoughts about an unmarried girl getting herself into such a situation, but after Karri has been so kind, she likely doesn't want to turn down my request. "Very well, Tessa," she says. "If you're sure you're feeling up to it."

In my willingness to make a delivery to the Royal Sector, I didn't consider that it would require passing the gates where Wes's body hangs, and it doesn't come to mind until the smell hits me.

I stop short on the path. My mouth goes dry. I can't do this.

I don't even know what I was going to do.

Deliver a package. That's why I'm here. That's what I need to do.

The discarded powders wrapped up in a muslin bundle can just sit in my apothecary pack next to my record books and the delivery I'm to make. I'll toss them into a fire. Then I'll toss myself into a fire.

An elderly man is driving a donkey with a small cart, and he glances at me as he goes past. "You get used to it after a while," he says.

No. I won't. And we shouldn't. We shouldn't get used to this.

Wes wouldn't hesitate. He *didn't* hesitate. He leapt over that wall because I needed him to. Because I wanted him to.

I square my shoulders and walk. There's a horrific buzzing in the air that finds my ears before I reach the gate, and it's not until I round the bend that I realize what the sound is: flies. They're everywhere, in the air, on the trees, feasting on the bodies—because of course there are more than one now.

There are six. I can't tell which were men and which were women.

I can tell Wes, though. His body has begun to decompose, the daggers beginning to slip from the loosened tissues of his eyes. The flower is gone. The rope of the treble hook has sunk into the gray skin of his wrist.

"It's not Wes," I breathe to myself. "It's not Wes."

Because it's not. It's a corpse. A body. Not the rogue who used to tease me and help me and protect me. Not the young man who pulled me against him and promised to return in an hour.

Do not cry. I don't.

Flies cling to me as I force my feet forward. I swat them away forcefully. One of the gate guards steps forward, swatting at flies himself. Sweat sits in a sheen on his brow, and he looks bored and irritated. I know I would be.

"State your business," he says.

I pull free the order that Mistress Solomon gave me. "I have a delivery in the Royal Sector."

He barely gives it a glance, then nods at the gates and returns to his post.

Well, I always knew it was easier to get in than it is to get out. A woman with a glistening purple carriage is waiting on the other side while guards search her belongings. Her skin is starkly pale, with rich red hair coiled in impossible braids. She stands to the side, haughtily checking her pocket watch. Diamonds sparkle in the sunlight.

That pocket watch alone would buy enough medicine for a family for months. I want to grab a fistful of the powder in my pack and shove it down her throat.

I shake myself. No. I don't. It's not her fault. She didn't put Wes up there. She can't help that she was born to privilege.

One of the guards opens the door to her carriage and bows to her. "Forgive the delay, Consul Marpetta."

A consul! I've never seen one up close, and I want to gawk. I probably *am* gawking. I try to force my eyes away.

She tosses him a coin. It winks in the light and then disappears into his palm. "I'd rather you search everyone than let a smuggler out," she says, her voice so soft I almost don't hear it. She climbs into the carriage, and he slams the door behind her.

As her carriage rattles past, the guard notices me staring. "Don't you have business here, girl?"

"Oh! Yes." I hurry away.

I'm no stranger to the Royal Sector, but I know it in the dead of night, when the streets are empty, dark, and silent. With the sun blazing overhead, everything gleams, even the gutters. Doorways sport gilded edges. Fountains splash merrily in front of the larger houses. The windows of the shops are all crystal clear, the cobblestones out front freshly swept. Electric lights blaze inside the fanciest establishments, but others are lit by oil lanterns. Doorknobs are edged in silver, carriages and carts are lined with leather and steel. Horses prance and shine, their harnesses richly detailed.

And the people! Women wear dresses with jewels embedded in the bodices, silver stitching glinting along the skirts. Men wear long jackets of brocade or silk or soft suede, their boots thickly heeled and polished. Fabrics burst with every color, brighter than any found in the Wilds, where dyes would be too expensive and too frivolous. At night, these swaths of pink and purple and orange are all muted shades of gray.

There are more common people, too, workers with duties like me, but they're hidden, invisible in homespun wool or gray trousers that seem to blend with the cobblestones or the brick walls of the storefronts. Even still, I see the differences here as well, from boots with thick leather soles, belts stamped with intricate leather-working, and buttons that have been made from a steel press, not carved from a piece of wood.

Despite all of the riches and perfection of this sector, I ache for the people dying in the Wilds, for the people struggling in Steel City or Trader's Landing or Artis. There is so much here. So much wealth, so much health, it's like a slap in the face.

What Wes and I took . . . they could afford to lose it.

And now he's dead, and they're prancing around as if Kandala weren't dying outside these gates.

I have to duck into a shop to ask for directions so I can find the address Mistress Solomon specified. The closer I get to the center of the city, the larger the houses grow. More gold, more silver, more wasted wealth.

I've never walked right up to one of the houses to ring the bell, and it feels unnatural, as if slipping through open windows and picking locks is the preferred means of entry. A steward answers and takes the parcel, looking down his nose at me haughtily. "This was to be delivered an hour ago," he says.

As if it matters. I hastily bob a curtsy, though he's probably not someone who deserves it. "Forgive me," I say. "Please don't tell my mistress, sir."

He huffs through his nose and closes the door in my face.

I give the closed door a rude gesture, then turn around.

Now what?

I have to walk. If I don't walk, that steward might come back out and call for a patrolman. There are fewer shops here and more houses. I try to backtrack to where I first asked for directions.

Instead I turn a corner and find myself staring up at the palace.

If the houses looked wealthy, the palace looks like an ostentatious abomination. It's massive, stretching four city blocks wide, with white bricks edged in lavender that practically climb into the sky. The front is wide and flat, with two towers at either end. Two massive fountains spray water high in the air, bubbling and splashing on the way down. Carriages roll past, and footmen leap into action, opening doors, carrying parcels, rolling out carpets.

The palace shouldn't be white. It should be red with blood, or black with death, or honestly, it should be a charred pile of rubble that I would skip through, and happily.

I slide my hand into my pack. The muslin of ground thimbleweed root is wrapped tight, but it's still there.

That's too much. You'll end up killing someone.

My feet carry me forward against my will. I don't want to be here, but it's almost as if my body is working against me. Rumor says that the Moonflower elixir they mix in the palace is ten times the strength of the crushed petals Wes and I used to steal. I'm not sure what I'm going to do—it's not like I can walk right in and ask for some.

But that guilt and loss is still pooled in my chest, wrapped up as tightly as the muslin pack. So many people are sick. I've left so many with no access to medicine. A small sample from the palace might be enough to cure ten times as many.

Much like in the shopping district, it takes me a longer moment to notice the commoners surrounding the palace, the laborers, the men and women working in drab attire, sweeping the streets and cleaning the gutters and brushing the horses. As I wander past them, I begin to feel invisible, too. I wonder if this is why it's so easy for the royal elites to ignore the people outside the walls of this sector. Are we all invisible to them?

A group of younger women in homespun skirts and wool trousers are walking toward the palace, and out of curiosity, I fall in behind them. The guards at the gate paid attention to me when I was gawking at the consul, but maybe they won't pay me any mind if I look bored and inattentive.

My heart is hammering in my chest as we approach the eastern side of the palace, but I keep my eyes forward, on the backs of the girls who are chattering away about some scandal involving Consul Cherry and Consul Pelham having secret meetings right underneath the king's nose. Another girl chirps that she's heard that one of the consuls is sneaking money to the rebels. I don't know any of the players, so I can't follow their conversation, but it doesn't matter anyway. I wait for a guard to shout out, or to stop me, or for one of the girls to notice that I'm following them, but no one says anything at all.

Just like that, I'm inside the palace.

It takes everything I have to keep from falling against a wall and pressing a hand over my chest.

I am *inside* the *palace.*

I have no idea what to do.

The doorway here leads into an area for servants, because, although the decor is still rather splendid, the floor is worn and the wallpaper scuffed in spots. The girls have moved into a room where uniforms are hung from racks along the wall, and they're quickly disrobing.

This is ridiculous. Someone is going to find me. I'm going to be dragged through the streets behind a horse or hung from the sector gates or something.

One of the girls must notice my attention, because she begins to turn. I quickly duck away from the doorway and hurry down the hall.

There are workers everywhere down here, some assembling cleaning supplies, others working on repairs to small bits of machinery, some polishing leather or mending clothes or embroidering finery. A few glance at me, but most are so wrapped up in their own duties that they pay me little mind.

I need to get out while I can.

I don't. I keep thinking about the elixirs and petals that must be stored here in the palace, the ones that can cure so very many people.

I keep thinking of the poison in my pack, of the fact that the king and his brother are likely somewhere inside these walls, plotting how they're going to execute the next smuggler.

The thought launches a swell of fury and fear into my chest, and I breathe deeply so I don't begin screaming.

Mind your mettle, Tessa.

Oh, Wes. My eyes fill. I press a hand to my mouth so I don't openly sob.

I need to find a place to hide. To think. To question my sanity.

And then, as if fate granted my wish, I notice a small closet filled with linens that seems wide and dark and cool. Without a thought, and while no one is looking, I close myself inside and tuck myself into the back.

CHAPTER TWELVE

Tessa

When I first locked myself in, I could hear the low rumble of people working in the hallways. I occasionally had to hold my breath when someone would come into this supply closet. Now, everything has been silent for so long that I've begun wondering if it's safe for me to take a chance at coming out. There are no windows, no way for me to measure how long I've been down here. I think of that pocket watch that the consul had, how just knowing the time of day is a luxury they aren't aware of.

It feels like hours.

I sneak to the door and press my ear against the wood.

Silence. Absolute silence.

It still takes a while for me to gather the courage to open the door. Everything feels different now. Earlier, I was burning with rage and exhaustion, full of exhilaration from being able to get into the palace so easily.

Now, my thoughts have caught up with me, and all that's left is panic that I'll be discovered and Wes's body will have some company along the gate.

My stomach rumbles, and my body alerts me that I have needs that haven't been addressed in hours.

I need to get out of the palace.

Finally, I pull at the latch, and the door swings open.

The hallway is empty and dim; only a few flickering lanterns are lit at either end. The few windows I can see are pitch-dark. It must be very late.

Good.

No, not good. When I reach the end of the hallway, I discover that the door at the end is padlocked shut.

Well, of course it is. It's the middle of the night, and the day laborers have gone home.

Voices suddenly echo down the hallway, and I duck into the room where the girls were changing earlier. My heartbeat is a steady thrum in my ears. Shadows appear in the doorway, and I bolt for the back half of the room. There's nowhere to hide.

There. A door in the corner. It must be another storage closet. I grab hold of the handle, whisper a prayer that it's not locked, and yank it wide.

It's not a closet. It leads to a lush staircase with red velvet carpeting and walls painted with a fancy hunting scene. The steps seem to lead to a hallway at the top. The lights blaze brightly, but the air is heavy and quiet.

That said, in my homespun skirts, I definitely wouldn't be invisible here, at this time.

I'm frozen in place and not sure what to do or where to go—but I definitely can't stay here in this stairwell. Part of me wants to dive right back through that door and into the changing room, but another part of me worries that those people will be there again, and I'll be walking right into discovery.

I need to move. Up I go.

At the top, I peek around the corner, but I find nothing. No guards, no one at all here, but I tiptoe forward regardless. My feet are practiced at sneaking, and I long for my mask and hat.

At the end of the hall, I peek around both corners, and again I see no one. I have no idea which direction is the correct way out of here, but based on how I got in here, heading right should take me toward the back part of the palace. Though the walls and flooring are more opulent here, this is clearly a servants' passageway. Maybe I can find another staircase and sneak back down to another area that won't be padlocked. Maybe—just maybe—I'll find where the Moonflower leaves are stored.

Maybe you can find the king and end his tyranny.

The thought hits me so hard and fast that it pulls me to a stop. I'm alone. This passageway is unguarded. I could find the king, and I could end his life.

But as badly as I want to avenge my parents and Wes, I can't bring my feet to move. I've spent the last few years risking my life to save others. I don't know if I could look down at someone—even the king or his brother—and kill him.

I think of those daggers driven into Weston's eyes. Nothing stopped that.

Not even me.

I swallow, my throat tight.

I wouldn't even need to do something violent. There's enough powder in my bag to lace the king's water pitcher if I wanted to.

Still, my feet won't move. I think of Wes standing in the workshop, declaring that he wasn't a smuggler, that he wasn't doing this to line his own pockets.

I'm not a killer.

The instant I have the thought, I can breathe again. My parents risked their lives to save others—and so do I.

I'm *not* a killer. I heal people; I don't harm them.

A door a short distance away opens, and a man steps through. He looks to be in his early twenties, with vibrant red hair, a scruff of beard growth on his jaw, and a half-buttoned green brocade jacket. He's carrying several books and papers, and he's reading one of them as he steps through the door.

For half an instant, I think he'll turn the other way without seeing me, that somehow my bizarre luck will continue. But his eyes lift, and he startles so hard that a few papers drift from the stack.

I take a step back and put up a hand. "I—I'm sorry—I—"

"Guards!" His expression has quickly shifted from surprise to alarm. He drops his books and throws open the door he just came through, but he doesn't take his eyes off me. "Guards! Secure the king! Secure the prince—"

"No!" I cry. "No—you don't—this was—this was a mistake . . ."

Run, Tessa. Weston's voice is like a whisper in my ears.

I dig my feet into the velvet carpeting and run. The stairs are behind me, but they only lead to a padlock, so I run directly at the red-haired man. He tries to grab me, but I throw a punch right at the base of his rib cage, and his grip slackens.

I'm loose and I'm running, and I'm about to burst through the first door I see. I thought my heart was pounding before, but now it's sprinting in my chest, pulling me forward.

Two other doors open, and guards appear in front of me, weapons drawn.

It startles a short scream out of me. My feet skid on velvet. There are too many of them. I don't even have time to fall on the carpet before two of them have a hold on my arms, and they're dragging me upright.

They're going to kill me. They'll do it right here. Daggers will be plunged into my ears or they'll cut off my head or they'll burn me in pieces while I watch. I've heard the stories. I've seen what happens to traitors and smugglers. My breathing is a panicked rush that won't let me speak. My vision goes spotty for a long moment, and I think I'm going to pass out. In a way, it's a relief. I don't want to be conscious. I don't want any of this to happen. But my body still has needs, and the only thing keeping me from wetting myself is the idea that I want to die with some shred of dignity. The stars in my vision clear.

The man with red hair steps in front of me, but he's looking at the guards. "Search the palace. She can't be working alone. Is the king secure?"

The one pinning my right arm nods. "Yes, Master Quint."

"I'm alone," I gasp, and my voice is nearly a keening wail. "I'm alone. Please. Please. Please. This was a mistake."

"It'll do you little good to beg from me." He's not even looking at me. "Search her things. Take her to the throne room. I'll speak to Prince Corrick."

Prince Corrick. My muscles go slack. Fear wins, leaving no room for humiliation.

Master Quint glances down, sees that I've soiled the velvet carpeting, and sighs. "I'll also send someone to clean that up."

—◆—

My underthings are wet and I can smell urine, but the guards have chained me tightly and left me lying facedown on the cold stone floor of what must be the throne room. I expected to be beaten and broken by now, but while they haven't been gentle, the guards have been practical and efficient, chaining my wrists behind my back with practiced ease and then lowering me to the ground to wait.

My breath shakes and shudders against the stone floor, but the guards say nothing and do nothing. This uncertain waiting is the worst torture.

No, surely the worst torture is yet to come.

I was so foolish. Wes would never let me hear the end of this. Maybe I'll find him in the afterlife, and he'll roll his eyes at me and say, "Lord, Tessa. You really did need me around, didn't you?"

Fresh tears squeeze free of my eyes.

I hear light footsteps approach, and I try to curl in on myself. I don't want to be afraid. I want to rage and fight, but I'm pinned in place, and there's nowhere to go. My eyes clench closed. "No," I say, and my voice sounds broken and raw. "Please. No."

"You have nothing to fear from me, girl." It's a woman's voice, her tone landing somewhere between frustrated and disappointed. When her footsteps come closer, I peek up, and I find myself looking at a stunning brown-skinned woman in a floor-length emerald-green gown. "I can't speak for anyone else in the palace, however."

"This was a mistake," I say to her. "I didn't—I don't know what I was doing."

"It's difficult to mistakenly find yourself in the middle of the palace at midnight," says a harsh male voice, and I clench my eyes closed again. The words are so cold and edged that a chill grabs hold of my spine.

Another man speaks with the deferential authority of a guard. "We have searched the palace, Your Highness. We found nothing else amiss."

Your Highness. That must mean Prince Corrick.

I was so stupid. I stood there and told Wes that we shouldn't keep hiding, but now that's all I want to do.

The woman straightens and says, "She's just a girl. Clearly not a trained assassin."

"You don't think girls are capable of violence and treachery, Consul?" Booted feet step closer, but he's behind me, so I can't look at him. His eyes were pools of black from across the square when he was going to execute the eight prisoners. I don't want to see what they look like up close. I'll do worse than wet myself.

"How did she get in here?" he says.

"We don't know." The guard sounds a bit hesitant now. "We have not been able to discover her point of entry."

"What are you doing here?"

It takes me a moment to realize that cold voice is speaking to me, and it's clearly a moment too long because the prince grabs hold of my hair and pulls tight. "Answer me."

It draws a squeak out of my throat. "I don't know—I don't know—"

His grip turns painful. "Stop saying you don't know."

I'm not sure if it's the command in his voice or the grip on my hair—or possibly just the sheer hatred I have for this man—but I grit my teeth and choke back my tears. My voice comes out like a broken whisper. "You killed . . . you killed my . . ."

"Who did I kill?" He says the words without any emotion.

I was wrong before. I should have tried to poison this man.

I would be doing the world a favor. A tear slips down my face. "My friend."

"What's your name?"

I hold my breath. I wish he would just kill me and get it over with. I'm shaking so hard I'm sure he can feel it through his grip on my hair. I feel like such a coward, but it's impossible to be brave.

His grip tightens until I'm sure hairs are beginning to pull free. "Your name."

I don't want to give it to him. All of Wes's warnings to protect my identity are rattling around in my head. But I'm dying, so surely it doesn't matter.

"Tessa." The word is almost forced out of my mouth.

The woman speaks again. "How desperate does someone have to be to challenge your laws? If you kill everyone who holds a grudge against your actions, Prince Corrick, your brother will have no subjects left."

He lets go of my hair and steps back. I can finally turn my head, but all I can see are his polished black boots.

"You overstep, Consul Cherry," he says, and somehow, his voice is colder. Darker.

"Do I?"

"What would you have me do? Should I send every assassin on their way with a bag of silver and some sugared pastries for their trouble?"

To my surprise, the woman laughs. "This girl was clearly not any threat to anyone in this palace," she says. "Your guards found no weapons."

"They found ground powders in her satchel," he says. "Do you suppose she was here to flavor Harristan's tea?"

Any laughter fades from her voice. "You attempted to execute eight people, and there were calls for revolution in the streets. If you hang a pretty young girl from the gates, I believe you will be dealing with more than you bargained for."

He's quiet for a long time. So long that I can tell he is thinking, and a new chill finds its way through my veins.

"Fine," he says, and his voice is resigned. "I'll leave her alive."

All the breath leaves my lungs in a rush. I don't know if this is worse or better.

"Should we take her to the Hold, Your Highness?" says one of the guards.

"No," says Prince Corrick. He sniffs at the air, and I cringe, wanting to curl in on myself again. "Have one of the stewards clean her up. Leave her in chains. Tie a sack over her head so Consul Cherry no longer has to see that she's a *pretty young girl*."

My blood turns to ice. I can't think. I can't see. I can't breathe.

"Your Highness—" Consul Cherry begins.

"You asked me to leave her alive," he snaps. "And so I will. Chain her in my chambers. Alive or dead, she can send a message that traitors are swiftly dealt with."

"No." I don't know if I say the word or only think it. I didn't think he could do anything worse than what he did to Wes, but he can. Almost subconsciously, my body tries to draw away from him. "No."

"Your Highness," Consul Cherry says more urgently. "What are you going to do?"

"I'm sure you can figure it out," he says. His booted feet are moving away. "Guards. You have your orders."

"No!" I scream after him as the guards take hold of my arms. I brace against the chains but it does no good. "No!"

All I see is the black of his jacket as he's walking away.

I spit in his direction. I mean for my voice to be strong, but it sounds broken and weak. "I hate you."

"Everyone does," he says.

The guards haul me up, and mercifully, I pass out.

CHAPTER THIRTEEN

Tessa

When I awake, I have one blissful, quiet moment when I think everything was a dream, and I'll blink into the morning sunlight and shudder over the tricks my mind played on me.

Instead, I can't blink the darkness away, because there's something over my head.

I can't move my hands because they're still chained, and the right one seems to have gone a bit numb.

My heart immediately leaps into action. I struggle to sit up, to right myself somehow, but I'm lying in what feels like a pile of pillows, and I can't gain any leverage or traction. The guards did exactly what he said, and there's a hood over my head, tied at the neck the way the prisoners wore them on the stage. I can't tell what I'm wearing, but the heavy warmth of my homespun skirts is gone. I'm not naked, but the idea of someone undressing me while I was unconscious, of being at Prince Corrick's mercy in that way, is . . . abhorrent. My stomach rolls and threatens to empty itself.

But my body doesn't feel abused, aside from the aches from being chained. And I feel dressed, just not in my own clothes. From what I can tell, I'm alone.

I choke down my panic, little by little, until I can force my thoughts to organize. I need a plan.

I'm chained and effectively blindfolded. No plan is forthcoming.

Think, Tessa. There's a fire somewhere to my left; I can hear it crackling. And I'm not sure how I can tell, but this room feels . . . large. Maybe I can roll myself somewhere that I can find . . .

Find what? A key? I'm not sure who I think I'm kidding, but Weston would find this hilarious.

What are you going to do?

I'm sure you can figure it out.

I can figure it out. I already have. Every time I think of it, the pit of my stomach gives way and I nearly vomit into this burlap sack. Just the memory of his terrible voice saying the words sets a tremor rolling through my body again.

No. A plan. I need one.

A door clicks, and I go still.

There's no noise—or maybe I can't hear anything over the rush of my heart. Tension holds my body rigid, braced against the chains.

Something brushes against my bruised and aching wrist, and I jerk so violently that I think I might break my arm. I drive my feet into the floor, only finding more pillows and no traction.

"No!" I cry out as a hand closes around my forearm. I'm choking on each word, pulling away, my head shaking violently. "No! No! No—"

"Mind your mettle, Tessa." The voice is low and soft and so

familiar that it forces me still the way nothing else would. "You don't want to draw the guards in here."

I'm frozen in place. I'm dreaming. This isn't real. This *can't* be real.

"Wes?" I whisper, and my voice is so soft.

"I'll unchain you, but you have to be absolutely quiet."

It's his voice. It's his *voice*. Maybe I'm hallucinating, but I'm nodding almost involuntarily. I don't know how he's alive, or where he found a key, or how he got in here, but I don't care. His hands, always warm and sure, brush my wrists, and the chains give way.

"Tessa," he says softly, "I need to tell you—"

I launch myself forward blindly and throw my arms around his neck. There's still a sack tied around my head, and one hand has all but fallen asleep, but the relief that courses through me is so fast and true.

"Please say it's you," I whisper. "Please tell me I'm not dreaming."

His hands come around my back, and he's holding me lightly. His scent is in my nose, comforting and familiar. I was shaking in terror before, but now I'm shaky with adrenaline and relief. Wes is here. I want to burrow into him.

"Easy," he says softly. "Easy."

I have so many questions that they all fight to get out of my mouth at once, and I draw back. I have to fight to keep to a whisper. "How? How did you escape? Who's hanging on the gate?" I start fighting with the knot at the base of the sack, but half my fingers are numb and refuse to work. I need to see him. Nothing matters now that Wes is here—now that we're together. "How can we get out? How long do we have before you're discovered? How—"

"Lord, Tessa." He brushes my hands away with typical Wes-like impatience. "Hold still."

I hear the swish of a blade and a quick rip of fabric, and the burlap sack loosens. Now I'm the impatient one, and I reach up to yank it free. I blink in the light as everything snaps into focus. I need to see the blue of his eyes and the stubble across his jaw and the few freckles the mask reveals and the—

My brain stops short.

The man in front of me isn't Wes.

Can't be Wes.

Every ounce of relief shrivels up and dies. Panic swells to fill the space. I try to shove myself back, but my feet are still chained and my body isn't ready for quick motion.

Regardless, he doesn't pursue me, just sits crouched in front of me, the length of his black jacket pooling on the floor beside his boots. Reddish-brown hair drifts across his forehead, and I know the pattern of those freckles. The knife hangs loosely in his hand.

I remember Karri's words from the day of the riots. *They're very handsome, don't you think?*

Prince Corrick.

My mouth is dry, my pulse a steady thrum in my ears. I can't comprehend how he'd know the right words or have the right voice or why he'd go to the trouble, but this is a trick. A manipulation. It has to be. His eyes aren't like Wes's eyes at all. They're cold, and shuttered, and completely unreadable.

But they're vivid blue.

When I don't move, he sheaths the knife and reaches for my ankles.

I shove myself back again, and it's easier now, my hands more willing to work—but there's a wall beyond these pillows and I don't go far. "Don't you touch me," I snap.

"I told you to keep your voice down." His voice isn't quite like Wes's now either. There's a command in his tone that Wes lacked. An edge. An impatience.

He reaches for my ankles again.

"No!" I kick out at him. He seizes the chain easily, taking hold of my feet, but my hands are free, so I lurch forward and punch him right in the face.

I think I genuinely take him by surprise. He swears and rocks back, and it grants me a few feet of freedom, but I don't get far before he grabs me again, so I swing around with my fist ready. This time I catch him in the stomach, but he deflects.

"Tessa! Enough." There's blood on his lip.

Good. I don't care. I throw a punch right at his crotch.

Direct hit. He doubles over. I scramble for the door.

My feet are still chained and I trip over myself, crashing to the floor. Corrick recovers faster than I'm ready for, and he takes hold of my shoulder and flips me over. I scream and kick at him again.

I hear the door click, but suddenly he's on top of me, his hips pinning my hips, his dagger—what I *hope* is his dagger—jutting into my abdomen. I shove at him, but he catches one of my arms and slams it to the ground. I cry out and try to wrench free. He doesn't give, but my shift does, and I hear fabric tear.

"I told you to be quiet," he growls, his face terrifyingly close to mine. I jerk back and more fabric tears, revealing my breast.

Something in my abdomen clenches, and my vision goes spotty, as I remember the cold note in his voice when he told the consul,

I'm sure you can figure it out. I'm wheezing now, and tears have filled my eyes. "No," I cry, trying to find leverage to strike at him. "No."

"Your Highness," says a male voice, and I freeze. The only thing worse than being assaulted by Corrick would be having it happen in front of an audience. But then the man says, "Are you in need of assistance?"

"Do I look like I'm in need of assistance?" Corrick snaps. "Get out."

The door clicks closed. Corrick looks down at me from inches away. Blood has smeared across his cheek. His weight still pins me to the floor. My breathing is a wild rush between us.

"You snuck in here to kill me and my brother," he says to me, and his voice is cold. "If you continue to fight me, the guards will continue to check. Their captain wanted to station a guard inside my quarters. Do you understand me?"

I swallow and shake my head. I don't understand any of this.

"Everyone in this palace expects the worst of me, Tessa." When he reaches for the ripped fabric at my shoulder, I flinch and shudder, but he simply pulls the cloth back up to cover any exposed skin. "The only place I can offer you safety is here, in this room."

Either I'm insane or he is. I don't know what to make of any of this.

I sure don't feel *safe*.

Maybe he can tell, because his eyes search mine. He sighs. "If I let you up, can you agree not to punch me again?"

I shake my head quickly, and he rolls his eyes—and all of a sudden, just for a flicker of time, he looks like Wes. "Well, that's true enough, I'm sure."

He lets me go anyway, rolling agilely to his feet. He tosses a small ring of keys onto the floor beside me. "Unchain yourself."

I try to pick up the keys, but my hands are shaking, and they rattle between my palms.

Corrick can surely hear it, but he moves away, toward a low table near the door. There's an array of bottles and glasses that sparkle in the light. He takes a glass and pours an amber liquid into it.

I've unchained my ankles, and I knot the fabric at my shoulder, but when he turns around, I coil the chain between my hands and glare up at him defiantly.

He raises his eyebrows, then drinks whatever he poured in one swallow. "Would you rather be thrown into the Hold?"

No. Yes. Maybe. I don't know.

Perhaps he can read that flicker of indecision that crosses my face because he nods. "Fair enough." He pours another glass. "Put the chain down."

I tighten my fingers on the links.

The corner of his mouth turns up, but he looks more disappointed than amused—and again, just for the briefest moment, he reminds me of Wes. "Lord, Tessa." He tosses back this drink just as quickly.

"Was it you the whole time?" I whisper.

"It certainly wasn't me half the time." He pours another drink. "Put the chain down. Now."

That cold tone of command has reentered his voice, and it speaks to a place inside of me that wants to flinch—but also wants to rebel. My palms have gone slick on the links, but I don't let go. He might have backed off for now, but he certainly wasn't gentle in the throne room, when he must have known who I was.

Betrayal burns in my chest—but it's also wrapped up in shock and disbelief. Wes is too kind, too compassionate, too . . . not this man.

"Prove it," I say, and my voice wavers, but I square my shoulders and keep my eyes locked on his. "Prove you're Wes. Prove you're not tricking me."

I expect him to refuse, because I'm in no position to make demands, but he sets down his glass and moves across the room to a low chest. He burrows through it for a moment, then draws out a length of black fabric and a hat.

He ties the mask into place, then eases the hat onto his head, giving the brim a tug in a way that's unequivocally Weston. My breath catches. The length of chain slips out of my fingers to rattle against the floor.

I don't know what this means. I don't know what to do. I press my hands against my mouth to keep from crying out. Too many emotions are warring in my chest. Relief. Fury. Despair. For days, I've been grieving Weston's death, and now, to discover that it was all a trick . . .

This is an entirely different kind of grief. An entirely different kind of loss.

When Wes died, I lost the hope of . . . of any kind of future with him.

With this discovery, it's like losing all of our history, too.

He takes off the hat and removes the mask, burying them down in the chest again. When he's done, he returns to the side table and picks up the glass with the amber liquid.

I expect him to toss this back as quickly as he did the others, but to my surprise, he approaches me and holds it out. "You look like you need this more than I do."

I don't want to take it—but he's not wrong. When he releases it into my hands, the liquid is trembling.

I close my fingers around the glass and breathe. I want to throw it at him.

As if he can read my thoughts, he says, "If you throw it at me, I'll cut your hands off."

I keep my hands clutched tightly around the drink. If he were Wes, I'd know he was kidding. But he's not Wes, he's one of the most feared men in all of Kandala, and I know for a fact he's done worse. I don't have to look farther than the men hanging from the sector gate.

I stare up at him and wonder who he killed to make this secret last.

I wonder why he kept this secret. Why he did this at all. Why he killed someone else to fake the death of Weston Lark. For as betrayed as I feel, the confusion about all of it is almost worse. What did he have to gain?

He's looking back at me without any hint of emotion on his face, offering no clues. So I keep the glass and I take a sip, and the liquor burns a path all the way down to my belly.

And then, because all of this fury and loss and anger and disappointment has to go somewhere, I draw back my hand and throw the drink right at him.

CHAPTER FOURTEEN

Corrick

For the last two years, every time a smuggler was caught, I'd be trapped with the secret terror of wondering if it was Tessa. I'd be called to the Hold, and the entire walk, I'd have to banish the thought of finding her broken and begging in a cell. Or worse, hearing about a corpse left in the dirt, the way Mistress Kendall was.

The past few days have been hell.

And now she's here. In my room.

Tessa has good aim. Brandy splashes across the center of my jacket, but I snatch the glass out of the air before it can shatter on the floor.

She's glaring up at me. Waiting for me to make good on my threat, I suppose.

I have no idea how to move forward from here.

I sigh and move to the side table, where I set the glass down next to the bottle, then unbutton my jacket and toss it over the back of a chair.

Everything smells like brandy now. I rub my hands down my face.

I don't understand how this all unraveled so very quickly. Harristan is going to come crashing in here at any minute and demand to know what I'm thinking, and I honestly don't have an answer to give him.

Steel rattles against the floor, and I look over. She's coiled the chain between her palms again, and her teeth are clenched.

Oh. She really *does* think I'm going to cut her hands off.

I'm used to fear and defiance, but this is Tessa, and I don't like seeing it in her. Shame swells in my chest, quick and hot and sudden. I drop into the chair. My emotions are a tangled mix. Anger that she was able to break into the palace. Excitement at seeing her again. Betrayal, because she clearly didn't come here looking for Wes.

Fear. Weston Lark tried to keep her safe. Prince Corrick can't show her mercy.

I brace my forearms on my knees and stick to business, as if she's any other prisoner.

"How did you get in the palace?" I say.

"Why did you trick me?"

"Do you have any concern at all for your well-being? Tell me."

She shuts her mouth and glares at me.

"What were you planning?" I demand. "They found powders in your bag." I think of her words on our final night together in the Wilds, about how we should be riding at the front instead of hiding in the shadows. Tessa wouldn't go for a weapon—but she has bottles and vials and powders and so much knowledge. I always worried she'd be caught for smuggling, but in a sudden whirl of panic, I wonder if she came here for something else altogether: assassination.

It's both disappointing and admirable, and my emotions don't know where to settle. My tone darkens. "Why are you here?"

Her eyes almost glow with defiance. She says nothing.

I wish I could turn off the lights and pull the mask over my face and turn back time. I wish we were back in the workshop, where she didn't fear me at all, and she'd answer my questions without hesitation.

Why did you do this? I would ask. *Lord, Tessa. I told you of the danger. I showed you what was at risk.*

There were times in the workshop where the distance between us was barely enough space to draw breath, and I crave that easy familiarity. That . . . friendship. That simplicity.

The distance between us now may as well be the width of Kandala. I'll never have any of it back again.

A knock sounds at the door, and the guard outside announces, "His Royal Majesty, King Harristan."

I stand, but my eyes flash to hers. There are a million ways this could go wrong, and a very short list of ways it could go right. "If you throw a glass of liquor at my brother, I really will have to cut your hands off. Keep your mouth shut."

Her eyes are wide and alarmed and locked on the door, so maybe she didn't need the warning. I don't have time to tell her anything else, because my brother storms into the room like a tornado.

"Corrick. What are you—" He stops short as soon as he crosses the threshold and sniffs at the air. "How much have you had to drink?"

"Not *nearly* enough."

His eyes sweep the room, and he stops when his gaze lands on

Tessa. She's drawn into the corner again, but she has the good sense to be on her knees. Her eyes are locked on the floor, and one of the silk pillows is clutched to her chest, as if that would provide any kind of defense against anyone at all.

She looks like a loud noise would cause her heart to stop beating. For half a second, sympathy joins the shame pooling in my chest, but then I realize the chain is nowhere to be seen, and I suspect she's hiding it.

Please, Tessa. If she attacks my brother, there is literally nothing I can do to save her.

Harristan barely looks at her. His incredulous eyes snap back to me. "What are you doing?"

"Allisander demands punishment. Arella demands leniency. I thought I might have discovered a happy medium." I move to the side table and fill a new glass, then hold it out to my brother.

He doesn't take it. "Arella hardly thinks what you're doing is lenient." His eyes search mine. "For that matter, neither do I."

It takes a moment for me to realize what he's saying. Harristan gives me free rein to do what needs to be done, but he doesn't like torture for the sake of pain and violence. He doesn't like prolonging the inevitable.

I drain this drink in one swallow like the others, then drop my voice so my words are for him alone. "As you said, brother, all that matters is what it looks like."

He frowns. "Cory. I don't like this."

I don't like it either. I look away.

He's watching me carefully, trying to figure me out. This isn't like me. I know it. He knows it. He's going to press me for more of an answer—or worse, for more of a decision. I'll have to tell him everything, and then Tessa will end up in the Hold, and later, at the end of a rope. I'll be right there next to her.

But then he coughs. It's not a small sound, like in recent days. It's a harsh cough that requires a breath of air that sounds as though it's pulled through a wet sieve. Then again.

"Harristan," I say in alarm.

He gives another short cough, then looks at me. "I'm fine." He clears his throat. "If she escapes your room, she's going to the Hold."

I make my voice hard, the way he'd expect it to be. "If she escapes my room, she won't make it to the Hold."

I expect him to say more, but Harristan nods and turns away. He's moving stiffly, his back tight as if he's trying not to cough again. I stand in the doorway and wait until he's out of earshot, then look to one of my guards. "Have the kitchen send a pot of tea to the king's room, along with a vial of the elixir."

"Yes, Your Highness." He bows to me, and I close myself back into my chambers.

Tessa is still in the corner, looking at me with wide eyes over the pillow.

"What?" I say flatly.

"The king is sick," she whispers.

"He is *not* sick," I snap. I stride across the floor, and her eyes narrow in a way that tells me she's going to drop the pillow and swing that chain.

I'm rattled and tired and full of tension, but on top of it all, I'm done with being struck. When she swings, I catch the end and jerk hard, looping it around one of her wrists and then the other so quickly that she cries out. Before she has a chance to fight back, I pin her against the wall, trapping her hands overhead.

She's breathing hard, her chest expanding rapidly into mine.

"You're not the first to attack me," I say.

Her cheeks are flushed, and I wait for her to fight me.

She doesn't. She stares into my eyes and we share the same air, until the moment shifts. Changes. Softens, though not in the way I expect.

"I wish I'd never let you kiss me," she says quietly.

I almost flinch. I should have let her hang on to the chain. Being hit with that would've hurt less.

"Now I understand why you wouldn't show me your face," she adds.

There's a note in her voice that makes me feel like a coward, and I don't like it. I have to fight to keep my eyes on hers.

"You didn't need to bother," she continues, and her voice is very low, full of censure. "I've only ever seen you from a distance." She hesitates. "*This* you, I mean."

"I couldn't take a chance."

"Because it's treason," she snaps.

I say nothing. It *is* treason.

"And now what?" she says. "You grew bored with me? With your game?"

My thoughts flash on our last night in the forest, when she was so determined to play a role in a revolution—when she was so determined to get herself killed. She was fierce and reckless and passionate, and for one wild moment, I wanted to stand at her side and believe we had a chance at changing everything.

But of course I couldn't. I can't.

She can't either. Especially not now.

Her heart is a steady thrum in her chest. I can feel it against mine. "I never grew bored with you, Tessa." Then I frown, my eyes narrowing. "What's your real name?"

She hesitates. "Tessa Cade." She swallows. "It is my real name."

I laugh, but there's no humor to it. "Of course it is."

"I'm sorry I'm not as good as you are at pretending to be some-one else." She hesitates, her eyes flicking to the door. "The king doesn't even know, does he?"

I don't answer, but I suppose that's answer enough. I don't like how easily she seems to see through me. She wrenches at the grip I have on her wrists, but I don't give an inch. She finally stops, her eyes boring into mine. She lifts her chin boldly. "Fine. Get on with it, then."

"Get on with it?"

"Whatever you're going to do." She's so brave. It's honestly astounding that she hasn't gotten herself killed before now. "Prove your point. Break my bones. Cut my hands off. Set me on fire. Take your dagger and write your name in my—"

"This all sounds like it's going to get rather messy."

"Do it."

"No." I glance up at her hands, one of which is turning an alarming shade of pink. "I'll ask again: If I let you go, can you agree not to strike at me?" She hesitates, so I add, "Most people don't get a second offer. I definitely won't give you a third."

She blanches a little at that, and I watch the battle in her eyes as she wars with who I *was* and who I *am*.

"Fine," she says, and her voice is breathy. "I won't hit you."

I release her hands and take a step back. I keep the chain and coil it around my hand. She stays pressed against the wall, but she's rubbing one wrist.

Despite all the defiance, she's still afraid of me. I can read it in the set of her eyes and the way she clings to the wall, waiting for me to do one of the things she said. As Prince Corrick, I can't fix that.

Again, I wish for masks, for darkness, for firelight and moonlit paths and everything we'll never share together again.

Wishing solves nothing. I learned that the night my parents died.

"Are you hungry?" I say to her.

She looks startled, then suspicious, then resigned. "No."

"I doubt that. You look like you haven't eaten in a week."

Her expression darkens. "It was hard to drum up an appetite when the King's Justice executed my best friend."

I'm used to having obscenities hurled at me, but her words hit me like the bolt from a crossbow, quick and painful, right through the chest. I have to glance away. I meant to protect her. I'm protecting her even now, and she looks at me like I dragged her out of the woods by her hair and strung her up on the gates myself.

I should have told her. That night, I should have told her.

Maybe I am a coward.

As the feared prince, it might be harder to fix what I've done, but it's easier to force doubt and sorrow out of my head. She's clutching her hands against her stomach, but I steel my thoughts against her judgmental expression. She can hate me if she wants. I'm used to it.

I move to the chair and my abandoned coat, then pull my pocket watch free. The jeweled face tells me it's an hour past midnight.

When I open the door, my guards clearly thought I was either asleep or otherwise occupied—because they were leaning close, speaking in low whispers. They snap to attention at once, and they exchange a glance across the hallway.

I've given the entire palace enough gossip to last a week, so I don't chastise them. "Send for a meal," I say. "Enough for two."

"Yes, Your Highness."

The door swings closed. I turn away and rub at my eyes. This day will likely never end. I can't sleep with her here. I'll wake up with that chain wrapped around my throat. Or worse, *not* wake up with that chain wrapped around my throat.

I lower my hands and study her. She still hasn't said what she was doing in the palace, and there's a part of me that isn't sure I want the answer.

Her expression has gone flat, her eyes closed off, and she's pulled into the narrow space between the hearth and the corner, in the shadows. After so many nights in close proximity, this distance feels unbearably far.

A knock sounds at the door, and I jump. It's too soon for food. My guard calls, "Master Quint requests an—"

I throw open the door before he can come barreling in here. "Quint. Not now—"

But he's already stepped past me, all but closing the door on my hand. "The Captain of the Guard said you refused to have a man stationed in your room. Honestly, Corrick, it should be two, at the very least—"

"Quint."

"Consul Cherry has already drafted a formal complaint. Word will reach the Royal Sector by morning, if it hasn't already." He sighs. "They do love a good scandal—"

"*Quint.*"

"But I need to have some awareness of your intentions here so I can address the inquiries—"

"I hardly have awareness of my intentions."

"When you have a girl chained in your room, it doesn't leave very much to the . . ." His voice trails off as his eyes fall on Tessa in the corner, then quickly snap to mine. "She snuck into the palace to kill you and you've turned her loose? Are you mad?"

"Very likely."

He sucks in a breath, and I know he's about to call for the guards, so I slap a hand over his mouth. "Shut up."

He shuts up.

I've never kept secrets from Quint, and I have no intention of starting now. "Quint." I lower my hand and sigh. "Allow me to introduce you to Tessa."

CHAPTER FIFTEEN

Tessa

I've learned too much in the last hour, and my brain can hardly contain it all. I feel as though I've spent the last few years underwater, and Weston—*no, not Wes, Prince Corrick*—just yanked my head above the surface. If I hold absolutely still, I can almost imagine that this is a terrible dream that I'll wake up from any moment.

But if I wake up, then Wes is still dead. I am still miserable. People are still dying. Kandala is filled with suffering. The prince and the king are still horrible men who do nothing to help their subjects.

Well, all of that is still true. Wes never really existed at all.

That's almost harder to accept than his death.

The man who's entered the room is the same man who first caught me in the hallway. Quint. He looks to be in his early twenties, with red hair and enough freckles to make him look boyish. He needs a shave more badly than Prince Corrick.

I'm clinging to the wall as if I can somehow pass through it and find myself on the outside, heading back to the Wilds and Mistress Solomon's and my friendship with Karri.

I'm such a fool. I'm never getting out of here.

When the prince says, "Allow me to introduce you to Tessa," the other man goes still, then sighs and runs a hand across his jaw.

"Tessa," he says slowly, giving me a clear up and down. He looks back at Corrick. "Your partner?"

Corrick nods.

And just like that, I realize Quint must know about Wes.

I can't decide if this is infuriating or a relief, to know that I wasn't the only one aware of Wes's existence, of the prince's trickery. I suck in a breath to protest, but Quint puts up a finger. His expression has changed from one of incredulity to one of thoughtful scrutiny. He gives me a slower, more appraising look as he walks toward me. I can feel the moment his eyes skip over the torn fabric at my shoulder, and I clutch it against my skin protectively. But his gaze isn't licentious, just . . . assessing.

Quint glances at Corrick. "Arella is livid. She thinks you're forcing the girl into bed this very instant."

The words make my stomach clench. Corrick hasn't harmed me—not directly—but that doesn't mean he can't, or he won't.

There's one thing he said that keeps flickering through all my worries: *The only place I can offer you safety is here, in this room.*

I have so many questions.

Corrick is clearly not answering. He's moved to the side table to pour yet another glass of liquor, as if I'm barely an afterthought. "Arella is livid about everything I do lately."

Arella was the woman who spoke to me when I was chained.

Before I knew who Corrick was. I don't understand why he'd be so terrible in front of her—in front of his guards, even—when he's made no move to harm me since I arrived in this room.

I open my mouth a second time, but Quint puts up a finger again. "Wait," he says. "I'm thinking."

He's stopped in front of me, and his head is tilted slightly, as if I'm a baffling puzzle he's been charged with solving. Even though he's a bit disheveled himself, I feel like I should adjust my clothes and stand straighter.

"Be careful," says Corrick. "She hits."

I narrow my eyes at him. "Only liars and villains."

He lifts his glass to me. "Cheers."

"Can you sing?" says Quint.

I blink. "Can I . . . what?"

"Sing. Or dance? Perhaps you know some sleight of hand?"

"I . . ." What is happening. "No."

"Quint." Corrick rolls his eyes.

"The king will never allow you to keep her here as some kind of . . . tortured concubine," says Quint.

"I won't allow it either," I snap.

He's not paying attention to me. "We'll need to come up with something else. Something that will satisfy Allisander yet appease Arella."

"I need to know why you were in the palace," says Corrick, and his voice has gone cold again, the way it was when he grabbed hold of my hair and jerked tight.

I swallow. "I told you. It was a mistake."

"Try again."

It's easy to see why people are terrified of him. It's not just his reputation. When his attention is so focused, it's hard to think of anything else. I want to rewind time to the brief minute when he was still Wes, unchaining my hands, letting me cling to him the way I've done so many times before.

I need to shake this off. Wes doesn't exist.

And Corrick is still waiting for an answer.

I glance between him and Quint. There's no use in lying, not when the answer is so boring. "I had to make a delivery in the Royal Sector. I made a wrong turn and found myself facing the palace. I knew—" My voice breaks, and I have to clear my throat. "I knew the supply of Moonflower petals here was more potent than in the other sectors, and I wanted—I wanted—"

"You wanted to steal right from the palace?" says Corrick. "Even *I* didn't take from the palace, Tessa."

"No—I know. I wasn't thinking. I didn't even plan it. There were—there were girls. Serving girls, I suppose. I followed them. I thought for sure the guards would stop me, but—but I guess one girl in homespun looks just like the others. I walked right in."

At that, Quint looks alarmed. Corrick's whole demeanor darkens.

Quint puts up a hand before he can say anything. "I'll find out who was stationed there at daybreak. You'll have names by breakfast."

I don't take my eyes off the prince. "You're going to kill the guard who let me past?"

"I'm certainly not going to write him a letter of gratitude."

I say nothing, but maybe my horrified expression conveys my thoughts anyway, because he sighs and looks away. "I'm aware of my reputation, but I don't execute *everyone*, Tessa." He pauses.

"Besides, I'm surprised you're sparing a thought to his defense. If he'd done his job, you'd be in the workshop right now, filling vials and loading your pack."

Hearing him talk about the workshop in such a flat voice makes my throat swell. Like it's something to be mocked, and not a space where we shared the most important moments of my life over the last few years. I have to press a hand to my eyes before tears can fall.

When I steady my breathing and lower my hands, trying to blink the tears away, I see that Quint is holding out an embroidered handkerchief, and his expression isn't unkind. It's so shocking that it drives back some of the emotion. I take it, clutching it between my fingers. It smells like cinnamon and oranges and feels like silk. It's quite possibly the most expensive thing I've ever held in my hands—with the exception of Moonflower petals. I hardly want to use it to dab at my cheeks. "Thank you."

There's a knock at the door, but Corrick doesn't move. "That will be supper," he says. "Enter," he calls.

A serving girl who looks a bit tired and rumpled carries in a tray. She sets it on the side table, then curtsies to the prince. "Your Highness. Master Quint." Her eyes land on me, and she quickly glances away. "Will you be needing anything else?"

"No," says Corrick.

"Yes," says Quint. "Prepare a suite for our new guest. Be sure the closet and washroom are fully stocked. Fresh linens, too."

"Of course." She curtsies again, then slips out the door.

"I'll leave you to dine," says Quint. "I'll speak with the captain for suitable guard assignments. I believe four should be enough to prevent any further . . . shall we say, wandering?" He looks at me pointedly.

"Wait. A room for me?" I squeak. Nothing here makes any sense.

They ignore me. "What are you thinking?" says Corrick.

"I'm thinking she shouldn't remain in your room any longer than necessary. It's the middle of the night, so rumors haven't had a chance to spread. You said she's been adjusting the dosages on your runs. Perhaps she could have brought some medicinal insight to the palace? Surely we can spin something better than a punishment of being chained to your bed."

"Surely," Corrick says woodenly.

Quint pulls a little booklet from his jacket and jots a note. "I'll draft an announcement by midday for you to review."

Then he's gone, and once again, I'm alone with the prince. Corrick moves to the side table, where a massive array of steaming food is making my mouth water. I can smell something sweet and something savory, and there must be fresh bread because the scent of the yeast is heavenly. My stomach reminds me that I haven't eaten. I don't want to move any closer to him, but I inhale deeply.

Corrick picks up a piece of fruit and holds it up to the light. The skin is glistening red. "Honeyed apple, Tessa?"

All of my hunger dies. "I hate you," I grit out.

He tosses it to me, and I catch it automatically, since the alternative is letting it smack me in the face.

"As I've said in the past," he says, "that will definitely work out for the best."

—◆—

A large, ornate table sits on the opposite side of the room. When I didn't move, Prince Corrick filled two plates and set them on the table, making a show of setting them across from each other, not beside each other. He holds out a hand to one of the seats and looks at me pointedly.

I really am hungry. Every breath reminds me of how little I've eaten lately. It took everything I had to set that apple on the floor.

I stick to the wall. "No."

"You decline an invitation to dine with the brother of the king?" He feigns a gasp. "What *will* the kitchen staff say when your plate returns untouched?"

"I don't think you want my hands near a knife right now."

That earns a rakish smile, and for a moment he looks so much like Wes that my heart swells and aches before shattering into a million pieces. Maybe he can read it on my face, because his mouth forms a line. "Sit. Eat. I know you're hungry. What's to be gained by refusing?"

Nothing, really. I don't have a good answer, and the question feels like a challenge. I take a deep breath and walk to the table. I'm sure there's some court etiquette I'm supposed to follow, but I have no idea what, and if he expects a curtsy, he's not getting one. My heart thumps along in my chest, and I have to remind myself that he's not Wes, he's the King's Justice. He's not a friendly outlaw. He's a cruel man with no empathy.

I ease into the chair, and he does the same. My spine feels like a steel rod. I can't relax. I pick up the roll from my plate. It's still warm, and dusted with salt. I tear a tiny piece and shove it into my mouth.

It's not salt. It's sugar, and it's everything. I want to shove the whole thing down my throat at once.

I can feel him watching me, so I keep my eyes on anything else. The filigreed place settings. The embroidered tablecloth. The gravy in a small pool beside four thick slabs of poultry.

I have so many questions, but they would all reveal my feelings about a man who doesn't exist, and I won't give any of that to Prince Corrick. He's already taken too much. I tear another small piece of bread and say, "Quint knows the truth. About you. And me."

"Yes." He pauses. "He is the Palace Master. And a friend. There is very little that goes on here that Quint doesn't know about."

"But . . . but the king doesn't know."

"No." Corrick glances away. "I never wanted to put Harristan in a position where he would be forced to deny it."

"If you were caught."

"Yes."

"I could tell everyone," I say, finally meeting his eyes with a glare. "Reveal your secret. The King's Justice is secretly a smuggler stealing from the royal elites."

"Go right ahead," he says mildly. "You wouldn't be the first prisoner to come up with a clever story." He slices a piece of meat. "If you decide you don't want to stay here, it's a good way to earn yourself a trip to the Hold."

"If I *decide*? Is that a joke?"

"I didn't lure you into the palace." His voice has turned hard. "In fact, when you forced my hand, I did my very best to convince you that tensions were high and you would do well to stay out of the Royal Sector for a while."

When I forced his hand. When we stood in the woods, and he didn't want to make a run for supplies. He tried to talk me out of it, and I shook him off and demanded revolution.

A revolution I now realize he could never be a part of.

Of course he had to kill off Weston Lark. I might as well have done it myself.

"And here we are," I whisper. Against my will, my eyes well again, and I sniff back the tears and shove more bread into my mouth. "Who did you hang in your place?"

"A true smuggler," he says easily. "He might have gotten away with Moonflower petals, but he thought to spend a few minutes taking advantage of the lady of the house, and her son heard the commotion and rang the alarm. I hear the man beat her rather badly before he was discovered."

I'm staring at him. I'm not sure what to say.

Corrick takes a sip from his glass. "Surely you don't think we were the only ones sneaking into the sector to steal medicine. It wasn't difficult to plant a mask on him."

I remember the alarms and lights from the night Wes went missing. I thought they were for him.

My mouth is hanging open. I snap it shut. "You . . . you said you worked in the forges. You said you were from Steel City."

He shrugs and runs a hand across the back of his neck, looking abashed. "It was as good a place as any other. I have an interest in metalworking, so I can speak to it a bit."

It's so difficult to remind myself that he's not Wes. His manner has changed again, and he's more relaxed now that we're alone and I'm not punching him in the crotch. I was wondering how he wore two faces, but after seeing him with different people, I'm thinking he has dozens of faces that he shows when the need arises. I have no idea which is real, but his easy manner is making it hard to remain tense and frightened. If I close my eyes, we could be back in the workshop, sitting by the fire, trading silly banter.

No. I can't. I can't forget that he's Prince Corrick. He could snap his fingers and have me executed right here.

I draw a shaky breath. "What—" I have to clear my throat. "When I was in chains—when you—when that other woman spoke for me—"

"Consul Cherry. Of Sunkeep." He takes another bite of food, as if my emotions weren't crumbling to pieces right in front of him.

My mouth stalls. I swallow. He was so harsh. That's what I'm having the hardest time reconciling. He was so playful and decent as Wes.

He sets down the fork and looks at me. That's almost worse. His eyes are so piercing. No wonder prisoners beg for death.

But then he says, "Ask your question, Tessa," and his voice is soft and low and familiar, no hint of ice or steel in his tone.

I draw a breath. "You knew it was me," I say. "When I was lying there in chains. I couldn't see you, but you could see me. You had to know."

"I knew."

"And . . . and you were so cruel." For all my rebellious bravado, my voice won't rise above a whisper now. I need to understand. I need him to explain it to me.

"I told you," he says. "Cruelty is expected. Necessary, in fact, in front of Consul Cherry." His eyes flick to the door and back to mine. "In front of my guards, who will gossip about whatever they see and whatever they hear."

I study him. I consider the way he threw me on the ground when the guard burst through the door. The way he adjusted the fabric over my shoulder once the door was closed.

The man on the gates was hung for being a smuggler, but he was caught raping and beating a woman. Isn't that what Corrick said? That part isn't public knowledge—just the smuggling.

Meanwhile, Corrick is allowing people to think he's abusing me—when he hasn't actually harmed me since the moment I woke up in the pile of pillows. I consider the food in front of me, or the way Quint is preparing a room.

"Why would you want people to think you're horrible?" I say.

He inhales as if to speak, then thinks better of whatever he was going to say, because he gives a slight shake of his head. "Why did you really sneak into the palace?" he asks quietly.

"I told you. I hoped—I hoped to steal medicine. I hoped to help the people we left vulnerable when Wes—when you—when *we* stopped."

"You made it into the servants' passageways, so you would have had quick access to our rooms." He pauses. "You know what they found in your pack. Did you seek to kill the king?"

I say nothing. My mouth goes dry. To even admit the thought crossing my mind is treason. It was only a moment, but I thought of it.

I wonder what my father would think of me right now. Did I fail? Or did I make the right choice?

"Did you seek to kill *me*?" Corrick adds.

I wet my lips. I won't say yes—but I can't deny it either. "I couldn't do it," I whisper.

"You're not a killer."

I nod. He knows I'm not.

His eyes go hard again, like twin slabs of ice in the moonlight. "Kindness leaves you vulnerable, Tessa. I learned that lesson years ago. I'm surprised you haven't."

Years ago. When my parents died?

No, that's ridiculous. That wouldn't have affected him. But I realize that I'm forgetting—again—that he's a member of the royal family, and he's faced his own losses.

So . . . when his parents died? What does that mean? He's changed faces again, and I'm not sure what's safe to say.

Corrick wipes his hands on his napkin. "Eat your dinner. I'll take you to your room so you can get some sleep. You'll need it. Quint will be banging on your door at sunrise."

CHAPTER SIXTEEN

Corrick

I don't want to take Tessa to another room. I want to keep her here, right here, where I know no one can hurt her. Where she can't take any actions that will force my hand.

I want to sneak her out of the palace and over the wall and back into the workshop, where we can stand in the quiet firelight as Wes and Tessa.

Where I can help my subjects instead of harming them.

What I want never matters, so I lead her down the hushed hallway, our feet making little noise on the velvet carpeting. She's barefoot, her hair long and unbound down her back, her hand clutching that scrap of fabric against her shoulder. My guards have the good sense to keep their eyes forward.

Quint has chosen the Emerald Room, which, contrary to its name, is decorated in shades of red and pink, from the satin coverlets on the bed to the heavy curtains that line the walls. The only element of green at all is the massive jewel hanging from the neck of the woman in the portrait over the fireplace. My great-grandmother. It's a good room, nothing too grand for someone who is ostensibly a prisoner, but definitely a sign that Tessa is not someone destined for the Hold.

Four guards have been stationed by the door, which feels like overkill, but then I consider how easily she got inside the palace and I say nothing.

We stop outside the door to her room, and she glances at the guards, her eyes a bit wide.

"They won't harm you," I say. "Unless you try to leave."

"That's it?" she whispers.

"If you wake early, the guards can call for food."

"You're leaving me here. Alone."

"Should I not?"

She shakes her head quickly, then steps across the threshold and turns to face me, as if she thinks I'm going to grab her arm and jerk her back out.

"And I can close the door," she says.

"I recommend it."

She stares at me for the longest moment, then grabs hold of the door and swings it closed softly. After a moment, I hear a key turn in the lock.

I glance at the man closest to the door. I don't know every single guard by name, but I know Lieutenant Molnar. He's older, well into his sixties, with thick graying hair. He served my grandparents, and then my parents, and now us. He's quiet, but he knows his job, and he does it well. He follows orders and doesn't gossip—and he's senior enough that he won't let the others do it either.

"You have a key?" I say to him.

"Yes, Your Highness."

"Good."

I should return to my own chambers, but I'm too rattled, too unsettled. I feel like I'll never sleep again.

I hate you.

When she said it to Wes, she never meant it.

When she said it to Prince Corrick, I could feel her conviction in every syllable. *I. Hate. You.*

I walk past my chambers, guards trailing me as I stride down the hallway. They don't usually shadow me everywhere, but I'm sure Tessa's sudden appearance has their captain spooked.

I stop in front of Harristan's door. His guards tell me he's asleep, but I'm the only person they'd allow through without protest. I slip through the door like a ghost, carefully easing it closed so the latch doesn't click. The only light in the room comes from the hearth, which has burned down to embers. A tray with teacups and saucers sits on the side table, but one is on the table near Harristan's bed. Good.

I can hear his breathing from here.

Not good.

I rub my hands over my face and sit in the armchair near his desk. A leather folio sits on top of all his other documents, the seal from Artis.

I ease it off the desk and flip the cover open. They've submitted an amended request for funding. Jonas is wasting no time. I pinch the bridge of my nose.

"Cory."

I glance up. Harristan is blinking at me from the bed.

"You're supposed to be sleeping," I say.

"So are you." He pauses. "What did you do to the girl?"

"She's sleeping in the Emerald Room. Under heavy guard."

"No." He gives me a look. "What did you *do*?"

"Nothing. I fed her dinner and sent her to bed."

He studies me. I study him back.

I want to tell him. I've wanted to tell him for years. He'd understand my drive to get out of the palace, to get out of the Royal Sector. He's the one who taught me how to sneak out, how to scale the wall and get lost in the pleasures of the Wilds. He's the one who always wanted freedom from this place.

I'm the one who got it, even if only for a short while, and it seems unfair to taunt him with the knowledge.

Even if it's over. I'm done.

Regardless, it's as treasonous an act as anything I could come up with. I was stealing from our subjects. I was acting in direct opposition to his orders—in direct opposition to orders I'm expected to enforce. If anyone found out, it would be a scandal beyond measure.

Harristan's gaze is heavy, as if he can pick apart my secrets with nothing more than his eyes, and I finally have to look away.

He clears his throat. "I find it hard to believe that you'd offer leniency to someone who snuck into the palace to kill me."

He's right, but I can offer him this truth. "She snuck in to steal medicine. She meant no harm."

"A smuggler?"

"Not quite." I think of the books in her pack, the way Quint thought we would need spin. "She has many theories about how to adjust the dosage of Moonflower elixir to make it more effective."

This isn't a lie, but it feels like one. I pause. "She steals medicine and distributes it among the people. For those who cannot afford it."

That turns him quiet for a long time, as I thought it might. Regardless of what people think, Harristan isn't heartless. The dwindling fire snaps in the hearth. "Do you think there are many who do this?"

I shake my head. "I have no idea."

"When the guards said someone breeched the palace, I thought revolution had finally found us."

I think of the true smugglers who escaped, the way the crowd called for rebellion. "It still might."

He falls quiet again, but this time, his eyelids flicker.

"Sleep," I say softly. I stand. "I'll leave."

"Cory." His voice catches me before I reach the door.

I stop and turn. "What?"

"There's something you're not telling me about her."

My brother rarely dwells in details, and it usually serves him well. But there are times, like now, when something earns his focus, and it's always hard to shake it loose.

I've been quiet too long, and the silence swells between us.

"I know people keep secrets from me," he says. "I didn't think you were among them."

If his voice was harsh or full of censure, I'd deny it. But Harristan is rarely like that with me, especially not when we're alone. There are few people who have his full trust in the palace. I might be the only one. For the barest instant, I wonder if this might chip away at it.

"I keep no secrets that put you at risk," I say.

"I know," he says equably.

Of course he does. But it puts my mind at ease.

But then he says, "I'd like to talk to her."

I wonder how that will go. I imagine Tessa throwing a punch at my brother, or tossing a drink in his face. There are a million things she could say that would end with her in the Hold—or worse. There are a million questions Harristan could ask—and a million wrong answers that will put Tessa in danger.

But he's the king, and no matter how much power I have, he has more. I nod. "I'll arrange it."

CHAPTER SEVENTEEN

Tessa

I should be in a prison cell.

Honestly, I should probably be hanging from the sector wall with daggers in my eyes, a warning to anyone else who might want to sneak into the palace.

Instead, I'm in a room that's six times the size of the one where I live. I have a washroom to myself, which I've never had in my life, and it's stocked with stacks of linens and towels, in addition to a dozen jars of soaps and lotions and crushed petals that smell of lavender and roses. There are two faucets branching over the tub, and I'm shocked to discover that one dispenses warm water. In the boarding house, if we want a bath, we boil water in a stockpot, then use the washtub behind the kitchen.

The lighting here is brighter than I'm used to. I know electricity runs in the Royal Sector, but seeing it from the shadows is different from sitting beneath an electric lantern and knowing it will never burn out or need more oil. Six small levers are affixed along the wall beside the bed, and I gingerly test each one, to discover that every lantern is connected to its own switch.

The closet isn't overly full, though it's been stocked with linen underthings, soft silken stockings, and half a dozen dresses made from miles of silk, lace, brocade, and satin. Lace-up boots and velvet slippers and shining shoes line the floor in three different sizes. Everything reeks of wealth and extravagance—and, to my surprise, modesty. The sleeves are tasteful and full. No neckline will reveal any more than a hint of cleavage. They're all beautiful, and the corseted backs will keep them from being shapeless, but after Corrick practically tore my dress off in front of his guard, they're not at all what I expected. Did Quint select these clothes? What did he say?

The king will never allow you to keep her here as some kind of tortured concubine.

No one will expect it either. Not in these clothes, anyway.

Every time I move, I expect a guard to come barreling into the room and rip my arms off. I locked the door, so I'll have at least a moment's warning.

Like that would help me do anything more than panic.

I remove the torn dress and slip into one of the sleeping shifts in the closet, then belt a dressing gown over the top of it all. I lie on the bed and turn all the switches off, then stare at the ceiling, flickering with gold from the firelight.

I'll never fall asleep here. I wonder if I'll ever fall asleep again.

I should be thinking of everything I've learned about Corrick and this twisted secret that allows him to torture his people in the daylight while saving them at night. I should be thinking of Karri and Mistress Solomon and how they'll react when I don't return. I should be thinking of how long I'll be kept in a room like this, before I'm ultimately tossed in the Hold.

I should be thinking of a way to get out of here.

Instead, my apothecary mind is thinking about King Harristan. I'm thinking about the way he started coughing and couldn't stop. I'm thinking of the note of fear in Corrick's voice when he said, "He is *not* sick."

My brain was still spinning with panic, but I know what that cough means.

I shouldn't care. I shouldn't.

I can't help myself. They have the best medicine here in the palace. They dose themselves three times a day, Wes used to say— which is probably true, since Wes was Corrick, and he was presumably receiving all of those doses.

Is the elixir beginning to fail? Is the king somehow more susceptible to the fever? Or is someone affecting his dosage of the Moonflower, like some kind of reverse poisoning, where they prevent access to something he needs? I have no way of knowing, and I'm certain no one will feed me the answers. I already slipped into the palace. I don't need to start inquiring about ways to make the king sick.

My brain won't stop working, though. My father used to talk about how too much medicine was sometimes worse than not having enough. Could the king be taking too much? They have the best apothecaries and doctors here, though. Surely. His dosage is likely well monitored.

If the medicine is losing its effectiveness . . . I don't want to think about the ramifications of that.

And if King Harristan dies, that means Corrick becomes king.

I don't want to think about the ramifications of *that* either. No matter what he said in his chambers or what he did as Weston Lark, he's still responsible for a great deal of suffering. Corrick can't undo that. He's terrifying enough as King's Justice. I can already tell that King Harristan has a limit. He didn't like the way Corrick was planning to . . . abuse me.

I have no idea where Prince Corrick's limits are.

I doubt I want to find out. I doubt anyone in Kandala wants to find out.

My belly is full, and this room is so quiet and warm, such a contrast to those minutes when I was pinned on the cold floor, Prince Corrick's fist tight in my hair. I shiver without meaning to.

But then he sat there at the dinner table, when it was just me and him, and for the briefest of moments he was like Wes again, a little funny and a little fierce.

I press a hand to my chest as my eyes well. My heart aches with each beat.

Wes isn't dead. My brain wants to rejoice.

But Wes wasn't real. A tear slips free.

"Miss." A hand rests on my arm. "Miss."

I jerk and shove myself upright. I didn't expect to sleep, but I must have. My limbs feel heavy and slow to work. The room is flooded with early morning sunlight—I didn't draw any of the curtains last night. I'm still in a sleeping shift and the belted dressing gown, but I never drew a blanket over myself.

A serving girl in a blue dress and a light-gray apron stands over me. She has ink-black hair tied into a tight twist at the back of her head, dark olive skin, and brown eyes. Something about her is familiar, but I can't place it. Maybe she was among the girls I followed into the palace yesterday.

"Forgive me, miss," she says. "Master Quint asked me to have you dressed and ready by half past eight. I've drawn your bath."

"I locked the door," I say.

"I knocked," she says. "But you were asleep." She pauses. "The guards have a key."

I'm not quite awake enough yet. I blink at her. She's young, maybe even younger than I am. I see that two guards are now inside the room, standing passively by the doorway. I wonder if they're here to make sure I don't get out of hand. They don't look too concerned, however. If anything, they look bored. I guess I'm not an exciting sleeper.

"How—" I begin. "What—"

"It's half past seven," the girl says. "My name is Jossalyn. We have little time."

"But—it's not going to take me an hour to bathe."

"No, miss. But you're meeting with the king at midmorning, so—"

"I'm what?" I scrub my hands over my face. Anxiety forms a pit in my stomach. "Wait. Did you say—the king?"

"Yes." She hesitates, then wrings her hands a bit. "I've called for breakfast. If you bathe now, it will be delivered by the time you dry."

I don't understand how she could say something like *you're meeting with the king* in the same breath as talking about ordering food, but I shove the hair back from my face. "I can't—" My voice breaks, and I clear my throat. "I can't meet with the king."

"It is by His Majesty's request," she says, as if that answers everything.

I glance at the guards by the door. They're both standing stoically, but I'm sure they're paying attention to every word we say now. One is older, and must be pushing sixty, though the other is younger and cast a long glance in my direction when I said I couldn't meet with the king.

I'm not sure how I can tell, but it's obvious that I'll meet with the king if they have to drag me there by my toenails.

My heart stops in my chest and takes a moment to start working again.

Wes. Help me.

There is no Wes. There's only Corrick.

I didn't expect to survive the night, but I've made it till morning. I press my fingers into my eyes and take a long breath. I would give anything to open my eyes and be back in Mistress Solomon's shop, Karri giving me a crooked smile.

"Miss?" says Jossalyn. She leans in until her voice is hardly louder than her breath. "The guards have been ordered to assist if you refuse to prepare."

I jerk my fingers down. "Right. Fine. Time for a bath."

━━◆━━

I haven't had assistance in the bath since I was a child, but Jossalyn seems unwilling to leave me alone, and I suspect my options are her or the guards, and I know which I prefer. I dunk my head under the water, and when I come up, she's ready to scrub my hair.

"I can really do this myself," I say.

"Yes, miss." She doesn't stop. Her fingers work my tangled tresses into a rich lather that smells of vanilla and sweet cream. In any other situation, this might be relaxing: the uncannily warm water, the soothing scents, the gentle pressure of her fingers. But I'm naked with a stranger, there are armed guards in the next room, and I'll be facing King Harristan in a matter of hours.

In the Wilds, a lot of people call him Harristan the Horrible. I wonder if he knows.

The instant the thought comes to me, I'm terrified I'm going to say it out loud. In front of him.

If you throw a glass of liquor at my brother, I really will have to cut your hands off.

My chest feels tight. I sit still while Jossalyn pours water over my head to rinse my hair, and I imagine my eyes are burning from the suds instead of everything else.

What does he want? Why would he want to see me?

Jossalyn laces me into a gown with fabric softer than I've ever felt against my skin. The bodice and underskirt are a rich purple, but the material stretched over top is sheer and white, floating in a dozen layers to create a finished product in lavender. The neckline curves gently across my collarbones.

Jossalyn lays a towel across my shoulders and unbinds my wet hair. "Come," she says. "Your breakfast awaits."

The food looks every bit as delicious as it did last night. Maybe more so. But I only nibble at a bit of sliced fruit because my abdomen is so tense. The room is so silent, with Jossalyn combing through my damp hair while the guards stand near the doorway.

This almost feels worse than prison.

No. That's such a stupid thought. The Hold would be awful. Probably.

"Be sure to take your elixir," Jossalyn says, and my eyes fall on the small glass cup near my plate. The color is dark amber, so much richer than what we mix in the workshop, which barely colors the water at all.

I take a sip. It never tastes good, but concentrated, it's worse than usual. I can't believe they drink this three times a day. I hope they don't make me do that.

Such a waste.

Jossalyn weaves my hair into a complicated braid that she pins in loops to the back of my head. Then she ignores my eating and begins smoothing a creamy lotion into my cheeks. I wonder if she's used to doing this, preparing women in the palace while they go about ordinary tasks like eating. I get the sense that I could be spinning in circles or having a lively conversation, and she'd be right there, patiently applying cosmetics.

Invisible, the way people were in the streets yesterday.

I glance at her and try to hold still while she works. I'm technically a prisoner, but she isn't treating me like one. She spared me any rough treatment from the guards, which I'm sure further hesitations would have caused. "Thank you," I say softly. "For your kindness."

"Yes, miss," she says absently, but I feel her hand hesitate as if I've surprised her.

"Do you . . ." I clear my throat. "Do you know if I . . . if I'm meeting with the king alone?" Her eyes meet mine, questioning, and I clarify, "Will Corrick be there?"

Her hands go still, and she glances at the guards, then back at me. "I do not know the agenda of *His Highness, Prince Corrick*." She says these last words with gentle emphasis. "Though Master Quint should, and you can inquire when he arrives." She dabs at my eyelids with her fingertips.

His Highness, Prince Corrick. I've never had to consider royal protocol, and even though I know Weston Lark was all a farce, it's hard to remember that I can't just call him Corrick either. I swallow. "And . . . how do I address the king?"

Her voice drops, and she swipes a small brush through a pot of pink powder. "You address him as Your Majesty, though you should wait for him to address you first." Her eyes meet mine for a moment. "No one addresses the king by name unless they have been invited to do so."

I nod quickly.

She shifts slightly closer, and her voice drops further. "It's intriguing to hear that you're an apothecary. The girls have been talking all morning about how you've brought news of a new elixir."

"I—what?" I think of Quint's musings last night, his need for spin.

"Surely it isn't a secret. The guards are the worst gossips anyway. My sister says they earn extra coin for whatever they bring back to their captain."

I'm not sure what to say to that. When I followed the serving girls yesterday, they were chattering about Consul Cherry and Consul Pelham, something about a scandalous carriage ride.

With a start, I realize I know Consul Cherry. Corrick called her Arella—the woman who spoke for me when he was being so cruel. She seemed forthright and determined—not the type to be embroiled in a scandal.

Then again, she was speaking in my defense—in defense of a presumed smuggler. Maybe that's all it takes to generate a scandal around here.

"Jossalyn," says the older man by the door.

She doesn't even flinch, simply brushing a stroke of pink along my eyelid. "Yes, Lieutenant."

"Master Quint inquires as to your progress."

"Nearly done." She sets the pot of powder aside and reaches for another.

The door opens anyway, and Quint enters the room. He's carrying what looks like a folded booklet. His jacket is buttoned nearly to his throat this morning, but he still needs a shave, and his red hair is already slightly untamed. "Tessa," he says. "I hope you've eaten."

"I—" I've hardly touched anything. "Yes?"

Jossalyn leans down and dabs color on my lips. "Stand up," she whispers under her breath.

I stand up so quickly that I knock my stool over. "Sorry. Your—" No. Wait. He's not royalty. "Ah—Master? Quint."

His eyebrows go up. Jossalyn giggles and rights the stool.

He glances at her. "You do lovely work, Jossalyn. She hardly looks like an apothecary from the Wilds."

She tucks her hands into her skirts and drops into a fluid curtsy. "Thank you, Master Quint."

I feel like I should be taking notes. Maybe she can go with me to meet the king. I want to grab hold of her hand.

Especially when Quint says, "Leave us. She will be returned to her rooms at sunset to prepare for dinner."

She curtsies again, then slips out the door.

"Thank you!" I call, but she's already gone.

The guards exchange a glance, then follow, pulling the door closed behind them.

I'm left staring at Quint. Jossalyn was so peaceful in her manner that I began to forget that I'm a prisoner here. This dress feels too tight to breathe in. I want to run, to burst through the door and bolt down the hallway and say a prayer for escape. I press a hand against my abdomen and draw a shaky breath.

"Be at ease," he says. "The Tessa I heard stories of could scale the sector walls without fear and pick window locks without leaving a scratch. Surely I'm not so intimidating."

No. He's not. I don't understand how a man like this can be a friend to a man like Prince Corrick. His voice is so gentle that my eyes begin to well.

He pulls a handkerchief free and holds it out. "Don't ruin Jossalyn's handiwork."

I take it but sniff the tears back. "Right."

Then I realize what he said. *The Tessa I heard stories of.*

Corrick talked about me? Every time I think I begin to understand him, something else comes along to shatter the illusion.

Quint flips open the book he carries. The pages are filled with notes that look hastily written, and I notice there are ink smudges on his fingertips. "As I'm sure Jossalyn mentioned, you are to meet with the king at nine, per his request—"

"Why?"

"He is the king. He doesn't need to say why. But likely about your medicinal insights." He looks at me pointedly, and I nearly choke on my breath, but I force myself to nod.

"Afterward," he continues, "Consul Cherry has asked to see about your welfare, if the king permits, which he likely will, as you seem quite well this morning—"

"Wait—I don't—"

"I have quite a bit to get through, my dear." Quint doesn't look up. "At ten, you will begin your lessons with Mistress Kent—"

"Lessons? Lessons in what?"

At that, he stops with his finger on the page and looks up at me. "Etiquette."

I open my mouth. Close it.

Maybe the Hold would be better.

"Followed by lunch in the hall," he continues, "and then the dressmaker will see you in her suite. Afterward, lessons with Master Verity—"

"More lessons?" I squeak.

"—on the current political climate of Kandala. If you are to be in the palace, you simply must know the key players. Once complete, you will return here to dress for dinner, which will likely be a private affair with Prince Corrick, though I have advised him it should be done in a public location . . ."

He keeps talking, but I've stopped listening.

A private affair with Prince Corrick. In a public location.

My mouth has gone dry. Last night was bad enough in the confines of his bedchamber. When we were truly alone, he wasn't quite as frightening, but that's like saying a ravenous wolf is only slightly less terrifying because it's in the midst of a meal.

I can only imagine what Corrick must be like in public, the King's Justice in the presence of his people.

With a start, I realize I don't need to imagine it. I watched the execution that ended in cries for rebellion.

I don't want to dine with that Prince Corrick.

"Tessa." Quint is looking at me. I don't know how much I've missed, but I'm guessing it was a lot.

I don't care. I force my eyes to meet his. "How can you be his friend?" I whisper.

Quint closes his little book and studies me. "You were his friend, too, weren't you?"

"No. I was . . . I was friends with a man who doesn't exist. A . . . a trick. An illusion."

"Are you so sure?"

Of course I'm sure.

But then I think of those few moments when the prince smiled, or when his voice gentled, or when he wasn't being violent and instead treated me with thoughtful consideration. *Ask your question, Tessa.* When the guise of Prince Corrick seemed like a mask that Weston Lark hid behind.

I'm not sure of anything at all.

Maybe he can read it on my face. Quint pulls his pocket watch free. "Shall we go?"

My heart wants to fall through the floor. "Is the Hold still an option?"

"The Hold is always an option." He offers me his arm.

I hesitate. I still want to panic and run. If this were Corrick in front of me, I probably would.

Quint leans in a bit. "I don't recommend it," he says softly.

So I steel my spine and take his arm.

CHAPTER EIGHTEEN

Corrick

I'm used to waking well before dawn. For years, because I would meet Tessa in the early hours of the day and we would make our rounds. Lately, I've been waking in the darkness and listening for the sirens, worried that she'd find herself caught by the night patrol.

This morning, I don't wake until the sun has fully risen, the hearth has gone cold, and my room is bathed in light.

Tessa is here.

She hates me, but she's here. She's safe.

It's reassuring, but it's also terrifying. I grab my pocket watch from my nightstand. It's nearly nine.

Nine! She'll be heading to meet with Harristan. I need to speak with her. I need to warn her of what to say. How to act. How to protect herself.

I stride across the floor to the door and throw it open.

Allisander Sallister is there, arguing with my guards, his voice a low, lethal hiss. "I've heard all about the girl he's taken. I assure you, the prince is *not* still sleeping, and you will—"

He stops short when the door is flung open. I watch as he takes in my bare chest, my loose linen pants. I very definitely need a shave, and at the present moment, my hair likely rivals Quint's.

"I was, in fact, asleep," I say. "And alone."

He clears his throat and straightens. "Forgive me." Though he says it to me, not the guards he was just dressing down. "Our supply run was attacked by vandals. The guards you provided were able to detain them. They've been taken to the Hold. I would like you to join me when we question them."

Oh, he would, would he? I run a hand across my jaw. I'd say it's too early for this, but it's really not.

"Send for breakfast," I say to my guards. "Tell Geoffrey I'm awake. Have a message sent to the king that I need to attend to business in the Hold." I glance at Allisander, who looks poised to step forward and wait in my chambers while I dress, but there's only so much of him I can take within five minutes of waking.

"Wait for me in the hall," I say to him.

He inhales to protest. I shut the door in his face.

I should be worried about whatever smugglers he's dragged into the Hold, or whatever he's going to say about last night, but I can only think of Tessa meeting with my brother.

She's smart and savvy and quick on her feet. I hope she has the good sense to lie. If she tells him the truth about everything, he won't believe her. I know he won't.

I hope he won't.

I press my hands to my mouth and breathe through my fingers. Tessa.

I have a thought, then dash to my desk, fish out a slip of paper, where I nearly spray ink all over the surface in my hurry to write. I fold up the parchment and take it to the door, flinging it wide as I did before, just as my steward, Geoffrey, is approaching with a shaving kit.

He and my guards all look at me in surprise.

I clear my throat and thrust the folded paper at the nearest guard. "Take this to Quint. Tell him it's for Tessa."

"Yes, Your Highness." He takes the paper and gives me a nod.

Geoffrey clears his throat. "I'll be quick, Your Highness." He pauses. "Consul Sallister told me you have business to attend to."

I'm tempted to tell Geoffrey to go shave that stupid goatee off Allisander's face, but I don't. He's already heard about Tessa, and he's definitely not happy about it. I sigh and take a step back. "We mustn't keep the consul waiting."

CHAPTER NINETEEN

Tessa

Quint must be used to filling uncomfortable silences. I'm holding on to his arm like it's the only thing keeping me upright, my breathing shallow and rapid, and he's waxing poetic about the historical relevance of the doorknobs.

"And you'll see," he's saying as we move into the central part of the palace, "the metalworking here turns from brass to gold-plated steel. Much of this area was destroyed in a fire a century ago, but the Steel City sector was just beginning to flourish, so King Rodbert ordered that all—"

"Master Quint." A guard has appeared in our path. My fingers tighten on Quint's arm.

Maybe Prince Corrick has changed his mind. Maybe this guard is going to drag me away. Maybe I'm going to be drawn and quartered. They'll do it in front of the king. Or on that stage where he was going to execute eight people. Or—

The guard extends a hand with an unevenly folded slip of paper. "From His Highness, Prince Corrick."

Quint takes it. "Thank you, Lennard."

The guard's eyes don't shift to me, but he says, "He asked that you give it to Tessa."

Quint offers the paper to me. I close my fingers around it. I have no idea what it could say.

That's not true. I can just imagine what it says. Probably a promise to break all my bones if I mess this up. I want to crumple it up without looking.

Quint is walking again, and the guard steps to the side to allow us to pass.

My hand is damp on the note, but I don't want to unfold it.

"Are you not going to read it?" says Quint.

I make a face. "It probably says something like, 'Say the wrong thing about me, and I'll use your limbs as firewood.'"

"I rather doubt it. I'm certain he would expect the guard to see it."

That draws me up short. I've never considered worrying about such a thing. My fingertips press into the paper, and I swallow.

Quint drops his voice. "Can you not read?"

I snap my head around. "What?"

"There is no need to be ashamed. I can arrange for tutors discreetly." His voice is still very low. "A delegate from Trader's Landing married a woman who had never learned her letters nor her sums, and within weeks—"

"I can read!" For goodness' sake. I hastily unfold the paper and stare at the words scrawled there. They stop my heart and coax it into beating again.

"Mind your mettle," I whisper. For a breath of time, I want to press the paper to my chest.

Weston Lark isn't real.

He's not.

But if he's not real, then Prince Corrick sent me the exact words I needed to hear at the exact moment I needed to hear them. Words that could sound like a warning or a threat or nothing of consequence at all.

I take a long, steadying breath. I square my shoulders and fold the paper into a rectangle in my palm.

"Steady on?" says Quint. His eyes are searching my face.

For all his endless prattle, Quint is sharper than he seems. I make a mental note to remember that.

"Steady on," I say, and to my surprise, I mean it.

"Marvelous! Now, allow me to draw your attention to the wall hangings . . ."

———✦———

The palace is enormous, and though it takes a while to walk to wherever the king awaits, it's obvious when we draw near. While we've passed guards and servants in the hallways, this door is surrounded by eight armed men: two on each side, with four directly across. These guards bear an extra adornment on their sleeves that I haven't seen on the others, a crown stitched in gold surrounded by interlocking circles of purple and blue. A footman in richly detailed livery stands to the side as well. The guards don't seem to move, but I feel their attention on me the instant we come into view. Every hair on the back of my neck stands up.

My finger's tighten on Quint's arm again, but my step doesn't hesitate.

"You'll stay?" I breathe.

"If asked."

The footman announces us. I think we'll be made to wait, but a voice calls from the other side. "Enter."

The door swings wide, and I find I can't breathe. Quint leads me forward. This is a different terror from last night, when I was certain I faced execution. This is fear wrapped up in silk and ribbons and etched with gold.

The room is smaller than I expect, with a marble floor and a long, shining glass table. The windows here stretch from the floor nearly to the ceiling, and curtains have been drawn wide, allowing natural light and warmth to swell in the room, making the sky-blue walls come alive with shadows. Flowers bloom in massive pots set against the wall, filling the space with warm and inviting scents. An actual tree towers in the corner, situated in a pot half the size of the table, and vines climb the trunk and stick to the wall, blooming with tiny pink flowers along the length. If a garden could be brought inside, I very much think it would look like this room.

Then my eyes fall on the king standing by the corner of the table, and it's a testament to the room that I didn't notice him first. I saw him last night, but my brain was clouded with fear, and my only thoughts were of escape and survival—to say nothing of betrayal. Now I can take in his height—slightly taller than Corrick, I think—and the breadth of his shoulders—slightly narrower—and the black of his hair and the blue of his eyes. He has a smattering of freckles like his brother, too, though his skin is more pale, and there's no hint of a smile on his mouth, so the freckles look like someone painted them on, an attempt to make a severe man seem more boyish. Four more guards stand by the wall at his back, and another footman waits in the corner by a table filled with drinks and delicacies.

I don't know if I'm supposed to kneel or curtsy or lie down on the floor and beg for my life. My mouth is dry. I wish Jossalyn were here so I could follow her lead. The king's eyes are on me, and I find I can't move.

"Your Majesty," says Quint. "May I present—"

"I know who she is, Quint."

"Ah, yes. And may I remind you that she is unfamiliar with court protocol—"

"I don't need to be reminded." The king's eyes flick to my left. "Out."

I suck in a breath, but Quint's arm drops from under my hand before I can dig in with my fingers. "Yes, Your Majesty."

And then he's gone, and I'm alone with the king. The door quietly clicks closed behind us.

No matter how much finery Jossalyn laced onto my body this morning, I feel like the ragged outlaw in torn clothes he saw last night in Corrick's chambers. My hands flutter over my skirts, unsure where to settle.

So many words want to escape my lips.

Forgive me. I don't know what I'm supposed to do.

Please don't kill me.

Please don't have Corrick kill me.

Please bring Quint back.

Please send me home.

Jossalyn's warning to wait until he addressed me is ringing in my ears. I bite into my lip from the inside until I taste blood.

The former king was well loved by the people. Kandala prospered.

To sit with Harristan's and Corrick's father would have been an honor. I wouldn't have been terrified. I would have been in awe. The envy of everyone I knew.

Then again, with the previous king, I wouldn't have been sneaking into the servants' quarters. I wouldn't have been smuggling medicine out of the Royal Sector. I wouldn't be here at all.

I'd be a lot better off than I am right now, because King Harristan is most definitely not well loved.

"What thought just crossed your mind?" he says.

I jump. "I—what?"

His expression doesn't change. "I know you heard me."

I can't very well say that no one likes him. "I was—I was—" My voice sounds like a wheezing whisper. I have to clear my throat, but it doesn't help. He's every bit as intimidating as Corrick. "I was thinking that King Lucas was well loved by the people."

King Harristan's eyes search my face, and his expression shifts in a way that makes me think he can read every thought I'm not voicing. "Yes, he was." He holds out a hand to indicate a chair. "Sit."

I have to force my feet to move. He's watching me, and after the way he said, *I know you heard me*, I don't want to make him wait again. He eases into the chair at the head of the table, but I drop into mine so quickly that I have to grab the edge of the table to keep from upending the chair.

Almost as if by some unseen signal, the footman moves out of the corner. He was standing so silently that I almost forgot he was there. He sets two glass goblets in front of us, then two china cups on delicate saucers. First the king, then me. He pours water into the goblets, and then tea into the cups. The tea is dark gray and smells heavenly. The footman pours milk into the king's tea and adds a small spoonful of sugar, then glances at me. "Milk and sugar, miss?"

I have no idea, but following the king's lead doesn't sound like a bad plan. "Yes. Please. Sir."

Once he's returned to the corner, King Harristan traces a finger around the rim of his cup but doesn't take a sip. "Did you know my father?"

It's a ridiculous question, but it sounds genuine, so I shake my head. "No. No, Your Majesty."

"It's easy to love your king when everyone is well fed and healthy," he says. "A bit harder when everyone is . . . not."

He doesn't say this in an arrogant way. More . . . contemplative. He's so severe that sentimentality takes me by surprise. I'm not sure how to respond.

He finally takes a sip of his tea. "Corrick tells me that you steal medicine and distribute it."

I freeze with my hand on the cup.

"You slipped into the palace, and your life has been spared," King Harristan says. "You may as well speak freely."

"Has my life been spared for . . . ah, ever?" I rasp.

"*Forever?* That is outside my power, I would think. But I would not have summoned you here if I wanted frightened lies." He pauses. "Is my brother mistaken about what you do?"

Mind your mettle. My brain supplies images before I'm ready. Wes in the workshop, helping me weigh and measure. The children we have to coax into taking their medicine. The women who cry on my shoulder when we appear with the vials, because they're so worried they'll lose their entire family. The men who want to skip their doses so others can have more.

"Tell me," says King Harristan.

The words aren't an order. They're a plea.

I blink at him, surprised. My brain supplies a memory from last night. Harristan and Corrick in close conversation, their voices low and intense. I wasn't listening. I wanted to escape. But my thoughts captured their words to replay later. To replay now.

Cory. I don't like this.

I wasn't wrong before. King Harristan has a limit. Not just a limit. A weakness for his people.

I think back to the moment in front of the sector gates, when the eight smugglers were set to be executed. King Harristan looked so cold and aloof. I thought it meant he was numb to our suffering, bored with our punishment. I thought it meant he was horrible, as so many of us believe.

But maybe he was so cold and aloof because he didn't want to be there at all.

What did Corrick say? *Kindness leaves you vulnerable, Tessa. I learned that lesson years ago.*

King Harristan would have learned that lesson, too. He also lost his parents—and inherited a kingdom that was on the brink of falling apart.

I don't want to feel any kind of kinship or sympathy for this man or his brother. They're cruel and cold, and they've caused so much harm. But it's one thing when I'm seeing the bodies hanging from the gate—and altogether another when Prince Corrick is telling me of their crimes.

I draw a long breath. "Corrick—ah, Prince Corr—I mean, His Highness—"

"I know who you mean."

"Right. Of course." I pause. "He's not mistaken. I do steal medicine. But I'm not a smuggler. I give it to those who cannot afford their own."

"Do you not think the people who have legally procured it have a right to their medicine?"

I hesitate.

His eyes bore into mine. "Truth, Tessa. If you will not give me the truth, you can spend the rest of your days in the Hold, and my brother's wishes be damned."

I stare back at him. I stood in front of Wes and said the time had come for revolution. I said we should step out of the shadows. Now I'm out of the shadows. I'm right in front of the king—and he's asking for the truth.

So I give it to him. "Your dosages are too high," I say. "You're taking more than you need."

"You cannot possibly know that."

"I *do* know that. My father was an apothecary, and I learned to measure doses myself. The people we are treating stay just as healthy as people taking six times as much." I'm saying too much, but now that I've begun, I can't stop. "My father used to say that too much medicine could be as harmful as too little. I sometimes wonder if you could heal all your people by virtue of regulating dosages more stringently. If you add a bit of roseseed oil to the elixir—"

"You and your father steal together?"

"I—what? No. My father—my parents are dead." I swallow. "They died two years ago."

To my surprise, he looks startled. He draws back in the chair. "You have my sympathy."

"Do I?" I say recklessly. "They were killed by the night patrol. *Your* night patrol."

"So your father was a smuggler? An illegal trader?"

"No!" The king might as well have slapped me across the face. I grip the edge of the table. "My father—he—he was a good man—"

"He was doing what you were doing?"

"Yes."

"Which, at its base, is stealing, yes?"

I glare at him. "It's not the same."

"It's the same to the night patrol." He takes a sip of tea.

I want to knock it right into his face.

Corrick might not have cut my hands off, but I have a feeling the guards standing by the wall would do it.

"My intention is not to upset you," says King Harristan. "But if you are to hold me in low regard for what happened to your parents, I would suggest that you consider the choices they made. Every smuggler has a story to justify their actions. The penalties are well known. How can I turn a blind eye to one type of thievery and not another?"

My fingers are clutching the edge of the table so tightly that my knuckles ache. He's wrong.

But . . . he's also not. I had this exact argument with Wes from the other side. *It's all the same to the king and his brother.*

"What choice do we have?" I snap. "People are dying."

"I know."

I freeze. That note is in his voice again. He does know. He does care.

"It might be all the same to the night patrol," I say roughly, "but it's different when someone just wants to survive."

"I believe the people who buy the medicine lawfully want to survive as well."

"If someone is starving and they steal a loaf of bread—"

"It is still stealing." His tone doesn't change.

"Have *you* ever been starving?" I say boldly.

Silence falls between us, sharp and quick. He hasn't. Of course he hasn't.

His eyes don't leave mine. "If you had this theory about Moonflower petals, about dosages, why did you not make it known?"

"To whom?" I demand. "I just told you, and you didn't believe me!"

He stares back at me impassively, running his finger around the rim of his teacup again.

I sit back sheepishly. "Your . . . um . . . Majesty."

"You said 'we.'"

"What?" This whole conversation is leaving me a bit breathless.

"Are you referring to the Benefactors?"

"No! I don't know who they are."

"You said, 'the people *we* are treating stay just as healthy.' Who is *we*?"

I frown. There are people in the sectors who think the king is a boorish fool who's lazy and frivolous, but sitting in front of him, I can tell that they're wrong. I don't get the sense that it's easy to lie to this man.

I do get the sense that he actually wants this kind of honest discourse, which is more surprising than anything else I've learned since coming here.

I take a deep breath. "When my parents died, I was there. I saw it. The night patrol—they're not . . . they're not subtle. I was blind with grief. I was going to run out after them. But there was a man in the shadows who caught me and trapped me in the darkness. I thought he was an outlaw. And he was. But not . . . not a smuggler.

He was saving lives with stolen medicine. He saved my life." To my surprise, my throat tightens. I feel like I'm grieving Wes all over again, in a completely different way. "We became . . . friends. We were partners. We helped people."

"And what became of this friend?"

I wish I still had Quint's handkerchief. I dab at my eyes with my fingertips. "The night after you tried to execute the eight smugglers, he wanted to stop. He said it was too dangerous. But I begged him to continue. I didn't—I didn't—" My voice catches. I can't breathe. I press a hand to my chest and close my eyes.

He wasn't real. Wes wasn't real. He didn't die on the wall. He didn't exist.

"He was captured," says King Harristan.

I swallow. Nod. Breathe.

"Look at me."

I have to force my eyes open. He's staring at me again, but his voice is no longer impassive.

"What of the people you were helping? What will become of them?"

I swipe at my cheeks. "They'll get sick and die," I say. "Or they won't. The same as will happen to anyone who doesn't have the elixir."

"Finn," he says, and it takes me a moment to realize he's not talking to me.

The footman peels away from the wall. "Your Majesty."

"Fetch Quint."

Quint must not have been far, because he appears in less than a minute.

King Harristan doesn't even give him time to speak, but Quint must be used to that, because he already has a pen in hand. "I would like a meeting with the palace doctors and apothecaries about the dosage levels in the Royal Sector. Tessa will present her findings to them tomorrow, and—"

"What?" I squeak.

Quint pauses in his writing to lift a finger to his lips, and I clamp my mouth shut.

"I would like a full accounting of the medicine dispensed in each sector by population, along with records of efficacy. Have Corrick review it. Issue a statement that our breech of security was a misunderstanding, that a concerned citizen, an apothecary herself, was merely trying to deliver a reporting of her research to the palace."

I'm staring at him.

King Harristan looks back at me levelly. "I can't grant you your life forever," he says, "but I can grant a few more days to corroborate your story. I am interested in hearing your theories in more detail."

I don't know what to say.

"She is overcome with gratitude, Your Majesty," says Quint.

The king grants him a withering glance. "Out of here, Quint. Take her with you."

"Indeed." Quint snaps his book shut and offers me his arm.

"Thank you?" I whisper. I'm not sure I mean it. I'm not sure if I want to.

Quint pats my hand where it rests on his arm. "Come along, my dear. Etiquette awaits."

CHAPTER TWENTY

Corrick

I'm rarely called to the Hold when the sun is in the sky, and now it's been twice in one week. It's never a particularly pleasant place, but during the nights it's usually cool, which keeps the odor manageable, and quiet, because even the most offensive criminals must sleep occasionally.

During the day, it's hell.

"You really must do something about the smell," Allisander says, a handkerchief masking his face as we walk through the gates.

Maybe it's only hell because he's here.

Or maybe it's hell because I am. I should be in the palace. I should be watching over Tessa. I keep thinking of the way she tossed that glass of brandy at me, and I imagine her doing something similar to my brother.

It's too easy to imagine. And despite all evidence to the contrary, I really am a lot more tolerant than Harristan is. *Lord, Tessa.*

"You haven't said anything about the girl," says Allisander.

The girl. I bristle at his dismissive tone, and it takes effort to hide it. The *girl* is brave. Brilliant. Strong. Compassionate. The *girl* does more for Kandala than the spoiled consul standing in front of me. "The young woman you assumed spent the night in my quarters?"

A guard steps forward to hold the door to the staircase.

"Well . . . yes," says Allisander. "According to Arella, you were—"

"I know what Arella thinks I was doing, just as I know what you think I was doing." I glare at him, and he has the grace to look surprised. "She was wrong. So are you."

He stares at me over the handkerchief. "Rumors say she snuck into the palace to kill Harristan."

There's an undercurrent of concern to his tone that makes me wonder, just for a moment, if the tiniest spark of their friendship remains. But then he adds, "She could have been working with the smugglers I captured, and now you've allowed her access to the king."

Ah. Of course. I keep my eyes forward and stride down the stairs. "She'd hardly be alive right now if that were true."

He's all but hissing at me behind his handkerchief. "Well, it's certainly not commonplace for you to bring a smuggler to your room—"

"Consul, I hope you didn't drag me to the Hold before breakfast for a discussion we could have had in the palace." We reach the bottom, and I glance at him. I need him to stop digging for information about Tessa—at least until I can find out what she said to my brother. "Tell me about your prisoners."

He huffs for a moment, like a discomfited toddler. "Well. They

struck in the Wilds. We had six wagons full between Lissa's shipment and my own. There were dozens of them, all at once."

I stop short in the final hallway before the turn into the lowest
level. A lone lantern hangs from the wall here, flickering shadows
across Allisander's cheeks. There isn't much that could drag my
thoughts away from Tessa, but that does it. "Dozens?" I say. "Your
supply run was attacked by *dozens*?"

"Yes. Far more than the small pack you unearthed from Steel
City." He coughs, and he must be grimacing behind the handkerchief. "We couldn't capture them all, of course. And lord knows
how many parcels they were able to escape with—"

"You don't keep an inventory?"

"Of course we do. But they set one of the wagons on fire—"

"On *fire*?"

"Yes. They had flaming arrows. Torches. They were organized,
and they must have known we were coming. We just authorized
this shipment two days ago, and because of its size, few people knew
we were coming." He makes a disgusted noise. "I knew those first
eight wouldn't be the end of it. There must be hundreds more,
waiting to destroy our supply runs. They endanger all of Kandala,
Corrick. They must be stopped."

"I agree." And I do. If Allisander and Lissa are spooked, they'll
stop making shipments at all. Or they'll require the sectors to
spend money and manpower they can't spare to come get medicine themselves. I wonder if any of the prisoners were those who
escaped during the riot. "I'll question them. We'll unearth what's
happening."

"Good."

We turn the corner. The smell is worse down here than usual.

It's quieter, too. For midmorning, I was expecting shouts and curses to be coming from the cells, but no one is talking. Four guards are stationed down here, and they nod to me, but they look . . . bored. I stop at the first set of bars and peer inside.

A young woman lies on the floor, facing the rear wall. I see brown hair first, in a messy pile beside her head. I'm so used to watching for Tessa among the smugglers that are dragged to the Hold, so for an instant, my stomach clenches. It's not her. I know it's not. It can't be.

This woman doesn't look quite right anyway. She's older than Tessa, with beige skin a few shades darker. Her jaw is bruised heavily, her lips cracked and bleeding. A fly alights on her mouth and she doesn't flinch—meaning she's unconscious or asleep. One arm seems twisted at an unnatural angle.

I can't shake the tension in the pit of my stomach.

I say nothing and move to the next cell. A man this time, easily in his thirties. Eyes closed, his nose crooked and crusted with blood. His clothes are torn and stained crimson in so many areas that I can't tell where his injuries originated. Both arms are definitely broken.

My jaw tightens.

Next cell. Another man, this time in his twenties. Broken, bloody, and bruised. Also unconscious. His leg is broken.

Next cell. A third man, even older. His beard is speckled with gray. The side of his face is awash with bruises and swelling, and it looks like his eye is crusted shut with blood.

A woman is in the next cell, her breathing rough and ragged. Her face is dirty but unharmed, and her feet are bare and bleeding. She's also pregnant. While I'm standing there, her eyes flutter open, and she coughs against the straw-covered floor. She sees me watching her, and I wait for fear to bloom in her eyes.

It doesn't. Resignation does. "I figured dying here would be quicker than the fever," she croaks, then blinks slowly.

Allisander said they were organized, that this was a planned attack, but none of these people look like organized criminals. I wonder if they're all sick.

"We'll make sure it's more painful," says Allisander. He kicks at the ground, sending a cloud of dust and grit rattling into the cell.

The woman coughs again, then spits blood onto the stone floor. "I figured. You proved that when we surrendered."

It takes a moment for the impact of that to sink in. I turn and look at Allisander. "They surrendered?"

"Of course. We had a heavy contingent of guards. Once we realized what we were under attack, we were able to corner half of them. Though most were able to escape into the Wilds."

The woman smiles, blood on her lips. "Thanks to the Benefactors, you'll see them again."

I freeze. I remember the shouts during the riot in front of the gates. "Who are the Benefactors?"

Her eyes fall closed.

Allisander slams a hand against the bars. "You will talk."

She doesn't.

Allisander inhales as if he's going to spew more vitriol, but she's not going to talk, and he won't be satisfied unless I start creating nightmares to get answers. I'll do it if I have to, but not for his private indulgence. I head for the next cell. Allisander shuts his mouth and follows. Another man this time. He's sitting upright in the corner, cradling his wrist in his lap, but his eyes are heavy-lidded. He's pale and sweating, his breathing a little too quick.

With a start, I realize he's a man Tessa and I used to bring medicine to. His name is Jarvis, and he has a pretty wife named Marlea. I wonder if I'll find her in one of the cells. They live in Artis, just outside the Wilds, and he works as a bricklayer while she mends clothes. He's large and thick with muscle, but he's also one of the most gentle men I've ever met. While most of the people who rely on us for medicine are quick to condemn the king—and me— Jarvis was one who'd always say, "I'm sure the man is doing the best he can."

I can't see him attacking a supply run.

Then again, I couldn't see Tessa sneaking into the palace either.

Tessa. Tension's grip on my insides grows even tighter. I look at the consul. "If they surrendered, why are they all so heavily injured?"

He cocks an eyebrow, like we're brothers-in-arms and I'll find all this amusing. "Does it matter?"

I don't play. "Yes."

What I can see of his face turns serious. I want to rip the handkerchief away. "Why?" he says.

"Because I can't question prisoners who are barely conscious." I pause. "My guards know that. If someone surrenders, they're brought to the Hold. Unharmed. Did you give them different orders?"

Allisander hesitates. He's trying to read my face.

I don't give him the chance. I look to a guard stationed by the wall. "Stanton. Have the prison doctor treat their wounds. Feed them all. I'll return late this evening."

He nods. "Yes, Your Highness."

Allisander has finally lowered that handkerchief. "You can't be serious."

"I am," I say. "If you want information, they need to be in a condition to give it." I turn for the stairs.

He's not following me. "First you bring an assassin to your room, and now you're caring for prisoners? Why isn't that girl down here in a cell, too, Corrick?"

I ignore him and look at Stanton again. "Have the guards who were assigned to the supply run report to the palace. I'd like to speak with them." Then I step close to Allisander, and I shove every thought of Tessa out of my head. I send my thoughts to the dark place that reminds me of how I felt after my parents were killed in front of me. "Would you like me to prove that I haven't turned soft, Consul?"

My voice is cold, but he doesn't back down. He may have been friends with Harristan, but his relationship with me has always been a bit more politically weighted. I sometimes think he avoids my brother, as if their standoff from so many years ago still stings, but he and I have always met on a level playing field. But now he looks like he wants to challenge me, and that is unlike him. I wonder how much gossip is already swirling in regard to Tessa. I wonder if the fact that prisoners escaped during the riots is being seen as a weakness on my part. I wonder if I'm going to be forced to do something terrible, just to quiet the rumors.

Without warning, my thoughts summon the image of Tessa on the floor of my room, shaking and terrified. Her thoughts are always of the people. Mine are too, but not the way hers are. She used to look at Weston—at me—with such devotion. I didn't deserve a moment of it then, and I deserve it less now.

The thought comes as a blow.

Something must flicker in my expression, something that exposes a flash of vulnerability or weakness, because Allisander steps forward and says, "Yes, Corrick. I would."

"Very well. You are banned from the palace until you can remember that I am King's Justice, and you are Consul of Moon-light Plains. You will not countermand my orders with guards I provided for your protection, and you will not—"

"You cannot ban me from the palace." He looks like he wants to knock me into the wall.

"Shall I find you a cell among your friends? They seem crowded. Perhaps you could share."

His hands have formed fists, and his eyes are cold. "No," he says through gritted teeth.

I raise my eyebrows.

"No," he says again, "Your Highness."

"Remember that," I snap. "Yours is not the only sector with the Moonflower." I turn and head for the stairs without waiting to see if he follows or not.

—◆—

I've been waiting for Harristan for twenty minutes, and I'm about ready to tear the wallpaper from the walls. Instead, I'm looking at stacks of paperwork that are accumulating in front of me: detailed accountings of each sector's medicinal allotment, along with the most recent census per town, as well as death records and health records and crime records. More information than I could ever care to need.

"What is all this?" I ask a page as he carries yet another stack into my quarters.

"By order of the king, Your Highness," he says, before offering a quick bow and leaving the room—just to reappear minutes later with more. He looks at the laden table doubtfully.

I want to tell him to toss it all in the fireplace.

"Just stack it on the floor," I say.

I sent word to Quint, hoping he'd bustle through my doorway with information about Tessa's meeting with my brother, but apparently he's been dealing with some kind of issue with the kitchen staff.

I have no idea what Harristan is doing—or why he'd send me all this. I sent word to him, too, and my brother's response was a terse, "Later."

I move to the side table and pour a glass of wine.

The page returns with another stack. Lord. I pour the wine back into the bottle and switch to brandy.

I enjoy details, and I'm not opposed to digging through mountains of documents, but this . . . this is a bit much. I'm not even sure of the purpose.

I want to send word to Tessa, but I can't think of anything to say that won't be read and gossiped about—and I need to know how her meeting with Harristan went so I can decide how I want our interactions to be viewed.

I also can't stop thinking about these Benefactors, and what that means. Is someone behind these attacks, these raids? For the people to take such a risk would require funding of some sort. Or medicine. Otherwise the risk to the people is simply too great.

If these attacks continue, Allisander will slow his shipments. The risk to Kandala is too great.

On my final night as Weston Lark, I asked Tessa if she knew who they were, and she didn't. She wouldn't have lied to Wes. I wish we'd had one more night, one more chance to talk to the people.

But of course I've undone any chance of that.

I drag my hands through my hair. I'm exhausted, and it's hardly the middle of the afternoon.

When the page appears with more, I snap, "Enough."

He flinches and almost drops them all.

I sigh. "Put them on the floor. I'll send for you when I've reviewed what you've brought."

In a year, most likely.

Finally, an agonizing hour later, the guards announce my brother. After the way he made me wait, I expect him to come storming in, but instead, Harristan strides into my room casually, letting the door fall closed behind him.

"Corrick." He takes one look at the stacks of folios and paperwork and frowns. "What's all this?"

"You tell me." I take a sip of my drink. "It was sent here by your order."

"Oh. Yes. The girl claims our dosages in the Royal Sector are too high. Will you see if we have data that may corroborate this? The palace physicians are looking into it, but you're better with all this." He waves a hand at the piles.

Meaning he doesn't have the patience—or the time—for it. I don't either, really. My heart is thumping at what Tessa told him. "And when would you like this analysis?"

He eases into the chair across from me and lifts the cover on a folio before letting it fall closed. "Tomorrow."

I choke on my drink. "An entire *day*, Harristan? Why not in an hour?"

"I will not have her staying in the palace if her reasons for being here are not valid."

I set my drink down and stare at him. He stares back at me.

Last night, in the quiet darkness of his quarters, he said that I was keeping secrets from him—but he didn't demand answers. He doesn't demand them now either. But his position is clear.

I am both surprised and not that Tessa was able to somehow convince my brother that her reasons for being in the palace were valid. Not just valid, but . . . beneficial.

"I'll go through the reports," I say quietly.

"Good." He reaches for my glass of brandy and takes a sip. "You do realize you can't ban Allisander from the palace indefinitely."

I grimace. "I didn't realize the news would reach you so quickly."

"He issued a complaint almost immediately."

"From the palace steps, I imagine."

Harristan doesn't smile. "As a matter of fact, yes." He hesitates. "Even if our dosages are faulty, we cannot alienate our primary supplier."

"Allisander grows too bold."

"For all of Arella's demands for leniency, her sector is not a major supplier for Kandala. Nor is Roydan's."

I know this. He knows I know this. He sets the glass on the table and I take it. "Stringing people up outside the gates hasn't stopped the smugglers," I say. "If anything, they grow bolder."

"For certain. They sneak right into the palace and find themselves in my brother's room."

I drain the glass and look away. "Lord, Harristan."

For a moment, I think he's going to press me for more information. My brother is no fool. He knows there's more to Tessa than what I've said. He admitted as much last night.

But he simply glances at the papers and stands. "You have much to do." He claps me on the shoulder before turning for the door. "I'll take care of Allisander."

"Thank you."

I can't say it aloud, but I'm thanking him for more than just handling an irritated consul. I'm thanking him for his trust. For allowing me to keep my secrets.

For allowing me to protect Tessa.

He knows it, too, because he offers a small smile. "You're welcome, Cory."

Then his smile is gone, and he's reaching for the door.

CHAPTER TWENTY-ONE

Corrick

Quint is sprawled in a chair in my quarters, eating strawberries while the sun sets in the window behind him. He's been talking about nothing for at least twenty minutes, and usually I don't care, but my nerves are so on edge that I'm ready to have my guards drag him out of here.

"And then," he's saying, "Jonas told the guards that the girl was his niece, if you can believe that. I don't know who he thinks he's fooling."

I fight with the gold buttons on my jacket, then jerk it off my shoulders to toss onto the bed alongside the others I've tried and discarded. "I feel like there must be a matter *somewhere* in the palace that needs your attention."

"More than likely." He picks up another strawberry and twists the stem free. "Try the black one again."

I frown. That's the jacket Geoffrey first pulled from my

wardrobe—and likely the one he expects that I'm still wearing. I yanked it off when I realized it reminds me too much of what I do for my brother, which makes me worry it will remind *Tessa* of what I do for my brother. I reach for the red one instead.

"Absolutely not," says Quint.

I sigh and set it aside, then run a hand across my jaw.

Quint sets the strawberry down and walks past the pile on my bed, heading for my wardrobe. "Honestly, Corrick. The girl has seen you in wool and broadcloth." He surveys the contents for a moment and pulls a garment free. "Here."

The jacket is a deep-blue brocade, with a faint pattern of leaves in a slightly darker shade, with a black silk collar and silver piping. The buttons are burnished silver. It's soft and simple and I've never worn it—it's nothing I would normally wear.

"No," I say.

"You don't want to be the prince. You can't be the outlaw. Shall we come up with another identity?"

"Quint."

He holds open the jacket like a valet. "You know the salon will be packed with courtiers at this hour. Do you want to leave your girl to the vipers?"

No. I don't. And he's right: it doesn't matter what I wear. I can't be who she wants me to be. I sigh and slip my arms into the sleeves. "She still hates me."

"She hates that you lied. There's a difference." Quint steps around to face me. He bats my hands away from the buttons, then takes them up himself.

"I had *no idea* you knew how to button a jacket," I say, feigning wonder.

"Hush." He finishes the last button, brushes invisible dust from my shoulder, and steps back.

I tug at my shirtsleeves and realize that he's studying me. This is what most people miss about Quint: he seems scattered and shallow, but underneath, he's a keen observer who sees everything and forgets nothing.

"What?" I say.

"I heard what happened in the Hold today. With Consul Sallister."

"How I banned him from the palace?" I grunt. "Harristan had a few words about that."

"No. About how you ordered that the prisoners be fed and treated."

I frown. "Sallister had most of them beaten half to death, Quint. If he wants to find out who's behind the raids on his supply runs, he needs to leave me someone to question."

He says nothing.

I roll my eyes and turn for the door. "*Now* you have nothing to say?"

"Tessa may be safe, and she may not like the truth," he says quietly. "But here, you can only be Prince Corrick."

"I know."

"You can only be the King's Justice."

I want to be irritated, but I'm not. Maybe I needed the reminder.

My voice is just as level as his. "I haven't forgotten."

"Of course not." Quint reaches for the door. "Your evening awaits, Your Highness."

———+———

Quint was right. The salon *is* packed with courtiers. I spot Jonas Beeching in the corner, and the consul is sharing a drink with a young woman with raven-dark curls that spill down her back. She appears to be half his age, and I wonder if this is the *niece* Quint mentioned. Jonas must feel my gaze, because he begins to look up, so I glance away. He'll want to emphasize the need for his bridge request for Artis again, and I have no desire to play politics tonight.

But then, just for a moment, I glance back, thinking of that moment at the table when Allisander mentioned that Jonas's request for too much silver might have something to do with the Benefactors who are funding the rebels. I turn that around in my head, and it doesn't quite seem to fit. Jonas is too complacent, too happy to allow the world to keep turning as it always has because nothing bad affects him personally.

I scan the crowd for Tessa, wondering if any of the ladies have sunk their claws into her yet. Gossip fills the air like a haze, and though voices drop when I draw near, I catch a few scattered comments as I stride through the room.

Apparently she's an apothecary.

I heard she spent the night with the prince.

I don't care what some girl says, my physician recommends four doses a day.

She'd better watch her throat.

I roll my eyes and take a glass of wine from a passing servant with a tray.

Maybe the king tried to sneak her into the palace.

Perhaps she's carrying his bastard.

I choke on my drink.

Well. That will come as a surprise to Harristan.

I don't see Tessa, and it takes effort to keep from pulling my pocket watch free. Across the room, Jonas looks like he's gathering the nerve to approach me. If Tessa doesn't show up soon, I'm going to have to find someone else to talk to or I'll be forced to listen to him.

"Your Highness."

The quiet voice speaks from beside me, and I turn to find myself facing Lissa Marpetta. She and Allisander control the supply of Moonflower in Kandala, but she doesn't annoy me half as much as he does. She doesn't annoy me at all, honestly. She's nearly twice my age, and she was once close with my mother. I often wonder if that's part of the reason she never pushes me or Harristan too hard. Many of the consuls think she is passive, a woman who was once close with the royal family, who later lucked into wealth and power. Harristan disagrees. He thinks she's clever. While Allisander has no hesitation in speaking out for what he wants, Lissa always seems happy to let him fight the battles while her sector reaps the rewards.

"Consul," I say. "I thought you'd returned to Emberridge."

"I heard there were developments in the palace, and Allisander sent word that I should return."

Of course he did. "A misunderstanding," I say smoothly. "The girl brought evidence to the palace that our dosages require a closer look."

She studies me. "You would believe the word of a girl from the Wilds over your royal physicians?"

"I believe we should listen to anyone who might suggest a way to make the medicine more effective."

Lissa hesitates. "With all due respect, Your Highness, I would suggest that you proceed with great care."

I take a sip of my drink. "You think I would be reckless?"

"I think your parents were too trusting of those outside the palace." She's quiet for a moment. "I was quite fond of your mother. I do not want to see the same fate befall you and your brother."

I look back at her, and some of my agitation dissipates. It's rare that any of them take a moment for sentimentality with us, especially now. I nod. "Of course, Consul."

She moves away, and I drain the last of my glass. I didn't need the reminder about my parents. I don't need the reminder that Tessa's theories are just that—theories.

A sudden hush descends on the room as someone new seizes their attention. I see a fancy dress, a fair complexion, and a pile of curls, and my eyes almost dismiss the newcomer as another courtier . . . until I realize it's Tessa.

She's been dressed in a striking gown of crimson velvet, though the skirts are split down the side to reveal a swath of sheer cream-colored voile when she moves. Her arms are bare, though someone has wound a lengthy stretch of red satin ribbon in a complicated pattern along her forearms, and it's tied off just above her elbow. Her expression is aloof, her mouth unsmiling, her eyes flinty. Led by guards, she could easily look like a prisoner, but instead, she looks like a queen.

Her steps slow as she enters the room, her eyes searching the faces.

The whispers have begun anew. Tessa's stoic countenance begins to give way, and I can tell she's hearing some of the comments. Her gaze begins to flick left and right, looking less aloof and more panicked.

I step across the room. "Tessa."

She gives a little jolt, then looks up at me. An attendant has lined her eyes with dark colors and brushed pinks across her cheeks. Her lips are a lighter red than the dress, and they part slightly when she gasps.

Tessa must realize she's staring, because her eyes go cool and she clamps her mouth shut. She takes hold of her skirts and drops into a curtsy that somehow manages to be both graceful and belligerent. Clearly etiquette lessons went well. "Your Highness."

Only she could turn a curtsy into an act of defiance.

I bow in return, then offer my arm. "Shall we?"

She hesitates, uncertainty flickering behind the boldness in her eyes. Every person in this room is watching her reaction, waiting to see how she'll proceed—and how I'll respond. Half are simply curious, but half are undoubtedly waiting for a bit of vicious entertainment, something they can whisper about once I'm gone. Some of them are probably hoping blood will spill.

Quint's warnings are loud in my head. *You can only be the King's Justice.*

Maybe Tessa can read the shift in my expression, because her hand lands on my arm weightlessly. I can feel her fingers trembling.

She's still afraid of me. That pierces a hole in all of Quint's warnings.

A part of me wishes I could undo it, but I have no idea how to undo all of what I am. I consider the way my parents died, and I don't even know if I would.

The doors swing open as we approach, the cool night air swirling against my skin. The cobblestone road in front of the palace is bustling with activity. Horses and carriages come and go, servants and footmen scurrying about. Somewhere, a horse whinnies, and a man shouts for a porter.

A footman stops in front of us and bows. "Your Highness. Your carriage is ready."

"A carriage," whispers Tessa.

"Did you think we would walk?" I say, leading her down the steps.

In the sunlight, my carriage is a deep burgundy, but in the moonlight, it looks black. Silver accents glint in the light from the lanterns. Four horses stand in gleaming harness, tiny bells jingling when they toss their heads. The footman holds the door, and I offer Tessa my hand.

She narrows her eyes at me, ignores my hand, and climbs inside.

I'm about to follow, but Captain Huxley stops beside the carriage. "Your Highness."

The captain of the palace guard is a large man with blond hair, ruddy cheeks, and a fondness for chocolates and bitter ale. He's an honest man, as far as I can tell, but he's known for taking bribes in exchange for bits of gossip about the royal family. He's been captain since my father was king, but when Harristan chose his personal guard, Huxley was overlooked, a slight I don't think he's ever forgiven.

We haven't forgiven him for failing to keep our parents safe, so I think we're even.

He's all but blocking the doorway. I barely glance at him. "What?"

He hesitates when he hears my tone. "This girl is unknown. I should ride with you."

"I will take it under consideration while you ride behind." I shift to move past him.

"Regardless of what stories she bears, she slipped into the palace—"

"Yes. She did. Walked right past one of your guards."

"Yes, well—that is—Your Highness—" he begins, blustering.

"I am very hungry, Captain."

He hesitates, then takes a step back. "As you say."

When I climb into the carriage, Tessa has taken the seat to the front, so I jerk the door closed and ease onto the velvet cushions on the opposite side. Her eyes are dark and cool as they regard me, but her fingers are twisted together, her knuckles pale.

I give her a wry glance. "Captain Huxley offered to ride with us," I say. "I declined."

"Is he worried about the dagger I've hidden in my skirts?"

"Say that a little louder and you'll find out."

The driver chirps to the horses and a whip snaps in the air, and suddenly we're rocking and swaying over the cobblestones.

A small lantern hangs above the window, throwing shadows across her cheeks and making the red highlights in her gown gleam.

I lean back into the cushions. "Tell me: Do you really have a dagger?"

Tessa turns to look at the window. "Keep your hands to yourself or *you'll* find out."

"For as much as you hate me, you can't be this upset about a fine carriage ride and a meal at the most exclusive establishment in all of Kandala."

Her eyebrows go up. "I can't?"

Lord, she is so brazen. "Fine. Perhaps you can."

She says nothing. I say nothing. The silence grows cooler between us, punctuated by the rhythmic clopping of hooves against the cobblestones.

"Forgive me," I say. "I should have started by saying that I owe you a debt of gratitude."

She whips her head around. She looks like she expected me to be teasing her, but when she sees that I'm not, her eyes narrow. "Why?"

"Because you didn't tell Harristan about . . . us."

She turns to look out at the night again. "I did, in fact." She pauses, her fingers flexing. "I told him the truth. I was partners with a man I thought was a friend, until he was caught by the night patrol and hung along the gate."

The truth. I wonder if that's the truth she's told herself, too. That it doesn't matter that I was Weston Lark—because he's dead. Now I'm just me.

She clears her throat. "I thought it wouldn't matter anyway, since no one would believe me."

"Harristan suspects . . . *something* between us."

Her eyes snap to mine. "What?"

"It's not like me to be lenient." I shrug. "He's not pressing me for answers."

Her fingers twine together again, like this is worrisome. "Why not?"

"Because he's my brother, Tessa."

She looks back at the window. "It doesn't matter. There's nothing between us."

"So I've heard."

Silence ticks along between us again. The night is very dark here, but ahead, fire flickers in a massive circle that appears to hang suspended above the earth. Despite her ire, Tessa shifts slightly closer to the window to see better. I've seen it all my life, but even still, the illusion at night really is quite spectacular. It's not a circle at all, but a large archway hung with a hundred torches, each spilling ash and sparks onto a glistening pond that reflects the light. Tessa's lips part as we draw closer, the light illuminating wonder in her eyes.

I shift to the opposite side of the carriage to sit beside her so I can see it as clearly, and she gasps and swings a fist.

Honestly. I catch her wrist. "Don't cause a ruckus in the carriage," I say. "I was serious about the captain." I keep hold of her arm and nod at the window. "Look, before we're past."

She inhales like she wants to snap at me, but we've drawn close enough to hear sparks sizzle as they strike the water, and the sound pulls her attention to the window again. It's too dark to see the woven branches that support the torches, and starlight twinkles beyond the suspended flames. Each spark that falls glitters on the surface of the pond before drowning.

"It's called Stonehammer's Arch," I say. "You can see it from the palace. It was built by my great-grandfather as a declaration of love for his bride. He said as long as the torches kept burning, so would his love for her. When we were children, Harristan and I used to dare each other to climb across."

She jerks her hand out of my grasp. "I hope you fell a lot."

I lean close. "Never once."

"I'm going to stab you."

"I don't really believe you have a dagger."

She draws herself up, challenge flaring in her eyes, brighter than the arch. This bickering reminds me of the way we'd tease each other in the workshop, and at once it's both disheartening and exhilarating.

But suddenly her expression shifts, turning pained, and she presses her hands to her chest, as if it's hard to breathe.

I straighten, alarmed. "Tessa—"

"How could you do that to me?" She shoves me right in the chest, and I can feel all of her sorrow in the motion. Her voice breaks. *"How could you?"*

I freeze. For a moment in the darkness, I forgot.

Maybe I really did need Quint's warning.

She's so tense beside me that it feels like a cruelty to sit here. I shift back to my side of the carriage and tug my jacket straight. Shadows fall across her face, reminding me of the mask she once wore.

"Do you have any idea what I went through?" she whispers, her voice thin and reedy. *"Do you?"*

"No," I say quietly. "Tell me."

She goes still and looks at me.

"You died," she whispers, as if it should be obvious. Her eyes fall closed, and she shudders. "You were my best friend. You were . . . I was . . . I was in . . ." She draws a breath. "Everything was so awful. I just wanted to help people. You did too—or so I thought. And then . . ." Her voice hitches. "You went . . . you went over the wall for me, and I heard the alarms . . ." She sniffs and dabs at her eyes. "And then, at daybreak, I saw . . ."

Her voice trails off.

I know what she saw.

She dabs at her eyes again and fixes her gaze on the window. Stonehammer's Arch is fading into the distance. We're nearing the end of the private road behind the palace now, and soon we'll be thrust into the midst of the elites again.

"Tessa."

She swallows so hard it looks painful. "Don't."

"I need you to understand something."

"I don't care."

I lean forward and brace my arms against my knees. "Do you know," I say evenly, "that every time I am called to the Hold, I worry I'll find you in one of the cells?"

"I suppose that would have put a quick end to your game."

"It wasn't a game," I snap.

She finally looks back at me. "Then what was it? You are King's Justice. You are the *brother* to the *king*. One death away from the throne yourself. You have more power than almost anyone in Kandala." She spreads her hands. "So what were you doing? Was it some kind of penance? Some way to assuage your guilt?" Her voice breaks again. "You've seen what's happening to the people! You've seen it with your own eyes! I can't blame your brother. He's surrounded by people who probably only tell him what he wants to hear. But you've *seen* the suffering, the deaths and the desperation, and still you lined those prisoners up on the stage, and you—you—"

"Tessa." Every word pelts me like a stone. My own chest feels tight.

She presses her fingertips to her eyes. "Why are you doing this to me?" she whispers. "Just throw me in the Hold with the others."

"I can't." My voice is rough and broken, and it gets her attention. She lowers her hands to blink at me.

"I can't," I say again, my eyes burning into hers. "I can't, Tessa. You don't know how many times I wished dawn wouldn't come so quickly. How many times I wanted to stay with you instead of returning to this. How many times I wished I were truly Weston Lark, that Prince Corrick was the fabrication."

She swipes a lone tear from her cheek angrily and gestures at the plush confines of the carriage. "You couldn't leave all this finery?"

"I couldn't leave my brother."

That draws her up short.

"I couldn't take him with me," I continue. "How would I? And even if I could, then . . . what? Leave Kandala to the consuls? I can barely negotiate a reasonable price out of Allisander Sallister for Moonflower petals as it is. He's worse than his father was. It's a delicate balance of keeping him happy and keeping our people as healthy as we can. He would volley for power, and considering all he has at his disposal, he'd likely get it." I pause, then run a hand across my jaw. "Yes. I saw the suffering, Tessa, the same as you. But if Allisander were in power, medicine would be twice as scarce, and the fevers would be twice as deadly."

She's staring at me now.

"You can hate me," I say. "Lord knows everyone else does. But you do not know this side of it."

She's gone completely still. The tears seem to have frozen on her cheeks.

I don't blame her.

But I can't keep her prisoner. She'll always hate me. She'll never trust me. Knowing she's safe in the palace isn't any comfort at all if she's hardly more than a dove locked in a gilded cage.

That's *my* life, not hers.

"I'm not going to kill you. I'm not going to throw you in the Hold." I blow a breath through my teeth. "Hell, if you want to leave, I'll call the carriage to stop. I'll step out to speak with the captain, and you can slip away."

I reach for my waist and slip the buckle of my belt, freeing my dagger. I hold it out to her. "I don't have a treble hook handy, but you can take my blade if you like."

She blinks at me like I've lost my mind. "This is a trick."

"I have *never* tricked you." I catch myself and roll my eyes. "Well. At any rate, I am not tricking you *now*."

She glances from the dagger to my face and then to the window. Her fingers are trembling again.

"Tessa," I say softly. "I let you think I died because I wanted you to stay out of the Royal Sector. I wanted to keep you safe."

I drop to a knee before her and press the dagger into her hand.

She glances at it and then up at me. "I can leave. Just like that?"

My chest has grown tight again, and my breathing feels shallow. I force emotion out of my head, reminding myself of who and what I am. The King's Justice spares no thought for loss or pity.

"Head southeast," I say brusquely. "There's a small gate in the wall where the terrain dips. It looks old and rusted, and there's a padlock, but the hinges are fake, and you can pull the pins from underneath. Do you understand?"

She nods, dumbfounded.

"Captain!" I call. The carriage lurches to a stop.

I pull a small pouch from my pocket and toss it into Tessa's lap, and it jingles with silver. "That should be more than enough to start over."

"Wait—"

I can't wait. If I wait, I'll change my mind. "You have five minutes," I say. "We'll be facing away from the carriage."

Without a backward glance, I slip the latch on the door and spring out.

CHAPTER TWENTY-TWO

Tessa

The door to the carriage slams, and I'm alone. My heart pounds in my chest. Again, too much has happened, and my world feels like it's been turned upside down for the tenth time today. The pouch rattles with coins when I lift it, and the dagger is heavy. When I pull it free of its sheath, it looks sharp and ready. I try not to wonder if he's ever used it on anyone.

I don't trust Corrick at all, but this . . . this doesn't feel like a trap. What would be the purpose? What would he have to gain?

I'm quick and sure-footed. This dress is dark. If the captain and his men are distracted, I could slip away like a ghost.

I couldn't go back to Mistress Solomon's, but I could find work in another city. Especially with a purse full of silver.

But then I think of my meeting with King Harristan. *It's easy to love your king when everyone is well fed and healthy. A bit harder when everyone is . . . not.*

He cares. What's happening in Kandala weighs on him. I'm not sure how I can tell, but I can.

Despite everything, I can tell it weighs on Corrick as well.

I have never tricked you. I've been treating him like the man who everyone fears, as if his entire life has been one big trick. But he's been progressively protecting me since the instant I arrived in the palace, from the way he provided me with food and a room to sleep in to the note he slipped me before his meeting with his brother. Prince Corrick has done a lot of terrible things, but his words rang true. Maybe I don't understand things from this side, just like they don't seem to understand things from mine. And maybe the king was just indulging his brother by allowing me to meet with the royal apothecaries, but it's an opportunity to tell people who *matter* that they could be doing better with the supplies they're given.

I can't keep stealing to help the sick, but maybe I can help them in another way.

Maybe.

It's a lot of maybes.

When Wes stood in front of me on our last night together, I said we needed to stop hiding and cause a revolution. Running now would be hiding. And this isn't the type of revolution I was thinking of . . . but maybe I can bring about change. Maybe I can show the king how badly his people are suffering.

Maybe this is a chance no one else would ever have.

I leave the dagger and the coin pouch on the seat, then put my hand on the latch of the door. I open it boldly, stepping onto the cobblestones with no effort to be silent.

The captain's head whips around. So does Corrick's.

"Ah . . . forgive me." My voice cracks, and I have to clear my throat. "Your Highness?" I curtsy for good measure. "It's been a long day, and I'm rather hungry. You mentioned you were as well."

Corrick looks at me across fifteen feet of darkness, his blue eyes dark and inscrutable. He's gone very still.

My heart is beating so hard that I can nearly taste it in my throat. I hope I'm not making a mistake.

"Indeed," he finally says. "We'll discuss the pattern of those search lights another time, Captain."

He walks back and looks down at me in the moonlight. In the dark it's easy to remember him as Wes: the way he moves, the way the stars glint in his eyes. Brocade and silver have replaced homespun wool and rough leather, but he's still the same man. This morning, I told Quint that my friendship with Wes was an illusion based on a trick, and he said, *"Are you so sure?"*

As always, I'm not sure of anything.

Corrick's eyes skim my face as the cool night air streams between us. "Dinner awaits," he says. Any trace of an edge has vanished from his voice.

A footman scurries forward to hold open the door.

Corrick offers me his hand to help me into the carriage.

This time, I take it.

We sit opposite each other again. A whistle and a whip crack later, and we're rocking over the cobblestones. Corrick settles back into his cushions, regarding me. There's no challenge in his expression now—simply consideration. He's obviously waiting for me to speak, to explain myself, but my tongue is twisted into knots.

Eventually, his eyes narrow just a bit. "Did you stay because you truly wanted to, or did you stay because you do not trust me?"

"Oh!" That didn't occur to me—but voicing either of those

options makes me feel too vulnerable. "I . . . I chose to stay. I have obligations in the palace."

His eyebrows go up. "You do?"

"The king asked me to speak with the royal apothecaries and physicians."

"Ah." He says this graciously, but his eyes search mine, and I can tell he knows there is more that I'm not saying. My thoughts are too complicated to put into words.

Maybe his are, too, because he says nothing more.

I pick up the small purse of coins and toss it back to him. He nimbly snatches it out of the air.

My fingers curl around the dagger, though, and I keep my eyes locked on Corrick as I tuck it into the side of my boot, then let my skirts fall to cover it. "You're not getting this back."

To my surprise, he smiles, his eyes lighting with challenge. "Consider it a gift."

———◆———

In the center of the Royal Sector sits the Circle, which isn't really a circle at all, and is instead a dais constructed of marble and granite in the shape of an octagon, stretching at least fifty feet across. Hundreds of years ago, it was used when the king wanted to hear from his people personally. Then Corrick's great-great-great-grandfather took a dagger in the neck, and it was decided that requests from the people should be made in writing and left at the sector gates.

Over time, the Circle became a convenient location for merchants to sell their wares. As the story goes, twenty years ago, an enterprising tavern owner at the edge of the dais set a few tables and chairs out and outfitted his serving girls in fancy dresses.

Within a year, he'd taken over the entire space. Now it's turned into a place where the richest elites gather to gossip and be seen spending their coins on things they don't need.

I've only ever seen the Circle in the early hours of the morning, and only when I'm sprinting through the deserted streets of the Royal Sector with stolen petals in my pack. In the dark, the dais is gray, the tables and chairs unremarkable, the pots of flowers drab and lifeless.

When Corrick leads me out of the carriage, I'm jolted by the difference.

Now, yellow and white roses spill from massive pots set among the tables, filling the air with a rich aroma. Stained-glass lanterns hang suspended on wires strung above the patrons, casting a flickering multicolored glow across the crowded space. No walls separate those dining from the cobblestone streets, but dozens of carriages line the way, bored attendants waiting with the horses. In the Wilds, it's rumored that the elites would spend a week's worth of silver just to dine here.

I look around at the painted faces, the elegant finery, and I think it might be true.

Every eye follows us from the carriage to our table.

Our presence here must have been prearranged, because our table is at one end of the dais, set apart from the others, with room for the guards to stand between us and the other diners. Wine has already been poured, and a basket of steaming bread sits between us. It's simultaneously private yet not at all. If the guards were steel bars, this would be a cage. Conversation is loud in the night air, but the space between us hangs heavy with silence again.

Corrick sits in his chair as comfortably as he lounged on the velvet seat of the carriage, and he takes a lazy sip of wine.

I'm perched on the edge of my chair, and I want to drain my entire glass and ask for a dozen more.

The prince is watching me. "Second thoughts?" he says.

"Quint said it would be public, but . . . I didn't realize it would be like this."

He lifts one shoulder in an elegant shrug. "We could have dined in the palace, but that would have been worse."

My eyebrows shoot up. "Worse?"

"Here, few people will dare to approach our table." He takes another sip of wine. "In the palace, we wouldn't have had a moment of privacy."

"And you think we have that now." I pick up my glass and limit myself to a sip.

"Not as much as I'd like, but Quint wants people to see you as a potential ally to the throne." His voice turns dry. "Not the outlaw who, according to rumor, slipped into the palace to assassinate the king."

I cough on a sip of wine. My rash decision to enter the palace feels like a nightmare I wish I could shake off. "Of course."

He glances past the guards, and his expression goes still. "Lord." He downs the rest of his glass.

"What's wrong?"

"Our evening is about to get less private."

I follow his gaze and see a man weaving between tables.

Corrick looks at me, and his eyes spark with devilry, reminding me of Wes. His voice drops, like we're co-conspirators. "If you want to throw a drink at *this* man, you have my full permission."

I blink. "Wait. What?"

But he's standing, smoothing his jacket, his face transforming into the darkly beguiling Prince Corrick.

If he's standing, I probably should as well. I shove myself to my feet. A man steps between the guards without hesitation, so he must be someone of importance. He's not much older than Corrick, maybe Harristan's age, with a goatee that's so thick it appears to be glued onto his face. It does nothing to hide the sour pinch to his mouth. He looks like a man who isn't attractive at all but clearly believes he is.

"Consul!" Corrick says joyfully, like he's greeting a long-lost friend. "Have you dined this evening? Join us."

The man stops short. His eyes narrow. "Corrick." He glances dismissively at me. "I didn't want to interrupt your dinner with your . . . guest."

He says *guest* as though Corrick invited a sow to leave a mud pit to sit at this table with him.

I don't want to throw my drink. I want to throw that dagger.

"Nonsense," says the prince. "Tessa, you have the honor of meeting Consul Allisander Sallister."

Consul Sallister. Moonlight Plains. The man who would volley for power if he could.

A serving girl appears with another chair for the table. Another fills Corrick's wineglass before vanishing. Invisible.

I wish I were. The tension between these two men is palpable. My heart thrums against my ribs, but I paste a smile on my face and curtsy. "Consul. I am honored."

He doesn't even look at me. "I understand from Harristan that our argument in the Hold was a misunderstanding."

"Our argument?" Corrick blinks as if startled. "Allisander," he says smoothly. "Did you truly think I would ban you from the palace?"

"I question your actions," the consul says, his voice low and vicious—but not so low that nearby tables aren't getting an earful. "I question your motives. Last week, you had eight captives and three escaped. Today, I brought you a dozen rebels and instead of interrogating them, you're coddling them." He glances at me pointedly. "To be frank, I'm surprised they're not at this table with you."

I flinch.

Corrick doesn't. "You brought me a dozen unconscious rebels," he says evenly. "I will question them and punish them in due course." He pauses. "I will not do it over dinner, however."

I shiver at the chill in his voice.

Consul Sallister leans in. "You promised my supply runs would be safe—"

"I promised *guards*, which you received."

"—and you promised an end to these attacks—"

"Which you know I cannot guarantee."

"—which you've made no effort to *stop*, if the new evidence of these Benefactors is to be believed."

Silence falls between them like a blade. Corrick's eyes are blue ice. The consul's cheeks are red, his shoulders tight. I twist my fingers together. I wish Quint were here to talk about the table-cloths or the design of the lanterns.

"Perhaps," I say, and my voice sounds wispy. I swallow. "Perhaps if word spreads that your apothecaries could make the medicine more effective, the supply raids will lessen."

The consul's eyes don't shift to me. "What is she talking about?"

"Tessa's arrival in the palace was unorthodox, I'll admit," says Corrick, "but she has presented evidence to Harristan that perhaps the dosages could be made more effective."

"Or more people could die," says the consul.

A new tightness wraps itself around my chest. He's not wrong. My theories are only that—theories based on the small population of people in the Wilds. More people could die.

"Or more could live," says Corrick. "Which I believe is an outcome we should all hope for." His tone is cold, and hope feels miles away. "Don't you agree, Allisander?"

"You are going to contradict the royal physicians for some . . . some *girl*? You go too far, Corrick. If there is another attack, I will halt my supply runs until you have determined who is responsible."

I suck in a breath. This man controls the greatest supply of Moonflower petals in Kandala. If he stops providing it, people will die.

I'm not the only one who thinks so. A whisper flies through the crowd beyond the guards.

Corrick takes a step forward, and the night is full of so much dangerous potential that I wonder if he's going to strike the other man or order the guards to put an arrow through his back.

Instead, Corrick drops his voice to a level that won't be heard away from this table. The edge leaves his tone. "It's been a long day for us both. I let my temper get the best of me earlier. I was angry that the Benefactors seem to be funding these attacks, and I can't force answers out of unconscious thieves. I shouldn't have taken my frustrations out on you." He pauses. "Let's not allow a few heated words to come between us." He gestures to the table. "Please. Join us."

The consul hesitates, but now he looks uncertain instead of furious. "My supply runs—"

"Allisander." Corrick claps him on the shoulder like they're old friends. His voice is no longer soft, and I can see necks craning to hear. "I'll grant you whatever you need to protect your people. As always."

Allisander clears his throat. "Very well." He glances at the table. "I will not intrude on your dinner."

"Will you be staying at the palace this evening?" says Corrick. "Perhaps a game of chess in the morning. We could discuss some alternative methods of protecting your deliveries."

"Good." Consul Sallister tugs his jacket straight and takes a step back. "Until tomorrow, then."

"I look forward to it," says Corrick.

After the consul leaves, I expect Corrick to look aggrieved, but he doesn't. He extends a hand toward my chair. "Forgive the interruption. Please. Sit. Have you tried the bread?"

I sit, but I stare at him. He's so formal and polite all of a sudden. This is like Prince Corrick Number Four. Or maybe Number Nineteen. I've lost track.

He must notice my bewildered expression. "I don't want anyone thinking I'm upset about what just happened," he says, his tone low enough that his words are for me alone, but as perfectly even as when he mentioned the bread. "The cheese is very good, too. Try some. I insist."

"Ah . . . sure." I tear a piece of bread, trying to remember which knife was for cheese during my lesson with Mistress Kent.

Corrick lifts one of his and taps it with his index finger, so I look for my own. Out of everything, these tiny kindnesses from him are the most unexpected. I follow his lead and spread cheese across the surface of the bread, then take a bite.

It's divine. The cheese melts onto my tongue, and I nearly forget what just happened.

But now that we're eating, the other patrons go back to their meals. Conversation regains the near-cacophony volume from before Corrick and Allisander argued.

I study the prince. He's such an enigma. Every time I think I understand the slightest thing about him, he does something new that doesn't quite make sense. I can't even tell who just gained ground—and who lost it.

He takes another piece of bread and slathers it with cheese. "I sense that you have questions."

"Who just yielded? Was it you or him?"

"He did," says Corrick. "But it looks like I did, which is what matters. I can't have the entire Royal Sector thinking Allisander will blockade access to the Moonflower petals. I'm surprised he didn't start a riot right here."

"He really controls so much?"

"Yes. But he also doesn't want to cease his shipments, because we'd be forced to rely on Lissa Marpetta alone, which would mean her prices would increase, and he doesn't want to give up one single coin of profit—or the illusion of control." Corrick sighs, looking irritated. "But if outlaws keep attacking his supply run, it won't be worth it to him. Especially if someone with money is funding the attacks."

Outlaws. My chest is tight again. "He said you have . . . prisoners."

"I do."

I keep thinking of the way King Harristan said, *It's the same to the night patrol.* I have to force myself to swallow the food in my mouth, because it's turned into a tasteless lump. "What . . . what are you going to do to them?"

"I'm going to question them and see what they know." He pauses, his eyes holding mine, his tone level. "And then I will act accordingly."

He doesn't say this in a challenging way, but I feel like he's thrown down a gauntlet anyway.

On the day of the execution before the gates, I remember thinking of how horrible the king and the prince were. Prince Corrick stood on the stage, so cold and uncaring. I longed for a crossbow to shoot them both, to free Kandala from their tyranny.

But I didn't know about Consul Sallister then. I feel like that shouldn't matter when people are dead . . . but after meeting him, I realize that it does.

I mentally realign everything that happened the morning before the execution that turned into calls for revolution—and the morning afterward. Wes was unsettled. Troubled.

I think that very few people truly deserve what they get, Tessa. For good or for bad.

I told him he only deserved good things, and he looked away.

He saved me on the night my parents died. He's saved me countless times since.

He's been responsible for the deaths of countless people, too.

The king's voice is loud in my memories.

Every smuggler has a story to justify their actions. The penalties are well known. How can I turn a blind eye to one type of thievery and not another?

There are too many layers here. I thought it was as simple as right or wrong . . . but it's not. My chest feels tight again, and my eyes go hot.

Corrick picks up his wineglass. "If you cry, I'll be forced to comfort you."

His tone says he's teasing—but also not. It helps chase my tears back. "However will you manage?"

"Well. Forewarning that I'll have to do something *truly* abhorrent to keep up my heartless reputation."

Something tells me he's not wholly teasing about that either. Any emotion dries up. A serving girl appears with platters laden with slabs of beef surrounded by root vegetables and a fluffy circle of pastry painted with honey.

Once she's gone, I look at Corrick, who taps his finger against his fork before picking it up.

I mirror his movements gratefully, and we eat in silence for a moment.

"Do you think the royal apothecaries will really listen to me?" I venture softly.

"Harristan has ordered it. They will." He rolls his eyes. "And he's delivered a room full of records for me to review by tomorrow, so if I can find any evidence to back what you've already discovered, it will help."

I straighten. "Really?"

"Yes. Between that and dealing with Allisander's prisoners, it'll likely take me all night." He gives me an ironic glance. "I'm so *very* appreciative."

"Why you?"

"Why not me? As much as you might like to imagine it, I don't ride around in velvet carriages and order executions *all* day."

He's challenging me again. Not directly, but I feel it.

In a way, that reminds me of Weston Lark, too.

Corrick slices another piece of food. "Don't pity me too much."

"I don't pity you." I feel a bit breathless again. Every moment I spend here changes the way I feel about him and the way I feel about myself. "If you're trying to figure out a way to make the medicine more effective for all of Kandala, I'm going to help you."

CHAPTER TWENTY-THREE

Corrick

The White Room is one of my favorite spaces in the palace. We're on the top floor, and the windows are massive, allowing the best view of the entire Royal Sector. Sunlight floods the room during the day, while the moon and stars gleam among a wide swath of blackness during the night. The walls are all white, but hung with abstract paintings in every color: swirls and slashes of yellows and reds in one, flickers of black and shades of pink in another. Wide stripes of gray and green and blue coat a wide canvas that hangs above the hearth. The room always seems to gather quiet and calm, a space for peaceful reflection.

When we were young and Harristan was in poor health, he would sit bundled by the fireplace, and our mother would paint with whatever colors he requested. I would grow bored and beg to leave, but he would sit for hours.

Harristan rarely comes here anymore. He says the room reminds him of what it felt like to be weak. I think the *truth* is what makes him feel weak: this room reminds him of our mother and what we lost.

Tessa turns a page, and I have to remind myself to focus. I had servants bring the stacks of paperwork here because the table is large and the lighting abundant—but my thoughts are full of uncertainty, and now I wish we'd remained in my chambers.

My attention should be on these documents. On the disparity between the deaths in far southern sectors like Sunkeep, versus those that lie closer to the Royal Sector like Artis, Steel City, and Trader's Landing. On Tessa's notes, and whether we can convince people to adjust their dosages. On Allisander's threats, made in the open air of the Circle. On the prisoners still waiting to be questioned.

My attention should be on Harristan, on whether his medicine is truly working.

Instead my focus is on Tessa, bent over a sheaf of papers in the drawing room, wisps of caramel hair coming loose from her pinned curls. My attention is on the tiny yet precise movements of her fountain pen as she takes down information as she reads. My attention is on the soft pink of her mouth and the gentle curve of her cheek and the determined look in her eyes.

My attention is on the fact that, out of every diversion available in the palace, she asked to read dry, boring documents.

My attention is on the fact that, instead of claiming escape, she stayed in the carriage.

Likely, neither of these choices have anything to do with me.

But still, she stayed.

"This would go a lot faster if you were reading, too," she says.

"I am reading." But I'm not. I have no idea how long it's been since I've turned a page.

"Hmm." Her pen keeps moving.

I can't decide if I'm amused or irritated. "Are you accusing me of something else?"

She ignores me and shuffles through the papers she reviewed earlier. "Sunkeep receives less medicine than the other sectors."

"Consul Cherry's sector has fewer people."

She frowns. "And significantly fewer deaths."

"Some speculate that the high heat somehow staves off the fevers."

She looks back at her notes. "But there are fewer deaths even in the winter months. If heat had anything to do with it, there would be fewer deaths in all sectors during the summer months. Artis seems to fare the worst in the summer."

"I didn't say it was *my* speculation."

She taps at her mouth, thinking. I can almost see the wheels in her brain turning, and the familiarity of it tugs at my heart. I have to shove the emotion away.

After a moment, she glances up again. "Consul Cherry. Arella."

"Yes."

"The girls were gossiping about her, how she was seeking additional funding for her sector."

"Gossiping? What girls?"

"On the day I was able to get into the palace. Serving girls. They said that Consul Cherry and Consul Pelham had to be hatching a plot to fleece silver from the king." She pauses. "I didn't know who they were at the time."

I want to roll my eyes at the idle gossip, but something about this lodges in my head for examination later. "All the consuls seek additional funds for their sectors. They expected Harristan to grant a funding request to Artis to build a new bridge, but it was declined, so I'm expecting them all to scramble to put a request together."

"You don't want Artis to build a bridge?"

My voice is dry. "Not one that costs four times as much as it should."

Her mouth twists as she considers the implications of that, but then she looks back at the papers in front of her. "So Sunkeep has few deaths, but Emberridge and Moonlight Plains seem to have a healthier population—"

"Because they control the medicine. Allisander can't guard his entire wall with dying soldiers."

She looks up. "I've spent two hours reading all this to come to the same conclusions everyone here already knows, haven't I?"

"Don't be ridiculous." I pull my pocket watch free. "You've spent three hours."

She glances at the pitch-dark window, then at the brightly lit chandelier overhead. "It's a wonder anyone here ever sleeps, when you can chase the night away." She stifles a yawn.

"You should retire."

"I thought you said this was going to take all night."

"I said it was going to take *me* all night." I set my own papers on the table. "I'll see you to your room."

"No!" She grabs hold of the armrests like I'm going to physically wrestle her out of her seat. "This is important."

"I know."

She narrows her eyes at me. "You *knew* people here were taking more medicine than they needed. Why didn't you do something about it?"

"For one thing," I say, "I don't know that. Not with certainty. You're the apothecary, not me."

"You do know it. You've seen it."

"Yes, I've seen it." I pause. "And I've still seen people die, Tessa."

She stares back at me, and I feel as though a wall of ice has formed between us.

"I'm not challenging your knowledge," I say. "But it wasn't enough. I didn't have proof. And where would I say I'd gotten it? Do you think the King's Justice could suddenly have suggestions on dosages and additives? We get hundreds of messages at the palace gates every day. A good portion of them declare the fevers are some kind of plot to keep the people subdued. Many promise miracle cures. None work."

Her eyes narrow further. "Mine isn't a miracle cure. It's better medicine."

"I know. But the Royal Sector is rationed just like all the others. Anyone who takes more than their allotted dose is spending their own silver. I can't control what people want to spend their money on."

"Your brother can."

"Oh, you think so?" My eyebrows go up. "I cannot simply take a hypothesis, snap my fingers, and have my brother turn it into a royal decree."

She frowns.

I lean in against the table. "Can you imagine the outcry if Harristan told his subjects they couldn't purchase as much as they want? Can you imagine Allisander's reaction? Or . . . anyone's, really? The hoarding, the panic? Every sector has pockets of wealth. Every consul purchases more than their allotment. There is too much fear already. Even if you are able to prove that we can make the medicine stretch further, it may not matter."

"But your brother is the king! Why can't he make Allisander provide *more*?"

"By law, the consuls can set the prices on their sector's exports. But say Harristan overturned that law, and suddenly Moonflower petals were free. Who pays the thousands of people who harvest the petals in Allisander's sector? What motivation does Allisander have to keep his fields in good condition?" I pause. "And then, what's to stop other sectors from hoarding their goods in fear that we'll seize *those* assets as well?"

I see her expression and sigh. "We buy what we can from the taxes we collect, and we distribute it among the people. But there is never enough: not enough silver, not enough Moonflower. Ruling a country takes more than just medicine, Tessa. We're stretched thin everywhere. Jonas asked for too much money to build his bridge—but he surely still needs one. His people are just too sick to efficiently build it."

Her frown deepens. "So you think this is hopeless."

"Sickness has plagued Kandala for years. If royal physicians and advisers have not been able to discover a pattern as to who is affected by the fevers, then we are unlikely to overturn it in this room in the dead of night."

She picks up her piece of paper again, sighing through her teeth. "Well, they haven't had to."

I've been in this room and gone through documents just like this many times. I've seen the same glimmer of hope that shines in her eyes die in a dozen others. I could call for the physicians and advisers to join us right this minute, and I'd watch it again.

I think of the way Harristan read every single request for leniency on the day we were to execute the eight prisoners, or the way he sent me all of these documents and granted Tessa an audience with the royal apothecaries. I've been thinking he was indulging me for keeping her here, but maybe it's something else.

"Harristan doesn't think it's hopeless," I say.

Her eyes lift. "How do you know that?"

"Because you're here."

She bites at her lip, considering that—but then she sets down the papers and rubs at her eyes. "Well. Like you said, I don't think the answer is in these documents."

"Very well." After the way she clutched at her chair, I didn't expect her to give up so easily. I'm surprised that I don't *want* her to give up so easily. "I'll see you to your quarters."

"Oh, I'm not done." She taps the table decisively. "I need to see a map."

———✦———

Sleepy servants bring half a dozen maps, as well as a tray of black tea and warm muffins, with pots of honey, milk, jam, and sliced berries arranged around a small pot of pink and lavender blooms. They set cups and saucers in front of us both, but Tessa ignores everything in favor of the first map. It unfurls across the next table, and she slides her fingers along the edge, surveying it.

"Tell me your thoughts," I say.

"Maybe it's not the weather in Sunkeep that makes a difference. They have the greatest exposure to the ocean." She points to the southernmost sector, running her finger along the lengthy border. "Which makes me wonder if there is something about the ocean that has some kind of . . . preventive effect."

"Emberridge, Artis, and Steel City also border the ocean," I say.

She makes a face. "Well, yes." She points to the eastern border, running her finger along the edge. "But these are cliffs along the oceanside of Emberridge and Artis, right? So they don't have as much access to the water."

"That's true." I pause, surveying the map. "But Steel City and Artis share a port where the Queen's River joins with the ocean." I point to it. "And the Queen's River runs straight through both Emberridge and Artis." I point to the western side of Kandala. "Here, the Flaming River runs alongside Moonlight Plains and the Sorrowlands and also joins with the ocean. Nearly every sector has direct access to free-flowing water."

She looks at me. "Except the Royal Sector."

"To prevent an attack by sea—but the Royal Sector is just as affected by the fevers, despite our water sources." Unbidden, my thoughts turn to Harristan. I've hardly seen him today, so I have no idea if his cough has returned. A small spike of fear enters my heart and lodges there.

He was fine when he came to my chambers. He must be fine now.

One servant has lingered, fastidiously wiping a drip of tea from the silver platter. Hoping to catch an earful of gossip, no doubt. "Leave us," I snap.

He jumps, then offers a quick bow and leaves.

I look back at Tessa. "Continue."

Her eyes are dark with reproach. "You don't have to be so cruel."

I drop into a chair. Worry for my brother has caused my mood to sour. "I didn't kill *you* and Allisander threatened to stop shipments of the Moonflower, so I beg to differ."

She glares at me.

I glare right back. "Continue."

She looks at the map, then back at me. The censure hasn't left her eyes.

"I bring nightmares to life," I say. "If you think a dark look will affect me, you will quickly learn otherwise."

She hesitates, then sighs. "Perhaps there is something different about the sea life, then."

It takes me a moment to realize she's talking about Sunkeep again.

"Mistress Solomon uses ground seashells in one of her fever lotions," Tessa continues. "It's ridiculously expensive because the shells have to travel so far, but it is one of her few concoctions that actually seems to make a difference. I always thought it might be the white willow bark, but maybe—"

"Wait." I sit straight up. "Something other than the Moon-flower can cure the fevers?"

"Well—no. But the lotion does seem to make the fevers more manageable, so the Moonflower elixir is more effective." She grimaces. "Maybe. Honestly, I think that all she's really selling is a cheaper version of hope to desperate people."

Desperate. Like I just was. I sit back in the chair and run my hands over my face. The room is so silent I can nearly hear the gears shift in my pocket watch.

I need to move. If I keep sitting here, I'll spin worry into a frenzy. I shove away from my chair and move to the window. The sky above is dark and thick with stars, but the Royal Sector makes for a fine match, random candles and electric lights twinkling throughout the city. The Hold is a massive rectangular building, easily spotted because torches burn all night beside the men standing guard. In the distance, the spotlights sweep along the wall.

Fabric rustles as Tessa leaves her chair and moves to join me. Her voice is very low, very quiet. "You're worried for your brother."

"The king needs no one's worry, least of all mine."

She hesitates. "Others must suspect he is sick."

"He's not sick." I want my voice to be hard, to scare her away from this line of conversation, but it's not. I sound petulant. Worse: I sound soft. Weak and afraid.

Without warning, her hand closes on mine, and she gives it a light squeeze.

I look at her in surprise, but her eyes are on the city lights, and she lets go of my hand so gently that it feels like I imagined the touch.

Especially when her voice is all business again as she says, "What about Ostriary?"

I blink. "What?"

Ostriary is the kingdom on the opposite side of the Flaming River, which runs along the western side of Kandala. The river is rough, fast-flowing, and wide—over fifteen miles wide in spots—which would make trade difficult in the best of conditions. But on the opposite shore, Ostriary's terrain is dense marshland in the south and mountainous in the north, making for treacherous travel. We don't have a hostile relationship with Ostriary—but thanks to the difficulty of travel, we don't have a very good one either. Our father had just begun sending emissaries into the region to see whether it would be worthwhile to try to establish trade routes, but then he was killed and Harristan was left to deal with a dying population.

"Are they affected by the fevers?" says Tessa.

"I don't know," I say.

"Don't you think it's worth finding out?"

I inhale to reject the notion—but it's not a bad question. I look at her. "Maybe."

"If the Moonflower grows in the north *here*, maybe it grows in the north *there*. And if they're not sick there, maybe you'd be able to get it for—"

"These are a lot of ifs and maybes." I pause, mentally tabulating how much silver it would take to outfit ships that could withstand the river current and hire people willing to take on the task of traveling and mapping unknown terrain. "It would be costly, too. I'm not sure Harristan would be able to justify the expense."

That said, Allisander would hate the idea. That alone makes me want to draw up a funding request this very minute.

Tessa sighs.

I sigh.

I wish she hadn't let go of my hand so quickly. The motion was meaningless, I'm sure of it. The same momentary compassion she would give to a worried mother when we wore masks and tried to help the few we could.

You don't have to be so cruel.

She may have felt something for Weston Lark, but she hates Prince Corrick.

"It's worth discussion," I offer.

She turns to look up at me in surprise, her eyes lighting up. "Really?"

She's so heartfelt about everything she does that I nearly smile at her reaction. "You're at court now, so you shouldn't be so earnest."

"What on earth does that mean?"

"You should say, 'If that's the best you can do, Your Highness.'" I say this with an intonation that sounds a lot like how I mock Allisander in my head. "Or, 'I suppose that will do for now,' with a heavy sigh so it's clear you're unsatisfied."

She folds her arms across her chest and looks back out at the city. "Well, that's just ridiculous."

I laugh.

She startles, then frowns.

A weight drops between us again, hot and sudden. I don't know what just happened.

Tessa swallows. "You remind me so much of Wes when you laugh." Her eyes gleam. "I can't tell who's real and who's the illusion."

Those words carry so much pain that I nearly flinch. I hold my breath for a moment.

I reach out and touch her hand the way she just did to me. The way we did a hundred times in the woods, when the nights were too difficult.

I wait for her to pull away, but she doesn't. I close my fingers around hers, and we stare out at the lights of the city.

"You see through all my illusions," I say, and my voice is rough.

She turns to look up at me, and I hate that there's hope in her eyes. It reminds me so much of our last night in the woods, when I promised to return—and then I didn't. I'm destined to disappoint her. There's a prison full of smugglers that are proof enough of that.

Even still, I can't let go.

I lift my other hand to touch her face, tentatively at first, but then more sure when she doesn't pull away. "You remind me of how it felt to be Wes."

Her breathing shakes, and her eyes fall closed. "I hate you."

"I know." My thumb strokes across her mouth, and her lips part. We're closer somehow, all but sharing breath.

Then her eyes open, and she gasps. She puts her free hand in the gap between our faces, her fingertips against my mouth. Her eyes blaze into mine.

I want to take her hand and push it out of the way. I want to press my mouth to hers. I want my hands on her waist, on her back, on every inch of skin this gown leaves bare—and some inches that it does not. I want her scent in my head and her taste on my tongue and her arms wound around my neck.

I can't move. I want her to want those things, too.

"You're *not* Wes," she whispers.

The words hit me like an arrow, and I step back. The distance between us is suddenly immeasurable.

Light and sound explode outside the window, so bright and loud that I jerk her away from the glass. We stumble back six feet, but nothing comes close to the palace. Fire has erupted a few blocks away, at the Hold, flames billowing high into the night. I can already hear shouts from distant parts of the palace, and people running in the streets down below.

"What—what's happening—" she begins.

"Guards!" I shout. The door to the room swings open, and guards burst in.

Another explosion in the city makes the windowpanes rattle. Near the Hold again. The flames are three stories high. The alarms in the sector start blaring.

Another explosion. I don't flinch this time.

Another.

A guard is speaking to me. "Your Highness. You should move away from the windows."

But I can't. I can't look away.

The Royal Sector is on fire.

CHAPTER TWENTY-FOUR

Tessa

The room was so silent and still when I was alone with Corrick, but now it's loud with guards and advisers who bustle in and out, carrying orders and messages. King Harristan joined us within ten minutes of the first explosion. He clearly dressed in a hurry, because he's in his shirtsleeves along with simple calfskin trousers and unlaced boots. He and Corrick are sitting at one of the long tables with Quint standing to one side, the Palace Master hurriedly scribbling notes that are taken by runners as soon as he tears them free. Several consuls are also in the room, including Consul Sallister, Consul Cherry, and Consul Marpetta, the woman I saw at the gates on the morning I came to the sector for Mistress Solomon. I don't know the others. At first they surrounded the king, arguing over whether the entire sector was under attack, over the best way to fight the fires, over who was behind the explosions. Harristan listened to their bickering for one full minute longer than I would have, then said, "Enough. If you have so much to offer, go find a bucket of water and get to work."

They all fell silent. Now they're sitting at the table closest to the hearth. Their voices are a low rush, and I can tell they're still arguing, but they have the sense to stay out of his way. I hear murmurs of funding and rebels and planned attack.

I'm clinging to a corner, hoping everyone has forgotten I'm here. The tension in the room is palpable, and I'd leave if I didn't think it would draw more attention.

It's hard to imagine that two days ago, I was sitting across a worktable from Karri, bleakly grinding roots and herbs into powder, and now I'm in a crimson gown on the top floor of the palace, staring out a window as fire rages in the city below.

I've overheard enough to know that this was a coordinated attack on the Hold, though flames have spread to nearby buildings. Explosives blasted through the front doors—but also the rear, causing a wall to collapse. The fires are so massive that workers seem to be having trouble putting them out. At first, there was some worry that the palace would be attacked next, which is why everyone is in this room, a dozen armed guards blocking the doors. But no further explosions have occurred.

A young man appears in the doorway, his cheeks flushed, sweat dampening his hair. His clothes are singed, his fingers a bit sooty. The paper clenched in his hand looks crumpled and damp. "Your Majesty," he says breathlessly.

Harristan takes the missive and reads it. After a moment, he sets it down and slides it toward Corrick. When the king speaks, his voice is resigned. "This wasn't just an attack on the Hold. This was a rescue mission."

At the table near the hearth, Consul Sallister stands. "*What?*"

Corrick runs a hand across his jaw. "Most of the prisoners escaped. They had help."

If I were in the workshop with Karri and I heard this news, my heart would leap with relief that people had escaped the cruel tyranny of the king and his brother. In a way, my heart leaps here, too. But I've learned enough now to know it's not as simple as *us* versus *them*, and I know this won't be seen as a relief by anyone else in this room.

For a moment, the room is absolutely silent, but then Consul Sallister approaches the table. "Escaped," he says, and his voice is low and vicious. "*Again*, they escaped." His face reddens. "Corrick, you said they weren't organized. You said they were 'roughshod laborers.' You said—"

"Consul," says King Harristan. His voice isn't harsh or sharp, but the other man goes silent anyway.

"This took planning," says Consul Marpetta. Her voice is very soft, but firm. "And funding."

"Yes," snaps Consul Sallister. "Funding, from some sympathizers called the Benefactors. What do you know about that, Arella?"

"Do you mean to accuse me of something?" she says levelly.

"Do you need to *admit* to something?"

They're both deathly silent for the longest moment, and I can feel their hatred from here.

"The gates are locked, I presume," says an older man at the table who sits near Consul Cherry. "Is the night patrol searching the sector?"

"Yes," says Corrick. He glances at the crumpled paper on the table. "Two have already been captured."

"Then execute them," says Consul Sallister. "Right now."

His voice is so cold. So callous. Almost as if he's not talking about people at all. Like he's talking about livestock.

King Harristan and Prince Corrick exchange a weighted glance. My heart seems to pause in its beating. So much has changed since I first slipped into the palace. I'm hopeful. I'm terrified. I'm . . . I don't know what I am.

Then Corrick stands up and says, "I'll see to it."

"No!" The word flies out of my mouth before I can stop it, and I gain the attention of everyone in the room.

Except Corrick. He doesn't look at me, doesn't turn, doesn't meet my eyes. "Consul," he says, his tone flat. He heads for the door. Consul Sallister follows. After a moment, so does Consul Marpetta.

I want to chase after Corrick. I want to beg him to stop. What did he say? *You remind me of how it felt to be Wes.*

He was Wes. He doesn't want to do this. I know he doesn't.

But he walks through the door. *I'll see to it.*

My fingertips are pressed to my mouth. I can't breathe.

I'm not invisible now. King Harristan glances at me and then at the Palace Master. "Quint."

Quint rises without hesitation and approaches me. "My dear, you must be exhausted—"

"Please," I whisper against my fingers. "Please. He can't."

The expression in his eyes tells me that Corrick can, and he will.

I'm so stupid. I let myself think otherwise for a bare space of time, but I knew who he was. I knew what he could do.

I should have run from the carriage when I had the chance.

I should have stabbed him with the dagger. I should have done something.

Instead I'm just standing here while Quint takes hold of my elbow.

He's going to kill them. Corrick is going to execute people right now.

I want to run. I want to scream. I want to throw myself at the king's feet and beg for mercy.

None of it will do any good.

Quint must be able to read the panic as it washes through my eyes, because he says, "Walk with me, Tessa."

Consul Cherry stands, and she glances at me before looking at the king. "I'm sure Prince Corrick will be able to learn a great deal about their operation once they're dead." She glances at the older man at the table. "Roydan. I'd like to further our conversation in private."

"A discussion that cannot be shared with your king?" says Harristan.

Roydan looks like he's going to say something conciliatory, but Consul Cherry faces Harristan boldly. "No, Your Majesty," she says. "It cannot." Then she offers a curtsy and turns for the door.

He inhales sharply, but before he can retort, he coughs hard.

Consul Cherry and Roydan turn to look at him in alarm.

In a heartbeat, Quint has let go of my arm and taken Consul Cherry's. "Arella. Where will you and Roydan be meeting?" His voice is louder than usual as he propels them toward the door. "I will have food sent. Perhaps a bottle of wine?"

They're through the door. A guard slams it closed behind them.

Harristan is still coughing. Two of his guards exchange a glance.

Maybe I've seen enough worried citizens exchange similar glances in my presence, but I know what that look means.

Is he sick? Should we do something?

The platter with a teapot and saucers is still sitting untouched at the end of the table, so I step forward and briskly pour a cup of tea, then add a dripping spoonful of honey. Vallis lilies and lavender are arranged in a tiny vase, and I try not to think of how long I'd have to work to buy a few lily petals for my apothecary kit when here, they're just being used for decoration. I break a few leaves of each free, crush them in my palm, and add them to the water. The spoon clinks against the china as I stir rapidly before moving to carry it to the king.

One of his guards steps in front of me so quickly that I gasp and almost pour it all over him. Some tea sloshes over the side of the cup.

"The—the vallis lilies," I stammer, suddenly realizing I'm alone with the king and his guards. "And the honey. For—for his cough. It'll help."

"No," says the guard.

"Yes," wheezes Harristan.

The guard blinks. He shifts sideways to glance at the king, who's holding a hand out to me, gesturing for the cup.

I ease it onto the table in front of him, wondering if this guard is going to cut my hand off. The cup rattles against the saucer. He takes a tentative sip and coughs again.

The guard is glaring at me as if I personally caused it.

But then King Harristan drains the cup and his coughing ceases. The room is abruptly so silent that I can hear my pulse thundering in my ears. The guard hasn't moved, and he's still partially blocking me from the king, but his expression isn't quite as severe as it was a moment ago. He's still tall and imposing, though, with light brown skin and close-shorn hair and arms so muscled that he could probably crush my skull one-handed.

As soon as I have the thought, I realize he hasn't moved because he's waiting for the king to tell him how to proceed. Corrick just walked out of here to execute the other prisoners. From what he said, few people suspect the king is sick, and I just witnessed his coughing fit. Maybe this man *will* crush my skull one-handed.

Much like the night I woke in Corrick's quarters, I'm simultaneously filled with fear and fury, but the fury takes over.

I glance between the king and his guard. "I was trying to help," I say in a rush, my voice hot with anger that has more to do with Corrick than the man in front of me. "Nothing more. I don't gossip, and I don't know anything. You can kill anyone you want, so I guess you can kill me too, but I'm just one person, and killing me isn't going to—"

"Enough."

King Harristan doesn't say it forcefully, but there's enough authority in his tone that my lips stop working. The guard's posture has turned from standing into looming.

I swallow and force myself to stand my ground.

"Rocco," says Harristan. His voice is slightly rough, just a bit weak, like the cough took something out of him but he doesn't want to reveal it. "Stand down."

The guard falls back to loom against the wall, and I'm left facing the king of Kandala in his shirtsleeves.

I felt a little more bold when there was a guard between us.

Maybe he and his brother took lessons in being intimidating while just sitting there, because they both manage it effortlessly.

"I'm not going to kill you," he says.

I'm not sure what the right response is to that. "Thank you?" I hesitate. "Your Majesty?"

His eyes flicker with something that's either irritation or amusement. I hope it's the latter, but I suspect it's the former, especially when he says, "Sit."

I drop into the chair closest to me, and he picks up the now-empty teacup. "One of your remedies?"

"It's just—" I have to clear my throat. "It's the vallis lily petals. They're very expensive—but they're good for a cough. Better than turmeric, even."

He's just looking at me, so I start babbling. "In Artis, a lot of the shipbuilders get a dry throat from their woodworking, so it's a quick remedy. Sometimes that can cause an inflammation that mimics the fever sickness, so there's always a lot of worry around the docks, but a little ginger and turmeric will usually draw it right out if there's no high fever."

He glances at my hand, and I'm embarrassed to realize that I was reaching for the king's forehead.

"Ah . . . sorry." I jerk my hand back down.

"Do I have a fever, Tessa?"

I go still. What a loaded question.

Is he mocking me? It doesn't sound like it.

Do I touch him? Do I feel his forehead to see?

And what if he does have a fever? Do I say yes? Do I say no?

I lift my hand again, and there's a spark of challenge in his gaze.

My fingertips gingerly graze his brow, but it's not enough to tell anything at all.

Mind your mettle, Tessa.

Shut up, Wes. Corrick. Whatever.

I grit my teeth and flatten my hand against the king's forehead.

No fever.

I'm so shocked that I rotate my wrist to use the back of my hand. Still cool. And I'm struck by how vulnerable he looks, sitting in the chair half-dressed, my hand against his face. I've been so awestruck by the fact that he's the king that I forgot he's a man only a few years older than I am.

"No," I say honestly, sitting back in my chair. "You don't."

For an instant, it feels as though everyone in the room lets out a breath. The wave of relief is that potent. Even the king himself seems to lose an ounce of tension.

I'm not immune myself: my heart slows. I can draw a deep breath for the first time in what feels like hours.

Then the king says, "How do you *really* know my brother?" and my heart wants to ricochet straight out of my chest.

Harristan smiles, but it's shrewd. "You wear every emotion on your face."

I slap my hands to my cheeks. "He said that, too," I whisper.

"Are you working in league with the people who attacked the Hold?"

"What?" I sputter. "No!"

"Who are the Benefactors? Are they responsible for this?"

"I don't know! I only heard of them at the riots. At the execution."

"What of the smugglers we captured? Were you to distract the prince?"

"No! I didn't—I don't—"

"You seemed distressed when he agreed to punish them for their crimes."

"Because I don't want him to *kill* anyone. I don't want—" My voice breaks. "Enough people are dying in Kandala. We shouldn't be killing our own people. Especially if they're just trying to stay alive."

And then, to my horror, I'm crying. I'm crying in front of the king.

Soft fabric brushes my fingers, and I blink. He's offered me a handkerchief.

I close my fingers around it. "Thank you." My voice sounds thick and nasally. I can't look at him now.

When he speaks, his voice is very low and almost gentle. "The King's Justice cannot be lenient to those who attack a building in the center of the Royal Sector." He pauses. "Surely you know this."

I press the handkerchief to my eyes. I do. I do know it.

That's the worst part.

"I know," I whisper.

"You could have poisoned me with the tea," says Harristan, his voice equally quiet.

I could have stabbed him too, but I don't say that. "I'm not a killer."

"Indeed not." He pauses and inhales, but whatever he was going to say is lost because Quint comes bursting through the door.

"Forgive me, Your Majesty," he says. "I was seeing Consuls Cherry and Pelham to another suite—" He sees us sitting and stops short. "Am I . . . interrupting?"

King Harristan looks at Quint. "Be sure the consuls know that my coughing was tempered by Tessa's assistance. I was lucky she was here. She formed a quick-acting tincture with few supplies—"

"It was just honey and—" I begin, but Harristan silences me with a look.

"—and I am grateful for her intervention," he finishes.

"Yes, Your Majesty," says Quint. He sounds nonplussed.

I feel the same way.

"See her to her room," the king says.

Just like that, I'm dismissed. A moment later, my hand is on Quint's arm, and we're in the hushed quiet of the hallway. To my surprise, the guard Rocco follows a short distance behind. Probably to make sure I get where I'm supposed to be going.

Every hour I spend here seems to turn my thoughts upside down and inside out, until I have no idea what's right and what's wrong. Maybe Quint can sense that, because he's not talkative as we walk.

Or maybe he's as tired as I am.

I can't decide whether I want to ask if he knows what Corrick is doing to the prisoners, and before I can make up my mind, we're at my door. Rocco speaks quietly to the guards standing there, and they disperse.

Quint turns to face me. "Jossalyn will have your agenda at daybreak," he says.

The very thought is exhausting. I can barely remember why anything felt like progress with Corrick when we reviewed the maps—because everything unraveled when the fires began outside the window and he marched off to kill prisoners. Much like this morning, I want to clutch at Quint's sleeve and beg him to stay, but I know there are much more pressing matters right now.

I force the thought out of my head and bite back a sigh. "Thank you."

He nods and turns away.

I pause with my hand on the doorknob. I look at Rocco, who's taken the place of the guards he sent away. My eyes flick across that royal insignia on his uniform. Maybe the regular palace guards are all busy chasing down escaped prisoners.

"It's your turn to make sure I can't get out?" I say to him.

His eyebrows lift. "To make sure you can't get out?" he echoes.

"You replaced the guards. You're my new jailor?"

"Ah. No." He reaches for the doorknob and holds the door wide for me. "You acted to protect the king," he says. "As such, you've earned his favor."

I glance at the door, at his hand, at the empty hallway. "I . . . don't understand."

"You're not a prisoner. You're not confined to your quarters."

"I'm not."

"No, Miss Tessa."

"Then . . ." I hesitate. My tired brain is too tangled up. "Then what are you doing here?"

"I'm a guard." He smiles. "I'm here to make sure no one gets in."

"Oh." I look at the door again. "Oh." I step across the threshold. "Thank you."

He nods and pulls the door closed, sealing me in with the silence.

I walk to the window. I can't see the sector as clearly as I could before, but it looks like the fires have been brought under control.

The alarms in the sector have been silenced, and the searchlights don't spin as frantically.

Somewhere in the darkness, Corrick is executing prisoners. I turn away from the window.

I should hate him, but I can't. I don't know what that says about me, and I'm not sure I'm ready to examine it too closely.

I wonder what my father would think of Prince Corrick, of the king and Allisander and this struggle among the elites that seems to cause the most suffering among the poor, who don't deserve it.

I wonder what my father would think about me, safe in the palace while the sector burns below.

I move to the closet and unwind the ribbons from my arms and pull the dress over my head, but my thoughts are far outside this room. The day Mistress Solomon made us attend the execution, I remember standing in the crowd and wishing Wes were there. I didn't know it then, but he was. I thought Prince Corrick was horrible, and in some ways he is, but maybe he was standing on that stage feeling as distressed as I was.

Then execute them. Right now.

He didn't even look at me before he left the room.

Jossalyn has left a sleeping shift hanging from a hook on the closet door, but I ignore it and paw through the closet until I find what's probably riding attire, but is definitely more comfortable than a gown: soft calfskin pants, a knit pullover, and a pair of boots.

Once I'm redressed, I throw open the door again.

Rocco is standing there, and his eyebrows lift as he takes in my attire.

"I don't have to stay in my room?" I say.

"No." He pauses. "I can send for a meal if you would rather—"

"No. Thank you." I have to clear my throat. "I'm not hungry. I want . . ." My voice trails off as I stare up at him. I might not be a prisoner, but he's still the king's guard. "Can you take me somewhere?" I say quietly. "Like . . . outside the palace?"

He frowns, which makes me think he's going to decline, but he says, "Where?"

I take a deep breath. "I want you to take me to Prince Corrick."

CHAPTER TWENTY-FIVE

Corrick

Scorched bricks and splintered wood litter the floor, and remnants of smoke form a haze around the one remaining torch in this part of the Hold. Guards removed the bodies a while ago, but they haven't returned. This part of the Hold isn't usable, and I'm sure they think I'm long gone.

Allisander is. He didn't last five minutes.

I'm glad. I don't want him here. I don't want anyone here.

When we walked in, the prisoners were bound on the ground. For a moment, I thought both men were dead, because their faces were black with soot and their clothes were charred. The scent of burned flesh was sickly sweet in the small space. It was obvious why they'd been caught so quickly. They probably hadn't made it out of the Hold.

But then I saw the rise and fall of one's chest, and the other made a pathetic keening sound.

Allisander was right behind me.

I wished they were dead. I wished they'd escaped. I wished Harristan would call a halt to all of this, instead of leaving me to prove how vicious we could be. I wished I were Wes, free to help, instead of Corrick, trapped by circumstance.

I wished. I wished. I wished.

All the while, Allisander was waiting.

I'm not usually the one with the blade or the arrow or the ax. I give the order and someone else provides the action. But tonight my thoughts were wild and scattered and if I opened my mouth to give an order, I worried I'd unravel everything my brother has worked so hard to hold together instead.

So I took a blade from the guard and cut their throats.

I held the weapon out for the guard to take it, but I kept my eyes on the consul. "Satisfied?" I asked him. My voice was rough, my hands sticky with blood.

He was breathing hard, his nostrils flaring like a panicked horse. Maybe he didn't expect me to be so quick—or so brutal. Maybe he expected me to shy away from the violence.

"Yes," he said.

"Good."

Then he was gone, and the guards were dragging the bodies out.

I'm sitting in the dust against the wall now. My hands are dark with dried blood, thick and black around my fingernails. The air feels thin and hard to breathe—but maybe that's my chest, which has been gripped with dread since the moment I heard Tessa cry out for me to stop.

Here, you can only be Prince Corrick. You can only be the King's Justice.

I know, Quint. I know.

I press my fingers into my eyes. As always, I envy Harristan. Not for his throne, but for his ignorance of all this. His distance. His privilege.

Maybe that's the same thing.

I keep telling myself that at least eight of them escaped, so it was only two. I keep telling myself that these men wouldn't have lived much longer. I keep telling myself that what I just offered was a *mercy*, not cruelty, but I don't know for sure.

I wish my head would empty itself of thoughts, that I could wrap my mind up in the darkness that lets me be who I need to be. Every time I try, I think of Tessa, her eyes dark with censure.

She'll never forgive me. She'll never let me touch her again.

I'll never be free of this. Of who I am. This will be my life as King's Justice: Cruel Corrick, the most feared man in the kingdom, and somehow also the most alone.

I want to scoff, but to my shock, my eyes prick and burn. I blink hard and swipe at my face. This is ridiculous. I haven't cried since the day our parents died. I don't want to cry now.

A tear falls anyway. I drag a sleeve across my face. It's damp, and I realize I'm dragging blood across my cheek.

I bring nightmares to life, I said to Tessa. I'm very likely the living equivalent.

Somewhere in the darkness, a boot scrapes against the stone floor, and I jerk my head up. One of the guards must be returning.

I scramble to my feet. Swipe at my face again. Grit my teeth against everything I feel.

A new thought enters my brain, almost worse than the sorrow and dread. Prisoners escaped. There was an attack on the Hold.

This might be someone other than guards. I reach for my blade automatically.

It's not there. I gave it to Tessa.

Alarm chases away the anguish. I grab a rock from the rubble and pull back into the shadows, peering through the hazy dimness, wondering if I've been very foolish in remaining here.

But then the light strikes a bit of silver and the shine of a black boot, and I recognize the palace guard uniform. I recognize Rocco, one of my brother's personal guards.

My breath catches. Has Harristan come looking for me? He's come here, to the Hold?

Relief hits me so fast and sudden it's like a blast of wintry wind against all the hot sorrow. I nearly leap out of the shadows. For once, I won't be alone here. I won't be alone in . . . this.

I drop the rock and start forward. I don't know what I'm going to do, but so much emotion has clawed its way up my throat that I'm worried I'm going to fall on my knees, clutch at my brother's hands, and beg for a release from all this.

But it's not my brother following the guard.

I stop short. My heart feels like it wants to explode from my chest. Every muscle tenses. That cool wind of relief turns into a hot wash of shame and vulnerability.

Tessa has stopped short, too, and I can tell from the shift in her expression that I was right: I am a living nightmare. Her lips part and her eyes widen and she sucks in a breath. "Oh," she whispers. "Oh no."

I want to be indifferent. I want to not care. I want so much that I can't have.

I look at the guard. "She shouldn't be here," I say viciously. "Why would you bring her here?"

"I asked him to," says Tessa—and for the first time, her voice isn't full of censure, it's . . . mollifying. She steps toward me.

I step back. I keep my glare fixed on Rocco. "Take her back to the palace. Now."

"No." Tessa steps forward again. "Just—"

"Stop." I pull back again. I can't meet her eyes. "You shouldn't be here."

"Please. It'll be—"

"Go," I snap. "Or I'll lock you down here forever."

"No, you won't."

She reaches for me, and I jerk away. My boot catches on that rock I dropped, and I stumble back, tripping over a splintered beam of wood. My shoulders slam into the wall, and my fingers curl into fists. I'm breathing hard like a cornered animal.

She has the good sense to stop pursuing me. We stand there in the flickering torchlight. Her hair is loose over her shoulders, her face clean-scrubbed, her clothes so simple I'm surprised she found them in her closet.

I'm wearing the same fine jacket I wore to dinner, but every inch of me is streaked with dirt and soaked in blood.

"No illusions now," I say.

"No," she agrees, her voice even.

I glance at Rocco who's waiting not far behind her. "How did you get him to bring you here?"

"I asked him to find you."

"Where is Harristan?" I look at the guard, and a new worry lances my heart. "Why aren't you with the king? What has happened?"

"His Majesty ordered that I attend to Miss Tessa," he says impassively.

"Your brother is fine," says Tessa, and her voice is careful. Again, she's seen through me. "He had a coughing fit after you left, but he doesn't—"

I push off the wall. "He *what*?"

"He's fine. No fever. I gave him some tea with honey and vallis lilies." Her hand closes on my forearm and gives a gentle squeeze. "He's fine."

Something about her touch forces me still. My breathing slows fractionally.

Her eyes are piercing, though, and I worry she's going to ask what I've done. She'll ask, and I'll tell her, and I'll destroy any remaining flickers of . . . whatever is between us.

I was ready to kneel at my brother's feet and beg for release.

I'm ready to kneel at Tessa's and beg forgiveness.

She slides her hand down my forearm and laces her fingers with mine. She doesn't flinch at the blood. My chest tightens at the thought of her touching it.

Please, I think. *Please don't ask.*

Please don't hate me anymore.

I hate myself enough.

I start to pull away, to draw back into the dark and shadows. Her grip on my hand forces me still.

"Walk with me?" she says.

I inhale to refuse. I want to sit in the dark and pray for the earth to swallow me whole.

Instead, I nod. She leads and I follow, and we step out of the crumbling bloodstained room and into the bright lights of the Royal Sector.

CHAPTER TWENTY-SIX

Tessa

I don't know where to take him, but I couldn't keep standing in that tiny room. The scent of blood and death was thick in the air. I wish we could walk straight out of the sector and get lost in the Wilds, but I already know he won't leave his brother.

Instead, I lead him toward the palace. The lights out front are bright, the cobblestones glistening. Horses and carriages still clatter over the cobblestones despite the late hour, as messages about the explosions are sent and elites come and go. When Harristan's guard led me out of the palace, the halls were busy with activity, and I doubt that's changed much.

I don't want to think about what Corrick has done. There's blood all over him, so I know it was violent. His blue eyes are hollow and haunted, so I know it was terrible. When we found him in the shadowed chamber of the Hold, a part of me wanted to run screaming—until I saw the anguish in his expression.

"Rocco," I say quietly. "We can't go through the main doors. He can't go through the palace like this."

"They know what I am," says Corrick. He still looks flighty, his eyes a bit wild, but there's an element of challenge to his voice. I wonder if this is how he convinces himself to do the things he does.

I ignore him. "Maybe a back entrance?" I say to the guard.

"No," says Corrick.

"We could enter through the servants' entrance," says Rocco. "The day staff is gone. There are washrooms and fresh linens."

"*No*." Corrick seems to draw himself up, but he's glaring at Rocco, not at me. "I will not sneak into the palace."

I can't tell how much of this is defiance and how much is some form of self-preservation. Either way, I should let him do whatever he wants. He's the prince, and I'm . . . no one. But I've only been here a day and I know how much rumor and appearances matter, and I know that right now, he can't afford to appear weak. Walking through the palace covered in blood certainly doesn't seem like a vision of strength. I consider the note in his voice when he realized I was with Rocco and not his brother.

"Would the king want you to be seen this way?" I say.

"Do I look so terrible, Tessa?" he says.

Yes. But not in the way he means. "You look . . . desperate."

That seems to hit him like a dart. The fight drains from his eyes. "Fine."

――+――

The servants' entrance is the same locked passageway I used when I first came to the palace, and it's just as deserted as it was when I snuck into the back stairwell. The washroom is massive, with electric lights and running water, and several large tubs. I see stacks and stacks of folded linens and a massive hearth and realize this is a room for laundry.

Well, of course. I wouldn't expect anyone in the palace to be scrubbing fabrics in the stream or hanging tunics in the sunlight. In the corner is a dress form with a maid's frock pinned to it, with a few sewing tables and yards of fabric strewn about. A long mirror is bolted to the wall, and Corrick walks past it on his way to one of the wash basins. I watch as his step falters and his eyes shy away, but he doesn't stop moving.

"Your Highness," says Rocco. "Shall I call for a steward?"

"No. Guard the door." He tugs at the buttons of his jacket just as fiercely.

I hover between the doorway and the basin. I don't know if he wants me to wait in the hall with the guard or if I should go back to my room—or if I should stay right here.

I don't know what *I* want to do.

"Why did you come looking for me?" he asks. His voice is a bit husky but a bit angry, too. "Did you think you could stop me?"

"I knew you wouldn't stop yourself."

His hands freeze on the buttons, and it's only then that I realize he's trembling.

I step over to him and place my fingers over his, tugging a button free.

"Stop," he says. "I can unbutton my coat."

I smack his fingers hard, like he's a child who's been told not to touch the hot stove but does it anyway. I think I shock him, because he jerks them away.

I sigh and pull the next button free. The fabric is tacky, and I try to ignore why, keeping my eyes on what I'm doing.

"If you know I can see through all your illusions," I say softly, "you might as well stop trying to throw them in my path. I know who you are. I know what you've done." I glance up, and I can't decide if I hate him or if I pity him—or something else altogether. "I see *you*. I see what this is doing to you. *Has* done to you."

He goes very still, but his breathing sounds shallow. He blinks, and to my absolute shock, his eyes fill.

He must realize it at the same time, because he jerks back, turning away, pressing the heels of his hands into his eyes. "Lord, Tessa."

Seeing his ready emotion summons my own, and I feel my chest tighten. He looked broken in the chamber of the Hold. He looks broken now, like sheer strength of will is all that's holding him together.

I touch his arm, and he jolts. His hands drop to his sides, forming fists the way they did in the shadowed chamber. His eyes are red-rimmed but dry. "Stop," he says.

The word sounds like a warning. A plea.

I stop.

He has all the power here, but he faces me like I do. He doesn't want to admit what he's done, and I don't want to ask, but the question is strung between us and someone has to grab hold. I have to clear my throat to speak. "Did you kill those prisoners?"

He doesn't look away, and he doesn't hesitate. "Yes."

The silence that follows that word fills the room until there's no air left to breathe. I think of Consul Sallister, who was so terrible at dinner, and the control he has over Corrick and Harristan. The control he has over the entire country.

I think of King Harristan's voice when he said that the King's Justice can't be lenient when people are bombing the prison.

Killing people is *wrong*. I feel that to my core. I couldn't kill the king when I had the opportunity—not even when I was certain he deserved it. But like the king said, the penalties for smuggling are well known. Some of the people in the Hold were true smugglers— but some weren't. Bombing the Hold was wrong, too.

Does any of that excuse Corrick's actions?

I can tell he doesn't think so. He wears the guilt like a mantle. I thought that all his power lay in his role here, as King's Justice, but it doesn't.

The only power he had was in the Wilds, as Wes.

And now that's gone.

I swallow. "What happened?"

"You heard Allisander."

"Yes. I did. What happened?"

He doesn't answer for so long that I think he's not going to. But then he says, "They were badly burned in the explosion." His voice is rough, like he's swallowed fire. "Hardly conscious. They weren't captured. They couldn't have escaped." He runs a hand through his hair, and it must be sticky because he grimaces and yanks it free. He's not looking at me now. "They wouldn't have survived the night."

"Why—" My voice cracks, and I take a breath to steady it. "Why are you—why are you—" I gesture at his clothing, and my breath shudders. "There's so much blood."

"Because I wanted it to be fast." His eyes meet mine now, and I'm sure he's seeing the horror in my expression. "I needed it to be fast."

There's a note in his voice that I can't quite figure out, but my heart must be ahead of my brain, because my pulse begins to ease, the panic draining out of my chest before I understand: he didn't want to do it, but if he had to, he was going to make it as quick and painless as possible.

In a way that looked as brutal as possible.

They wouldn't have survived the night.

He made an execution out of an act of mercy.

I wonder how many times he's had to do that. How many times he's had to choose the lesser of two evils, because the option was to execute a prisoner or to watch more people die for lack of medicine. It's a terrible choice to have to make. A terrible position.

I think back to the moment we were poring over maps, when the tiniest bit of hope flickered in the air. I wonder if the explosions burned it out, if there's nothing left.

"Don't pity me," Corrick says. "If you pity anyone, pity them."

"I do," I say. But I pity him, too. I can't hate him anymore.

He sighs and leans back against the wall. He presses the heels of his hands to his eyes again. "Leave me alone, Tessa."

I blow a breath out through my teeth and step forward, catching the edges of his jacket between my fingers.

He startles and jerks his hands down.

"Mind your mettle," I say as I work the buttons.

He blinks. Scowls. "I told you—"

"You told me a lot of things. Maybe you could shut up for a minute and let me think."

He shuts up, but I don't think. Not really. I keep my eyes on my task until the last of the buttons slip free. "Take that off," I say as I turn away to tug at the chains that will make the faucets run. The rush of water roars in the silence.

"Wash your hands and face," I say. I plug the drain and dip my hand in the water to check the temperature. Flecks of blood and dirt had clung to my fingertips from where I touched him, but they swirl away into nothing. I start to turn back around. "I'll see if I can find a wash—"

I stop short. The breath rushes out of my lungs.

He hasn't just removed the jacket. He's removed his shirt, too, leaving his upper body bare, his trousers hanging low on his hips. He doesn't look like a blood-soaked villain anymore; he looks warm, somehow simultaneously vulnerable yet fierce. Muscle crawls across his shoulders and down his arms, revealing various scars, from what looks like a puncture wound in his abdomen to what must have been a knife or a dagger bisecting his bicep. My eyes lock on to the faint tracing of hair that starts below his navel and disappears under his waistband.

Corrick clears his throat, and I jerk my gaze up. My cheeks are on fire.

"Mind *your* mettle," he says.

"I hate you."

"Hmm. Not too much, it seems." He steps into my space, and I nearly trip over my own feet to get out of his way, but he's only moving to thrust his hands under the flow of water.

I'm such a fool. I can't be lusting after him. Not now. Not ever.

My heart doesn't care. Other parts of me don't care. My whole body is a traitor.

"Didn't you say you were going to find a washrag?" he says pointedly.

"Oh! Yes. Of course." This time I do stumble over my feet. But I find a washrag and bring it back to him, trying not to look at the long slope of his back, or the way his waist narrows beneath his ribs, or the long jagged scar that's partially hidden by his waistband.

"You have a lot of scars," I say.

"Smugglers aren't generally a very agreeable sort." He bends over the basin, soaks the rag, and scrubs at his face. "Sometimes I try to ask questions and they have other ideas."

Interesting.

But it gives my brain something to latch on to aside from wondering what his skin feels like. My cheeks are burning, but I keep my eyes locked ahead, on the far wall. "Did you get a chance to question the prisoners who escaped tonight?"

"No. I was busy reading maps with you and watching the sector go up in flames."

"So none of them?"

He scrubs at his face with the rag again and turns to look at me. "No. Why?"

"Consul Sallister made a comment about 'roughshod laborers.' All the rumors said the smugglers from Steel City were young and disorganized." I consider the explosions outside the window. "This seems really organized."

"Yes," he agrees. "They're getting money from somewhere. These Benefactors must be well funded. There are many theories that the money is coming from inside the palace." He ducks his head to splash more water on his face.

I think back to the conversations we had as Wes and Tessa, when he so adamantly declared that he wasn't a smuggler and he wasn't in this for personal gain. He'd looked haunted then, and I thought it was for the same reasons I was. Now I know the truth. "Did you question them? The prisoners from Steel City?"

"Yes. No one led me to believe they were part of some master plot." He rakes his hands through his hair, which is now dripping water onto his chest. "They called for revolution and . . ." He shrugs. "You were there."

The execution turned into a riot. Prisoners escaped.

I wonder how Corrick was planning to execute them. I'm scared to ask.

That tempers some of my flames.

He tugs at the chains to stop the flow of water, then turns around to lean back against the basin. "If there's an underground network of smugglers funded by these Benefactors, they're too well hidden. No one will admit anything to the night patrol. No one will speak to me, certainly."

Funny how that happens when you kill everyone. The words sit on the tip of my tongue, but I don't say them. I don't think he needs me to.

I don't want to stare at him—well, my traitorous eyes do, but that's not going anywhere good. I turn away and find a soft towel on a shelf, then turn to bring it back.

He's standing right behind me.

I suck in a breath and shove it against his chest. "Here."

"Thank you." But he doesn't move.

"What will Allisander do now?" I say.

Corrick shakes out the towel and drags it across his skin. "He vomited in the hallway of the Hold, so hopefully I was convincing that I'll take a hard line on any further attacks."

"Which means you think there will be more."

"Yes." He finally meets my eyes. "I think there will be more." He pauses. "And I think, after today's attacks, they will be more violent and even better planned. Word will spread quickly that this rescue mission was successful. The people will be emboldened. This isn't just about funding rebels. If we have organized attacks on supply runs in addition to calls for rebellion in the streets, well . . ." His voice trails off.

"You think Allisander will stop supplying the Moonflower."

"No. I think we'll face a full-on revolution."

What did Harristan say? *It's easy to love your king when everyone is well fed and healthy. A bit harder when everyone is not.* He's not wrong. But seeing things from this side makes it all so much more complicated. Revolution will mean more deaths—not just from violence, but from the fevers as well, as medicine becomes restricted.

I look into Corrick's eyes and remember how I stood in the darkness with him and begged for revolution. I begged him to stand at the front with me—but I didn't have a plan. I don't have one now.

Now I understand what he was telling me that night. *Rebellion won't stop the fevers, Tessa.*

A revolution might remove Harristan and Corrick from power, but it won't stop the illnesses. It won't force Allisander to provide more medicine. If anything, it'll be harder to come by.

And if the king is busy fighting a revolution, he won't be able to spare the expense to look for alternate ways to cure the fevers. Kandala will tear itself apart.

"Roydan and Arella have already begun to have secret meetings," Corrick says. "It's possible the other consuls have, too. Allisander and Lissa have a private army. If this comes to revolution, it might not just be the people against the throne."

"It might be sector against sector," I whisper. "It really is hopeless."

Corrick nods.

"But if we stop the attacks—"

"It won't stop a rebellion. Again, that's a big *if*. I can hardly stop them now."

He's right. I know he's right. And like he said earlier, if royal advisers haven't been able to solve the problem, it's unlikely we're going to solve it in the dead of night in a washroom.

The blood is gone, and Corrick's hair is slicked back, but the haunted look hasn't left his face. I watched his eyes light up when he saw Rocco in the Hold. Was he hoping for Harristan? Is the king not involved in what Corrick is tasked with doing? Does he deliberately keep himself at a distance, or does Corrick try to shield him from it? I can't decide which is worse, but I watched his eyes fill a few moments ago, and I think both options are horrible.

"The night patrol will be more brutal now," I say quietly.

He looks back at me for the longest moment, his expression inscrutable—then scrubs his hands over his face and makes a sound that's half aggravation, half anguish. "I can't call them off, Tessa. I *can't*. Allisander would stop his shipments. Harristan would—"

"I know."

"—never be able to back it. The rebels set fire to the sector—"

"I know."

He breaks off, breathing heavily. "I don't know how to stop it," he says. "I can't even figure out who's funding these rebels—or why. Is this an attack on Harristan? Or is this a bid for medicine? Or both?"

So many questions—and as usual, no answers. I put a finger to my lip to think. A week ago, I might have been fighting on the side of the Benefactors. After seeing the destruction they've caused, I don't know if that's the right side either.

But Corrick is right: if he can't stop the attacks, he has no leverage—and no way to stop the violence on either side. We need to find out who the Benefactors are.

As soon as I have the thought, I realize how to do it.

"People will talk," I say suddenly.

"Of course," he says. "Everyone talks."

I shake my head quickly. "No—I mean you've been going about this the wrong way. You've been interrogating people as King's Justice."

"Shall I have Harristan do it?" He rolls his eyes and turns away. "I'm sure that will be much less threatening."

"No." I catch his arm, and he turns back to look at me. "Not Harristan."

"Then who?"

"You and me."

His expression turns skeptical, so I rush on. "Not as prince and . . . and apothecary." I take a deep breath. "As outlaws."

"As outlaws."

"Yes." I pause and stare up into his blue eyes, remembering the way they looked behind a mask. "We talk to people as Weston Lark and Tessa Cade."

Chapter Twenty-Seven

Corrick

It's nearly dawn by the time I crawl into bed, but that doesn't stop the guards from rapping at my door at an hour past dawn, announcing that Consul Sallister has arrived.

"I believe we were to play chess, were we not?" Allisander calls.

I wish I could order *his* execution.

But we play in my quarters, the fire snapping in the hearth, a serving girl bringing us sugared pastries and boiled eggs and pouring cup after cup of black tea. I expect Allisander to be full of demands, seeking promises, but he's oddly quiet. Tension hangs over the room, and I can't tell if it's between me and him, or if it's all in my head. Every move we make on the chessboard feels like a precursor to battle.

I think of Tessa's censorious eyes last night, and I have to shake off her judgment. As much as I hate Allisander, I need him. Kandala needs him.

For now.

The thought makes my heart pound. Harristan can't undermine his consuls, but if we can stop the attacks and find out the source of funding—if we can ease some of the tensions in the sectors—then maybe we can formulate a new way to move forward.

But tensions are higher than ever, and the night patrol is on high alert. If Wes and Tessa return to the Wilds, the risk would be immense.

I look at the self-indulgent man in front of me. The risk is immense either way. The Benefactors have to be connected to someone from the Royal Sector—I just don't know who else would have the silver to spend on revolution. But the consuls are all close to Harristan. I can't imagine any of them paying citizens to revolt when any of them would have an opportunity to put a knife in my brother themselves. It would be cheaper. Simpler. Faster.

I think of that stack of letters Quint brought to Harristan on the day we were set to execute eight smugglers. Nearly two hundred letters—a lot of unhappy people crying for change.

Arella's was among them. Her feelings about the executions have been made quite clear. She would never attack Harristan.

But she's got a soft spot for the people, for those who are suffering.

And she's been having secret meetings with Roydan.

They all ask for money when someone is denied funding. Allisander implicated Jonas Beeching—but Arella was pretty quick.

I've fallen so deep in thought that I'm startled when Allisander speaks into the silence. "I'm surprised you had time for a game, Corrick."

"I made you a promise," I say breezily.

"You make a lot of promises."

My hand goes still on a chess piece. There's a note in his voice I can't quite figure out, and it draws my gaze up from the board. "I do my best to keep them all."

"Indeed? To whom?"

He looks . . . smug. Or something close to it. He's honestly a terrible chess player, but I've been letting him win for the last half an hour simply because I didn't think it would be a good idea to poke at his pride.

Now feels like a good time to stop.

"I don't know what you mean." I move my rook in position to capture his king. "Check."

He moves his king one square to the right. "I've looked into this girl of yours."

My blood goes cold, but I shrug and study the board. "She is not *mine*."

He leans in, his eyes seeking mine with vicious intensity. "She isn't an apothecary. She works for a charlatan who peddles cheap skin remedies."

I'm frozen in place. I don't know what to say. I knew Tessa was her real name, but the shop where she works is outside the Wilds, well away from here. She never worried about anyone we were helping identifying her, surely.

Or maybe she never worried because she wouldn't have been at risk the way I was.

I move my rook again. "Regardless of her employment, she has brought theories to Harristan. Theories that may—"

"The woman who owns the shop indicated that Tessa was

distraught after the failed execution. She said that the girl told her friend she was pregnant with a smuggler's baby."

Of all the things he could have said, that's the most unexpected. I almost burst out laughing. "Truly, Allisander? You believe she's pregnant with a smuggler's baby and she found herself in the palace for . . . what, exactly? Last night in the salon half the courtiers thought she was pregnant with *Harristan's* baby, so perhaps we should make a wager—"

"I'm not a fool, Corrick." His voice is level and cold.

I draw myself up and stare back at him. He's too close to the truth. If it were about me, I'd laugh him right out of my quarters. But it's not about me. It's about Tessa.

"Arella and Roydan have made it very clear that they do not take issue with these smugglers," Allisander says, his tone unchanged. "Consul Craft overheard them getting into a carriage together. They clearly believe the Crown has taken too harsh a stance on thievery and illegal dealings."

"This is idle gossip, Allisander. Consul Cherry has made no secret of how she feels."

He pushes his chess piece one space to the left, then brings his gaze to meet mine again. "After your behavior in the Hold, I suspect you have begun to think the same."

He's drawing the wrong conclusions in so many ways—but the worst part is that I can't give him the right ones. My heart pounds against my ribs as I remember the way I slit those throats last night. I'm beginning to wonder if Allisander will never be satisfied until we're executing anyone who dares to look at him askance. "You saw me in the Hold last night."

"I did. You looked like you wanted to cry."

"*You* looked like you wanted to vomit. Ah, forgive me. You *did* vom—"

He slams a hand on the chessboard, and the pieces rattle and topple. My king falls to the floor. He inhales fiercely.

But then he stops.

The anger in his gaze speaks volumes, however, and I hold my breath and wait. I'm not sure what he was going to say, but I hope it's something so brutally treasonous that I could call a guard in here to run him through on the spot.

But he doesn't. And I don't. We sit there in frozen fury for the longest moment, until the guards rap at my door to announce Harristan.

I want to wither with relief. My brother could ask me to read every single document in the palace while standing on my head, and I'd do it willingly if it would get me out of this conversation with Consul Sallister.

Harristan doesn't wait for a response; he just strides into my quarters before the guards have finished speaking.

Allisander rises to his feet and smooths his jacket, any hint of anger vanishing. "Harristan."

I can't read his voice. I don't know if he's glad my brother is here—or disappointed. But Harristan looks back at him, and his voice is even. "Consul."

For one brief second, I think Allisander is going to needle him the way he was needling me. But he must still hold some respect for my brother, because he takes in Harristan's curt response and cold demeanor, and he turns wicked eyes my way. "Thank you for the game, Corrick. We will pick it up at another time."

I don't know what to say, and he doesn't wait for an answer. He exits through the door, and I'm alone with my brother.

I'm surprised to find the air between us is as prickly as it was with Allisander. It must be on my side: displeasure tinged with disappointment that my brother wasn't the one to find me in the Hold. It's ridiculous and foolish for me to have even hoped for such a thing—but I did, and I can't seem to let it go.

Then my brother speaks.

"Rocco reported that he found you in a destroyed section of the Hold last night, with no guards. What were you doing?"

This is startling, and not at all what I expected him to say. I begin gathering the marble chess pieces to place them in their velvet and gold box. "Your guards gossip worse than mine do, Harristan."

"You didn't answer my question."

I don't know how to answer his question. We can't afford to appear weak now, of all times. Each chess piece clinks into the box until Harristan steps over to the table and snaps the lid closed.

"Talk to me." There's a tone of command in his voice, one I'm used to hearing—but never directed at me.

Two chess pieces remain in my hand, and I slide them over each other in my palm. I give him a sidelong glance. "Am I speaking to my brother, or am I speaking to the king?"

"Both."

Maybe I was wrong before. Maybe the tension isn't all on my side.

I stand and set the chess pieces on the table, then offer him a flourishing bow. "Forgive me, Your Majesty. I had no idea this was an official meeting."

"Corrick." His tone is unyielding.

I didn't want to kill those prisoners.

I don't want to do this anymore.

I don't want you to need *me to do this anymore. This can't be how Father would have wanted us to lead.*

I can't say any of that. "There were few guards left in the Hold after the attacks," I say. "The few that remained were needed to remove the bodies." I pause. "Are your guards to be your spies now?"

"Do they need to be?"

I don't have to pretend to be offended at the question. "No!"

"That girl didn't want you to kill those prisoners—"

"Neither did Arella and Roydan," I snap. "Send your guards to eavesdrop on them."

"—and she asked Rocco to take her to find you in the Hold. Why?"

Because she saw through me. Because she knew I was a breath away from shattering. Because her hope hasn't burned away into nothing.

I can't say any of that either.

Harristan takes a step closer to me. "I thought this was a simple dalliance," he says, his tone low. "An infatuation, maybe, that got away from you. I was willing to overlook it."

I move to the side table and uncork the brandy. I want to pour it straight down my throat, but I have the sense to use a glass. "But your guard has convinced you otherwise?"

"You spend a great deal of time in the Hold, speaking with smugglers. I find it an interesting coincidence that when the night patrol caught a small operation, half of them were able to call for rebellion and escape. And when Allisander caught another group, they were able to set the sector on fire while being rescued."

My hand goes still on the glass as the impact of these words becomes clear. Even still, I can't quite believe it. I turn around. "What are you asking me, Harristan?"

"Are you involved with these smugglers somehow? Do you know anything about the thieves who've been plaguing the sector?"

The world seems to tilt on its axis, just for the barest moment. I'm destroying myself for the sake of my brother, and he's all but accusing me of treason.

The worst part is that he's not wrong. Not entirely.

I drain the glass of brandy and pour another.

He moves close. His voice drops. "Tell me, Cory. If you're doing this—whatever they've promised you—"

All of my anger flares. I whirl, plant my hands on his chest, and shove him as hard as I can. "*Get out.*"

He stumbles back a step, surprise plain on his face. Then he coughs. Hard. He puts a hand to his chest.

For an instant, panic replaces all the anger. He sucks in a breath, and it sounds like he's breathing through a cupful of water.

"Harristan," I whisper.

He grabs hold of the back of a chair and fights to breathe.

I did this. I did this. Tessa said he was fine, but he's clearly not. I move to surge past him to shout for a physician.

Harristan seizes my sleeve and draws me up short. "Tell me," he gasps. His eyes are dark and intent on mine.

And a little desperate.

"I'm not working with the smugglers," I say. "I would never betray you. I have never betrayed you. I swear it."

He stands there fighting to breathe, until his grip on my sleeve feels less like a demand and more like a plea.

"I swear," I say again, my voice softer. "I swear."

For the first time in what feels like an hour, he draws a full breath. His grip eases. He nods and straightens.

He's not dying. I didn't kill him. Relief is potent, but some of my rage slips back into my chest, turning my voice rough. "Why would you think that?"

"Because you're hiding something from me." He hesitates. "And Allisander expressed concern—"

"That son of a bitch."

"You can't blame him. You've changed these last few weeks."

My brother's voice is still a bit thin, a bit reedy. I look at him. "I have always worked in your interest, Harristan. Always." I pause, remembering the moments I stood in the deserted chamber of the Hold and wished for my brother to appear. How I wished for him to see how this was destroying me as effectively as the fever is destroying all of Kandala.

But he didn't. He's not seeing it even now.

I straighten, and I don't even have to try to tinge my voice with regret. "Sic your guards on me if you must. Measure my every movement. Attend every interrogation. Tether your horse to mine if you like. I commit very little treason on the toilet, but if you want to be *absolutely thorough*—"

"Cory." He draws a breath, then hesitates.

I stare back at him, and I wonder if he can read the emotion in my eyes. I remember when we were young, how we'd sneak into the Wilds, how he'd lead and I'd follow, but I always felt an obligation to protect him. Some of it was due to growing up beside a brother whose health was monitored and protected and worried over for so long. Some of it was due to the fact that he would one day be king, and I would not. It's an obligation I still feel, and it seeps into every action I take. I thought he knew that.

For the first time, I feel as though *he* has betrayed *me*.

Maybe he can see it, because he lets that breath out slowly. He claps me on the shoulder, giving my arm a gentle squeeze. "Forgive me. Please."

I nod.

But something has fractured between us.

I think he must feel the same, because he holds on for a moment too long, then steps back and turns for the door.

I should tell him everything about Tessa. About Weston. The words burn in my throat.

Then again, maybe that would confirm all his worries. *I am committing treason, brother, I've been committing it for years.*

I swallow the words. I swallow my anger. I swallow my disappointment. When the king pauses at the door to glance back, the King's Justice looks back at him.

Once he's gone, and I go for the door to have a message sent for Quint, I find Rocco there guarding my door.

———◆———

Hours pass. Quint doesn't arrive.

I'm not desperate enough to send word to Tessa, because every syllable will be scrutinized and reported back to my brother, and I can't think of anything to say that won't bolster his suspicion. I also don't want to leave my room with my brother's guards trailing behind me, because I know it will generate gossip: either people will think we're more at risk because of the explosions at the Hold, or they'll think Harristan is doing exactly what he's doing.

I don't like either option.

I'm also petty enough to like the idea of Rocco having to

stand outside my door for hours on end, because it's interminably boring.

Only slightly more boring than sitting in here by myself. I've been spending the time reviewing the documents that Tessa abandoned, and discovering nothing new. Tessa was right: no one will speak to me like this, but they'll speak to Wes and Tessa.

I'm fidgety and eager for nightfall.

Quint finally appears when I'm debating whether I'm going to eat dinner in my quarters alone, like a prisoner.

A guard announces him and swings the door wide.

"Quint," I say. "Finally."

"Forgive me, Your Highness," he says. "The king required my services for much of the day."

His tone, the formality, draws me up short. I glance behind him at the door that's falling closed slowly.

"No apologies are necessary," I tell him. "I wanted to request additional reports on the fevers—"

The door clicks closed.

"What's wrong?" I whisper.

He doesn't move from where he stands. "Someone has suggested to your brother that you're involved with the smugglers." He pauses. "That you are working with these Benefactors, if not funding them yourself. That you deliberately allowed the prisoners to escape on the day of the riots. That you enabled the attacks last night."

I go still. It's very different to hear this from Quint than from my brother. When Harristan spoke of treason, it was between us. Now . . . it's not. "Someone." I scowl. "It's Allisander."

"It may not be him alone." Quint pauses. "Some have suggested that you may have confided in me."

I study my friend. For the first time, I realize he's not in disarray. His jacket is buttoned, his hair is combed.

His eyes are tense and uncertain.

"Are you unwell?" I say. A flicker of fear ignites in my chest. "Is Tessa unwell?"

"Tessa is fine." He pauses, then steps toward the table, but he stops before reaching it. His voice is very soft. "Corrick—I've kept many secrets for you."

"For which you have my gratitude."

"For which I could be executed, if these rumors are true."

I stare at him. "Quint." If Harristan has gotten to Quint . . . I'm done for. "Quint, what have you done?"

"No, Corrick. What have *you* done?" His eyes are intent, piercing mine.

We stare at each other across the room, and the fire snaps in the hearth. Tension holds my heart in a vise grip. I think of every story I've ever told Quint, every transgression I've ever committed. The names I've given him of families near death. The times I truly *have* allowed prisoners to escape. The homes I've broken into when I steal Moonflower petals. The way I've evaded the night patrol or the way I get over the wall. All I know about Tessa and every action we've taken together.

I was angry that Harristan would believe a rumor like this.

It's a different feeling that Quint would.

"Shall I call for a guard to take my head right now?" I say flippantly, while inside I'm reeling. "I'm sure Rocco would be willing."

He stands there and evaluates me. It's not a good feeling, because I know how much he sees. I know how much he knows.

"You were my confidant, Quint." I pause. "More than a confidant. You were my friend."

"*Were?*"

I tug at my sleeves and don't look at him. "Did you sell me out to Harristan?"

For the first time, anger flares in his eyes. "Do you think I would?"

I take a step toward him, and it requires effort to keep my voice down. "Do you think I'd help rebels and smugglers while pretending to distribute medicine to those who need it?"

He stares at me. I stare back.

Finally, he sighs. "No. I don't." He pauses. "And I didn't sell you out to your brother when he asked."

I don't move. "What did you say to him?"

Quint looks back at me squarely and folds his arms. "I said you've never spoken a word of treason in my presence. That you've been loyal to the kingdom in every action I've seen you take."

I inhale what feels like the first deep breath in hours. I press my hands together in front of my face and try not to rattle myself apart.

Quint risks his neck by keeping my secrets. He always has, but I've had contingency plans for my morning activities. I've never been directly accused by my brother. I've never been suspected by any of the consuls.

Now . . . now the risk is very real.

"Leave," I say to him, and my voice is not unkind. "I will not speak to you except in public, and only for official business. I will not—"

"Corrick." He unfolds his arms and moves to the side table to pour a glass of brandy for himself. "Honestly. I know the risks I take."

"I'll take your involvement to my grave, Quint," I say.

"Well," says Quint. He drains the glass, which is very unusual for him. "Let's hope that's more than a day away."

"You trust me, then?"

"I've always trusted you." He hesitates, then glances at the door, and his voice grows very quiet. "If you were assisting these smugglers, I know you would have a reason." He pauses. "I thought perhaps you no longer trusted *me*."

"I tell you everything." My voice grows rough. Some days he feels like my only friend here, the only person who's ever known all sides. "Everything."

He pours another glass, and I think he's going to toss it back as quickly as the first, but instead he holds it out to me. "Then I ask forgiveness for doubting you."

"You're probably the only person in the palace who doesn't need to ask forgiveness for anything."

He laughs at that. "That's hardly true." He pauses and loses the smile. "We'll have to be careful," he says. "Tensions are high right now."

We. We'll have to be careful. It's more than I deserve. I drain the glass he gave me.

"I have a plan," I say huskily.

"Of course you do."

I hear the tension in his voice, and it makes me hesitate. "Do you want out, Quint?" I pause. "You don't need to risk your neck for me."

"It's not just for you, Corrick." His eyes hold mine. "Tell me your plan."

I tell him about Tessa's suggestion, that we go into the Wilds as outlaws again to see if people will talk about what's going on and who's behind the attacks.

When I'm done, Quint strokes at his jaw, thinking. "You'll have to convince people that you were being held captive in the Hold, and you escaped during the explosions. That will explain your absence." He pauses. "You can slip out the window as usual, but Tessa's rooms are along the side wall, and she'll be visible."

I can't invite her here either, because my brother's guards would definitely report it.

"I'll see if I can distract the guards for a moment," says Quint. "Is she as quick and sure-footed as you said?"

My heart pounds. "Yes."

He pulls his pocket watch free. "Be ready at midnight. I'll make sure she has a mask."

CHAPTER TWENTY-EIGHT

Tessa

It's been a day of dresses and curls and lessons and so many curtsies that I want to lodge a protest.

I haven't seen Corrick.

I haven't seen the king.

I've hardly even seen Quint, and during the few moments he did appear, he seemed tense and distracted. The attacks on the sector have everyone on edge—including me. Rocco hasn't been outside my door at all, but the guards who replaced him have the same purple and blue royal insignia on their uniform.

The entire day has carried a sense of anticipation. Of waiting. Of something to come.

But now it's nightfall, and nothing has happened.

I haven't spoken to the royal apothecaries—though I'm sure the king has more important things to do right now. I have no idea whether Corrick will take a chance as Wes again. Last night, he didn't give me an answer, and I began to wonder if that's answer enough, especially as the day wore on.

I'm not a prisoner, but today, I feel like one. Rocco willingly took me out of the palace, but I wonder what would happen if I asked the guards to take me out of the sector. I imagine showing up at Mistress Solomon's in one of these silly dresses, how surprised she would look. I imagine wrapping Karri up in a hug. She was such a good friend—and then I vanished. I wonder what they think has become of me. Is there gossip in the sector about me breaking into the palace? If so, I'm sure it's been eclipsed by everything that happened last night. Will there be another attack? Will Consul Sallister stop providing Moonflower to the sectors? Will he be able to, if his supply runs keep getting raided?

I have so many questions that they tangle up in my thoughts and keep sleep a far distance away.

Jossalyn took down my curls hours ago, leaving me with a hot cup of tea and a tray of baked twists of dough dusted with sugar. A vial of the elixir sits beside it, so much darker than the ones I mix. I swirl the liquid in the vial and wonder how much of this concentrated Moonflower would save families in the Wilds.

But then I consider Harristan's cough last night. He didn't have a fever—but he's still not wholly well. He's the king of Kandala, so he's certainly receiving more than enough himself. I don't understand.

When I climb into bed, I don't think I'll sleep, but I must, because a sound wakes me. My room is cloaked in darkness, and the hearth has fallen to embers.

A hand comes over my mouth.

I suck in a breath to scream, but then Quint's voice says, "We have less than a minute for you to get into Corrick's quarters. There is no time for questions. Can you run?"

My thoughts spin, but I nod against his hand.

He lets me go. The door is open and unguarded. I run.

The hallway is empty somehow, and I sprint like a ghost. This stupid palace is entirely too big, because Corrick's room seems to be a mile away, and my bare feet skid on the velvet carpeting.

Just as I hear a male voice saying, "Master Quint, there doesn't appear to be anything amiss," Corrick's door swings open and I run smack into him.

He catches my shoulders and holds me upright. "Quiet."

I'm gasping for breath. "But—"

"I said *quiet.*" He shoves me into his room and leans out into the hallway. "Guards! What is going on?"

My heart won't stop pounding. I hope the guards know what's going on because I sure don't.

A male voice calls back, "Master Quint thought he saw suspicious activity in the streets."

"The sector was attacked last night. Doors should not be left unguarded," Corrick snaps. "Return to your posts at once."

"Yes, Your Highness."

He lets the door fall closed, then turns to look at me.

I'm still a bit winded. He's dressed in finery again, all velvet and leather and brocade, which is quite a shame after I've seen him shirtless. His eyes are as cold and hard as the first night I arrived, which makes me want to back away.

He sure doesn't look ready to play the role of Wes.

I swallow and try to calm my heartbeat. "What's happening?"

"Quint got you out. It'll be a real challenge to get you back in, because they won't fall for that twice, but we'll worry about that then."

"What are we doing?"

He grabs two leather packs from beside the hearth. He tosses one at me, and I catch it against my chest. Then, without a word, he moves to the window, swings a leg over the sill, and disappears into the darkness.

All the air leaves my lungs in a rush. I sling the pack over one shoulder and peer out the window after him. There's a thick, heavy rope attached to the ironwork below the window, and it creaks with his weight.

My heart is in my throat again.

This was my idea, but it's terrifying.

"Remember how to climb a rope?" he whisper-calls up to me.

"Did you think I'd forget in two days?"

He grins, and in an instant Cruel Corrick is gone, leaving Wes in his place. "Then step quick. We've got rounds to make."

———

The night air is cool, with a bit of wind to grab tendrils of my hair and toss them into my eyes. The dark sky hangs heavy with clouds, only a bit of lighter gray in the distance to reveal the location of the moon. Rain feels like a distant promise that might not be kept. Far across the palace grounds, flames flicker against the sky and my heart stutters, thinking of the attacks, but then I remember the arch of torches we spotted during our carriage ride. Stonehammer's Arch, the proclamation of love his great-whatever-grandfather once made.

I hope you fell a lot.

Never once.

I'm barefoot, dew clinging to my feet as I slip through the darkness to follow him. I can't tell who he is tonight, or which personality is going to show itself when he decides to let me know what's going on. He's moving so silently that I don't dare to make a sound either. I have no idea what guards patrol out here or who we might encounter.

I sure hope he doesn't expect me to play the role of outlaw in my nightgown. Then again, he's not dressed like Wes. There must be clothes in these packs.

The farther we walk, the darker the night gets. Grass and dirt squish between my toes, turning Corrick into a shadow, while I'm a ghost in my pale-green nightshift. My hammering pulse has long since slowed to a normal pace. Gradually, the lights of the palace become smaller as the flaming torches of the arch grow closer, dripping sparks.

"Here," he finally says, slowing to a stop. We've been silent for so long that his voice is loud to my ears. He turns to look at me, and there's tension around his eyes.

"Here what?" I whisper.

"You don't need to whisper. There are no guards along the rear wall of the palace, because they guard the wall surrounding it. But I wanted us to get closer to the arch in case anyone was looking out the window."

"You . . . you want us to be visible?"

"The opposite, actually." He unbuttons his jacket and slips free of the sleeves. "Haven't you noticed yet that when you look at the light, the nearby darkness seems darker?"

"No, I never really—" The breath leaves my lungs in a rush. He's pulled his shirt over his head.

Corrick's eyes flick skyward. "Maybe you should focus on changing."

I focus on the shadows and lines of his chest in the darkness. "Uh-huh."

He throws his shirt at my face, and I laugh under my breath, ducking to unbuckle my own pack. There's a homespun skirt in some dark color, along with thick socks, rough boots, and a gray stitched chemise. With a start, I realize these are the clothes I was captured in. Freshly laundered, obviously, because they smell like roses and sunshine.

I glance up to find Corrick staring at me. He's pulled a black shirt over his head, but that's all. I can't read his expression in the darkness.

I straighten. "What?"

"You laughed. I wasn't sure that would ever happen again."

I blush and look down, glad he can't see my face. "Well."

I'm not sure what else to say.

Well, I don't feel like a prisoner right this moment.

Well, I forgot that Weston Lark was an illusion.

Well.

I've grown too quiet, and so has he, and the air seems weighted with . . . something. I shiver and shake out my skirt.

"Turn around," I say.

"Why?" he says brightly.

What a scoundrel. I throw his shirt back at him. "You know why."

He smiles wolfishly, but he turns around. I dress with extra care anyway, slipping the skirt under my nightclothes, then pulling the shift out through the neck of my chemise. The palace clothes were more lovely than anything I've ever worn, but there's something comforting about slipping into the old Tessa. I use the shift to dry my feet and then turn my back for him, balancing on one foot to pull on my socks and lace up my boots. Fabric rustles as he finishes changing behind me. I keep my eyes fixed ahead, on the flickering torches of the arch, watching how embers fall in tiny bursts, defying the night before burning out in the water below.

"Ready?" he says.

I turn around. My breath catches again.

He's not shirtless. He's not the King's Justice. He's . . . he's Wes.

I've known the truth for days, and he proved it once before, but this . . . this is like seeing a ghost. His mask, his hat, his clothes. He's Wes. *He's Wes.*

It's too much. I can't help it. I stumble forward and throw my arms around him. My breath is hitching, and I'm trying to stop tears from falling. I'm failing.

He catches me, and at first I think he's going to set me upright or make a bratty comment about how I really need to stop crying on his shoulder, but he doesn't.

He doesn't say anything. He just holds me, his arms tight against my back.

Eventually, my breathing steadies, but I don't raise my head. He's warm and sure and real against me, his breath whispering against my hair.

"Forgive me," he says quietly, and his voice is rough. I squeeze my eyes closed again. His thumb drifts across my cheek. "Please, Tessa. Forgive me."

I take a deep breath—but there's so much. Too much? I don't know.

I think of that moment when the Hold exploded, how he was about to kiss me, and I stopped him.

He's not Wes, not really.

I'm not quite ready to let him go yet, though.

Eventually, I remember that we have things to do and lives to save. I draw back and look up into those eyes I know so well. "We can't stay here."

He nods, but his gaze doesn't leave mine.

I blink the last of my tears away. "Do you—" I have to clear my throat. "Do you have a mask for me?"

"Yes." He pulls one from his pack, along with a hat.

I tie it into place and swallow hard against the lump in my throat.

Now he's staring at me the way I was just staring at him, and I have to force myself to look away and tie up my pack. "Where . . . um, where are we leaving these?"

"There's a chest outside the gate. Do you remember how I told you to escape from the carriage? That's my exit."

I nod and sniff and shoulder the pack, then fall into step beside him. We slip silently through the grass.

The dark and silence begins to feel too weighted, so I say, "What if someone comes to your room?"

"Quint will stay in my quarters and periodically call for food and wine until we return, so it will give the impression that I'm toiling away over those reports. My brother retires early, so he's probably asleep."

"What if someone insists on speaking to you?"

"The only person who can truly *demand* my presence is Harristan, and that's rare." There's a note in his voice that belies how casually he answers. "Quint has a cache of answers anyway. I've been called to the Hold, I've been asked to review a funding request before it's submitted to the king, I've been asked to mediate something that doesn't need mediation . . ." He shrugs.

I glance at him. "Why does Quint cover for you?"

"In the beginning, I think it was because I convinced Harristan to let Quint have his job. He's young for his role as Palace Master, and you can already tell my brother doesn't suffer fools. But Quint is more savvy than he lets on, and he took me by surprise when he caught me sneaking back into the palace. I'm not sure what he thought I was doing, and at first we were both a little wary about it, but gradually I started to take him into my confidence." He pauses. "Quint is a good friend."

That heavy note is back in his voice.

"Something is wrong," I say softly.

"No." He glances at me, then gives a self-deprecating laugh. "Well, not any more than usual."

"Tell me."

He says nothing for so long that I begin to think he won't answer, and when he does speak, he only says, "Look. The gate."

It's exactly as he described, and it's smaller than I expected: only about three feet high, barring the way to what appears to be a dark tunnel. As promised, there's a wooden trunk that appears to be decaying with rot, but when Wes—*Corrick*, I sheepishly remind myself—throws open the lid, the interior is dry and clean.

The tunnel is black and our breathing echoes, and I'm glad for his company, because this narrow space would be terrifying alone. Something skitters over my boot and I gasp, but he grabs hold of my hand to steady me, and I continue on.

"This used to be a spy tunnel," he whispers, but his voice is loud anyway. "A hundred years ago, there were a dozen, all over the

Royal Sector. Some have caved in, but there are a few, like this one, that prove useful for any princes-turned-outlaw." He pauses. "Harristan and I used to use them all the time."

"He did this too?" I say, surprised.

"No. When we were children." Another pause. "Harristan was often unwell, and our parents would dote on him. He was never allowed to do anything. It drove him crazy. He'd convince me to sneak into the Wilds with him. It would take him twice as long to scale the sector walls, but he's the one who taught me how to do it."

I imagine the king and the prince as boys, sneaking through this tunnel, eagerly whispering, daring each other, challenging order and rules the way Corrick does now. It's harder to imagine Harristan as a sickly child, but I consider his coughing fits, and my apothecary brain wonders if he has some lingering illness that's masquerading as the fever.

That note is back in Corrick's voice, but for the first time, I can identify it. Longing. Loss. Sadness. Regret.

"Something has happened with King Harristan," I whisper.

"He thinks I'm working with the smugglers," he says simply.

"Wait." I wish I could see his eyes, but the tunnel is pitch-dark, and his expression is a mystery. "What?"

"You heard me." Corrick takes a long breath. "They've been pointing fingers since we first learned of the Benefactors, but I never expected anyone to suspect *me*. Allisander suspects that you're a part of it, too. That's why I couldn't come to you today. Harristan all but accused me this morning. His guards are reporting to him on my movements. He tried to get Quint to talk."

My chest is suddenly tight. "But—but you're not! You're—you're—"

I break off. He might not be the kind of smuggler Harristan is imagining . . . but Corrick isn't completely innocent either.

"Tessa. I know."

We walk in silence after that, our feet scraping against the walls of the tunnel, until we eventually burst free into the woods. It's misting rain now, and I don't recognize where we are, but I'm sure we're nowhere near the workshop. He wouldn't have been that careless. Not to keep this secret for so long.

My chest is still tight. His brother accused him. The king accused him.

And still he's here.

"I don't have a lot of petals," he says, "because I couldn't risk someone alerting Harristan to my request. But Quint was able to gather enough for one round of doses."

I bite my lip. "This . . . this is treason."

"It always was, Tessa."

I think of all the times we spoke ill of the king, of the cruel prince, of the way people were executed for doing exactly what we're doing. I swallow.

"You're risking yourself," I whisper.

"Yes. So are you." His eyes hold mine. "Let's make it worth it."

Chapter Twenty-Nine

Corrick

When we were children, Harristan and I would climb out of the tunnel and leave our royal lives behind like shedding a skin. He might have been slower to run and climb, but he was always better with the people. Merchants would sometimes see a boy with too many coins for his own good and they'd try to con him out of them, but my brother could never be tricked or swindled. He used to say that being coddled and sheltered and wrapped up in blankets gave him a lot of time to study people. It's truly a miracle I was able to keep Weston Lark a secret from him for so long.

No. It wasn't a miracle. It was trust. He trusts me.

He *trusted* me.

I'm not sure I'll ever be able to erase the memory of the look on his face when he asked me if I was involved with the smugglers. It's etched as deeply as the moment I heard a boot scrape against rock in the Hold and I hoped he would appear through the haze of smoke.

Tessa looks at me, and I can feel the weight of her gaze. Always before, it was easy to forget everything that awaited me in the palace and lose myself to the persona of Weston Lark.

Today, it's not. Tessa knows too much, and everything is at stake.

I suppose it always was, for her.

"If we discover who's behind the attacks," she says slowly, "what will you do to them?"

"It depends."

She gives me a look, and I lift one shoulder in a shrug. "It does." I glance down and meet her eyes. "I can't allow them to continue. You know that."

"I do. I know." But she swallows, and I realize this bothers her.

"Even if we stop the attacks, it won't cure the fever," I say. "But right now, Allisander has the right—and the motive—to restrict access to the Moonflower. I can't do anything if he locks himself up in his sector. If I can prove to him that his supply runs are safe and that I'm not a rebel myself, I can work with Harristan to figure out a more equitable way to distribute the elixir, especially if you can prove that we can do more with less."

"That's a lot of *ifs* again." She draws a long breath that shudders a little. "And it might not stop a revolution."

"Tessa." I look down at her and think of Quint sharing his worries in my quarters. If she runs, it would be nearly impossible to explain away, but I won't force her to do this against her will. "I have a pouch of coins. If you want out—"

"No." She shakes her head a little. "I want to do the right thing."

"Hmm." I look straight ahead. "The problem is that we all have different ideas of what's right." I sigh. "Including my brother. To say nothing of Allisander."

"Sometimes things are just *right*," she says forcefully. "It's not fair that people are dying when we can help them. It's not fair that Allisander can control so much—just because he has land and money. It's not fair that you're expected to—"

"Allisander is motivated by silver, so he'd likely consider it very fair—"

"I'm not talking about Consul Sallister. I'm talking about the king."

Those words drop like a rock, and I'm not sure what to say. "It's not a matter of expectation, Tessa." My voice turns rough against my will. "It's a matter of need."

"When we were in the carriage, you told me you couldn't leave him behind." She pauses. "Do you think your brother is weak?"

I think of the way Harristan reads every plea, how the deaths of our people seem to weigh on him. How he rarely wants the details of what I do to maintain the illusion of control.

I think of how he dove to cover me when our parents were slaughtered.

Or how, afterward, he stepped into his role as king.

"I would never call him weak," I say.

She's quiet for a while, and then she says very gently, "Do you think, if you were no longer King's Justice, that your brother would be able to maintain control?"

I'm not sure how to answer that either.

I suppose that's answer enough.

She keeps her gaze forward. "When my parents died, I wasn't sure how I would survive. It was all I could do to remember to eat. Sometimes I think that meeting you for . . . for *this* . . . was the only thing that forced me out of bed." She pauses. "I can't imagine having to run a country."

"The consuls worried Harristan was too young, and they tried to make a claim for ruling in his stead, but he was nineteen and they had no legal right. And after Consul Barnard was outed as being behind the plot to kill them, we didn't trust any of them. At every meeting, every *interaction*, they looked for weakness. They waited for us to fail. We had no one." My throat is tight, and I wish this conversation weren't summoning memories I try to keep buried. "We only had each other."

"Barnard wasn't working with any of the others?"

"We could never find evidence of it." I shrug. "And then the fevers began to spread more widely, and . . . well, you know how Kandala has fared."

"The morning I met with Harristan, he said that it's easy to love your king when everyone is healthy and well fed, but a bit harder when everyone isn't." She sighs. "And I know what Consul Sallister would do if he were in charge. He talked about the prisoners like . . . like they weren't even people."

"His father was no better. Lissa Marpetta is greedy, but she's never been like Allisander. She's content to follow his lead when it comes to maintaining control, however. A bit of a silent partner."

"It's all so . . . so cold."

"I know."

She glances up at me. "You said you and Harristan used to sneak out when you were children, but no one was sick then. Why did you start bringing medicine into the Wilds?"

"I didn't start with medicine." I study her in the darkness, the way the shadows trace her features. "That came later."

"Then how did it start?"

I shrug a little, but it's more to cover my own discomfort. None of these memories are good. The early ones strike the hardest, like the day my parents were killed.

"When Harristan first named me as King's Justice," I say quietly, "I was fifteen. I knew what the role required, of course, but in the beginning, the people weren't very sick. No one was stealing Moonflower petals. I was never forced to do anything truly terrible. I thought I could skip being cruel by being *creative*, like sentencing people to chisel a thousand bricks from the side of a mountain. I never had to order an execution. I never *wanted* to order an execution." I snort at my naivete. "I remember thinking that maybe we'd get lucky, that no one would ever do anything truly *bad*."

We walk in silence for a moment. She's patient, waiting for the rest of my story.

But she knows where I ended up. Maybe that's what's making all of this harder to say.

"More and more people began to get sick," I say, "and the Moonflower was found to cure the illness. Suddenly, it was a commodity." I draw a long breath, remembering the fights that would break out in the street over *rumor* of a few petals. "The entire country was falling apart. Homes were being raided, false cures were being spread, Moonflower was being stolen. We were getting reports from consuls daily, about violence in their sectors as people fought to get access to a cure." I shake my head, remembering one of the letters had a streak of blood down the side by the time it made its way to the palace. "It was . . . horrible."

"I remember," she whispers.

Of course she does. She was in the thick of it.

"Harristan had to take a stand," I say.

"Which means *you* had to take a stand."

I nod. I want to leave it there, but I still haven't answered her question. "The first—" I hesitate. "The *first* . . . was a man who'd killed a child. His name was Jarrod Kannoly." I don't remember all their names, but his will be forever etched into my memories. "He said he didn't mean to, that it was an accident, but . . ." I shrug and run a hand across the back of my neck. "Everyone says they *didn't mean to*. But a woman had bought enough Moonflower for her family, and the man heard about it. He grabbed the little girl and said he'd cut her throat if the woman didn't give him half."

Tessa is staring at me. "And he *did*?"

I nod. "It happened in the Royal Sector, so they brought him right to the Hold. He was coated in blood."

I still remember Harristan's voice when he heard about it. *Cory. We have to do something. The consuls are demanding action. We have to stop this.*

We have to do something.

Meaning *I* had to do something.

"It was awful," I whisper. There have been many since then, but the memory of that one is always the hardest. Maybe because it was the first. Maybe because of what he'd done. Maybe because of the knowledge that no matter what I did to him, it wouldn't bring that little girl back to her mother.

I shake off the emotion. "I snuck out of the palace that night," I say. "There was a part of me that wanted to run, to lose myself in the Wilds. But I couldn't leave Harristan. You know."

"I know."

"I had silver in my pockets, and I just started leaving it any-where it seemed it could do a bit of good. On windowsills, in door-ways, in the pockets of laundry left out to dry. As many coins as I could carry." I pause. "It was never enough. And I'd see the elites buying *so much*, so much more medicine than they needed."

She stares up at me. I stare back.

I take a long breath. "And then there was a night that I saw a man and his wife sneaking medicine, and at first, I was so angry." My jaw is tight. "I thought they were more smugglers. I didn't know what I was going to do, but I followed them out of the sector. And then—and then they met up with a girl—a girl about my age—"

She sucks in a breath. "You're talking about me. My parents."

I nod. "Yes. I saw what you were doing. I figured it out." I pause. "I wanted to help. I didn't know *how* to help."

She's still staring up at me, and I wish I could see that night through her eyes. I was keeping my distance, always so wary of getting tangled up with the night patrol, because I knew my actions would bring down Harristan. I remember how they dragged Tessa's father out of the shadows, how he fought back. How her mother fought back. The crossbows fired before I could even get to them. I remember dragging Tessa away, clamping my hand over her mouth, trapping us both behind a copse of trees. She was shaking against me, tears soaking into my hand.

"I did what I could," I say to her now, and my voice almost breaks. I have to take a shuddering breath. "I do what I can. And every day, I regret that it's never enough."

Moonlight sparks in her eyes, but I can't read her expression. We stand there in silence, sharing breath.

A twig snaps, and voices carry through the trees.

I swear, grabbing hold of her hand, pulling her off the path. "Listen."

Booted feet clomp along the path, with men speaking in low

tones. I can't tell if it's the night patrol, but we're deep in the wooded part of the Wilds, so it's unlikely—though not impossible, since we've doubled the number of patrolmen. I hold my breath as they draw close.

Then I recognize the men. Dorry Contrel and Timm Ballenger. Both middle-aged forge workers from Steel City who have wives at home and half a dozen children between them. Hardworking men who grunt and moan about the king and his brother, but worry more about feeding their families and keeping them healthy than anything else. Tessa and I have brought their families medicine in the past, when they haven't been able to manage food and tea leaves on their monthly wages.

It's unusual for them to be out at this time of night.

I think of Jarvis, the man in the cell when I visited with Allisander. I was surprised to find him caught among smugglers, too.

I strain to listen, but I can't make out much of what they're saying, and the words I do catch aren't incriminating. They're heading our way, though, toward their homes.

Once they're past, Tessa peers up at me in the darkness. The weight of everything I said hangs between us, but she only whispers, "Why are they out at this hour?"

I shake my head. "Let's see if we can find out."

We don't follow the men straight to their homes. If they were out and about for anything untoward, I don't want to spook them. Instead, we begin on the north side of the village. The first house is tiny, with hardly more space than our workshop. The roof leaks during the spring rains, but Alfred and Tris, the man and woman who live there, are in their late seventies and can't climb up there to do any repairs. Months ago, I brought them a stretch of sailcloth with their medicine and within a day, others from the village had nailed it across the worst spots. Tris repaid me with fresh eggs, which Tessa took and boiled and brought the next morning for us to share in the workshop.

It's been weeks since I was here, but it feels like years. My chest grows tight.

"I'll keep watch," Tessa whispers as we near the house. Her eyes are shadowed behind the mask, her lips a pale curve in the darkness. She must catch sight of my expression because she frowns. "What's wrong?"

Everything.

I shake my head slightly. "Nothing."

She squeezes my hand and slips into the shadows. I tap at the door lightly, three short raps followed by two more deliberate ones. It takes a moment, but eventually the door creaks open.

It's Tris. She looks like she's aged a decade. Her hair is thinner, her cheeks more sunken.

Her face breaks into a wide smile when she recognizes me. The joy and relief in her eyes is fleeting on her side, and gutting on mine.

"Weston," she whispers. "We've been so worried." She steps forward, her arms wide. No one reacts like this to my presence in the Royal Sector. Then her arms close around me, and it's like being embraced by a ghost.

"Tris," I say softly. "Have you been eating?"

"Here and there." She doesn't let go of me. "I forget sometimes without Alfred to remind me."

I go still. I knew our disappearance would have wide-reaching effects. I didn't expect it to strike the first house we visited. "Alfred is gone."

She finally draws back and nods. Her eyes well.

"Here," I say, gesturing toward the room behind her. I sweep my gaze across the room, wondering if I can get her to eat something now. "Sit."

She hobbles into the room, dabbing at her eyes. She eases into a rocking chair beside the bed.

There's a heel of bread on the table, and I bring it to her, then hang her kettle over the fire.

"I'm sorry," I say quietly. It doesn't feel like enough.

It never feels like enough, but tonight, I feel it more acutely.

"It's been about a week," she says, and a tear streaks down her face. "I didn't want him to go."

I drop to a knee in front of her and pull an apple from my bag, pressing it into her hands. People in the Wilds tend to look out for each other, so I'm sure she hasn't been starving, but the kitchen pantry looks barren. "I'll try to bring more food the next time I come."

I've fallen back into my role as Weston Lark, as if no time at all has passed, so I say the words automatically.

I'm a fool. There might not *be* a next time.

She squeezes my hand. "You've always been such a kind boy." She swipes away a tear with the back of her hand. "Alfred will be sorry he missed you. I thought you might have been captured, but he always says you've got a good head on your shoulders. Is young Tessa with you?"

Wait. "What?"

"Tessa? I always thought she might be sweet on you. She hasn't been caught by the night patrol, has she?" She wrings her hands.

"No, I— Tessa is fine. But did you say Alfred would be—" I break off. I must have misheard her.

But Tris nods. "Sorry he missed you. I was so worried when I heard of the captures during the raids yesterday, but Lochlan said everyone from our village was accounted for, and Alfred wouldn't be in direct danger."

I stare at her. "Alfred isn't dead?"

"What?" She blinks. "Oh, I hope not!" She wrings her hands again. "Have you heard news?"

I can't tell if she's addled or if we're speaking of different things.

"Tris," I say as gently as I can. "Did Alfred die of the fever?"

"Oh, goodness no. When we agreed to help with the raids, Lochlan said the Benefactors would give us enough medicine to survive, and he was right. We're always a bit tight for food, but we've made it work. It was such a blessing, after you and Tessa had to stop coming. Look." She hands me a small pouch.

Lochlan. The name tugs at my memory, but I can't place it. I take the pouch and tug at the strings. Dried petals are gray and white at the bottom of the bag.

"Take it," says Tris. "I have plenty, thanks to Alfred."

"Wes." Tessa hisses at the door. "The night patrol."

"Get back into bed," I say to Tris. I pocket the pouch of petals. "I'll be back when I can."

I'm out the door and in the shadows with Tessa before I draw a full breath. My thoughts are churning with what Tris said, but I can't make sense of any of it.

The night patrol clomps between the trees a short distance away, and we crouch together in the darkness against the back wall of the house, huddling against the stacked stones of the chimney. We always stay close when we hide, but tonight I'm very aware of her breathing, of the scent of her skin, of the way her shoulder brushes against mine.

I should move away. I should harden my eyes and turn off the churning emotions in my chest. I should have left her in the palace and done this alone.

I can't even convince myself. I can't imagine ever doing this without her at my side.

I don't dare speak. I wish I could share my thoughts.

Forgive me.

Please, Tessa.

I would give anything.

"You there!" a man shouts, and I jump and shove Tessa behind me, pressing back against the wall of the house.

But we haven't been discovered. Three patrolmen have crossbows trained on a boy with a pack a short distance away. He can't be more than thirteen or fourteen, and I suddenly realize I know him. His name is Forrest, and he lives with his parents on the far side of the village. His eyes are wide, his cheeks stark white in the moonlight. He's right at the edge of the tree line, and he must have walked right out in front of them.

I remember Mistress Kendall crying over Gillis, and I wonder if there will be another mother sobbing over her son, getting slaughtered in the darkness when she screams at the night patrol.

One of the patrolmen grabs Forrest's satchel and yanks it open. "A bit young to be smuggling, aren't you, boy?"

At my back, Tessa is breathing shallowly, her fingers in a death grip on mine now.

I've never interfered with the night patrol as Wes. The risk was always too great. Tessa and I hide, and we do what we can.

Tonight, the stakes feel different.

Forrest swallows and stammers, "I'm not—I'm not—I'm not—"

"We know what you are." The patrolman lifts his crossbow. Another grabs the boy's arm.

Tessa gasps. Forrest screams. "No! Da! Help me!"

I burst from our hiding place. "Stop!" I shout. "Stop!"

One of the patrolmen looks my way, but the other doesn't hesitate. He pulls the trigger on his crossbow. I leap for the boy.

Forrest falls when I slam into him, and for a moment, I'm worried that I've been too late, that I've just tackled a corpse. But my arm burns like fire, and Forrest is gasping against the underbrush.

I ignore the pain in my arm and spring to my feet, only to find a crossbow leveled at my chest. "Good," grunts the patrolman. "I'll get a bonus for catching two of you."

Then he pulls the trigger.

CHAPTER THIRTY

Tessa

Everything is happening too fast. I've got a rock in my hand and I'm racing at the patrolman, but my thoughts are a tangled mess of panic and horror. Then I'm leaping, jumping, swinging the rock as hard as I can. I hear the *swick* of the crossbow, then the crunch of my rock against the patrolman's head. He goes down.

A shadow rolls into me, and suddenly Corrick has the fallen patrolman's crossbow, and he's reaching for an arrow.

He's not going to be fast enough. There are three of them, and the other is already pointing, ready to shoot.

"No!" screams Forrest, surging off the ground to tackle the patrolman around the waist.

The man stumbles back a few feet, but Forrest isn't big enough to bring him down. The patrolman pulls a dagger. "You filthy brat—"

Corrick shoots him in the face.

The man jerks and goes down. I gasp, choking on my breath.

But there's still one more, and he's managed to reload. Corrick is fighting for another arrow, but his movement is slow and clumsy. He'll never be fast enough.

I yank the dagger from my boot, the gift Prince Corrick gave me during our carriage ride. I know the worst spots for a dagger to hit, and I don't bother to aim carefully. I plunge the dagger into the patrolman's neck. He collapses.

The silence is sudden and weighted.

Forrest is panting, his breath coming in rapid, panicked gasps.

I might be doing the same thing. My fingers are sticky with blood.

Corrick finishes loading the crossbow, and he seizes another two arrows to shove under his belt. "Forrest," he says, and his voice is shockingly quiet after what just happened.

The boy's gasps have turned to dry heaving, and his hands press tightly against his abdomen.

"Forrest," Corrick says again. His voice is cool and authoritative, which shouldn't be a surprise, but it is. Now I know why Wes was always so calm in the face of violence. He puts a hand against the boy's shoulder. "The bodies need to be burned. Is your da home? Strip their uniforms and hide them. If anyone sees the smoke, say they died of the fever—"

"I'll help him."

The male voice comes from behind us, and Corrick whirls, the crossbow raised.

A young man has come through the trees, but he sees the crossbow and he lifts his hands. He's wearing a hooded cloak, so I can't make out much of his features in the dark, but his arm is thickly bandaged, the fingers stiff and swollen. He doesn't look afraid. If anything, he looks long-suffering, like he's used to weapons being pointed at him.

"Go ahead," he says to Forrest, nodding toward the village. "Get your da to help drag them to the pit."

The boy nods quickly and bolts.

Corrick hasn't moved. The crossbow is leveled with deadly aim.

"I'm Lochlan," the other man says. He offers half a shrug. "You can put down the bow. We're all doing the same thing." His eyes narrow. "Or were you looking to steal the boy's pack?"

"No." Corrick still hasn't looked away, and his voice is very low, very quiet. "Tessa. Are you all right?"

I haven't given a moment's thought to myself, and I'm frozen by the unexpected tension that seems to have overtaken this small clearing. "I—yes."

"Tessa?" says Lochlan. His tone is lazy, musing. "Would that make you Wes?"

"Help Forrest get rid of the bodies," says Corrick. "We have rounds to make."

Lochlan keeps his hands up, but he moves closer, peering at *Wes*. "I've heard a lot of stories, but rumor said you were killed."

"Still alive," says Corrick. He doesn't lower the crossbow.

"There's something . . . familiar about you," says Lochlan. "Have we met?"

"No." Corrick jerks his head toward the trees. "Tessa. Head for our place."

I don't understand what's happening, but I can hear the urgency in his voice. I don't want to be unarmed, though. I have no idea how to use a crossbow, but I reach for the dagger and pull it free. It jerks out of the patrolman's neck with a horrific squelching sound.

Lochlan's eyes follow the motion. "That's a fancy dagger."

Something about the way he says it feels dangerous. "Stolen," I say quickly.

Too quickly. His eyes narrow further.

I think of the prince cautioning me in the room of the palace. *You're too earnest.*

Lochlan takes another step closer. His eyes have shifted back to Corrick, lit with careful scrutiny.

"Tessa," says Corrick. "Go. Now. I'll follow."

I'm not sure what's happening, but I don't want to leave him. My heart beats hard in my chest.

But Lochlan takes a step back, tossing sandy hair back from his eyes. Any tension drains from the air. "Go ahead," he says. "If you're leaving the boy's pack, I've got no trouble with you." He glances at the bodies and spits at the night patrol, then looks right back at Corrick. "I'll clean up your mess."

Corrick doesn't move.

I reach for his arm, and it's only then that I realize a wide swath of his shirt is blacker than the rest, and the sleeve is torn. Was he hit? I don't see an arrow. But now I see that his hand is trembling, and his jaw looks more pale than it should be. "Wes," I say. "Wes, come on."

For an instant, I don't think he's going to follow. But then he steps past Lochlan, giving the other man a wide berth, and we let the darkness and the trees swallow us up.

—+—

Corrick's manner is tense and prickly, and he keeps casting glances over his shoulder, so I stay silent and close. He holds the crossbow assuredly, like he's ready to fire a bolt at any moment. I've never seen him hold a weapon.

I've never seen him kill anyone, for that matter. Not like this.

I saw the aftereffects of what he had to do in the Hold, but that was different. *This* is different. The night patrol would have killed that boy. They would have killed Corrick and me, too.

I swallow, tasting blood on my tongue. I don't know if I've bitten my lip or if it's just the scent in the air. My hands are still sticky with the patrolman's blood.

I'm trying not to think about the fact that I killed someone, too.

I try to force the image out of my brain, but it doesn't want to shake loose. It's too tangled up with the sound of the boy screaming for his father. Did we do the wrong thing? The right thing? I have no idea.

We reach a small clearing, and Corrick puts up a hand for me to stop. We're not far from the workshop now, but I'm savvy enough to know he thinks we might have been followed, so I stay silent and still while we wait.

Minutes tick by. I study the tear in his sleeve. His arm is awash with blood, and he hasn't let go of the crossbow, so it must be mostly superficial. Still, he needs a bandage, and maybe a sling. I remember the way his fingers trembled when he held the weapon upright.

Then I realize I'm being foolish. He can't have a sling. How would Prince Corrick explain that away?

Everything happened so fast. *Too* fast.

Finally, an eternity later, Corrick nods to me, and we stride across the clearing. The crossbow hangs at his side now, in the hand of his good arm. His shoulders are a bit less tense. Moonlight traces every inch of him, though, and I can see the hard set of his jaw, the tension that hasn't quite escaped his eyes.

"Who was he?" I say softly, because it's obvious that Corrick has some history with Lochlan.

"A prisoner in the Hold," he says, his voice barely more than a rasp on the night air. "I broke his wrist."

I swallow. Every time I want to forget who he is, fate seems determined to remind me. "Why?"

"He was trying to kill Consul Sallister." He pauses. "He was one of the three who escaped. During the riots."

"Oh." The sound eases out of me as I work that through in my head. "And he's smuggling again."

"I spoke with Tris. Alfred is doing something for him. And we saw the other men in the woods." Corrick sighs tightly. "I wanted to talk to others, to see if I could find out more."

I consider the way Lochlan watched me pull the dagger out of the patrolman's neck. "You think he recognized you?"

"I think he was *close* to recognizing me."

"Does it matter? You said no one would believe me if I accused you—"

"I'm not worried about him accusing me." He breaks off and tugs at the brim of his hat, then winces. "You know who I am, Tessa. If I'm caught by smugglers—"

"They'd kill you."

He snorts. "No. I'd wish for them to kill me. They'd torture me and use me against Harristan."

He says it so simply, while a chill grips my spine at the thought.

I hadn't even considered. I remember the night he "died," how he made a comment that he was surprised I wasn't waiting to turn him in to the night patrol. A part of him really *was* worried. Now I see why he was so tense, thinking Lochlan might have followed.

Corrick looks down at me. "I'm worried more about what they'd do to you."

A shiver runs through me.

"I don't like being out in the open," he says. "Let's get to the workshop."

The workshop is cold from the night air, with a thin layer of dust on everything. It's clearly been left untouched since we were last here. He drags wood from the pile and tosses it into the hearth one-handed, which makes me think his arm is bothering him more than he's letting on. He strikes a match and lights the fire while I use the broom to get rid of the worst of the cobwebs and dust. It's not long before the workshop is warm, lit with a glow.

Wes leans against the table, his eyes shadowed under the brim of his hat. The crossbow sits right beside him.

Not Wes. Corrick.

I clear my throat and look away. "Do you want me to take a look at your arm?"

"The arrow clipped me. I'm fine." He tosses a small pouch onto the table. "Tris said the Benefactors have been distributing medicine."

I pick it up and shake it out. Gray and white petals flutter to the table, each one long and curved, though some are shorter, with a bit of a sharper angle at the top. I frown, but at my side, Wes is flexing his arm like it hurts.

I roll my eyes and step over to him, ignoring the petals. "Don't be foolish. I've been watching you favor this for the last twenty minutes." I tear the gap in his sleeve wider. The arrow sliced through the side of his upper arm, and he likely needs stitches, but I don't have any supplies here.

"Take your shirt off," I say. "I have some muslin. I'll wrap it."

He removes his hat, then drags his shirt over his head, and again he's shirtless in front of me. I've seen the show before, but he's got the mask on, and now it's like *Wes* disrobing, and for a long, awkward moment, my voice doesn't want to work.

I focus on the wound, fetching water from our rain barrel to clean the blood away gently. I listen to him breathing, inhaling the scent of him in the warm closeness of the workshop.

This is too intimate. Words need to happen.

"Where did you learn to shoot like that?" I say.

"I'm the brother to the king, Tessa." He says this like it's amusing.

"You've never interfered with the night patrol before."

That draws him up short, and he looks away. "It's . . . different now." He pauses. "And they're not supposed to slaughter people in the streets. It's part of why I was so angry at Allisander for having his guards rough up the last round of captives. It's one thing for me to issue an order of punishment, but I don't torture people for the sport of it. My guards in the Hold aren't cruel. The night patrol shouldn't be either. Forrest is a boy. They could have arrested him."

"Well. You saw what they did to Mistress Kendall."

"She attacked them."

I try to remember. All that comes to mind is her grief. Does that matter? I can't tell.

My parents attacked them. I remember that.

It's the same to the night patrol.

I dry his arm carefully and tear long strips of muslin to make a bandage. "No matter what you *say*, if *your* actions are cruel, those who act on your behalf will do the same."

I expect him to deny it, or to offer some kind of rebuttal, but he doesn't.

Instead, he says, "So I've seen."

I meet his eyes. Cool blue stares back at me, no deceit or cunning in those depths.

"You make me want to do better," he says suddenly, and his voice is thick with emotion, so I go still. "You make me wish Weston Lark was real, because you will never look at me the way you look at him. I don't know how to fix everything I've done wrong, Tessa. I don't even know if I *can*. But I want to try."

I don't know either. And no matter what he does as King's Justice, it won't cure the fevers. It won't fix access to the Moonflower. It won't stop the cries for revolution. He and Harristan have set things in motion that may never stop. Or maybe the execution of their parents did. Either way, the people of Kandala will never go back to the way they were before all of this happened.

But then I realize he's not just talking about fixing everything for the people of Kandala.

He's talking about fixing everything for *me*.

I tie off the bandage, but my fingertips linger on the muscle of his bicep.

"Does it hurt?" I whisper, and I'm not entirely talking about the wound to his arm.

"Very much."

Neither is he.

I lift a hand, pressing it to his cheek, and his breath hitches, just a little. His skin is warm against my palm, just a little rough. My thumb brushes along the curve of his lip, and I swear he stops breathing. My fingers tease at the edge of the mask the way I've done in the past.

I wait for him to duck away, to hide, but he doesn't move. My fingertips slip under the edge of the fabric. It lifts by an inch, then two, then reveals one blue eye smudged with kohl.

His gaze never leaves mine. His lips part, and a breath escapes.

And then he reaches up to tear the rest of the mask away, and I'm left facing Prince Corrick in the tight warmth of our workshop.

The mask drops on the table beside the crossbow. His chest is rising and falling rapidly, and his hands look like they want to reach for me, but he's waiting. For me.

I've spent so much time wondering how a terrible man like Prince Corrick could spend hours secretly helping the people of Kandala, when I've been looking at it backward all along. I should have been wondering how a man who wants so badly to be kind and good, to do *right*, would be able to hide the truest parts of himself away to support his brother and protect his people.

"Hello," I say softly. "Corrick."

A light sparks in his eyes. "I don't think I've heard you say my name before."

"Corrick," I say again, and his eyes close for a moment while he takes a long breath.

I press a palm to his cheek again, and now there's no mask between us. His eyes flick open, and he's closer suddenly. I don't know if that's his doing or mine.

"Corrick," I whisper.

His hand lands on my waist, very lightly, very gently. The other strokes a line across my cheek, and I remember I'm still wearing a mask.

He gives it the slightest tug. "May I?"

I hold my breath and nod.

He's slow and delicate and it's torture. We're close enough that I can feel the heat of his body. He unties the knot, and my mask slips away.

He leans in to pull the cord that keeps my braid in place, and my hair slips across my shoulders. His breath caresses my ear. "Say it again," he whispers.

"Corrick," I exhale. His thumb strokes across my lower lip, and my breath shudders.

He's so close that my fingertips find the bare skin of his chest, and it lights a fire in my belly. "Cory?" I try.

A low sound escapes his throat. "Lord, Tessa." His hands lock on my waist, and his lips find mine.

His touch was so slow and tentative that I expect his kiss to be the same, but his mouth is sure and determined. When my lips part, his tongue teases at mine, drawing a gasp that he inhales. He tastes like cinnamon and sugar, and my hands stroke up the length of his chest to find his broad shoulders, his sloping neck, his muscled arms. I expect to feel hesitant, the way I did in the palace when he almost kissed me, but I don't.

Because this is different. This is our space. He's not Wes, because there is no Wes, not really. He's Corrick. He's *always* been Corrick. Everything we've done together is a part of who he is.

Without warning, his hands close on my waist tightly, and I'm lifted to settle on the table. My legs fall apart, and he steps into me, my skirts bunching around him, his mouth finding mine again.

He's closer now, his hands freer. I explore the warm stretch of his waist, the curved muscle of his back. His lips drift down my jaw, his teeth dragging at the sensitive skin below my ear, nibbling along my neck. Every nerve ending in my body is firing, and I want him closer. My hands slide along the waist of his trousers, the skin there softer than silk.

One of his hands finds my knee, his fingers drifting along the outside of my thigh. I suck in a breath and pull him closer, and he buries his face in my neck to make a sound that's very much like a low growl. Our hips meet, and I cling to him, my fingers digging into his skin. His hand skims higher along my thigh, until I see stars and shiver. This time when he kisses me, he's slow and sure, one arm holding me against him so tightly that I can feel his heart beat against mine.

"Tessa," he whispers, and my name sounds like a plea. "Oh, Tessa."

"Say it again," I tease, and I feel his smile against my lips.

The alarm in the Royal Sector pierces the night, and I freeze. So does Corrick.

His breathing is shuddering. I have to close my eyes.

"They've caught someone," I whisper.

Someone he'll have to deal with. Someone he might have to execute. I pull my hands to my chest.

After a moment, Corrick's gentle fingers settle on my wrists. His lips brush against my temple.

He sighs. I sigh.

"We need to finish our rounds," he says. He finds his shirt and slips his arms through the sleeves. "We'll head toward Artis and see what we can discover before daybreak."

And after that, we'll have to go back. He'll need to be the King's Justice.

I don't need to say it. He knows it, too. The disarmed look is gone from his eye, and cool Prince Corrick looks down at me.

He scoops me off the table, setting me on my feet. He draws my hand to his mouth and kisses it. Then he grabs his mask and ties it in place. "Yours too," he says.

I rebraid my hair, trying to ignore the tightening of my throat. My fingers are trembling and don't want to work right.

Maybe he can tell, because Corrick takes the ends of my mask in his fingers and ties it gently.

"You were right," he says. "I should have listened to you in the beginning. When it comes to revolution, we should be riding at the front."

I widen my eyes as my head spins. "You mean as outlaws?"

"No. I mean as Prince Corrick and his brilliant apothecary. Weston Lark can't step out of the shadows." He pauses. "But the King's Justice can."

My heart skips.

"Don't worry," he says softly. "I'll be better." Then he drops one last kiss on my lips. "We'll pick that up later," he says in that rough-growl voice, and goose bumps spring up everywhere. I shiver as he reaches for the door to swing it wide.

On the other side, backed by eight men, stands Lochlan, his crossbow pointed right at Corrick.

CHAPTER THIRTY-ONE

Corrick

I knew I should have killed this man when I had the chance.

If I were alone, I'd fight. I'd run. I have a dagger and my treble hook. I could bury the weapon in Lochlan's belly and escape into the woods, then be over the wall in the blink of an eye.

But I'm not alone. At my side, Tessa's breathing is quick and shallow, and she's shifted closer to me.

It seems unfair that fate would put her in my arms at last and then deliver this fool to our door.

I glance at the crossbow and then back up at Lochlan's face. "You said you didn't have a problem with me."

"I don't have a problem with some bleeding heart named Wes. I do have a slight issue with the King's Justice, Prince Corrick."

"So do I," I say easily.

He snorts, then glances between me and Tessa. "I knew I'd heard your voice before. It took me a bit, but that dagger was just too fancy. No way that didn't come out of the palace." His expression darkens. "Tricking your people into thinking someone was helping them? You're even more disgusting than I thought."

I ignore him and look at the other men. "You know me. You know us. Put down your weapons and walk away."

The men exchange glances. Lochlan knows who I am, but I can feel their uncertainty in the air. They've known Wes and Tessa for years. Thunder rolls overhead, and rain begins to spit between the trees.

Lochlan keeps the crossbow trained on my chest, but he looks at Tessa. "Who is he?"

"He's Wes." She's such a terrible liar. Her voice is breathy and afraid. "Weston Lark."

"Tell the truth or I'll shoot him."

"He's Wes! I promise, he's Wes!"

"You're a liar, and you don't matter." He turns the crossbow on her.

"No!" I shout. Without thought, I tackle him. Even though one of his arms is injured, he's stronger than I expect. We roll in the wet underbrush, grappling for control, until I hear Tessa scream.

It's all the distraction Lochlan needs. He grabs the crossbow and bears down. "They'll kill her," he says. "Now tell the truth."

Rage colors my vision. I try to shove Lochlan off me, but now he has me pinned. Somewhere behind me, Tessa squeals, and I hear a punch land.

"Fine!" I shout. "I'm Prince Corrick," I grind out. "I'm the King's Justice."

"No," gasps Tessa, and I wonder if they're choking her. But then she says, "Corrick, no."

All the ways she said my name, and this time breaks my heart.

"Surrender," says Lochlan, and in his eyes, I can see the promise of everything they'll do to her if I don't.

I lift my hands, and it costs me everything. "I surrender."

—+—

We're forced to walk through the woods, heading east this time, which means we're not going back to the village where we first met Lochlan. My hands have been bound, the ropes tied so tightly that my fingers are already tingling no matter how much I flex against the bonds. The point of a crossbow keeps jabbing me in the back, and I can tell it's intentional. I grit my teeth against saying anything, because they've got Tessa walking somewhere behind me, and Lochlan already made it clear that if I don't do what he says, they'll take it out on her.

He's the one jabbing me with the crossbow.

Rain falls steadily through the trees now, turning the footing slick and challenging, especially in the dark. Especially with my hands tied. My pulse beats at a rapid clip, sending little spikes of anger and fear through my bloodstream. I pray for the night patrol to find us.

Then again, maybe that would be worse. I don't look like Prince Corrick right now, and I don't know every single patrolman in Kandala. They were going to shoot that boy in the village. I have no doubt they'd shoot me for daring to impersonate the king's brother.

And if they did believe me, being found among smugglers couldn't be explained away.

I don't know why I'm even thinking like this. I know what men like Lochlan will do with me.

"You can't possibly think you'll be able to collect a ransom," I say. "Harristan will never yield to your demands."

"I don't care about a ransom." He jabs me so hard that I stumble and nearly go down.

The rain intensifies, beating down, making me shiver against my will. I try to listen for Tessa behind me, but the hiss of rain through the trees makes it impossible to hear anything that's not right next to me. I peer up at the sky through the trees, and it's pitch-dark with clouds and rainfall. Sunrise is still hours away, but I rather doubt I'll be climbing that rope back into my quarters.

I hope Quint returns to his rooms. I hope that he claims ignorance.

I hope Harristan doesn't grant this man one single request.

I hope they let Tessa go.

I hope. I hope.

My father once said that hope can be powerful, but it's worthless without action. If Lochlan doesn't want money, what else could he want? A pardon? He has to know that would never work.

"Tell me what you want," I grind out.

"I want you to shut up."

"You'll never get anything out of the king without my participation."

He punches me right between the shoulder blades, and this time I stumble freely, slamming face-first into the mud so hard that it rattles my jaw. I roll to my side, but he's already got the crossbow pointed down at me. "All I *want* is for the King's Justice to stop sentencing people to death." He glares at me. "Guess I'll get what I wanted."

"Corrick!" Tessa shouts worriedly from somewhere in the darkness behind him. "Corrick, are you all right?"

I spit blood at the ground. "Oh, I'm doing splendidly, thank you."

Lochlan kicks me in the stomach. I don't even see it coming, but that doesn't help. His boot plows into my midsection, and I'm suddenly choking on nothing. Stars fill in my vision. I don't even realize that Lochlan has grabbed hold of my shirt until he slams me back against the ground. I'm wheezing in the rain, blood on my tongue.

He holds me there, his eyes like fire as he glares down at me. "I should just kill you right now," he says, his voice low and cruel.

"I should have killed you when you attacked the consul." I load my gaze with every ounce of brutal promise I can muster. "I should have killed you on the dais before the crowd. I should have killed you in the village an hour ago."

I expect him to step back and pull the trigger on his crossbow, or maybe kick me again, but he doesn't. His eyes narrow. "Why didn't you?"

Because I don't want to be a killer.

I don't say it. I don't think I need to.

"Hey," says a man behind him. "Lochlan. What are we doing?"

Lochlan lets go of the crossbow to hang at his side, then grabs my arm with his uninjured one. "Get up," he says. "Walk."

I get up. I walk.

I've lost my hat in the scuffle, and half my face is slicked with mud. Something must have broken the skin, because every drop of rain stings when it strikes my cheek. The mask has twisted the tiniest bit, narrowing my field of vision by half an inch. It's enough to add another dose of misery when everything is awful.

"Let Tessa go," I say.

"I told you to shut up."

"You must want something from Harristan," I say. "If you let her go, I can intercede for you—"

"This is what's wrong with all of you in that sector," he sneers. "You think everything is about money. You think everything is about what you can get."

"Again," I say, "you're a *smuggler.*"

"Because I had no choice. None of us have a choice if we want to survive."

"Ah, so you were raiding shipments out of the goodness of your heart. Silver had nothing to do with it?"

He jabs me in the back with his crossbow. "*Shut up,*" he growls.

"No matter what you do to me," I say, "you've attacked too many runs. You've spooked the consuls. You attacked the sector. They'll stop supplying Moonflower. You'll have nothing."

"I'll have plenty. We'll *all* have plenty."

There's a note of certainty in his voice that gives me pause. Who is funding this? Who is distributing medicine and silver to such an extent that the people are so willing to risk their lives?

Or have people grown so desperate that they have no choice?

I consider the men at my back. None of these people are skilled strategists, not even Lochlan. If he were, he'd be planning to use me to force Harristan into something. He'd be using Tessa to force *me.* I questioned Lochlan weeks ago, when he was first captured, and even then, I didn't get the sense that they were well organized.

I honestly don't get it now.

That must mean he's taking me to someone. Someone who *is* planning this. Funding this.

Someone who will have a plan for how to use me. Even if it's one of the consuls, they'll know what to do with leverage.

The thought should be chilling, but instead, it's somewhat stabilizing. "Who are the Benefactors?" I say. "What have they promised you?"

"No one needs to pay me to do this."

I don't believe that for a second. I try to think who might be behind all of this. Paying in silver and medicine wouldn't be cheap. Few consuls would be able to manage it. Jonas was desperate for silver to build his precious bridge, so I can't see him spending it to fund rebels. Leander Craft is the consul of Steel City, but he's always been rather conservative politically, never taking a stand against Harristan. He doesn't like the idea of unrest, especially because his manufacturing and steelworkers supply much of the entire country. He has the money, but . . . he simply doesn't seem like the type. Truly, the only people with both the money and the resources to fund raids would be Allisander Sallister or Lissa Marpetta, and they've been after me to stop the attacks.

Harristan and I have been watching two unlikely consuls work together for weeks, though.

Consuls who just asked for more funds.

Roydan and Arella.

But . . . why? Hurting Allisander hurts us all. Surely they can't hate him *so* much. It's not possible to hate him more than I do, and I manage to keep from destroying the entire country's medicinal supply because of it.

A whistle splits the night. Lanterns twinkle between the trees. I don't know where we are, but we're still in the Wilds.

"It's Lochlan," my captor shouts. "We've brought you all a present."

He jabs me in the back, and I stumble forward, into a clearing strung with canvas tents and crudely built lean-tos. There must be dozens, if not hundreds. People begin emerging into the rain, some with lanterns, some with nothing more than sticks or axes, shovels, and brooms. They're dirty and tired, from what I can see, but no one is coughing. No one is sick.

Many—*many*—are familiar.

"It's Wes!" calls a little girl named Abigale. "Wes and Tessa! They're not dead!"

Her mother picks her up, shushing her.

More people begin to spill from the tents and shelters, until we're surrounded.

No Roydan and Arella.

We've brought you all a present.

Tessa is shoved into place beside me, and I can hear her breathing shaking.

"Are you hurt?" I say. "Tessa, are you hurt?"

Her eyes peer up at me from behind her mask, which is as sodden as her hair and clothes, but I see no injuries. "No. No, I'm not hurt."

Lochlan walks up to me and rips the mask off my head. It takes blood and a clump of hair with it. One of the other men pull the mask off Tessa's head, but he's not as rough about it.

"Sorry, Miss Tessa," he says, and his voice is low and repentant.

"It's all right," she whispers, but she's wrong, because nothing is.

My heart is hammering in my chest. Lochlan is glaring at me, and nothing about his posture is repentant.

"Tell me what you want," I say to him.

He spits in my face.

I have a limit. I surge forward and slam my forehead into his.

He stumbles back. Someone grabs my arm. Tessa says, "Corrick, no!"

A gasp goes up from the crowd.

Lochlan finds his footing, and he wastes no time. He strides forward and punches me right in the stomach.

My hands are still bound, and I take the hit fully. It brings me to my knees, but someone's got a grip on my arm, so I don't go down. I can't breathe. The trees spin.

"Please," Tessa is begging. "Please stop this. Please."

"You heard her," Lochlan yells to the crowd. "You heard his name. You know who he is."

That gasp turns into a nervous murmur.

"He's been tricking you," Lochlan shouts. "He's been pretending to help you, while using your trust to execute more of you."

"No," I rasp. "No."

"No!" cries Tessa.

Lochlan punches me again. I swear I hear a rib crack. I don't realize I'm falling until my face slams into the sodden leaves underfoot. I cough and taste blood.

"Who's lost someone to the night patrol?" Lochlan shouts. "Who's lost someone to the Hold?"

A few cries go up from the crowd. Lochlan kicks me in the shoulder.

I was so stupid. I was so sure this was part of some mastermind's plan.

I was sure they'd want something from Harristan. From me.

They do, but it's not something I'm going to enjoy giving.

"Let her go," I spit out. "Please, Lochlan. She had no idea."

"She had no idea!" he cries. "Do any of you believe that? Do you believe she's innocent? They've been working together for years."

"To help!" Tessa cries. "To help!"

"He's the King's Justice," yells Lochlan. "You've all heard of the things he's done, haven't you? Done to people you love? To people you care about?"

"Yes!" they cry in return. The clearing seems brighter.

He's got the crowd.

I close my eyes. Maybe this is fitting. Maybe this is what I deserve.

"You know what he's done," yells Lochlan. "So let's give him a dose of his own justice."

The crowd roars, and the pain begins.

CHAPTER THIRTY-TWO

Tessa

When the crowd surges forward, I'm sure they're going to attack us both, but their target is Corrick, only Corrick. My hands are bound, my fingers numb, and someone has a grip on my arms to hold me upright. My throat feels raw, and I don't know how long I've been screaming. My ears hurt from all the shouting. I can't see him. Too many bodies are in the way. I can hear them, though, the sound of punches and kicks. The sounds of people calling for vicious violence.

This is worse than the riot in front of the gates. This is worse than the execution.

Is it because it's Corrick? Is it because I know him? Does that make me weak?

A week ago, if Prince Corrick had been dropped on the ground at my feet, I might have been a part of the mob.

Now, I have no way to help him. Begging hasn't worked. Screaming hasn't worked. They know what they're doing.

I spot a woman in the crowd. Her name is Bree. She has five sons, all under the age of ten. She was afraid to take medicine from us until her husband died of the fever and one of her boys started coughing the next day.

She's behind some of the men, her fists clenched, her eyes clouded with fear and anger.

"Bree!" I call desperately, and she looks at me in surprise before turning away.

I shout at her anyway. "Bree! Stop this. Wes helped you. *Prince Corrick* helped you. He used to let your boys tackle him in the yard. You begged for medicine after David died, and of course we brought it to you."

She's looking at me again. She's stopped trying to surge forward.

"He did what he could," I yell. I look for someone else I recognize. "Niall. Niall—stop. Listen. When you broke your arm last winter, Wes spent two hours splitting firewood in the dark because a storm was coming. *Prince Corrick* did that."

He hesitates, his eyes finding mine.

I look for someone else. "Percy Rose! Percy! Remember when your wife was up coughing all night, and Wes and I sat with you until it eased? That was *Prince Corrick*." I search the crowd. "Yavette! You were worried you wouldn't live until your wedding! Wes and I made you take the medicine every day. *Prince Corrick* did that. And now you're expecting a baby!"

I don't know if the shouts are quieting. I don't know if I'm making a difference. I keep searching. I keep begging. My tears keep flowing.

"Zafra! Prince Corrick used to bring you squares of fabric for your winter quilts. Norman! Prince Corrick used to give you an extra dose for your sweetheart in Artis. Warley! Prince Corrick helped you fix that door when the hinges rusted off."

"Da!" shouts a little voice. "Da, he stopped the night patrol."

Forrest. The boy we rescued earlier. My throat chokes on a sob.

His father is a burly forge worker named Earle, and I find him in the crowd. He grabs the arm of a man who looked to be ready to throw a punch. He's big enough to force his way through the people, shoving them back, shoving them away. His voice is bigger than mine. Louder than mine.

"He saved my boy," he says, his voice grave. "And he saved a lot of you, too. They both did."

The shouts have dimmed. Rain drizzles from the sky. Everyone is mud-splattered and breathing heavily.

And staring at me.

I can't look for Corrick. I'm terrified of what I'll find. There are so many of them, and he's only one man.

I steel my nerve. "I know—" My voice breaks, and I gasp and try again. "I know Prince Corrick has done a lot of awful things, but he's also done a lot of good. He risked so much to help you. To help all of you. He's not an awful man. The fevers are awful. The situation is awful. This—" I have to take a deep breath. "This . . . what you're doing . . . this is awful. He helped you. I helped you. Please stop. Please."

"Cut her loose," says a voice, and to my surprise, it's Lochlan.

A knife brushes my skin, and the ropes fall away. No one grips my arms.

I don't want to look. I have to look.

As if following my gaze, people step aside, and there he is, a pile on the ground. It's dark, and his clothes are torn, blood stark against the paleness of his skin. Half his face is shadowed with dirt and blood and bruises. There's a laceration across the bridge of his nose that narrowly missed his eye and bisected his eyebrow. Blood has caked on his eyelashes. I thought there was no way he could look worse than the way I found him in the crumbling ruins of the Hold, but I was wrong.

I stagger toward him and drop to my knees in the mud. "Corrick. *Corrick.*"

He doesn't move. His eyes are closed, but he's breathing—thank goodness. It's a rough and raspy wheeze. He's half curled, his body twisted in a way that makes me worry that his spine is broken, and his hands are still bound, his wrists raw and bleeding. His fingers are pale blue, and I think he's shivering.

"Cut him loose," I call. "Someone—please—"

"Here." Earle drops to a knee beside me, a knife in hand. When he cuts Corrick's wrists free, his arm flops limply, slapping into the ground with a sickening sound.

I press a hand to his cheek. My fingers are trembling. "Corrick. Can you hear me? Open your eyes."

His eyelids flutter, and he makes a low sound in his chest, but his eyes don't open, and he doesn't move.

I don't know what to do. My breath hitches. I look up at the faces—most familiar, some not—around me. Some still hold weapons. Most look bewildered, though some are regretful. Some are ashamed. Some are doubtful.

Some are cynical, including Lochlan, and that freezes my tongue on any requests for help. I don't want to give anyone an excuse to start beating him again.

I can't carry him back to the palace on my back. I can't carry him back to the palace at all. Not like this.

Earle looks up at the crowd. "Percy. Help me carry him." He looks at me. "We've got a girl here who's been patching people up."

They say it as if Corrick has a little scratch, instead of looking like he's a heartbeat away from a coffin, but I nod.

They lift him carefully, and I stay close. My heart is still pounding, waiting for them to change their minds.

To our left, a few people are jostled, and then a young woman pushes through. I throw up my hands as if she's going to attack, but then I recognize my friend.

"Karri?" I say, and shock is enough to chase away some of my panic.

"Tessa! Oh, Tessa!" She throws her arms around me, then just as quickly holds me at arm's length. Her dark-brown eyes trace my features, and I have no idea what she sees.

The men are moving away with Corrick's body. Lochlan is following.

"Karri," I say, and my voice is a broken mess. "Karri, I have— I have—I have—"

"Come on," she says, tucking my hand into the crook of her elbow, then tugging me to follow. "I brought some supplies. Let's see what we can do."

My brain refuses to process this. "Wait—you're—"

"Working with the rebels? Yes." She glances over again, and her eyes are just as keen and bright as they were when we worked across from each other at Mistress Solomon's. Her gaze flicks to the men carrying Corrick and then back to mine. "Just like you."

—⊷—

Corrick's back isn't broken, but his shoulder is dislocated. Karri and Earle jerk it back into place, and that's so painful it brings him around long enough to cry out and try to fight them off. His injuries must catch up with him, though, because he drops fast. We're in a small lean-to at the edge of the village, hardly bigger than the workshop, but there's a fire and it's dry and warm. A small bed sits against the wall, and Earle eases Corrick onto it.

The prince doesn't move.

I stand beside him, my hand hovering near his face, unsure if I should touch him. His eyes are already shadowed with bruising, and his breathing is too rapid, too rough. I don't want to hurt him more.

I have to keep my eyes on Corrick, because Lochlan is standing by the door, and if I look at him, I'm going to tear him apart with my bare hands.

A few hours ago, Corrick was promising me he could do better, and now I want to be the vicious one.

"Here," says Karri. She's brought a kettle and a low pan, along with some squares of muslin.

I dip one and touch it to Corrick's brow, where dirt has crusted with the blood along the cut over his eye. He flinches and sucks in a breath, blinking at me before his lids fall closed again.

"Shh," I say gently. "It's me. It's me."

He nods, and it's such a tiny movement, such a trusting movement. This time, when I tend to the cut, he holds still.

"It needs stitching," says Karri from behind me.

I know. I can see that myself.

"I can do it now," she says, "while he's barely awake."

Corrick's eyes crack open a fraction and find mine before fluttering shut.

"I'll do it," I say. "Do you have a needle?"

I've stitched people up a dozen times before, but this is different. I'm so uncertain about the people in this room, and very aware that while Earle and Karri are helping, Lochlan hasn't left, and I have no idea who might be waiting outside the door. I focus on threading the needle, listening to Corrick's breathing.

Karri stands beside me, taking the muslin scraps to clean his less serious wounds.

"So he's the father?" she whispers.

I almost drop the needle. "What?"

She glances at my abdomen and back at my face.

"Oh!" I'd completely forgotten the story I told her and Mistress Solomon. "No. That—no. I'm not pregnant. I was never pregnant." I tie off the knot in the thread. "He made it look like he was captured and killed. I didn't know he was the prince. He was always Wes to me."

"He was always Wes to us, too," says Earle.

"Well, he was always Cruel Corrick to a lot of people," says Lochlan.

I look at him. "Shut your mouth or I'll stitch it closed."

He doesn't look impressed. "Go ahead and try, girl."

"Stop it," says Karri. She casts a glance at the doorway where Lochlan looms, then presses the damp cloth to Corrick's cheek, dragging the dirt away from the small cuts there.

"How long have you been working with them?" I say quietly.

She doesn't look at me. "A few weeks."

"Karri!"

She shrugs. "After the riots in the square, my parents heard of an opportunity to get enough medicine for our whole family." She looks over to meet my eyes. "We've always had enough to support ourselves, but . . . the woman next door broke her leg and couldn't work. She helped my mother so much when we were growing up. She's been like a grandmother, really." She turns back to her work, rinsing the cloth and moving to the rope burns on Corrick's wrists. "My parents have never been rebels, have never done so much as speak out against the king, and they were too scared to do anything. But I . . . you'd clearly been in love with a rebel, and you're one of the kindest people I know, so I thought I'd try to help. And here I am."

Her eyes find mine again. "I kept hearing about Wes and Tessa, how they'd disappeared, and everyone thought you'd been captured by the night patrol. You were so upset at Mistress Solomon's, and I began to wonder if Wes was the man you wouldn't tell me about."

"Oh, Karri. I'm sorry. I . . ." I swallow. I would have told her. I should have told her.

"I'm not my parents," she says. She cleans another wound with such care. "I think it took me a little while to figure that out." She nods at the needle in my hand. "Do it before he wakes."

I look back at Corrick. His eyes are closed, and his breathing has slowed.

I don't want to hurt him.

Karri is watching me. "I can do it," she says softly.

"No—it's all right." I touch my fingers to the wound, pressing the edges together. Corrick doesn't move, not even when I press the tip of the needle against his skin. I bite my lip and push through, making more blood flow. I loop the thread quickly, tying off a knot that Karri slices with a knife.

"So you're doing what we were doing?" I say to her as I place the next stitch. "Stealing to give to people who have nothing?" I want to cast a glance at Lochlan. Corrick said he was one of the men raiding shipments. Is that what he is doing, too?

She nods. "Yes. There's a wealthy man and woman who've been providing silver and Moonflower petals to anyone willing to raid the shipments, but they don't want the medicine. They just want the attacks."

"Why?"

"They have a grudge against the throne." She slices through my next thread automatically. "I don't know who they are. But many people call them the Benefactors."

"Karri," says Lochlan, his tone low with warning. "He's the King's Justice."

"He's half conscious," she says.

"I don't care."

I place another stitch, but I realize a bloom of sweat has formed on Corrick's forehead, and his fingers are clutching at the sheet. He hasn't moved, but he's not unconscious.

He's . . . he's *listening.*

I can't decide if this is brave or stupid. Probably both. I put the needle against his skin again, but hesitate. My palm turns damp. I can't do this if he's awake. I can't.

I try not to think about the fact that I already was.

"He's helped us for years," says Earle. "I've heard about what he's done out there, but I know what he's done here, for us." He pauses. "And sometimes people go too far."

"On both sides," says Lochlan.

"Are you going to finish?" says Karri, and I almost jump. I push the needle through, and a muscle in Corrick's jaw twitches. I have no idea how he can stay silent through this, but I can do him the favor of being quick. I loop and tie off the knot, and she cuts the thread.

I take the muslin from Karri and wash the fresh blood away. Corrick doesn't move. His grip on the sheet has gone slack. I can't tell if he's passed out again or if he's just relieved that I'm not shoving a needle through his eyebrow.

"You all bombed the Hold," I say.

"There's a group from Trader's Landing that brought supplies from the mines," she says.

"Karri," snaps Lochlan.

"How did you get in?" I say, as I rinse the muslin and squeeze out the excess water. "The gate guards search—"

A hand closes on my arm, fingers digging into the muscle. "What do you think you're doing?"

Lochlan. He's right at my side. I gasp and try to jerk away. "I'm not—I'm not—"

"Let her go," snaps Karri.

"Lochlan," says Earle. "Leave her be."

Lochlan shifts closer to me, until standing turns to looming. He's no fool. "What. Are. You. Doing?"

I wish I had the needle in my hand again, instead of this useless crush of muslin. I'm ready to punch him in the crotch, but he suddenly cries out and lets me go, falling back a step, colliding with the small side table. A bowl overturns and shatters on the floor. White petals flutter wildly, and some end up on the bed beside Corrick.

Corrick has grabbed hold of Lochlan's broken wrist where it hung beside the bed, and he's twisting his grip. His eyes are full of pain and exhaustion but are as cunning and keen as ever.

"You'll keep your hands off her," he says, and his voice sounds like he's speaking through ground glass.

Lochlan is all but doubled over. He's gasping, making tiny keening sounds with each breath.

Karri and Earle have stepped forward, and their eyes go back and forth as they try to figure out who to help.

"Corrick." I have to clear my throat. "Corrick. Let him go."

He lets go, and Lochlan falls to his knees, cradling his arm against his belly. When he glares up at Corrick, his eyes are like fire.

Corrick's gaze is worse, his blue eyes like ice, carrying a promise of every cruel thought that can make its way through his head. I'd forgotten he can look like that.

Karri surges forward to scoop the Moonflower petals into a new bowl. They remind me of the ones in the workshop, the ones Wes took from Tris. Some are slightly narrower than I'm used to, and even in the midst of everything, my apothecary mind can't help but wonder why. Have they been cut smaller? Where did they come from? Do the Benefactors have access to a new supply, a new cure? The thought lights me with hope and fear simultaneously.

Corrick puts a hand against the bed and levers himself to sitting. Once he's upright, he braces his hands against his knees and clenches his jaw. His eyes are shadowed in a way that tells me they'll be blackened tomorrow, and his jaw is swollen on the left side. He's hunched over, and I wonder if he has cracked ribs.

Earle takes Lochlan's arm and helps him stand. For the first time since helping, he looks uncertain. Karri appears at my side with a cup of tea, the air thick with the scent of the herbs she's added. Ginger and turmeric, along with some lemon and rosemary.

"For the pain." She hesitates, then bites at her lip. "Your Highness."

Corrick takes the tea. He doesn't look like Wes anymore; he looks like the King's Justice, his eyes shadowed and closed off, even wounded. But he says, "Thank you."

He doesn't take a sip. He doesn't trust her. He doesn't trust any of them.

I probably shouldn't either, but I've known Karri for years, and I don't think she'd try to poison him—but then I'd never expect her to be working with rebels either. I've lived in the Wilds and worked in Artis side by side with these people all my life. But even though they seem to want to help right this second, Lochlan kidnapped me and Corrick. The crowd tried to kill Corrick, knowing full well who he was.

I suddenly feel like I have a foot planted in each world, and I'm not sure how to move forward.

From the expression on Earle's and Karri's faces, I don't think I'm the only one.

I thought things had turned in our favor, that I'd changed the minds of the crowd, but I'd forgotten, again, that Wes was never just Wes, and Corrick is . . . well, the brother to the king. They can patch him up, but they can't undo what's been done.

King Harristan's voice was so gentle when he spoke to me after the explosions in the Royal Sector, when he said, *The King's Justice cannot be lenient to those who attack a building in the center of the Royal Sector. Surely you know this.*

I do know it. I also know the King's Justice can't be lenient when he's been kidnapped and beaten nearly to death. He might agree with the rebellion, and he might be willing to change things from the inside, but that doesn't mean he'll turn a blind eye to everything done here.

Even if he would, I doubt these rebels would believe him.

I stopped the attack, but I didn't stop anything else. They're still rebels. To everyone here, he's still the prince whose duty it is to punish them. My pulse tumbles along, begging me for action, but there's no action to take. I place my hand over his.

Lochlan and Earle exchange a glance.

Karri won't meet my eyes.

Corrick looks at Lochlan. "Fetch a crossbow. Do it now." His eyes shift to Earle. "Take Tessa away from here."

My brain can't keep up with the sudden onslaught of emotion. "Wait. Corrick—Corrick, no—"

Earle takes my arm. "Come on, Tessa." His voice is low and sad.

Lochlan has already gone through the door. I struggle against Earle's grip. My eyes are on Corrick, broken and bleeding, but sitting upright out of sheer force of will.

"Stop," I say to him, and to my surprise, I'm crying. "Corrick, no. What are you doing?" I twist free of Earle's grip suddenly, and I throw my arms around Corrick.

He makes a small sound, and I know I've hurt him, but I don't care. "I'm sorry," I say. "Please—please don't—"

"Tessa." He speaks right to my ear, his voice just for me, and it forces me still. He has a plan. He must have a plan.

But then he says, "I told you what they'd do."

They'd torture me and use me against Harristan.

He did tell me. He sacrifices everything for his brother. This is no different.

I choke on my breath. I can't let him go. I can't. I burrow my face against his shoulder.

After a moment, his arms come around me, and I can feel him shaking.

His lips brush against my cheek. "Mind your mettle, Tessa."

My breath catches, and I draw back to look at him. "I can't lose you twice."

He flinches. "Forgive me."

The door slams, and I jump. Lochlan is back. Earle takes hold of my arm again.

I tighten my grip, and Corrick winces. "Tessa. Please."

"I can shoot you both," says Lochlan.

"No!" says Karri.

"Please, my love," Corrick whispers into my ear. "Please."

I draw back. There's nothing cold about his eyes now.

If he can be brave about this, so can I. I allow Earle to pull me back.

"I'm all right," I say to him, and my voice trembles. "I can walk."

He lets me go, but I was wrong. I'm not brave. I can't breathe. I can't walk.

A shout cries out from outside the shed. Then another. Then a shrill whistle.

"The night patrol!" someone screams.

Lochlan swears. He lifts the crossbow.

"Wait!" says Corrick.

I throw myself at Lochlan. It's not like when I did the same in the clearing earlier, when we saved little Forrest. I don't have a rock. But his shot fires wildly, and the bolt lodges in the ceiling.

He fights for the weapon, but he only has one working arm, and I have two. I jerk the weapon away from him. Outside the shack, more and more people are screaming. I hear pounding hoofbeats and someone official shouting orders.

Lochlan shoves me off him and bolts through the door. Karri and Earle are already gone. I can taste my heartbeat in my throat.

Corrick is off the bed and standing, but he's gone pale. All of his weight is on one leg. "Tessa."

"I'm here." I move to his side. "Lean on me."

His arm comes around my shoulders. He must be more hurt than he's letting on, because he feels unsteady against me.

Armed men burst through the door, crossbows aimed, and I jump. It's not the night patrol—it's the royal army.

They recognize Corrick, because they lower their weapons almost immediately.

"Your Highness," one says, and he sounds shocked.

"Lieutenant," says Corrick. His voice is weaker than it should be. "You have *exceptionally* good timing."

"Commander Riley!" calls another. "We found the prince."

Another man comes through the door, with blue and purple ribbons adorning each shoulder. His eyes go from Corrick to me and back.

"Your Highness," he says, and he sounds equally shocked.

"The prince is hurt," I say. "He needs a physician."

"Yes, miss." His eyes narrow a bit. "Are you . . . Tessa?"

"Yes."

"Why?" says Corrick.

"Forgive me, Your Highness." Commander Riley hesitates. "We didn't expect to find you here. But since we have . . . I have orders to take you both into custody."

CHAPTER THIRTY-THREE

Corrick

I thought I knew the Hold from every angle.

This is the first time I've seen it as a prisoner.

I'm locked in a cell on the lowest level, where smugglers and illegal traders are usually kept. It's either ironic or poetic justice; I can't decide which. Maybe simple necessity, after the front half of the prison was damaged in the attacks. The halls are torchlit, but the cells are shadowed and dim, and as usual, the smell leaves something to be desired. The stone floor is strewn with a thin layer of loose straw, but the walls are stained with every bodily fluid you can imagine.

I thought for sure we'd be taken to the palace, where I'd have to face my brother's accusations. Instead, we were brought here, where one of my guards stammered through reading me my charges. He kept glancing up, looking at me, then at Commander Riley, as if he expected the officer to let go of my chains and explain this was all a big prank.

Smuggling. Sedition. Treason. I've heard the words before, on a nearly daily basis, but they've never carried so much weight.

At my side, Tessa was trembling in her shackles, her breathing quick and shallow.

"They won't hurt you," I said to her softly. "They're good men. Just do what they say."

"No talking," the guard snapped, but then he blanched a bit and added, "Your Highness."

Tessa is in a cell at the opposite end of the hall now, on the opposite side. The guards haven't been rough with either of us, but I don't want to give them cause, so I haven't tried to yell to her. I can practically feel her worries from here.

Or maybe what I'm feeling is my own worries.

I don't know what Harristan will do.

I know what he'd expect *me* to do, and that's not very comforting.

I never realized it, but the straw on the cell floors is truly torture. It does nothing to spare me from the cold hardness of the stone, and itches through my clothes when I move. I feel every bruise acutely. My shoulder hasn't stopped aching, and the wound Tessa stitched over my eye is throbbing, matched only by the pulsing pain in my swollen ankle. My stomach has been making a case for breakfast for a while now. Without sunlight, I have no way to mark the passing of time, so minutes feel like hours. I know the guards change shift at midday, but when it happens, it comes as a surprise anyway, somehow feeling both earlier and later than I expected.

I don't expect to sleep, but my body has other ideas. I doze fitfully, waking with a jolt every time I hear a boot scrape on stone, but no one comes to my bars. No food, no water, nothing.

By the time the guards change shift for the evening, I'm ready to beg.

I press my forehead against the floor and bite at my lip, clenching my eyes closed. I survived what happened in the village; I can surely survive a day without food and water.

But I was wrong about the straw. This thirst is worse. My head pounds now, and the guard's hesitant voice is loud in my memories.

Smuggling. Sedition. Treason.

I stood in my quarters and swore to Harristan that I wasn't involved. And I'm not. Not the way he thinks.

What did he say to me about my feigned friendship with Allisander?

All that matters is what it looks like.

My throat tightens. I'm used to people hating me, but this is altogether different.

I'm not used to my brother hating me.

I've stopped hoping he would send for me, and I've begun dreading it. The thought of his disappointment weighs on me more heavily than every bruise the rebels gave me. Everything I've done to protect him, and I undid it all with pure selfishness. I didn't need to leave the palace. I didn't need to spend hours in the Wilds every morning. What did I do? Help a few dozen people prolong the inevitable?

And now Tessa is in the Hold. The one thing I always hoped to avoid.

I wonder who Harristan will choose to dole out punishment. Who will replace me as King's Justice? My brother's circle of trust is not broad.

A name pierces my thoughts like a needle.

Allisander.

Harristan doesn't trust him any more than I do, but I can see the consul using his significant status to force my brother's hand. It would make Allisander the second-most powerful man in Kandala. He could take whatever action he wanted against the smugglers—and he's been desperate to do so for months now. My heart thrums along at a rapid clip.

Allisander would make an example of me. I have no doubt.

Maybe he already is. Maybe that's why there's been no food, no water. I never starved my prisoners, and he made his thoughts very clear about that.

The thought of Allisander in my place makes my chest tight, and it's painful to swallow. I spent my life trying to protect my brother, but Allisander would spend his life trying to undermine Harristan at every turn. Against my will, my eyes burn.

Footsteps echo in the hallway, and I try to calm my hitching breath. The guards are changing again. It must be midnight. Shame curls in my belly, and I want to roll into the darkened shadows. With each new guard, it's a new moment of gawking, the fearsome prince reduced to powerless captive.

I press my fingers into my eyes. Poetic justice, for sure.

"Corrick."

I jerk my hands down. Harristan stands on the other side of the bars, flanked by his guards. His expression is cool and still. Unreadable.

I'm not facing my brother. I'm facing the king.

I wait for him to say something else. He doesn't.

That's not reassuring. A tremor rolls through me, a clenching in my chest. I struggle to force myself upright. I've been lying on the cold ground for hours, and none of my joints want to work. By the time I'm on my knees, I'm lightheaded and breathing heavily. Harristan watches this impassively.

I don't know if I want to cry or if I want to beg for my life. So many times I wished for my brother to come to the Hold, to witness what I was forced to do.

Now he's here, and I wish he were anywhere else.

"Your Majesty," I say, and my voice breaks. My breathing won't steady. I can't look at him.

He glances at the guard by the corner. "Open the gate."

The man scurries. When Harristan enters the cell, two of his guards come with him, as if I'm a threat. One of them is Rocco.

Maybe my brother is going to have them execute me right here. My heart races in my chest, but I keep my eyes on the straw, on the boots of the guards.

When Harristan's fingers touch my chin, it's so unexpected that I jump, but he's simply lifting my gaze.

"You're injured," he says, and the way he says it is interesting, like he had no idea until this very moment. Which is possible.

He casts a glance around the empty cell. "You outfit your prison rather sparsely. Have you no chairs?"

I frown. "What?"

He looks at Rocco. "Send for food."

"Yes, Your Majesty."

To my surprise, Harristan drops to a crouch to look at me eye to eye. He's so out of place here, resplendent in green brocade and shining silver buttons, while I'm covered in dust that clings to dried blood and sweat. My face is surely a mask of bruises and cuts, while his is unmarred perfection.

I still can't read his expression, and for a long moment, we stare at each other.

"You swore to me," he finally says.

I look away. "I did so truthfully." But my words sound hollow. I know where I was found. I know how it looks.

"I've had Allisander in my face since before dawn, insisting you're behind the attacks on his supply runs. That you've been funding the rebels."

I jerk my head around. "No! Harristan, I—"

He puts up a hand, and I stop short.

"You weren't in your quarters," he says. "You were nowhere to be found. So I sent soldiers into the Wilds."

Where they found me.

I swallow, and my throat feels like it's lined in parchment. Maybe it would have been better if Lochlan had killed me.

"I wasn't working with the rebels," I say, and my voice is rough and shaking. "Please, Harristan." I sound like every single prisoner who's begged at my feet. "I have nothing to do with the attacks on Sallister's supply runs."

He says nothing, just regards me silently.

Rocco reappears. "Your Majesty." He's holding out a leather satchel and a full water skin. I'm so thirsty I can practically smell it. "This is from the Hold stores. Shall I send for more from the palace?"

"Not yet."

Harristan takes the water skin and offers it to me.

I drink too fast, sputtering on the water like I've never tasted a drop, but I'm too thirsty to care. When I finally lower it from my lips, I hold it out to my brother. I have no idea when I'll get more, so it takes literally everything I have to say, "Will you please send some to Tessa?"

He studies me for a moment, then nods, handing the skin to Rocco, who leaves the cell.

Harristan looks over his shoulder at the other guard. "Retreat to the hallway. Have the prison guards keep their distance."

They do. I hold my breath almost involuntarily.

Once they're gone, Harristan sits down in the straw in front of me, then gestures for me to do the same. I stare at my brother, who's never set foot in the Hold, who's now sitting on a cell floor. I don't think *I* have ever sat on a cell floor.

Well, until today.

He pulls a small length of bread from the satchel, followed by some overripe pears and a slab of cheese that looks a bit spotty.

He breaks the bread in half and looks at it dubiously, but then extends a piece to me. "Here. Eat, Cory."

I tear a piece free with my teeth. "You could have had me brought to the palace."

"I was too mad at you for that."

"Are you still?"

"Maybe." He splits the cheese, too. "Do you remember that time those boys from Mosswell dared us to race all the way to the river?"

"I do." It was years ago. I was twelve or thirteen, so Harristan must have been sixteen or seventeen. There was a large stable on the edge of the Wilds that kept ponies for hire, and the boys would slip a few out of the paddock and take them galloping through the woods at dawn. We'd only ever ridden the sleek and polished horses from the royal stables, well-trained and well-bred animals who never took a step wrong. The ponies were fat and furry and ornery, but Harristan has a competitive streak, and we were riding double with nothing more than a halter and a rope, galloping out of the paddock before the other boys had even climbed over the fence.

I remember clinging to my brother's back, getting whipped by branches and leaves, laughing every time that pony tried to put its head down to buck, because Harristan would jerk its head up and swear in a very unprincely fashion.

I also remember Harristan aiming for a narrow ditch that any horse in the royal stable would have leapt over without hesitation, because that ridiculous pony skidded to a halt, and Harristan and I did not. We went flying headfirst into the mud. We had to tell our parents that we were climbing trees in the orchard and we fell.

"It's the last time I've seen you so bruised," Harristan says now.

"Lucky me."

"Stupid pony," Harristan says.

"Stupid princes, more likely," I say. I put the cheese in my mouth, and it's awful, but I don't care.

"Did the guards do this to you?" he says quietly.

I tear another piece of bread. "No. Those rebels you thought I was *helping*."

He inhales sharply and straightens.

I meet his eyes. "I'm very glad you sent the soldiers," I say, and despite everything, I mean it.

He holds my gaze for a long moment, and I can feel every question he's not voicing. "Quint has been in my face much of the day, too," he says, his tone musing.

I've been worried about Quint since the instant I was locked in this cell, but I've been afraid to so much as breathe his name. "You've loved every moment of it, I'm sure."

"He insists you've never had one truly treasonous thought cross your mind."

Only Quint could think of the perfect way to phrase that to Harristan, because every syllable is absolutely true. "He's right."

"He says that every secret you keep is an effort to protect me."

I should double Quint's salary—if I ever get out of prison. My throat feels tight again, and to my absolute horror, I feel a tear make its way through the dirt on my cheek. "He's right about that, too."

Harristan waits, but I say nothing. I swipe the tear away, and no more dare to follow.

My brother sighs, then reaches out to ruffle my hair affectionately, like I'm a boy.

"Ow," I say.

He stops with his hand on my head and levels me with his eyes. "Tell me the truth."

I hesitate. "I think Arella and Roydan are funding the rebels. It would explain their secret meetings—"

"Corrick," he snaps. "I meant the truth about you."

"I know what you meant." But the truth won't help him, and it certainly won't help me.

"Don't be a fool. I can't bring you back to the palace if I don't know what you're doing."

"I was apprehended in a rebel camp," I say. I want to shake him. And he wonders why I keep such secrets. "Harristan, you can't bring me back to the palace *at all*. How would you appease Allisander? How?"

A muscle in his jaw twitches as he sits there regarding me, but he must see the truth in that, because his shoulders droop and he runs a hand across his jaw. "Very well. But I can make sure you're fed." He looks at the cut over my eye. "And treated." He casts another glance around. "And perhaps provided with a *chair*, at the very least."

"The prisoners use furniture as weapons."

He looks startled, and I shrug.

When he stands, I do as well, and I limp behind him to the doorway. He hesitates, but I slam the gate closed between us.

He looks at the lock and then back at me. "I will leave Rocco to ensure you are left unharmed."

"Ah! My best friend."

He gives me a look. "Mother and Father tried to protect me, too," he says.

"I remember. So does the pony."

"You might think you're the clever and brave one, little brother, but don't forget." He smiles. "I found a way around them both."

CHAPTER THIRTY-FOUR

Tessa

When Rocco appears at the bars of my cell with a water skin, I think my eyes are playing a trick on me. The stone floor is freezing cold, and even though I tried to sweep the loose straw into a pile, I've been shivering for hours. I blink at him, once, twice, then a third time, like my eyes refuse to believe it.

"Miss Tessa," he says, holding the skin through the bars.

"Rocco." My mouth is dry. I get to my feet, and it takes more effort than it should. My joints are sore and achy, and my head spins. I have to hold on to the bars to take the water skin from him.

I don't know why he's here, and right now, I don't care. I drain the whole thing in a minute, then press my forehead against the bars, panting.

It takes me a moment to notice there are other royal guards in the hallway. Corrick's cell door looks to be open, but I can't see him. I can't see what's happening to him.

My heart stops, then restarts itself at twice the pace.

"What's happening?" I say to Rocco.

"The king is speaking with the prince."

"*Speaking,* speaking, or . . . or . . ." My words trail off, because I don't want to put voice to anything else my imagination is supplying.

"The king is speaking with the prince," Rocco says again, and I realize that's all the answer I'm going to get.

I swallow. Corrick said his brother had accused him of treason before we left the palace. We've been down here for nearly a full day now, and I have no doubt that King Harristan has known about it. None of that can mean anything good. The smell of this cell has given me a clue to what's been done within these walls, and I don't want to think about any of it. I don't want to think about Harristan ordering those kinds of things done to his brother.

Exhaustion and fear have caught up with me. My throat tightens against my will, and I close my eyes and breathe against the bars.

Please, my love.

A tear slips down my cheek, and I make no attempt to brush it away. Did I prolong the inevitable? Did I save him in the village only to watch him face a worse fate here?

Booted feet scrape against the stone floor, and my eyes flick open. Rocco has stepped back, standing at attention, and to my absolute shock, I find myself facing the king.

I must be speechless for a moment too long, because King Harristan gives me a quick up-and-down glance before looking at Rocco. "Remain with Corrick. I will send supplies and further orders." He turns his gaze back to me. "Can you walk?"

I have no idea. *Remain with Corrick. I will send supplies and further orders.* What does that mean? What has he done? My mouth has gone dry again, and I take a step back from the bars. "I—I—"

He looks at one of his other guards. "Thorin. Carry her."

They open the gate, and I put up my hands before the other man can touch me. I don't know what's happening, but I do know I don't want to be carried into it. "Wait. Stop. I—I can walk."

"Good," says King Harristan. "Come with me."

————

I don't know where I expected to go, but that guard, Thorin, loads me into a carriage just outside the Hold. I've completely lost track of time, because I was ready to step out into sunlight, since it was dawn when we were first taken, but the night sky is ink-black and twinkling with stars. The king must take a separate carriage, because I'm alone with Thorin in this one. He's not as friendly as Rocco was, and sits stony-faced across from me.

I clench my fingers in my skirts, which are dusty and stained with Corrick's blood.

I don't know if Thorin will talk to me, but this silence is so full of tension that it's going to rattle me apart. "Where are we going?" I say.

"To the palace."

I want to ask why, but I remember Quint chastising me when he said, *He is the king. He doesn't need to say why.*

Once we're there, I expect to be thrown on the floor like I was on the night I was found in the hallway, but to my surprise, I'm taken to my room, where a sleepy-eyed Jossalyn waits to give me a bath. Thorin stands beside my door—to make sure I obey, I suppose.

Jossalyn ignores him and looks at my face, and then at my clothes, and she frowns. "Where are you injured?"

"I'm not." I swallow. "It's not my blood."

She glances at the guard, then nods to me. "Out of those . . . clothes then, miss."

I feel like I haven't slept in days, so when Jossalyn scrubs at my skin, I let her. I wish there were food here, because the water skin woke my hunger with a vengeance, but there's none. Jossalyn roughly towel-dries my hair and braids it wet, pinning it up in a complicated twist that I'd never be able to replicate. I don't know what to do. I don't know what to say.

What happened between the king and Corrick? Did the king torture him? Will he torture me? I don't know who to ask. I don't know *how* to ask. I wish I could talk to Quint, but I haven't seen him since the night he helped me into Corrick's quarters. I'm tired and starving, but in less than thirty minutes, I'm in a royal-blue dress, being escorted back to the room where Corrick and I watched the Hold go up in flames while consuls argued and guards and messengers bustled about.

Tonight, there is no one but King Harristan. He's standing by the massive windows, backed by the starlit sky. Food has been arranged on the table in the center of the room, and it must have been recently, because everything is still steaming. Roasted poultry and root vegetables, pastries with sugared crusts, sliced breads with little pots of jam and honey. There's even a small bowl with Moonflower petals, too, more than enough for half a dozen people, along with a mortar and pestle and a steaming teapot. One plate has already been prepared, silverware sitting ready beside glasses filled with water and wine.

My mouth waters almost instantly, and I have to swallow and press my hands to my abdomen. I can't tell if it's the lack of food in my belly or the presence of it in this room, but I feel lightheaded.

Behind me, the door slams shut, and I jump. To my surprise, I'm alone with King Harristan.

He studies me from across the room, but he doesn't hesitate. "Sit," he says, and while there's no warmth in his tone, his voice isn't unkind. "Eat."

I sweep my eyes around the room, as if there's an unsprung trap waiting, but we're the only ones here. Not even a lone guard or a footman. The king doesn't move from the window.

I ease into the chair at the table and pick up the fork.

Other people might have stronger willpower, but I don't. I'm starving. I shove an unladylike amount of meat into my mouth. Then half a roll of flaky pastry, followed quickly by the other half. I load the fork with vegetables until it won't hold anymore.

When he approaches the table, I hurriedly set down my fork and wipe at my mouth, then begin to force myself to my feet.

Harristan lifts a hand. "Sit," he says. He takes the chair across from me and gestures to my plate. "Continue."

I can't. Not now.

He's going to want something from me.

"What did you do to Corrick?" I say, and my voice sounds so small and frightened that I want to start over.

But the king blinks in surprise. "To Corrick?"

To my horror, tears fill my eyes, blurring my vision with fear that quickly coalesces into anger. "He said you accused him of treason, and I know—"

"Tessa."

"—where you found us, but he's not a traitor; he's not a smuggler." I should stop, should shut up, but now that I've started crying and talking, the words fall out of my mouth of their own volition. "Corrick is not a villain. He's—"

"*Tessa.*"

"—trying so hard to protect you, but you have to know it's destroying him. And now . . . what? What are you doing to him? Are you torturing him? Are you—"

"*Enough.*" His voice is sharp, like a slap. "You will not *accuse* me."

I go still. His eyes are so hard and cold. My hands are clenched on my silverware. I'm afraid of him and angry at him and hopeful and worried and a whole host of broken emotions that have my stomach tied in knots.

"He's not here," I whisper. "I am. What did you do?" My voice wavers on the last words. "What did you do to him?"

He stares at me for a moment, then sighs and sits back. He runs a hand across his face. "Lord, Tessa. He's my brother."

The king sounds so much like Corrick in that moment that I startle, forgetting my tears. He says this as if it means everything, and in a way, it does. I'm reminded of the night I rode in the carriage with Corrick, when I demanded to know why he wouldn't leave this life if he hated it so very much.

I couldn't leave my brother.

"I didn't harm him," Harristan continues. "I wouldn't have even if he deserved it, which he very well might." He pauses. "I offered to release him from the Hold, but he refused. When

Thorin brought you here, I had food and supplies sent back for Corrick."

I frown. "He . . . refused?"

"He says that Consul Sallister would not stand for his release." He pauses. "And he's not mistaken."

I look back at my plate. The worst part is that I can see Corrick saying that. He lay on that bed and let me stitch up his eyebrow so he could listen for more information. Of course he'd choose a cold cell over angering a consul who could endanger the entire country.

"He wouldn't say much else," Harristan says carefully. "But I brought you here in the hopes that you would."

I glance back up and meet his eyes. "That I would what?"

"That you would tell me what he's been doing."

I go very still. *This* is the trap.

Harristan is studying me. "I'm not asking you to betray him."

I look away.

"There are very few people I trust," he says. "But Corrick is one of them. He trusts you. That carries weight with me."

I don't know what to say. This still feels like a betrayal.

Harristan leans in against the table. His tone is beseeching. "You said yourself that I have to know it's destroying him. I don't know. I *should* know." He pauses. "Help me to know."

He means that. I can hear it in every syllable. Corrick doesn't want to be cruel. This man doesn't either.

A tear slips out of my eye, but this time there's no anger behind it. Only sorrow. *Oh, Corrick.* I don't know what the right decision is.

"If he's trying so hard to protect me," says Harristan, "perhaps I should have the chance to do the same for him."

That hits me like an arrow. I look up and meet his eyes. "I can only tell you half of it," I say, and my voice is rough and uncertain.

"Only half?"

I nod. "My half. If you want the whole story . . ." I take a deep breath, hoping I'm not making the wrong choice here. "Then you need to send for Quint."

CHAPTER THIRTY-FIVE

Corrick

Within an hour, my cell has a mattress, heavy blankets, and not one, but two chairs. A fresh change of clothes has been provided, so I no longer need to sit here in torn wool that's stained with my own blood. A basket sits in the corner with bottles of water and wine, along with rounds of cheese, perfectly ripe honeyed apples and sugared pears, fresh breads that are still warm from the ovens, and dried beef—more food than I can eat in a week. The rats will probably make a meal out of most of it before I can, but I do appreciate my brother's tending. It's very likely more than I deserve.

I also have company of a sort in Rocco, who stands in the shadows of the hallway, leaning against the wall across from my bars.

I don't know whether I should be relieved that Harristan took Tessa out of here—or worried. He obviously hopes to question her to find out what I was doing.

He should be questioning Arella and Roydan. He should be

confining them to their quarters and reading any messages they send. He should be calling a meeting of the consuls to let them make demands of each other.

I keep thinking back to Jonas's request for a bridge for Artis, the one that Harristan denied. Jonas hates Allisander, so I could see him attacking the supply runs on principle alone, but he doesn't have any silver to spare. Artis is struggling if the fever is running rampant among the dockworkers. Most of his sector is dependent on those who work along the water.

Arella made a request later that day, though. She also put in a formal request to pardon the prisoners before the execution that never happened. I don't know why she and Roydan would want to interrupt Allisander's supply runs—but if she were paying off common folk, it would explain why she needed more silver. Sunkeep and the Sorrowlands both border Trader's Landing, and the consul from there was responsible for killing my parents. Roydan and Arella have softened their borders to account for the lack of a consul in Trader's Landing. Have they turned against us as well? Is there something about that sector that bears discontent for the Crown? I don't know.

That girl with the rebels said that explosives came from the mines of Trader's Landing, too.

I wish I were in the palace. I wish I had my records and a map. I wish I had Quint, who'd be gossiping endlessly, but knows everything about everyone.

Instead, I have Rocco.

I limp to the bars and offer him an apple. "Peace treaty?"

He doesn't move from his spot on the wall. "Are we at war, Your Highness?"

"You're my brother's spy. You tell me."

"I am no one's spy." He looks at me dispassionately. "The king asks questions, and I answer."

I shouldn't be irritated. I know all my brother's guards, and I know where their loyalties lie. This is just the first time it's ever put me at odds with them. I toss him the apple. "Will you answer mine?"

He catches it easily. "Certainly."

"What are your orders?"

"To ensure you're unharmed."

"The Hold guards won't harm me."

"An easy night for me, then."

"Are Arella and Roydan still in the palace?" I say. "Have they had any more secret meetings today?"

He frowns slightly. "I don't know. I was off duty until dusk, and I have been with the king since then. He has only met with Consul Sallister."

"What did they talk about?"

"I was not privy to their conversation."

I give him a look. He gives me one right back, then takes a bite of the apple.

I sigh and press my forehead against the bars. I don't know what I'm doing. Like when Tessa was stitching up my forehead, I'm grasping for information, and I don't know what I can do with any of it. Before, I was facing death, and now I'm facing . . . what? An eternity in the Hold? Harristan can't let me out of here unless we can determine who's truly behind the attacks. Even then, there's already been enough talk. I was found with rebels. It doesn't matter what they were doing to me—just that Harristan sent the army looking, and they found me.

Light flickers in the stairwell, men's voices echoing. I wonder if my brother might be returning, or possibly Tessa, but then Allisander himself turns the corner.

I jerk back from the bars automatically, but there's nowhere to go. That's the problem with a cell.

Allisander stops in front of me, inches from the bars. He's holding a handkerchief over his face as usual. "I had to see it for myself," he says.

For the first time in my life, I make no attempt to hide my dislike of this man. "Allisander," I say. "I'd think you would have learned your lesson about standing too close to the bars."

He doesn't move. "I'd think you would have learned your lesson about smuggling."

"I'm not a smuggler."

His eyes trace the walls. "Your current accommodations suggest otherwise."

"What do you want?"

"You've stolen from your people, Corrick, while punishing them for the same. I want your brother to make an example of you."

"I'm not behind the raids on your supply runs."

"It doesn't matter if you are or not. The people of Kandala must see a show of strength. They must see that the king will not stand for insurrection—and we all know Harristan isn't going to do anything to you. Something must be done—and it's clear that you and your brother are no longer the ones who should be doing it." He pauses for one long, vicious second. "Many of the other consuls agree." He *tsks* mockingly. "Perhaps you should have granted Jonas the funding for that bridge."

A cold lick of fear races down my spine. I need to get to my brother. All this time I've been worried about rebellion from the sectors, when I should have been paying attention to what was happening with the consuls. I think of Arella and Roydan, and I can't believe my options are siding with them or siding with this man. "Not *all* of the consuls agree."

"Enough of us do. And we have enough of a force to do what we see is necessary."

I stare at him. "Most people don't boldly admit to treason in front of my guards, Allisander."

"*Treason*? Kandala stands on the brink of revolution. The elites were woken by explosions in the streets two nights ago. Rebels have formed packs in the Wilds. The King's Justice has been found to be a hypocritical traitor—and the king himself hides a cough that grows worse by the day. No one is safe. There's nothing *treasonous* about protecting our people." He steps right up to the bars. "Especially when you and your brother sure couldn't do it."

I punch him in the face.

He rocks back, blood flowing freely from his nose. "Guards!" he shouts. "Guards, you will punish him!"

They don't move. They don't even look over.

I stand against the bars and flex my fingers. "You don't seem to have much willing help right now."

Allisander swipes blood from his face and surges forward, his hands balled into fists.

Rocco catches him from behind. "Consul. You will keep your distance."

Allisander glares at me. There's blood smeared across his cheek. "Fine. Let me go."

Rocco looks at me.

I shake my head. "Put him in a cell," I say coolly. "He's conspiring against the throne."

Allisander fights the guard's grip. It makes his nose start bleeding again. "This won't work. We'll see you hanged, Corrick," he snaps. "I'll do it myself—"

Rocco shoves him into a cell, and one of the Hold guards slams the gate.

"Do you know who I am?" he yells. "You will all be put to death. This man has no power any longer. He is a *criminal*—"

I ignore him. "Rocco," I say urgently. "You need to go back to the palace. You need to tell Harristan what he said. The consuls can't be trusted. I don't know what they're planning, but you need to go back."

Rocco stands in front of my bars. "My orders are to keep you safe."

I swear and hit the bars, and they rattle with an earsplitting clang. "The hell with your orders! You have to protect the king!"

"Yes, Your Highness. I will." He looks to one of the Hold guards. "Unlock the gate."

"What?" I whisper.

Allisander isn't anywhere near as quiet. "*What?*" he demands. "What are you doing?"

The guard puts a key in the lock, and I stare at Rocco. "What *are* you doing?"

"Returning to the palace, as you requested, but I must take you with me." The lock gives, and he swings the door wide.

"You will hang for this," Allisander says. "He is a traitor."

I'm staring at Rocco like this is a trap.

"His Majesty told me to ensure you are unharmed," he says. "Your Highness, he never said *where*."

CHAPTER THIRTY-SIX

Tessa

The king makes for an intimidating audience, even with Quint at my side. It doesn't help that the Palace Master looks as anxious as I feel. I speak haltingly at first, the crackling of the fire under-scoring my words, but King Harristan says nothing as I tell him the story of my parents again, how they were killed by the night patrol—and Corrick stopped the same thing from happening to me. I tell him about the workshop, and the people we helped, and how I didn't know who Prince Corrick really was until the night I was captured in the palace.

The king listens to all this patiently, and when I finally fall silent, he says, "How did you come to be in the rebel camp?"

I swallow. "Consul Sallister was threatening to withhold medi-cine if Corrick didn't put a stop to the attacks on his supply runs. We've heard some whispers about the Benefactors, and I thought . . ." My mouth goes dry. "I thought people might talk to us if we returned as outlaws."

He considers this for a moment. "And how did you leave the palace without being seen?"

My eyes flick to Quint before I can stop myself.

The king follows my gaze.

Quint inhales like he's going to spin this, but King Harristan's gaze is unyielding, and Quint sighs. "I helped."

"And not for the first time, I'm assuming," says Harristan. "Or Tessa would not have asked for you to be here."

Quint glances at me. "No, Your Majesty," he concedes.

"I'm sorry," I whisper.

"This is not a time for apologies," says Harristan. His eyes are on Quint now. "For how long?"

"For . . . years."

"Years," echoes Harristan. He frowns. "*Why*, Quint?"

"In the beginning . . . well, simply because Prince Corrick is the King's Justice." He says this as if it explains everything, and in a way, it does. "I wasn't helping so much as turning a blind eye to his mysterious early morning absences. But then came a morning when he didn't show for a breakfast with one of the consuls. I went to inquire, and his guards said he hadn't left his quarters all morning. When I knocked, he let me in, and he was . . . in a state. He was filthy, with blisters on his hands. He'd watched a child die. A baby who coughed so hard she couldn't breathe."

"I remember that," I say softly, and I do. The mother had the fever all through her pregnancy, but she kept taking the teas we brought, and the baby was born perfectly healthy. But within a week, the infant had a fever, and she succumbed to the cough right in front of us. I swallow. "He was filthy because he helped the father dig a grave."

"Yes," says Quint. "He told me. He told me everything." He

glances at Harristan. "He was helping his people, Your Majesty. How is that treason?"

The weight in the room is potent.

Harristan runs a hand over the back of his neck. "I hate that he wouldn't tell me."

"He *couldn't*—"

Harristan silences me with a look. "I know," he says evenly. "I know what he risked." He looks at Quint. "You should have told me."

Quint says nothing. He doesn't look afraid. He looks resigned.

I glare at the king. "You don't make it easy to tell you anything at all," I say.

"Tessa," breathes Quint.

"I'm not just talking about Quint," I continue. "I'm talking about Corrick, too. You said you know what he risked, but I'm not sure you do. He let those rebels beat him nearly to death because he didn't want to be used against you. He was willing to sacrifice his life to protect you. He doesn't want to be cruel. He doesn't want to kill anyone. He does these things to spare *you* from doing them. He wants to be *honest* and he wants to be *just* and he wants to be *better*. Not just for you. For all of Kandala. And you—well, you are a—"

"Tessa."

It's not Quint's voice this time. It's Corrick's. He stands in the doorway, Rocco at his back. He's a bit pale, the bruises on his face stark in the artificial light here in the palace. His hand is braced on the doorframe, his knuckles white where he grips the wood.

"Corrick," I whisper.

He limps to the table, and I stand to help him, but he stops by my side. He brushes the back of his uninjured hand against mine, looping our fingers together, causing my heart to skip a beat. But his eyes are on the king. "You should be questioning Arella and Roydan, not chasing down my pastimes."

Harristan looks from Corrick to Rocco. "What happened? Why are you here?"

"Allisander came to my cell. He said he plans to force you to make an example of me, or he and the other consuls will stand against you. He says he has enough of a force to pull it off."

The king's expression darkens. "He grows too bold."

"I agree. Which is why he's locked in a cell."

"Corrick! You cannot—"

"This is *beyond* bold, Harristan. This is revolution, and it's coming from all sides. I don't know who he's working with, but he's talking about an attempt to remove you from power. The rebels in the Wilds have explosives from Trader's Landing. We have no idea how they were able to get enough into the sector to attack the Hold, which means they could attack any other part of the sector, including the palace. We have no idea which consuls will ally with Sallister—or if they would even stand with us against a rebellion."

I glance between him and the king. "You said Consul Sallister has his own army."

"He does," says Harristan. "Consul Marpetta has quite a force protecting Emberridge as well, but Lissa has always seemed content with the status quo." He looks at Quint. "Which consuls are in the palace?"

"Nearly all of them," says Quint. "Lissa Marpetta is the only one who returned to her sector."

"The people of Artis are struggling," I say. "I don't know of any military force, and when I worked for Mistress Solomon, we would have heard of such a thing."

"He wanted silver for a bridge," says Corrick. "Allisander said we should have granted it. Remember when you told me that *in public is all that matters*? You were talking about me and Allisander—but I think they're pretending to *hate* each other. I think Jonas is working with him."

The king looks at him. "But they *do*—" He breaks off with a cough. His fingers grip the edge of the table.

All the men exchange a glance, and Harristan doesn't miss it. He glares at Corrick. "Stop it. I've told you before, I don't need—" He coughs again.

"Here," I say. I seize the teapot and pour hot water into a china cup, then add honey. I don't have a scale, but I toss a few petals into the mortar bowl to grind them up. But as soon as I see the petals against the stone, I hesitate.

Harristan coughs again.

"Tessa," says Corrick.

"Hold on. I need to think." I glance up, surveying the array of food. There are no vallis lilies this time, but there are sprigs of thyme on the edge of one of the platters.

I shake the petals out onto the dark tablecloth, grind the thyme, and add it to the cup with the honey. "Here," I say to Harristan. "Drink that." Then I look back at the white petals.

"What are you doing?" says Corrick.

"The petals are different." I quickly divvy them up. "Look." I point. "Those are clearly Moonflower. Those are . . . I'm not sure."

"They are very similar," says Quint. Even Rocco draws close for a look.

"The petals were like this in the rebel camp, too," I say. I feel like I'm close to figuring something out, but I'm not quite there. "The ones they would have gotten from the Benefactors."

Corrick's expression is grave. "Or the ones they would have gotten from stolen shipments." He pauses. "They're very close, Tessa. This could be a growing anomaly, or—"

"No! You were never the one to grind and measure. But there's never been a . . . a growing anomaly." I pause. "Corrick, you once said you never stole from the palace. Maybe—maybe—" My thoughts trip and stumble as I try to figure this out. "I need my books. My father used to keep track of new herbs."

Harristan coughs again, but it's not as strong. "What does this mean?"

"You drink the elixir here three times a day. What if . . ." My thoughts churn. "What if someone realized you don't really need as much? If you were sickly as a child, maybe you really *do* need more to keep the fevers at bay, but if someone is tampering with your supply . . ." I let my voice trail off.

"Wake the consuls," says Harristan. His voice is rough. "We need to determine which shipment these petals came from. We need to determine if the supply was contaminated, or if someone—"

A shout echoes from the hallway, and he freezes. Another shout, followed by a crash, and then splintering wood. Then a woman's scream.

Harristan and Corrick exchange a glance. Rocco goes for the door.

An explosion rocks the palace, causing the floor to shake and the china to rattle. The lights flare with blinding brightness before dying altogether, plunging the room into sudden flickering shadows from the hearth. Shouts and screams erupt in the hallway before another explosion occurs, somehow closer, making the windows rattle.

"Guards!" a man is shouting, but my heartbeat is so loud in my ears that everything is muffled. I'm distantly aware of a hand closing over my wrist, pulling me through the shadows. Something is burning, somewhere, a scent distinctly different from wood smoke, a bitter taste in the back of my throat.

Another explosion, and the windows shatter. I jump and scream.

Hands catch me, pulling me close. "Tessa." Corrick's voice in my ear, low and urgent. "Tessa, we have to run."

Then I hear the voices, the shouts in the hallway. Many are panicked, people terrified of the explosions.

Some are not.

"Find the king," a man yells, and I'm not sure how I can tell, but it's not a guard.

"Shoot anyone you see," calls another.

Smoke is filling the hallway now, and I hear glass shattering. A woman's scream is abruptly silenced. Corrick tugs at my hand, and I follow into the darkness.

CHAPTER THIRTY-SEVEN

Corrick

I knew revolution would find us.

I didn't expect it to be so soon.

I didn't expect it to be from all sides.

Alarms blare in the sector, but I have no way of knowing if they've attacked anything more than the palace. After Allisander's comments, I don't even know if this attack is the work of rebels or consuls.

The hallways are full of smoke and darkness, but I can sense movement, and I can hear the shouts and fighting. We have the advantage of invisibility, but so do they. I keep the wall at my back and head right, away from the noise. I've lost track of Rocco and the guards who were in the hallway, but Harristan and Quint are somewhere ahead of me. Tessa grips tight to my hand.

"This guard's got the king's mark," calls a man. "He must be close."

I freeze. Tessa's fingers bite into my palm. I don't dare say Harristan's name.

The voices fall silent, and I know this is not a good sign. They're hoping to use the darkness against us. The smoke tickles my throat, and I try to breathe shallow breaths.

Harristan coughs.

"There!" shouts a man, and I hear the *swip* of a crossbow. It hits something, but I have no idea what. A man cries out ahead of me.

A rush in the darkness tells me an enemy has drawn close, and I leap forward to tackle them. An elbow drives into my ribs, and my earlier injuries scream at me. We crash to the ground, and I realize I'm not going to be fast enough to do anything but die.

But then the body is jerked away from me, and I hear the unmistakable sound of a blade piercing flesh, followed by a body hitting the floor beside me. A man groans. There's a scuffle, and I roll just before a booted foot strikes my shoulder. Something—someone—hits the wall with a sickening thud.

I brace my hands against the wall, waiting for a clue about what just happened.

"Corrick?" Tessa's voice cries out from the darkness. "Corrick."

A hand brushes my shoulder, and I jerk away. It's too much fast movement at once, and I have to brace a hand against the floor. I inhale a lungful of smoke and cough.

"Your Highness?" Rocco. His voice is closer, and I realize it was his blade that rescued me, his hand that found me in the darkness.

"I'm all right. Harristan?"

He doesn't answer, but he coughs again, hard.

"We have to get out of the corridor," calls Quint, and his voice sounds more distant.

I find my knees, then the wall again. "Get to my quarters," I call. My room is along the back wall of the palace, which hopefully hasn't taken as many hits as the front half. I have ropes in my chest to go out the window, but I don't want to shout that into the darkness.

Crawling through the smoke seems to take an hour, but no further voices cry out in the dark. But then my hand finds the familiar edge of a doorjamb, and we push through the doorway.

At first I'm not entirely sure it's my quarters. The lights here are as dead as they are in the rest of the palace, and while the smoke is nowhere near as dense as it was in the hallway, the room is still cloudy with a haze, even though a fire burns low in the hearth. But my stinging eyes begin to adjust, and I can make out my side table, my bed, the low chest along the wall.

I can make out Harristan, who's not still coughing, but I can hear his wheezing from here. Quint, who's got a hand braced against the wall. The guards Rocco and Thorin, who are already dragging a chest of drawers in front of the door.

Tessa, whose eyes are full of questions I can't answer.

"Who?" says Harristan between gasps.

"I don't know," I say truthfully. I look at the guards. "Could you tell?"

"Just men," says Thorin.

"With crossbows," says Quint, and a strain in his voice forces me to look back over. That hand braced against the wall is leaving a dark handprint, and his jacket is unbuttoned, showing a spreading stain near his waist.

"Quint!" I say in alarm. I remember the sound of that first arrow hitting something when Harristan coughed.

Quint waves me off. "I'll be fine."

The doorknob rattles, and Thorin and Rocco exchange a glance, just before something heavy slams into the door. The chest of drawers gives half an inch before they both brace against it.

Tessa looks at me. "Can we go out the window again?"

I limp to the back wall and peer out into the darkness. In the distance, Stonehammer's Arch is blazing against the night, but the palace grounds are pitch-dark. The alarms in the sector are loud and relentless, and smoke fills the air every way I turn.

The rope Tessa and I used to escape is still pooled on the floor by the window, triple knotted around the ironwork along the sill.

Something heavy slams against the door again. Wood cracks, and the chest of drawers whines against the floor. Rocco swears.

Tessa appears at my side. "Can you climb?"

"Yes," I say confidently. Though . . . I probably can't. Even if I can bear the weight of a rope around my boot, my shoulder will never be able to support my weight. Then again, I'd rather free-fall out this window than take an arrow in the face, which seems like more of a certainty if we don't get out of here.

My brother has crossed the room as well, and he coughs again as he peers out into the darkness with me, then inhales deeply of the night air.

"Harristan, do you remember how to climb—"

"I taught *you*, Cory," he gasps. He takes hold of the rope.

"One of us should go first, Your Majesty," calls Rocco. Wood splinters as the rebels slam into the door again.

"Then hurry," I say. I head for the chest of drawers and brace my shoulder against it. I don't know how many men are on the other side, but it must be half a dozen. "Go, Thorin."

"No!" calls Harristan.

"You're the king," I say. "Go. Get out."

Thorin disappears out the window, followed swiftly by my brother. Tessa and Quint are both beside the window.

"Go," I say to them. Another slam against the door. Flaming cloths are shoved through the opening this time, landing on the chest and catching almost immediately.

"No," calls Quint. "Corrick, you're—"

"Go!" I shout at him. My bad ankle keeps threatening to give out, and I have to readjust my shoulder against the chest. Flames feel close, and I'm afraid to look to see how close. I grit my teeth against the pain and the heat. "Go now, Quint. Go, Tessa."

The rebels slam into the door again. More wood splinters. The wall has caught fire behind me. I can hear shouts.

Quint and Tessa go out the window.

I look over at Rocco, braced against the chest like I am. Sweat threads his hair and drips down his cheeks.

"Run, Your Highness," he says. "I'll buy you time."

"You go," I gasp, trying to hold my grip as the chest begins to shift along the floor. "Go after them. Harristan will need another guard."

He gives me a withering look, but before he can say anything, I add, "That's an order, Rocco."

"I can't leave you here."

"Well, I can't run." I give a humorless laugh. The chest slips another inch, and I choke on my breath. "And I can't climb." Another inch, and I press my forehead against the chest. The room is filling with smoke, and I know I won't be able to hold this door much longer. "Please, Rocco."

"Very well, Your Highness."

He lets go of the chest. It skids six inches, and I cry out. I had no idea he was holding so much weight. Men shout in victory on the other side of the door. I'm not going to be able to hold this much longer—or it's not going to matter, because they'll be able to get through the space.

I should have told Rocco to leave me a weapon.

Then again, maybe quicker is better.

An arm hooks under mine, pulling me away from the chest, lifting me to my feet, dragging me forward. I trip over myself for a few feet before I realize Rocco is supporting my weight, half carrying me across the floor.

"I told you to go," I say.

"Execute me later." He takes hold of the rope. "Can you hold on to me?"

The door explodes inward. Rocco doesn't wait for an answer and swings us onto the rope, and for a terrifying moment, the world spins wildly, the flaming arch swirling through my vision. The rope brushes my fingers, and I grab hold with my strong hand, trying to support some of my own weight, but we still descend too quickly. Rocco's legs hit the palace wall as he rappels downward.

I hear the *swip* before I recognize the sound, and in the darkness below, Tessa cries out. A man is in the window with a crossbow.

"Run!" I cry. "Tessa, run!" She should have gone with Harristan. She shouldn't be here.

The rope jerks, and Rocco swears. We bounce against the wall one more time.

Then the rope gives altogether.

We hit the ground. It hurts *spectacularly*. I try to roll, as if that will somehow make it hurt less, but it doesn't.

"Corrick." Tessa's voice, low and desperate in my ear. "Corrick, you have to get up."

Swip. I feel the rush of an arrow near my head, but I can't move. I hear a crossbow snap close by, and I flinch, but I blink and realize it's Thorin and Rocco, returning fire. Men above are arguing, shouting at each other about who cut the rope.

Then I'm lifted again. Someone has an arm under mine. My vision goes spotty, flaring with light. Flames have erupted from dozens of windows along the back wall of the palace. The alarms keep blaring, and I want to lie down right here. I don't know who has me, but if it's Rocco, I'll have to stop hating him.

Then I hear Harristan's voice in my ear, rough and ragged. "Race you to the gate?"

It's a taunt from when we were children. His voice is so low and close that I realize he's the one holding me up. I blink at him. His face is smudged with soot, but his eyes are dark with concern. "You'll win this time," I say.

"Come on, Cory," he says, and he takes a step forward, supporting my weight, gasping from the effort. "Let's make it a tie."

CHAPTER THIRTY-EIGHT

Tessa

The workshop was always tiny for me and Wes. With four of us, it's downright crowded. It feels like a risk after the rebels found us here last time—but we're outside the sector, and I don't know where else to go. The guards are outside, Rocco at the door while Thorin walks a perimeter. The king doesn't want to risk a fire, but we have candles that Quint lights along the table, so we're not trapped in complete darkness. Corrick is upright in the chair, but his breathing is shallow, and he's got an arm across his abdomen like everything hurts. It feels like weeks ago that we were kissing in this room, his hands and his mouth warming me from head to toe, when it's hardly been a day.

The sector alarms haven't stopped ringing, but they're not as loud from here, and they don't inspire panic when the only person I used to worry about is here within these walls.

I pull a low stool next to Corrick's chair and sit beside him. "I still have some herbs here," I say softly, touching my hand to his. "But I can't brew tea without a fire."

Corrick shakes his head, but his fingers close around mine. His eyes keep falling closed.

Harristan glances at the door, then at the window. He runs a hand across his face and looks down at his brother for a long moment.

"I should have told you," Corrick says, as if he can feel the king's gaze. His words are slow and heavy. "I'm sorry."

"As am I," says Quint. He's leaning against the wall in the corner.

I know they're not apologizing for their actions, just the secret, but I'm not sorry about any of it. I'd do it all again, without hesitation. We couldn't help all of Kandala, but we helped those we could—and we did it without hurting anyone.

Harristan sighs. "Well, whatever you were doing, you didn't cause this revolution."

Corrick says nothing, and I wonder if he's fallen asleep. The shadows under his eyes seem darker. He said he didn't think his ankle was broken, but he couldn't put weight on it during the walk to the workshop, and he sweat through most of his clothes by the time the guards got him through the door, so I know he's more hurt than he's letting on.

Harristan is watching him too. With another sigh, he tugs at his jacket buttons, then slips his arms free. He lays the garment over his brother, then retreats to sit along the hearth. We sit in silence for the longest time, and it presses in around us, thick with worry. I wonder how many people were in the palace, and how many were killed—or how many were able to escape. Corrick said that rebellion was coming from both sides.

I wonder if Karri was part of the attack. Lochlan. Earle. All the people we once helped.

I think of what they did to Corrick, and the attack on the palace doesn't seem too far off.

Corrick's hand goes slack within mine, and I glance at his face in alarm, but his breathing has deepened. He's asleep.

"Quint," Harristan says softly, breaking through my thoughts.

"Your Majesty?"

"You're still bleeding."

"Oh. It's nothing." But Quint's voice is softer than I'm used to. "It's from the exertion."

Harristan has already uncurled from the hearth, and he stops in front of Quint. The Palace Master was sitting with his arms folded, but now I realize he was pressing his hand against a wound.

"Quint," I whisper. I should have noticed. I should have seen. My focus has been on Corrick, and now a wash of guilt sweeps through me. "You should have said something."

"Prince Corrick was *by far* more—"

"Show me," says Harristan, and as usual, his voice leaves no room for argument.

Quint hesitates, then lowers his arms and draws his jacket to the side. The entire left side of his shirt is dark with blood. The king peers at it for a moment, then looks at me. "Do you have supplies here?"

"Nothing for stitching," I say. "I have muslin to wrap it." I fetch the roll of fabric I used to tend Corrick's arm, along with the small scissors we kept for cutting bags of dried Moonflower.

"Honestly," says Quint. "It's barely a scratch—"

"Sit," says Harristan. "Remove your jacket."

Quint sits. Obeys.

I expect Harristan to move out of the way so I can treat the wound, but instead, he holds out a hand for the supplies.

I inhale to say I can do it, but then I think better of it and give him what he asked for. He unrolls a long strip of cloth and slices through it neatly.

Quint watches this, then glances at me and back at the king. "You are the king," he begins. "If I may—"

"I know who I am, Quint." Harristan's voice isn't impatient, the way I've heard him before. He sounds . . . thoughtful. He lifts the edge of Quint's shirt, and I wince as I get a closer look. An arrow cut straight across the side of his abdomen, causing a wound at least five inches long. I can't tell how deep it is, but it's bled enough to tell me that it won't heal well without stitching. He's probably right that exertion made it worse than it would've been.

Harristan rolls up the muslin to press it tightly against the wound, and Quint hisses a breath. But the king is quicker than I expect, and he wraps a length around Quint's waist swiftly, holding the bandage in place. His fingers are sure and gentle as he overlaps it twice, before tying it off with a well-placed knot.

"You're very good at that," I say, and I mean it.

Harristan glances at me. "I was sickly as a child. I spent a great deal of time among the palace physicians." He looks back at Quint. "That should hold until it can be treated properly."

Quint's expression flickers into a frown. "Thank you, Your Majesty."

"Thank *you*. That arrow was meant for me." Harristan says this as if it's nothing, then rolls up the remaining muslin in his hands and looks at me. "Who else knows of this place?"

"The rebel Lochlan," I say. "And the men who came with him."

"And what do they want?" he says.

I stare at him. "I don't know what you mean."

"They have attacked the palace, Tessa." He pauses. "What do they want from me? Do they want silver? Medicine? A full pardon?"

I think of all the people who were attacking Corrick. He was so sure that they'd use him against Harristan, but then they didn't. They just wanted vengeance. "I don't know who these Benefactors are, but the people just . . ." I swallow. "They want to stop dying."

He looks away, and when he speaks, his voice is low. "I want that, too."

I hear the truth behind every word. I've heard it since the first day I faced this man in the palace. I saw it in the way he patched up Quint's wound. He and his brother have spent years doing what they felt they needed to do to survive, and they've been destroying themselves in the process.

"Corrick implicated Arella and Roydan," says Quint.

The king runs a hand across his jaw. "Yes. He did. And while I can see Arella taking a radical stance, I can't see Roydan going along with it. Then again, I can't see the other consuls taking such a strong stance against *me*, and clearly they are." He shakes his head. "I can't stay here. I will not hide in the shadows while the sector burns."

"You cannot return, Your Majesty," says Quint. "It's too dangerous."

"I believe I've spent too much time allowing others to do what they think is best." Harristan looks at me. "And what about you? Where do you stand?"

I stare back at him. "I want people to stop dying, too."

"I can't cure the fevers, Tessa. I would if I could." He pauses. "Where would you be in this revolution, if my brother had not tricked you?"

Tricked. I take a breath and think of my last conversation with Weston Lark. My voice is soft yet strong as I say, "I'd be lighting the explosives myself."

The king smiles, but it's a little grim. "Far easier to start a war than to end one." He pauses, his eyes skipping across my form in a way that's coolly assessing. "These rebels tortured Corrick, but not you."

I glare at him. "And you think I was somehow a part of it?"

"No." He steps right up to me, and his eyes are as chilling as Corrick's can be. "One day we will have a conversation that does not end in accusations," he says. "What I mean is that they did not harm you." He pauses. "They did not trust the King's Justice. But they trust the outlaw Tessa."

My breath catches. Yes. They do. I remember Earle's gentle hand on my arm when Corrick was begging Lochlan to end his life quickly. Even Lochlan himself was gentler with me, having one of the men cut me loose after I got them to stop beating Corrick.

"What are you saying?" I whisper.

"I am saying that civil war will kill far more people than the fever ever could. I am certain my soldiers have already begun a defense. People are likely dying in the streets as we speak. On both sides. If I cannot restore order, this will spill outside the Royal Sector." He pauses. "I have yielded to Consul Sallister's demands for far too long. I have yielded to the demands of the elites for too long. I will hear from my people."

I stare at him.

"I don't know what I can promise," he cautions. "Change is never quick or easy. But I would like to try. Will you help me?"

My mouth is dry. I glance at Corrick, who's well and truly sleeping now. I'm not sure what to say. The rebels might not hate me—but they might not listen to me. I'm not entirely sure I trust Harristan either. He might want his people to stop dying, but we have very different ideas of how to accomplish that. I know he can't snap his fingers and change everything, but I'm not naive enough to think he'd do that even if he could.

I think of my father, acting in defiance of the throne. Would he do this? Or would he be disappointed I'm not running the streets with the rebels myself?

King Harristan is watching me, and I'm sure he can read every emotion as it crosses my face. His expression is as sly and calculating as ever. "Perhaps I should have started by asking what it is that *you* want."

I smooth my sweaty palms along my skirts. "I want . . ." My voice is breathy again, and I clear my throat. I want people to stop dying. But we all want that.

I take a breath and look at him. "I want a pardon for the rebels. Or . . ." I search for the right word. "Or amnesty. Both." I glance at Corrick again, asleep under his brother's jacket. I have to steel my nerve to add, "Including the people who hurt him."

Harristan's expression hardens, and I rush on, "They won't listen to you at all if they think you're going to execute them for hurting the King's Justice."

"Very well," he concedes. "What else?"

I can't believe I'm negotiating with the king. I don't know what else to ask for. Medicine for everyone? I know he can't grant that. Then a thought occurs to me.

"I want you to let Corrick stop being the King's Justice," I say softly.

At that, Harristan frowns. "I did not force him into the role. He is not indentured in some way."

"I know. I know." I take a breath. "But . . ."

My voice trails off.

"If I may," says Quint, "at the risk of interrupting your negotiations . . ."

"Please," I say, just as Harristan says, "No."

I fold my arms.

Harristan smiles, and for the first time, it reaches his eyes. I wonder if he hides as much as Corrick. "Go ahead, Quint."

"Prince Corrick may not need your permission," says Quint, "but I believe it would mean a great deal to know he has it."

"Fine," says Harristan. His gaze hasn't left mine. "Anything else?"

I think. "No."

"Nothing for yourself? What I have asked of you is not a small thing, Tessa."

For half a second, my thoughts whirl. He's the *king*. But I've never done any of this for financial gain, and I have no desire to require it as part of helping him negotiate peace. Then I consider Mistress Solomon's, and how I likely no longer have a position there.

"I'll need a job," I say. "And lodgings. Nothing . . . nothing grand, of course. But you were going to give me an opportunity to help improve dosages before." I hesitate, wondering if I'm asking too much. "I'd like to have a chance again. When all this is over."

"Done," he says. He straightens. "Quint, remain with Corrick. I will leave Rocco at your disposal."

Quint stands, and he looks startled. "But—Your Majesty—"

"You are injured, and so is he. If this place is as remote as it seems, you will be safest here." He looks at me. "Are you ready to play liaison?"

I feel the blood rush out of my face. I would've been brave enough to light the match to ignite the flame. Somehow extinguishing it seems more frightening.

But the king offers me his hand, and much like Corrick, I have a choice in what I'm going to do.

I reach out and take it.

Chapter Thirty-Nine

Tessa

I'd envisioned climbing the walls or returning through the tunnel with the king, but instead of heading toward the Royal Sector, Harristan chooses to head deeper into the Wilds. He said he wants to enter the sector through the gates, to have more guards at his back before we step into the fray. He left his jacket over his brother and stripped the rings from his fingers, then traded his jeweled dagger belt for the less adorned one that Quint wore. Thorin still has his weapons, but he's also in his shirt-sleeves because Harristan didn't want anyone to see the royal insignia. In the dark, no one will know him. Hopefully, no one will look at us twice.

I've traveled these paths a million times with Corrick, but it's entirely different to walk with Harristan. The horns in the sector have gone quiet, but I can see the searchlights skipping over the wall at regular intervals. I keep glancing over at the king as if he's going to vanish, like maybe everything has been a dream up till this point. The first shadow of beard growth has grown to cover his jaw, making him look younger, less intimidating somehow. I consider Lochlan and some of the others, and I don't know if that's a good thing. The farther we walk, the more I become aware of the sound of his breathing, the wheeze that's not quite a cough but sounds like it needs one.

"Do you need to rest?" I ask carefully, then quickly tack on, "Your Majesty?"

He glances at me. "No. Do you?"

I frown but keep walking.

"And you can't call me that," he says. "Not here."

"Of course. I'm sorry."

"What did my brother call himself?"

I almost don't want to tell him, because for a fleeting moment, I'm worried he'll want to adopt it for his own, and Corrick's secret persona is something precious that only belongs to me. But that's silly, and I'm too tired to think of a good lie, so I say, "Wes. Weston Lark."

The king startles. *"Really."* He gives a soft laugh. "I suppose I shouldn't be surprised."

"Why?"

"Because that was his name when we would sneak into the Wilds as children." He's quiet for a moment, probably remembering it. "Do you know—well, I suppose you wouldn't. Weston and Lark were the names of Father's hunting hounds."

I giggle in spite of myself. "He named himself after dogs?"

"He did indeed."

"What was your name?"

"Sullivan, after the fastest horse in the stable. Corrick used to call me Sully for short."

The fastest horse in the stable. I almost snort before catching myself. They were such *boys*.

The thought, once it strikes me, is surprising for some reason. I've seen it in a dozen ways since I first snuck into the palace, but their closeness is still startling. It's the most humanizing thing about them. It's the most . . . *gentle* thing about them.

"Tell me your thoughts, Tessa," says Harristan, and because he doesn't say it like an order, I do.

"I was thinking that you could be loved," I say softly. "Even if your people are sick."

He looks over at me and says nothing.

I blush and turn my eyes forward. "I was thinking that you're *not* horrible, not really. And he's not cruel. I have no idea what it was like to lose your parents, but I know what it was like to lose mine. I can't imagine having to . . . to rule a country after that. When my parents died, I hated the night patrol. Who did you hate? Everyone in the palace?"

"Yes," he says simply. His eyes are in shadow now, but the memory of loss is thick in the night air. "Well. Almost everyone."

Corrick.

I reach out and touch his hand, giving it a sympathetic squeeze. It's automatic, the way I'd do for Corrick—or anyone, really.

But the king looks at me in surprise, and I let him go. "Forgive me, Your—ah, Sully. Sullivan."

I swallow.

He says nothing. Thorin, walking at our back, says nothing.

When my parents died, I had Corrick. In a way, he had Quint, and he had me.

Corrick hid so much of himself from his brother. To protect him, for sure, but it created a barrier between them. When their parents died, I wonder who Harristan had. I wonder if he had anyone at all.

When I glance at him again, he's still watching me.

"I'm the king," he says. "I don't deserve anyone's pity."

"I don't pity you."

"You're a terrible liar, Tessa." He shakes his head and looks forward—then stops short so suddenly that Thorin draws a blade behind us.

But the king is merely staring. We've reached the clearing before the gates. It's deserted—which isn't too surprising for the middle of the night. The sound of shouts and screams echo from farther into the sector. But here, the gates have been blown off their hinges, and they're lying in mangled twists of steel on the ground. The guard station is deserted.

The bodies that once hung beside the gates are gone, replaced with huge white sheets painted with one word.

Revolt.

"I'd hoped for guards," King Harristan says. He looks at Thorin. "Advise."

The guard takes no time at all to consider. "We can travel through side streets, though we don't know how much damage has been done to the sector. There may be looters." He pauses. "I don't like the idea of being on foot. We could try for horses at Fosters' Livery—but it's not far from the palace, and it will be a risk if the rebels have been there first."

"I don't think rebels will go for the horses," I say, and they both look at me. "Not many people in the Wilds know how to ride—and I didn't see evidence of horses in either of the rebel camps I saw." I pause. "It wouldn't occur to me to get a horse. People in the Wilds are used to doing everything for ourselves—including walking."

The king nods. "Fosters' Livery it is."

CHAPTER FORTY

Corrick

When I wake, my head is pounding so hard that I want to cut it off. My mouth tastes like something died inside it. I'm disoriented, my vision a bit fuzzy, but I recognize the walls of the workshop. Three small candles are lit on the table, and when I sit upright, I discover Quint is half asleep on the darkened hearth.

But no one else.

"Quint," I say.

He startles and straightens immediately, but then he grimaces as if in pain, and presses a hand to his side. "Corrick. Rocco brought some water from the barrel. Let me—"

"Where's Tessa? Where's Harristan?" I blink at him and try to make my brain work. "What happened? Are you hurt?"

"They're gone," he says. "Your brother left to negotiate with the rebels."

I stare at him. I force myself to blink twice. "Am I still sleeping or did you just say my brother left to negotiate with rebels?"

"Tessa has gone with him to help."

I press a hand to my face. "They what?" My thoughts refuse to focus. "He left us here alone?"

"No, he left his guard Rocco, who—"

"Rocco!" I call.

The door opens almost immediately. "Your Highness?"

"Do you know where my brother went?"

"To attempt to stop the rebels in their attacks."

"As I said," says Quint.

I have to rub at my eyes. Finally, I can peer at the guard. "Rocco, we need to get back into the sector. We need to help him."

For the barest moment, I think he'll refuse. He's of my brother's personal guard, and they won't take action that would upset Harristan. But maybe he's equally worried for the king, because he says, "Yes, Your Highness."

I force myself to my feet and my head swims. I have to grab hold of the table.

Rocco steps forward to catch me.

I look up at him. "I'm sorry you're not getting that easy night you hoped for."

"I did not hope for that."

"Oh good," I say. "Quint, are you coming? We're going to need to find horses."

CHAPTER FORTY-ONE

Tessa

I was right. The livery is untouched. The streets here are deserted, but the scent of smoke is thick in the air. I can see a red glow beyond the nearest buildings. The searchlights have stopped spinning entirely. I expect the night patrol to be in the streets, or even soldiers, but maybe they've all headed for the palace. Even the stables are unmanned.

"People are afraid," says Harristan, when I comment on it.

They're the richest people in Kandala, but they're hiding from the poorest. All this time I've thought that the people within the gates were the most powerful, but maybe I was wrong. We all have power.

I don't know how to ride, but Harristan swings a leg over the back of a small black palfrey, then pulls me up to sit behind him. I don't want to do anything inappropriate, but he clucks to the horse and we lurch forward, so I grab the king around the waist automatically.

"I won't let you fall," he says, but that's not reassuring as the cobblestone streets rush by alarmingly fast. I jerk my eyes up.

Thorin rides ahead, almost invisible on his horse. It's so dark here. I've only been in the palace for a few days, but I'd almost forgotten what the sector looks like in the middle of the night. All silent gray, no color. We're not too far from the wall here, and it takes me a moment to realize we're not heading for the palace.

"Where are we going?" I say.

"We're going to approach the palace from the north," he says. "We'll loop around the Circle toward the army station. It's our best bet to find guards and soldiers."

"Do you think they'll listen to you if you show up with an army?"

"Do you think they'll listen to me if I'm dead?"

I want to disagree with him—but I can't. I was in the palace when they attacked. The king and his brother may have done terrible things, but this attack on the palace isn't better.

I think of all the innocent people in the palace. The invisible people. Jossalyn's gentle smile flickers into my thoughts, and my breath hitches.

I know the rebels are fighting for change, but they have Harristan's attention. Now it's time to forge a better path. Not . . . this.

"Don't cry yet," says Harristan, but his voice is more prudent than kind. "We've come this far."

It reminds me of Corrick's practical voice when we had dinner at the Circle. *If you cry, I'll be forced to comfort you.*

The sounds of shouting have grown louder, and Harristan pulls the horse to a halt. I look up in alarm, but this street is as deserted as the others.

Then I see the bodies, and I gasp. A man and a woman, crumpled in a doorway. Elites, from the look of their clothing. Blood has already pooled among the cobblestones. The woman is wrapped around the man in a way that makes me wonder if she was trying to protect him—or save him. Their throats are slit.

Thorin looks at the king, and Harristan points, then makes a circular motion with his hand. The guard nods and heads into the shadows, the darkness swallowing him up.

The king hasn't made a sound, so I don't either. I'm sure he can hear my shaking breathing, just as easily as I can hear the steady thrum of his heart, or the way his lungs seem to struggle for every breath. We're so still and quiet that when Thorin's horse trots out of a side street, I jump and give a little yip, causing our horse to shy and prance. True to his word, Harristan keeps the animal under control, but I redouble my grip on his waist.

Thorin's voice is very low. "The rebels have taken over the Circle. They have hostages. Several of the consuls, and half a dozen courtiers and advisers. The army can't get close."

"How are they holding the space?" says Harristan.

"They're surrounded by fire. They have small weapons that seem to explode with metal and glass when they throw them. The casualties are many."

I close my eyes and swallow.

I know what I said about lighting the explosives, but I wish I could take it back.

I want to go back to the Wilds. I want to go back to Corrick.

I want to go back to Wes and Tessa.

But everyone was sick. People were dying. Everything seemed bad.

This isn't better.

I take a breath and steel my spine. "Let's stop this," I whisper to the king.

"Indeed." He clucks to the horse, and we spring forward.

———

Hearing about the carnage from Thorin was vastly different from seeing it with my own eyes. Bodies litter the ground as we get closer to the Circle. The fires are massive, filling the air with light and smoke. The rebels keep adding fuel, sending sparks flickering into the night air. The lanterns that seemed so beautiful when Corrick and I had dinner are lit now, and they throw garish colors across the faces of the rebels on the dais. There are hundreds of them.

At the edge of the dais, two dozen people are on their knees. Many are wounded or bleeding.

Every single one of them is bound, with a blade or the point of a crossbow against their neck.

It's a macabre re-creation of the execution Corrick was expected to perform.

Hundreds of soldiers stand just outside the reach of the explosives.

"You will bring us the king," a rebel man shouts. He throws something that glitters in the firelight but explodes when it hits the ground, sending glass and flaming steel flying into the air. The soldiers closest skitter back.

"The king and his brother!" shouts a woman.

Harristan guides the horse wide, well away from the flames. As soon as the soldiers spot us, a dozen crossbows are jerked in our direction.

"Hold," says Thorin, and his voice isn't loud, but it's loud enough to stop any triggers from getting pulled. "You face your king."

The weapons are lowered immediately. The soldiers look from us to the flames.

"We will begin killing the consuls," the rebel shouts, and I realize it sounds like Lochlan. "You will bring us the king."

"If you begin killing consuls," shouts a soldier, "we will have no reason to hold."

"Bring us the king!" shouts another rebel. "Bring us the king!"

They quickly take up the chant. More explosives are thrown.

A soldier steps forward. "Your Majesty," he says. "Allow us to take you to safety. They intend to kill you."

"They've made no secret of that." Harristan swings a leg over the horse's neck and drops to the ground. "Bring me armor." Then he holds a hand up to me. "For Tessa as well."

"Armor?" I say. But soldiers are used to taking orders, and they're already pressing a steel breastplate to my chest, buckling it in place. The heat from the fires is intense, and sweat drips into my eyes. The armor doesn't help. My breathing is shaking.

The rebels haven't stopped chanting. *Bring us the king! Bring us the king!*

"I warned you!" shouts Lochlan.

A crossbow snaps. One of the prisoners jerks, then falls. I stop breathing.

"It's Craft," one of the soldiers says. "Consul Craft."

The other hostages start screaming. Many are begging.

The army seems to take a collective breath, men readying for violence. Harristan shouts, "Hold!"

They hold, but they shift unhappily.

The king's expression is as hard as granite, his eyes ice-cold. He looks at me. "Amnesty, Tessa? Really?"

I swallow. "Do you want them to forgive *you*?"

He stares back at me, and I remember his voice when he said, *It's the same to the night patrol.*

"Not all of these rebels deserve forgiveness," I say. "But not everyone who was captured deserved punishment."

"Bring us the king!" shout the rebels. "Bring us the king!"

Harristan's jaw clenches, but he nods. "I've agreed to your terms. Come. Let's make them believe it."

When he strides forward, I walk at his side. The men of his army yield space, opening up a path for us. The roar of the rebels is loud, pounding into my ears over every step.

When we reach the front of the soldiers, Harristan stops. I didn't think the heat could get more intense, but I was wrong. The fires rage around the rebels, and I can see sweat dripping from the faces of the hostages. I recognize Consul Cherry and Consul Pelham, whom Corrick suspected were working together—but they look terrified now. I don't recognize any of the other hostages— but I recognize plenty of the rebels. My heart is in my throat.

"Bring us the king!" the rebels shout.

"I'm here!" Harristan shouts back.

The shock is palpable—even among the army. Clearly not all of the soldiers had even realized we were here. The rebels are silent for a long moment, and then they cheer.

And then their chant changes.

"Kill him! Kill him! Kill him!"

"If you kill me, I can't help you," he shouts back.

They throw one of those glistening bombs, and the king jerks me back a few yards before it can land. Glass and shards of steel scatter along the cobblestones.

Harristan glances at me. "Your turn."

My heart stops in my chest. I don't know how to do this. I'm no one. This is different from when they were attacking Corrick. That was me and him. This is . . . this is a revolution. I don't know how to stop a revolution.

I think of what the king said. *Far easier to start a war than to end one.*

I take a steadying breath and step forward. "Please!" I shout. "Please listen to him! You know me. You know what I've done for you all!"

Kill him! Kill him! Kill him!

"Please!" I cry out. "He is willing to offer amnesty. He is willing to pardon you all. He is willing to offer *change*."

"Kill him!" they shout.

"He came here to talk!" I gasp and choke on my heartbeat, aware that I'm speaking through tears now. There are rebels with crossbows leveled at us both, but I take a step forward. "Please. Please stop this."

A man steps off the dais, stopping on the other side of the flames. Through the haze of smoke and flame, I make out his features. It's Lochlan. He's got a crossbow in his hands, pointed directly at me.

I raise my hands and take a shaky breath.

"Please," I say to him. "Please, Lochlan. He came here in good faith. Please."

"He came here because we're killing his consuls."

"If you kill any more," Harristan says behind me, "my offer of amnesty is revoked."

Lochlan's eyes don't leave mine. "What a surprise. He's already changing the terms."

"He's trying to stop you from killing any more people." I take a step closer to the flames. "Which is what you said *you* wanted to do."

"So, what? We go back to the Wilds and he goes back to his palace, and we all keep dying? I don't think so." His eyes flick to Harristan. "I don't trust you."

"But you trust *me*," I say desperately. "I know you do." I glance at the people behind him. "Because they trust me. And they trusted Corrick."

He studies me through the fire. For all the crimes he's committed, for everything he did to Corrick, I should hate him. But I can't. We're on opposite sides of the same coin.

Lochlan straightens. "Prove it," he says to Harristan.

"How?"

"Call off your army."

"Release your hostages."

"No."

Harristan's voice is like steel. "Then *no*."

I turn to look at him. "Can't you give them *anything*?" I hiss. "Can you have the army back off?"

"I came in good faith, Tessa. He must meet me halfway."

"He's not shooting you."

"He's no fool. If he kills me, this army will eviscerate them all. He's banking on my wish to save the consuls. It's literally the only leverage he has." Harristan looks at Lochlan and raises his voice. "I'll have my army retreat fifty yards if you release one hostage."

"You have archers," says Lochlan. "Fifty yards is nothing."

"Are we at an impasse?" Harristan spreads his hands. "I am willing to hear your demands."

"We want medicine," says Lochlan. "Medicine for *everyone*. We want to *survive*."

Harristan hesitates.

This has always been the crux of it. Lochlan doesn't understand. I didn't understand.

"Is that a no?" says Lochlan.

"I can't promise medicine," says Harristan, "but—"

"You can't move your army. You can't promise medicine." Lochlan takes a step back and looks over his shoulder at the rebels trapping the hostages. "Shoot another one."

"No!" I scream, but it's too late. The crossbow has already snapped.

CHAPTER FORTY-TWO

Corrick

We're able to find horses on the outskirts of the sector, but the army stops us before we can get close to Tessa and Harristan.

We can hear their shouts to the rebels.

We can hear the crossbow snap when Lochlan says, "Shoot another one."

The army surges forward, but Harristan calls for them to hold. The tension in his voice is potent. I saw Leander Craft fall earlier, the consul from Steel City. This time it's a young woman in a sleeping shift, and it takes me a moment to place her. She's the "niece" Quint saw with Jonas Beeching—confirmed when Jonas screams in rage.

It's a calculated strike. Another dead hostage, but not a consul.

I draw up the reins of my horse and look at Quint and Rocco. Quint is a bit pale, and he's gripping his side. I turn to one of the soldiers. "Help Master Quint down from his horse. He needs a physician."

"Yes, Your Highness."

Quint doesn't protest, which tells me he's more hurt than he's letting on.

I look at Rocco. "Let's go."

"Go?"

"Harristan isn't going to make any headway like this. He needs something tangible to offer them."

"What can he give them? The consuls are already held hostage."

I cluck to my horse. "Not all of them."

——+——

Many of the Hold guards have abandoned their posts, either out of fear or necessity, but a few still stand. The prison is dark and quiet as I limp down the staircase to the lowest level where Allisander is locked in a cell.

He scrambles to his feet when he sees me.

"Corrick," he seethes. "I cannot *wait* to see you at the end of a rope."

"Same," I say. "Rocco. Go in there and break his arms."

Allisander stumbles back from the bars so quickly that he trips over his feet and falls down. I must be pretty convincing—or Rocco's lack of hesitation is—because the consul keeps shoving himself backward through the straw.

"Enough," I say, and Rocco stops with his hand on the gate.

Allisander freezes but then gets to his feet. If his eyes were weapons, I'd be impaled.

But I think of Tessa and Harristan facing down the rebels and

I want to break his arms myself. I hook my fingers on the cell bars and hold his gaze. "You said you've allied with other consuls to overthrow Harristan. Who?"

"I'm not telling you anything."

"Do you recall asking if I torture prisoners during questioning?" I say, and I feel that familiar cool distance wind through my thoughts, the one that allows me to do what needs to be done. With Allisander, I hardly need it. "Would you like to find out?"

He steps forward like he's going to attack the bars, but Rocco is through the gate and stops him before I can blink.

He twists Allisander's left arm up behind his body, probably using a little more force than necessary, because the consul gasps and hisses a breath through his teeth.

Based on the look on Rocco's face, I don't think I'm the only one who doesn't like this man.

"Tell me," I say.

"No."

My eyes flick up to Rocco. "Break a finger."

The guard shifts his weight, and Allisander cries out before he catches himself. A sheen of sweat blooms on his forehead. "I'm going to hang your body on my gate, Corrick."

I don't look away from him. "Break another one."

This time the snap is audible. There's blood on Allisander's teeth. He must have bitten his tongue.

"Tell me," I say.

He glares at me, his breathing rapid and fractured.

I glance at Rocco. "Another one."

"All right!" Allisander shouts. He's almost keening now. "Leander Craft! Lissa Marpetta!"

I'm not surprised about Lissa. Leander is lying dead on the dais of the Circle, so I'm not worried about him either.

"What do you know about Arella and Roydan?" I say. "What are they doing?"

He's panting, and I wonder if Rocco is putting pressure on another limb. "I don't know," he says swiftly. "I don't know."

"Break another finger—"

"No!" he pants. "Corrick, I swear it. I swear to you. Arella has been going through documents from Trader's Landing with Roydan."

"What kind of documents?"

"Shipping logs. That's all I know."

Shipping logs. That doesn't seem important enough to warrant secret meetings. "Are they funding these raids?"

"No!" He gasps, then swallows. "I mean—I don't know."

Rocco looks at me. "Consul Cherry does not keep company with Consul Sallister."

That's true. Arella and Allisander are most definitely not friends.

"Do you know what's been happening while you've been locked down here?" I say to him.

"No." A fresh bloom of sweat appears on his forehead.

"Rebels have attacked the palace. They've taken the other consuls hostage. Harristan is trying to negotiate for their release."

His reaction is . . . not what I expect. He blinks at me in dismay. "They've attacked the *palace*?"

"Yes. Leander Craft is dead. So is Jonas Beeching's niece. Possibly more in the time you've been stalling." I pause. "You should be thanking me for locking you down here."

"They weren't supposed to attack the palace."

The impact of those words takes a moment to hit me.

They weren't supposed to attack the palace.

"Allisander," I snap. "What have you done?"

He says nothing. Rocco makes a small motion, and the consul cries out.

"Please," he whimpers. "They were supposed to attack the supply runs. Leander was a good man. They weren't supposed to come into the sector."

I stare at him. "You—you were working with the rebels? To attack your own supply runs?"

"It was just a little bit of medicine here and there," he says. "They'll do anything for it, Corrick. It was easy, really, and they don't—"

"But—" Maybe I'm too tired or too injured or too overwhelmed, but my brain can't make sense of this. "But *why*?"

"Because Harristan wouldn't pay a higher price if my shipments weren't at risk."

I have to take a step back from the bars.

I want to kill him myself.

"You did it for silver?" I demand.

"No. I did it because *this* time, I could force him to give me what I asked for."

I freeze.

"I see the way you manipulate the consuls," he says, "making us volley for funds. I saw it when I was a boy, when we asked for part of Lissa's lands."

"He was your friend, Allisander!"

"No. He was *not* my friend. A *friend* would not have humiliated me before half the nobility. A *friend* would have found a way to help me save face in front of my father. Harristan is no one's friend, Corrick. Not even yours. Look at the way he left you in prison for an entire *day*."

My fingers tighten on the bars.

"Do you know how much convincing it took for me to get him to accuse you?" he says. He leans in, his voice turning vicious. "It wasn't much at *all*."

I have to shake off the doubts he's putting into my mind. I know my role here. I know what I've done.

I'm only beginning to clearly see what Allisander has done.

I think of the prisoners we were set to execute, the ones led by Lochlan. I kept saying they weren't organized, because they *weren't*. They were innocent people lured into smuggling by Allisander—a man who was urging their punishment from the other side.

He was giving silver and medicine to desperate people. He was urging them to rebel—right when they needed little urging. And he was giving them the means to do it.

I think of Tessa splitting the petals before the explosions in the palace. I put my hands over my mouth and try to force my brain to think.

"You weren't even giving the rebels real medicine," I say softly.

"Why would I risk *real* medicine?" he demands. "Lissa has been supplying it to the palace for *years*."

I take a jolting step back. Lissa, who never demands anything. Lissa, who's always happy to maintain the status quo.

Lissa, who stood in the salon and tried to convince me not to trust Tessa. It had nothing to do with her being a girl from the Wilds.

It had to do with knowledge, and information, and access to everything Lissa was doing wrong.

It's just like Tessa said before the rebels attacked the palace. We're not getting a full dosage. Of course we need to take it three times a day in the palace.

Of course Harristan always seems on the verge of illness.

"You started this revolution," I say to Allisander. "Out of petty revenge."

"We all helped start this revolution," he snaps. "You too, Your Highness. *You*, the King's Justice. I gave them the means. *You* gave them the reason."

I flinch. I can't help it.

But then I take a breath and look at him. I can't undo what's been done, but maybe I can help stop what's been set in motion. "The rebels will not yield to Harristan. He can't promise access to the Moonflower—not when you're refusing to send shipments that are at risk."

"I don't care if Harristan falls to the rebels or to the consuls," Allisander says. "Either way, your brother will not be in power for long."

I slam my hand against the bars and the clang echoes throughout the prison. "Are you not hearing me?" I say. "Are you not listening? *They will kill the other consuls.* They have set the palace on fire. If we cannot find a way to undo this mess that you had a hand in creating, then there will be no Royal Sector to spend silver on your precious shipments."

He blanches at that.

"I will not bargain with smugglers," he says.

"You already have. And I don't want a bargain. I want medicine, and plenty of it. Harristan needs to be able to buy time."

"Absolutely not. You will not have one single petal—"

"Shut up." I look at Rocco. "Bring him."

Rocco drags Allisander out of the cell. He screams and thrashes the whole way, but the guard is impassive and unaffected, even when we move to climb the stairs.

I think of Tessa and Harristan facing down the rebels. I think of Arella Cherry begging for leniency, even though it pitted her against the other consuls, every single time. I think of Jonas Beeching pleading for more silver, and how Allisander accused him of cheating the system to buy more medicine.

And all the while, Allisander was trying to inflate his own prices.

I should tell Rocco to knock him down the stairs.

When we get out of the prison and onto the streets, Allisander shuts up. I don't know if it's the smoke in the air or the fact that we can see that fires still burn in the east wing of the palace, but I'm glad something made him stop.

"They did this?" he says, and his tone is strangled.

"You gave them the means," I snap.

Rocco binds his hands while I climb onto my horse, and then I take the rope and give it a jerk, nearly knocking Allisander off his feet. "Walk," I say to him.

"I absolutely will not—"

"Suit yourself." I loop the rope through the pommel of my saddle and cluck to the horse. The rope jerks tight.

Allisander swears and stumbles and almost falls, but he must decide walking is better than being dragged. "This is extortion," he snaps at me.

"Medicine," I snap back. "How much can you provide?"

"None."

I look at Rocco. "Fancy a gallop?" I draw up my reins. The horse begins to prance, eager.

"Fine," Allisander grits out. "A week of medicine."

"Eight weeks."

"I cannot provide medicine to all of Kandala for eight weeks—" But he breaks off as we sidestep a pair of bodies in the street. Two members of the night patrol. One took an arrow through the chest, though the other looks like he took an ax to the head. Tissue and bone glisten in the moonlight. Allisander realizes he's walking through blood and probably other things and sidesteps quickly.

His breathing has gone shallow and ragged. He probably wants his precious handkerchief.

"There are more," I say. A dozen yards ahead, we stumble upon three more. One woman, two men. A wide swath of blood streaks across a wall, black in the shadowed street.

"Two weeks," Allisander says, and it sounds like the words have been forced out of his mouth.

"Six," I say.

"Four."

"Six."

"Four, Corrick! I can't do more than that, and you know it."

I look down at him. "Yes. You can."

"I will agree to six if Consul Marpetta will agree to the same."

"She usually follows your—" I break off. What did Lochlan and Karri say in the hut when Tessa was stitching me up? *There's a man and a woman. We call them the Benefactors.* I thought it was Arella and Roydan. And Lissa was one of the few consuls who left the palace before any of this happened. "Allisander," I demand. "Is Lissa doing this with you?"

He doesn't say anything. He doesn't need to.

"Six weeks," I say to him. "And you'll be lucky if Harristan lets you keep your head at the end of it." I give the rope a sharp tug. "Hurry up. We need to stop a war."

CHAPTER FORTY-THREE

Tessa

We've retreated back to stand among the army. The rebels haven't killed any more consuls, but they seem to have an endless collection of their glass explosives, because they toss them at anyone who rides close. They've built their fires ever higher, and their chants vary between *kill the king* and *we want medicine*.

I'm on the fringes, but the king is surrounded by advisers. "The long bowmen can take out some of them," an army captain is saying to him, "but they'd be able to kill the consuls before we could save them all."

Harristan runs a hand along his jaw. His eyes are hard and tired.

He doesn't have to say it, but I know the truth anyway. If they storm this dais, they'll kill everyone.

I look back at the Circle. I can see the shadows of people moving around. They must be equally tired—and frightened.

I wonder if Karri is a part of it.

I step away from the army, and no one stops me. I ease silently over the cobblestones to stop in front of the flames where I know Lochlan waits.

A glass bomb comes flying out of the smoke, and I jump out of the way. Flaming bits strike my skirts anyway.

"Hey!" yells a soldier, but I put my hands up and face the flames.

"Lochlan!" I shout. "Lochlan, please. Please talk to me."

The shadows move and shift, and then he's visible, but barely.

"I have nothing to offer you," he calls.

"The king wants to find a solution," I say desperately. "Please. He doesn't want a war. He wants to help."

"He had time to help."

"He's going to kill you," I cry. "Do you understand? He's offered everything he can."

"He's already killing us," Lochlan says, and I can hear the matching emotion under his words. "You know that, Tessa."

"I know. I know." And I do know. That's always been the problem. There's never enough medicine to go around. "But . . . maybe . . ."

"Maybe what?" Lochlan calls. "Maybe the rich people will have their way and we'll go back to the way it was? No, Tessa. No."

"No," calls a man's voice from behind me, and I have to do a double-take when I see that it's Corrick. He's on horseback, leading a man through the haze by a rope.

Then I have to do a triple-take, because that man is Consul Sallister.

"You'll have medicine," says Corrick. "Eight weeks. From Allisander Sallister himself. He's pledged his assistance in finding a way to make Moonflower petals available to all."

"I said six," Allisander hisses, and Corrick kicks him in the shoulder.

"Tell them," Corrick says. "Tell them you will grant eight weeks of medicine to all citizens if they will stand down."

"Yes," Allisander calls. "I will grant eight weeks of medicine to all citizens."

A few people have moved forward to join Lochlan at the edge of the dais. One of them looks like Karri, and she's moved close. I watch as she intertwines her fingers with his.

Oh. I somehow missed that.

"We're already receiving medicine," calls Lochlan. "From the Benefactors."

"It's tainted!" I call back. "It's laced with something else. You've been tricked."

A murmur goes through the crowd, both the army at my back and among the people on the dais.

"Lies," says Lochlan, but for the first time, his voice falters.

"You have to have noticed," I say. "Tris said it herself, that the people have grown more desperate." My voice breaks. "There are more fevers, aren't there?" I say to him. "Aren't there?"

Another murmur goes through the crowd.

A boot scrapes against the cobblestones, and the king himself appears beside me. "Eight weeks of medicine. Real medicine. Enough time to form a new plan. A better plan." He pauses. "And I will not just meet with my consuls. You are not the only ones who have been tricked. I will meet with you as well. A council of the people."

Lochlan hasn't moved. He's not staring at the king. He's staring at me.

I glance at Harristan. "Amnesty," I whisper.

He takes a heavy breath. "If you release your remaining hostages and agree to leave the sector peacefully, I will have my army stand down. I will grant amnesty up till this very moment, but not one second longer."

Lochlan glances at Karri, then back at me.

But still he doesn't concede.

Shadows on the dais shift and move beyond the fire. Someone has approached Lochlan. After a moment, I realize it's Earle, with little Forrest beside him. My heart kicks. There's so much violence here, so much danger.

But then Earle says, "Tessa." His voice booms over the crowd. "When you spoke for Wes—for Prince Corrick—you spoke of all the things he did for us."

"Yes," I say. "Yes, he did it for you."

"Even while he did all of that, he was still the King's Justice."

I have to swallow past the lump in my throat. "Yes." My voice breaks. I can feel the sudden tension in the army behind me. This is all going to unravel again. They have no reason to trust King Harristan or Prince Corrick. "Yes. I know."

"But you weren't," Earle says.

I hold my breath. "What?"

"You were . . . just Tessa."

A woman approaches them, and I almost don't recognize her through the soot on her sweaty cheeks. Bree, the young widow. "Tessa." Her voice isn't as loud as Earle's, and I lean in to hear her. "You spoke of all the things Wes did. But . . . but you never talked about the things you did." Her voice breaks. "You set my boy's arm when he broke it falling from the tree. You showed me how to make a poultice."

"You saved Forrest," says Earle. "From the night patrol."

Another man steps forward. "You stitched up my hand when I sliced it on the ax."

An older woman. "You brought me blankets when the mice chewed through mine."

One by one, more rebels approach the edge of the dais, each one announcing something I've done to help them.

"You brought us medicine."

"You helped me birth that calf. I thought I was going to lose the cow."

"You taught me how to salve a burn."

My throat is tight, and a tear streaks down my face, but they keep going.

"You showed us how to make the medicine last."

"You helped us save ourselves."

"There are so many of us here. Because of you."

A boot scrapes on the cobblestones beside me, and I look over to find Corrick at my side. His rough fingers lace through mine. "You don't trust me," he calls to the rebels. "I don't expect you to trust me." He glances at me, and his blue eyes are full of emotion. "But you trust Tessa."

"I trust Tessa," says Earle.

"I trust Tessa," says Bree.

Slowly, it turns into a chant that tightens my chest and makes it hard to breathe. They have so much faith in me—and they're all a heartbeat away from being slaughtered by this army if they don't lay down their weapons.

Lochlan is still staring at me. "You trust the king," he calls to me.

"I didn't before." I pause. "But I do now." I swallow. "Lochlan. Please. There are so many people here. Please don't risk them all."

Lochlan looks at Harristan. "Amnesty?" he says. "And eight weeks of medicine?"

King Harristan nods. "You have my word. It has been witnessed by the consuls."

He sighs. "Fine. Let's hope we're not both fools." He sets down his crossbow. The other rebels do the same.

For a breathless moment, Harristan says nothing, and I wonder if this was all a trick, if the army is going to start picking off the rebels one by one.

But then the king turns to face his army. "Stand down. Allow them to leave."

I'm suddenly giddy with relief. I turn to look up at Corrick. His eyes are full of pain, and I realize he's bearing no weight on his injured leg, and the cut over his eye is bleeding.

"You shouldn't be here," I say. "You're injured."

His hands close on my waist, and they're trembling a bit, belying his confidence. "Someone once told me that we should be riding at the front, not hiding in the shadows. I couldn't let you and Harristan have all the fun."

He leans down to press his mouth to mine, but just for a fleeting moment before he pulls me against him. His arms are warm and sure against my back, but he's heavy with exhaustion. Behind us both, the army retreats as the flames die and the rebels allow their hostages their freedom.

Tension fills the air around us, but for the first time, it's undercut by a tentative hope.

CHAPTER FORTY-FOUR

Corrick

The east wing of the palace has significant smoke and fire damage, and it is uninhabitable, but the west side fared much better. There were many casualties, but due to the late hour of the attack, many of the palace staff had already left for the night. By the time we return to the palace with Tessa and the consuls, I'm shocked to discover that Quint has already given orders and had rooms prepared—before apparently collapsing on a chaise longue in the dimly lit salon.

The consuls shuffle off to their rooms, but Harristan hesitates in the hallway. He studies Quint, sound asleep to the point where he's almost drooling.

"I'll wake him," I say.

"No. Let him sleep." Harristan shifts his eyes to me.

I can't read anything in his expression, but his eyes are piercing. We may have stopped the rebels—for now—but there is a lot left unsaid between us. I want to collapse onto that chaise beside Quint, but I brace myself.

Harristan inhales, but Tessa holds up a hand. "Tomorrow," she whispers.

My brother shuts his mouth, but now his gaze shifts to her.

Tessa almost falters, but then she steels herself. "Tomorrow. Your Majesty. If you please. If . . . ah, if I may add to my list of demands."

"You may," he concedes.

I look at her, and even battle worn and road weary, she's more lovely than I've ever seen. "Your demands?"

She blushes, then bites at her lip.

Before she can say anything, Harristan claps me on the shoulder. "You heard her, Cory. Tomorrow."

Tomorrow comes, but Harristan doesn't visit my chambers. Not the following day either. He sends me a message to rest, to recover, to wait. I hear from the guards that he is meeting with each of the consuls individually, discussing plans to move forward. Lissa Marpetta has retreated to her sector, and Harristan has sent an army regiment to bring her back to the palace to answer for the fraudulent Moonflower petals.

Consul Sallister attempted to leave, but he was stopped at the gate. Every message he sends is scrutinized. Every shipment of Moonflower petals is inspected before it's distributed.

Tensions in the sector haven't lessened. The people are afraid of the rebels—and they're afraid that the supply of medicine will stop. There's a nervous hum to the city that's very different from before.

But I hear of no attacks. I hear no alarms.

I hear of no one in the Hold either. No summons for the King's Justice.

Quint doesn't visit me much, but he's as busy as my brother, arranging for tradesmen and carpenters and steelworkers to rebuild the east wing.

Tessa visits me often. Every break during her time with the palace physicians, every dinner, every spare minute. I teach her to play chess, and she immediately beats me in a game. She tells me that the palace apothecary was killed in the attack, but there are rumors that he was working with Lissa Marpetta.

I soak up every bit of gossip, and I worry for my brother. I worry for Kandala. I worry that we won't have any way to move forward, that we'll hit the end of the eight weeks and we'll be no closer to a solution.

Tessa worries about the same.

I send my brother messages, requests, inquiries.

Demands.

His response is always the same: *Tomorrow.*

At first, I enjoyed the respite.

By the seventh day, my ankle doesn't pain me, and most of my bruises have faded. I'm ready to don my mask and hat and stride into the woods as Wes, just for a chance to break the boredom.

When yet another deferral is delivered to my chambers— *Tomorrow, Cory, if there is time*—I crumple it up and toss it into the fireplace.

Then I stride down the hallway to his room.

Rocco is on duty, and while my brother's guards have never stopped me from entering Harristan's quarters, I wonder if things have changed.

But Rocco gives me a nod. "Your Highness. The king is dining with Master Quint."

"Marvelous. I'll join them." I grab hold of the door handle.

Harristan is talking and Quint is writing when I barrel into the room. They both look up at me in surprise.

Quint stands at once. "Your Highness."

"Corrick," says Harristan. "I sent word that we could meet tomorrow."

"Hmm." I move to the side table and pour myself a glass of brandy. "I believe I've heard that before."

"Shall I allow you a moment of privacy?" Quint says. He gathers his papers.

"Yes," I say.

"No," says Harristan. "Corrick, we can meet tomorrow—"

"I am the King's Justice," I snap, "and half the consuls were embroiled in a treasonous plot against you, Harristan. I should be a part of your meetings." I step close and slam my glass down on the table. "I should be interrogating them. I should be reviewing their holdings and their dosages and their—"

"Enough." Harristan puts up a hand. "You're right. The King's Justice should be doing those things." He pauses, and there's no censure in his voice. "But from what I've learned, you were unhappy in that role."

My brother's voice is quiet, but full of weight. The room seems to tilt, just for a second.

I don't know what to say.

I don't know what I *want* to say.

To my horror, my chest tightens, and I have to look away.

Quint finishes gathering his papers. "I will have another meal sent." But as he approaches the door, he stops beside me. "Before you went to the Circle with Tessa, I said you can only be the King's Justice." He pauses. "I was wrong. You should be Corrick." He glances at Harristan and then back at me. "Especially here. Especially now. You've come too far."

I have to swallow. "Thank you, Quint."

"Always."

Then he's gone, and I'm alone with my brother.

I take a long breath, then down the glass of brandy. I move back to the side table to pour another.

Harristan appears at my side, and he takes the bottle out of my hands. "Cory."

"Who will you choose in my place?" I say, and my voice is harsher than I expect. "You know, Rocco is more savvy than I gave him credit for, and he wouldn't flinch from violence—"

"I'm not replacing you."

"Ah, so you're going to leave me to rot in my chambers?"

"No." He sighs. "I was trying to see if I could understand what it is that you do."

I freeze. "What does that mean?"

"It means I've been interrogating the consuls. I've been to the Hold. I've been—"

"You've been to the *Hold*?"

"Yes. You were correct about prisoners using chairs as weapons."

Against my will, that makes me laugh. "I told you."

He doesn't smile. His eyes search mine. "I'm not replacing you. But I don't want to return to the status quo. I don't want to hide behind the King's Justice."

"You never hide, Harristan."

"Father did." He pauses. "And I wonder if that's part of why they were killed." Another pause. "There are very few people in the palace whom I trust. I would never replace you."

That sentence doesn't sound complete, so I raise my eyebrows. "But . . . ?"

"But . . . I do not want you to think you must hide your true intent from me." His voice sharpens. "I do not want to think that you would lie to me."

I swallow and look away. I think of that moment in the Hold when Allisander declared that my brother was not my friend, that he left me in the Hold for an entire day. He wasn't wrong about that moment—but the choices that put me there weren't Harristan's. The blame was mine. "Forgive me."

He hesitates, then reaches out to ruffle my hair, the way he did in the Hold. "You're forgiven."

I roll my eyes and duck away. "So . . . you don't want me to be Cruel Corrick anymore?"

He grimaces. "There is so much gossip and unrest. If even a fraction of it is true, I think you'll have plenty of opportunities to be Cruel Corrick. But . . . we have focused on the crimes of those who have little, those who commit crimes of desperation. The true insurrection was here in the Royal Sector. With us."

"Do you have any ideas?"

"I was giving them to Quint before you burst in here." He sighs and pours himself a glass of brandy, then smacks my hand away when I reach for the bottle. "I still have no idea why Roydan and Arella have been meeting secretly to review shipping logs. And we'll have to do something about Leander Craft's sector. I can't have two sectors without a consul. Those explosives came out of

Trader's Landing, so we'll need to discover how they were smuggled out. I suspect we may have more traitors in our midst than just Allisander." He runs a hand through his hair. "We'll need to appoint someone to oversee—"

A knock sounds at the door. "Your Majesty," a guard calls. "Another meal has arrived."

I smile at my brother. "Let's get to work."

CHAPTER FORTY-FIVE

Tessa

A week after the rebellion, King Harristan shows me to a new room in the palace.

"Nothing too grand," he says as a guard swings open the door. "As you requested."

My eyes almost bug out of my head. It's grander than anywhere I've ever lived in my life, including the small suite where I've been staying since the rebels bombed the palace. This is just down the hall from where Corrick sleeps, and the hallway alone is so lavish that I always feel like I need to whisper when I'm up here. The room is so immense that I can't take all of it in at once. Glistening marble and gleaming wood and lush wall hangings and a bed the size of an ocean. It's three times the size of the Emerald Room, where I first stayed the night I snuck in here. It's too plush. Too big. Too much.

Definitely too grand, and he very well knows that.

Or . . . maybe he doesn't. Maybe that's part of the problem. Not just with him. With all of the elites.

"It's lovely," I say haltingly. "I just meant—I meant—"

"Corrick and I have been discussing the consuls and the rebellion and how we shall proceed from here. We suspect Allisander and Lissa are not the only people who were working against the Crown, so I will not be inviting the other consuls. We have not stopped a revolution yet, Tessa. We have merely . . . delayed it a bit."

I stare at him. "Yes, Your Majesty."

He's not done. "As the consuls cannot be trusted, when you are not working with the royal physicians, I will trust you to be my personal adviser in dealing with Lochlan and the other rebels." I blanch, and he adds, "You did request a job as well, did you not?"

And yes, I suppose I did.

Then he leaves me there in the hallway, my mouth hanging open, and he goes on his way.

"Thank you?" I whisper, but he's already gone.

Much like the new room, this feels too big. But I wanted to be a part of the change, and I wanted to be leading the way.

I've been having breakfast with Corrick and Quint every morning. The Palace Master is full of gossip about the consuls and their loyalty, about Allisander and his hardly veiled insults about Harristan and Corrick, about who can be trusted and who can't. While there's hope in the air, there is fear, too, and it's obvious the guard presence in the palace has been doubled.

My days are busy with meetings, but my favorite part of the day is when the sun has fallen from the sky, and I walk with Corrick under the stars, the moonlight tracing his features in shadow.

Tonight, the weather has cooled, the sky overhead deepening to a blue so dark it's nearly black. We're nearing the fiery arch, and sparks sizzle as they fall onto the pond below it.

I shiver, and Corrick wordlessly slips out of his jacket to drape it over my shoulders.

"Thank you," I say.

"It suits you better anyway," he says, and I smile.

He doesn't.

I know he's met with Harristan, and he says that they're committed to making things better in Kandala. But that doesn't mean they've made things better between themselves. I remember walking with Harristan in the Wilds, when he said that the king deserves no one's pity.

I wonder if Corrick feels that way, too.

I lace my fingers with his. "You seem worried."

"Harristan said that he doesn't want to hide behind the King's Justice."

I wait for him to say more, but he doesn't, and I frown. "I think that's wise."

"I don't think he ever hid, Tessa. We never hid who we were." He hesitates. "There's so much at stake. Allisander and the others were going to try to overthrow him. I'm worried that if there's no more King's Justice, they'll try again."

I stop short and stare at him.

He must see my expression. "What?" he says, and he almost sounds petulant. "That's what happened to our parents."

"Do you know what you just said?"

"If there's no more King's Justice—"

"No! You said *we never hid who we were*." I want to shake him. "Corrick! You hid *everything* that you are. I think Harristan did too."

He startles, then sighs. He seems like he's going to start walking again, but I hold fast. He looks down at me, his eyes heavy and intent.

"The people loved Wes and Sullivan," I whisper. "Give them a chance to love Harristan and Corrick."

He traces a thumb over my mouth. "They loved Tessa Cade, too, remember."

"You can do this," I say quietly.

He shakes his head a bit, then brushes his lips over mine. "*We* can do this."

Then his hands find my waist, and I drown in his eyes and inhale his breath. The darkness closes in around us until there's nothing but the warmth of his hands and the sound of his voice, low and teasing in my ear. There is so much to be done, so many things to hope for.

But just for a moment, I close my eyes, lean into his touch, and remember what it was like when it was just the two of us against the night.

ACKNOWLEDGMENTS

From the moment I first watched (and fell in love with) the Disney animated version of *Robin Hood*, I've always loved stories about supposed "outlaws" who are secretly doing the right thing for the populace. I grew up watching and reading every rendition of these kinds of stories I could find, from Kevin Costner's *Robin Hood* to the old black-and-white episodes of *Zorro* to YA novels like Cynthia Voigt's *Jackaroo* or Lynn Flewelling's *Luck in the Shadows*. When I envisioned the characters of Tessa Cade and Weston Lark stealing medicine to help the people of Kandala, I knew what their journeys were going to be right from the beginning, and I completed the first draft of *Defy the Night* in early autumn of 2019. I then had to turn my attention to drafting *A Vow So Bold and Deadly*, so when my first editorial letter from my amazing editor came in January of 2020, it sat in my email in-box until I finished *Vow*.

And then, in March of 2020, the COVID-19 pandemic hit.

Since *Defy the Night* deals with a kingdom suffering a mysterious illness, I know there will likely be comparisons, and I'm already anticipating the questions of whether this is a "pandemic book." If you've made it this far, you know that it's not, but the way COVID-19 affected the world absolutely changed the way I looked at the kingdom of Kandala and what responsibilities rulers have to their citizens, especially in times of tremendous challenge and strife. My editor and I did several rounds of revisions to create what is now the finished book you have in your hands, and as usual, Mary Kate wouldn't let me stop until it was perfect.

So that's where I'm going to start. Mary Kate Castellani, my phenomenal editor at Bloomsbury, always takes my work to the next level, and then she somehow sees even more potential and pushes it even higher than that. I am always so grateful for your guidance and support, and I am so glad we have more books to look forward to in the future.

Huge thanks and gratitude go to my husband, Michael, who is quite possibly the most supportive husband in the world. I will never forget the time way back when I was first beginning to research literary agents, and he said, "Do you really think your writing is good enough that people would pay money to read it?" It was such a pivotal question at such a pivotal moment, and I thought about it for a second, then said, "Yes. I do." He simply nodded and said, "Let's get it done, then." Ever since that day, he's been 100 percent behind me, and I appreciate every single second we have together.

The entire team at Bloomsbury continues to blow me away with their incredible dedication to the books they publish, and I am so grateful for everything. Huge thanks to Adrienne Vaughan, Erica Barmash, Faye Bi, Phoebe Dyer, Claire Stetzer, Beth Eller, Ksenia

Winnicki, Rebecca McNally, Ellen Holgate, Pari Thompson, the copyediting team, the art department, and every single person at Bloomsbury who has a hand in making my books a success. Special thanks to Lily Yengle, Tobias Madden, Mattea Barnes, and Meenakshi Singh for their incredible work on managing my Street Team.

Speaking of the Street Team, if you're a part of it, thank YOU. It means so much to me to know that there are *thousands* of you interested in my books, and I will never forget everything you've done to spread the word about my stories.

My agent, Suzie Townsend, of New Leaf Literary Agency, has been an absolute rock for me since we began working together. Suzie, thank you so much for your time and your guidance as we bring more books into the world. Additional thanks to Dani Segelbaum for handling so much behind the scenes.

Huge debts of gratitude go to my close writing friends, Gillian McDunn, Jodi Picoult, Jennifer Armentrout, Phil Stamper, Ava Tusek, and Amalie Howard, because I honestly don't know how I would get through the day without your support. From reading my manuscripts to virtually holding my hand to listening to me and talking to me and supporting me, I am so grateful to have you all in my life.

Several people read and offered insight into parts of this book while it was in progress, and I want to take a moment to specially thank Christina Labib, Shyla Stokes, Reba Gordon, Ava Tusek, and Isabel Ibañez.

Special thanks to my "quaranteam" moms for helping me get through 2020 (and now into 2021), Christina Labib and Siobhan Reed. You're not writers, but you kept me going through a really challenging year, and I'm so grateful to you both.

Additional thanks go to everyone who helps to spread the word about my books, whether you physically put a book in someone's hands, or if you use book blogs, Twitter, Tumblr, Instagram, Facebook, and now TikTok. This includes readers, reviewers, bloggers, librarians, booksellers, teachers, artists, and cosplayers. Thank you all so much for helping to make my dreams come true. I know reading and reviewing and selling and creating can all feel like a thankless job. You have my full gratitude and appreciation for all you do.

And many thanks go to YOU! Yes, you. If you're holding this book in your hands, thank you. Thank you for being a part of my dream. I am honored that you took the time to invite my characters into your heart.

Finally, tremendous love and thanks to the Kemmerer boys for following in Daddy's footsteps and supporting me every bit as much as he does. You surprise me every single day, and I am so very lucky to be your mom.